WARRIOR'S WOMAN

by Phyllis Leonard

PREY OF THE EAGLE
PHANTOM OF THE SACRED WELL
WARRIOR'S WOMAN

WARRIOR'S WOMAN

PHYLLIS LEONARD

Coward, McCann & Geoghegan, Inc.
New York

For permission to quote from copyrighted material, the author gratefully acknowledges Editorial Minutiae Mexicana, S.A. de C.V., for excerpts from *A Guide to Mexican Poetry*, translated from the Nahuatl by Irene Nicholson. Reprinted with permission of the publisher.

SBN: 698–10843–4

Library of Congress Cataloging in Publication Data

Leonard, Phyllis
  Warrior's woman.

  I. Title.
PZ4.L5852War [PS3562.E57] 813'.5'4 77–4822

Printed in the United States of America

Dedicated to my dear friend and mentor,
Dorothy Torreyson, Ph.D.,
Professor Emerita of Spanish,
Los Angeles College System

*Those having torches will pass them on
to others.*
—PLATO

BOOK ONE

The Spaniard's Mistress

Come live with me, and be my love;
And we will all the pleasures prove
That valleys, groves, hills, and fields,
Woods or steepy mountain yields.
                    —CHRISTOPHER MARLOWE,
          "The Passionate Shepherd to His Love"

PROLOGUE

April, 1519: aboard *La Marquesa,* three weeks out of
Cádiz, Spain, bound for the Indies

The galleon reeled under the onslaught of a savage sea. Horses penned on the open deck neighed shrilly with terror, and their cries pounded at Alana MacKenna's heart and conscience as fiercely as waves pounded the vessel.

Accompanied by a huge dog, the young Irishwoman struggled from one stall to the next, trying in vain to calm the animals. She winced as sails burst like claps of thunder and narrowly escaped a barrel that caromed across the planking. Gasping with fright, Alana slipped and fell. She threw her arms around the wolfhound, hugging him close for their mutual protection. Finn weighed far more than she did, and his giant frame acted like an anchor, holding her fast.

The captain had ordered every passenger below, but she had returned to the deck. If death came, Alana refused to be trapped like a rat in the hold. After all, the horses were in this predicament because of her. Staying with them was the least she could do.

Seville, north of Cádiz, had long been a market for fine stallions and

9

brood mares such as she and her father before her had raised near Kildare in Ireland. But she hadn't been satisfied with that. Oh, no! Alana MacKenna had to gamble her future on a journey to the Indies where it might—and might not!—be possible to earn a fortune.

It was true there was a scarcity of good horseflesh on the Spanish islands of Hispaniola and Cuba, even though Hispaniola possessed royal breeding farms. Sturdy, hardy animals had been developed in the tropics since 1494, but demand continued to outstrip supply. The more aristocratic horses remained rare and costly because of the perils of oceanic transport, but daring traders lucky enough to enjoy quick crossings reaped a bonanza.

Yet what a reckless, impulsive act for a woman. Only a romantic fool quit home and hearth to go adventuring . . . and never mind that no one cared. Weren't her dear parents gone from the sweating sickness and her husband-to-be with them? By all that was holy, it would be a faraway day before the right man came along again.

Despite her misgivings, Alana had always had the wanderlust. And how very much she wanted to see the fabled cities of gold where jewels dangled from silver trees, where barbaric kings held sway over mountains of spices and bales of silk!

The Irishwoman was not alone in this desire. Tales of the New World wafted across the Old like erotic perfumes promising wealth, land, women, and slaves for the taking. Every ship setting sail for the western horizon carried the bold and the daring, from soldier to scoundrel, from priest to prostitute.

Alana huddled next to the dog and pulled a shawl over her nose and mouth. Wasn't the storm ever going to let up? She couldn't remember having been so miserable, wet, cold, and cramped. And hungry and thirsty, too! She could hardly wait to set foot on solid ground. Once she was home, by heaven, she would never put to sea again.

Crossings early in the year were infrequent because of inclement weather, but *La Marquesa* had raised the Indies less than three weeks out of the Canary Islands. The usual trip took sixty to ninety days, and Alana had worried at first about getting becalmed in certain latitudes. She knew horses often died there of thirst or ship madness or were thrown overboard to conserve water.

But the voyage had been uneventful this spring of 1519, and she had gladly joined fellow travelers in a thanksgiving service. Captain and crew had grinned broadly, their teeth bone white in bronzed and bearded faces. Good winds and friendly waters, *gracias a Dios!*

Alana lifted her head, letting the shawl drop away. Had the storm abated, or was it just her imagination? The waves seemed less violent, and there were tantalizing glimpses of the island through a slackening downpour. She peered longingly at its green vistas, so lush and reminiscent of Ireland.

The horses could swim that distance, she thought idly, remembering the times they had played in the River Liffey. It had been her father's theory that beautiful stock with astonishing endurance resulted from aquatic exercise, as well as Kildare's grass, which was rich in bone-nourishing limestone.

She heard a sailor in the bow shout with alarm. *Holy Mother of God, what now?* Only last evening at dusk, the ship had been approaching the roadstead of Santiago de Cuba, the island capital. Everyone had been eager to set foot on land. Then the freakish storm had hit. It had been so unexpected and vicious there was no time to man the clumsy capstan and drop anchor. *La Marquesa* had been blown among the reefs like a wounded bird among thistles.

At least the rain was tapering off. And there came the sun! Then there was a sudden lull. Noises smothered earlier by the howling wind now became painfully loud. Somewhere a man groaned, and injured livestock echoed his agony. Broken spars banged rhythmically overhead against the masts. The ship creaked and shuddered as if in premonition of its fate.

Alana stood up and walked past the stalls, her skirts heavy and sodden. Crooning to the four stallions and the mare, she tried to comfort them. They nipped at each other irritably, exhausted and agitated by the buffeting.

Pausing to examine a cut on the mare's shoulder, Alana listened carefully. What was the sailor yelling about this time? *Large heads of coral!* Her blood ran cold. If the wind shifted, the ship's tallow-coated hull would be ripped open like a hunter-gutted deer.

The mare whickered, an oddly feminine sound. Alana patted the sleek neck. "No, *mavourneen*, not yet. If the ship strikes, then I'll cut you loose." She gripped a dagger sheathed at her waist, reassuring herself of its presence.

The wolfhound should be freed from his leash, however, just in case of trouble. "There, Finn. Now you'll be able to swim better, although God forbid you have to."

As Alana smoothed the dog's head, the watching crewmen muttered uneasily. They had said all along she was a witch. Wasn't it common knowledge that those animals understood her words and talked to her in the night when no one could hear? Look at her now! Body of Christ, the woman showed no fear. Perhaps she and her four-legged familiars would turn into gulls and fly away from the stricken galleon.

While they cursed and gossiped, Alana marveled at the clarity of the atmosphere. On a beach to port she saw a carriage sheltered beneath an immense tree. Someone certainly had been anxious for the ship to dock to have driven down the coast this morning.

A lover waiting for that Castilian girl who shrieked with hysteria? A relative of her bead-telling chaperone? An impatient husband expecting his beloved? Alana wished she were in that carriage, drinking wine, eating meat and fruit, and laughing at the sallies of a flirtatious man.

A slight smile dissolved the strain on her face. The ship's pilot, who wished to repay a debt, was taken aback when he came across the deck. The blonde had the bravery of a Spaniard! It was his highest compliment.

"*Señorita*," he said, breathing hard from exertion. "Look over there to port. To the left. See?" He pointed at the island.

She had diagnosed his chronic dyspepsia a few days out of Cádiz. She had only told him what he knew, of course. He was getting too old for beef and pork pickled in brine, for cheese, onions, garlic and dried peas and beans. And the less said about ship's biscuits, the better. The pilot was grateful to her for an herb tea which relieved the pains in his gut. She had also supplied him with leaves for the voyage home and the name of an apothecary in Seville. He felt uncomfortable about the crew, but he planned to return the favor.

"See the channel of pale-green water coming right under the keel?" When she shook her head, he grasped her arm. The wolfhound growled. Hair rose on the nape of the pilot's neck, and he released Alana instantly.

"Quiet, Finn." She squinted against the sun. "Oh, yes, I see it now. What about it?"

"If your horses stayed in that channel, they could swim right into shore. There's coral on both sides—and sharks out there in deeper water—but I think they could make it without any problem."

"*Muchas gracias, hombre.* I'm very grateful for that information."
Alana gestured nervously. "Is there any chance of getting my baggage or
saddle gear?" Except for the money pouch in her voluminous skirts, her
possessions were stored below.

"Best to claim them later from the customs officials in Santiago."

"Will you be sailing back to harbor there?"

"No. Our canvas is too badly damaged to come about. We'll have to
wait for help, and a following sea or strong winds aft may drive us between
those coral heads before that comes. Then we'll be in real trouble." The
pilot belched and rubbed his abdomen. "One way or the other, your animals are going to have to swim for it."

A slight breeze stirred the ragged sails. Alana made her decision.

"Put the ramp in place, if you please." She pointed at the stalls. "I'll
ride the black stallion with the white blaze on his forehead. Can you get the
others into the water?"

The Spaniard nodded. "I've done it many times. Don't worry. But stay
in the channel, *señorita.* I'd hate to see you make a meal for the sharks."

"So would I!" Alana smiled, but her heart fluttered with fear as the man
busied himself.

Conn, the big stallion, was released from his stall while sailors set the
ramp against the railing. The horses had already been bridled the day before; Alana stepped up onto a box and mounted bareback. The horse was
surprised to land in water, but he rose quickly to the surface, snorting and
blowing. The warm Caribbean soothed his skin, and he began to swim
strongly, delighted to be off that terrible floor which had swayed continuously.

Halfway to the island the stallion found a footing. Plowing through
chest-high swells, he turned occasionally to beckon the other horses and
the dog paddling close behind. Twisted about on Conn's back, Alana gritted her teeth as each horse plunged into the sea, but once over the initial
shock they swam successfully through the channel and stumbled ashore.
The young mare sank to the ground with a groan, while the four stallions
remained standing, as wobbly and awkward as colts. When Alana dismounted, she, too, walked as if still accommodating her gait to a pitching
deck.

A hasty examination of her charges revealed scrapes, gashes, and a few
swellings that appeared insignificant. Finn had stepped on a broken shell,

but by and large the animals were unharmed. Rest, fresh feed, and a good grooming were all they needed.

She had no injuries either and suffered nothing more serious than consuming hunger and thirst and a fervent wish to wash away the salt water and get into clean clothes.

Alana dropped to her knees in the sand. She could see *La Marquesa* plainly, as well as several small craft approaching from the harbor. A frail cockleshell indeed to have carried its cargo of people, animals, and goods safely across the Atlantic. She smiled as a rainbow arched over the ship. A good omen!

Pulling a rosary out from under her bodice where it had been tucked for safekeeping, she thanked God for deliverance and asked his blessing and guidance for the future. That done, she sprang to her feet, her eyes sparkling with excitement.

For better or worse, Alana MacKenna had arrived in the New World.

I

The inquisitor general relieved himself while Negro coachmen supported him with discreet hands beneath his elbows. Expressionless, the twins
stared straight ahead until he had finished and then solemnly assisted him
back into the carriage. As the door closed, their eyes met in silent fury.

So far it had been an irritating day for the Bishop Bartolomé de Zamora.
Pain from gout had nagged him awake before dawn. Nuns had been cack-
ling in the audience room about alleged mistreatment of Indian slaves, and
now the sherry and madeira ordered months ago were in that stupid ship
out there. He bumped his inflamed foot on the hamper that overflowed with
wine bottles and delicacies. Sweet Mary in heaven, that a simple ride in the
country should end up like this!

The prelate sulked in his luxurious carriage. He was large and corpulent,
with a pudgy, waxlike face that seemed to melt slowly as he grew older.
He hated the sun, and his skin was pale like the smoothly shaven skull beneath the wigs he so vainly affected in the Cuban heat.

Those who hated him whispered he looked like a slug or, they sometimes snickered, a eunuch. There *had* been stories. . . . But when those
black eyes landed on them with the sting of a lash, rumor died and contri-
butions to the cathedral increased.

15

A gentle scratching on the door panel interrupted the bishop's thoughts. "What is it?"

"A woman with a dog and some horses has jumped off the ship. They are swimming this way."

His curiosity strongly piqued, the bishop pulled himself over to the window. Rings of heavily wrought gold inset with emeralds and rubies glittered on his big hand. The Spaniard prided himself on a classical bent, and although they were profane, he secretly enjoyed stories of pagan gods and goddesses. When he saw Alana rise from the waves seated astride a noble beast, he was immediately reminded of Amphitrite, wife of Poseidon, ruler of the sea and god of horses and horsemanship.

His appetite was further whetted by white flanks and knees revealed between boot tops and hiked-up skirts. And those proud breasts so pleasingly outlined by wet material. Although the bishop's attention seldom wandered above a woman's collarbone, he noticed that this face was pretty even from a distance. How extraordinary to find such an attractive woman unchaperoned, alone and riding like a man!

When she sank to her knees to pray, he nodded righteously. Proper. Very proper. A devout female—and extremely handsome horses. Island-born stock brought high prices these days, but such imports were worth a great deal more. That brute of a dog would also bring a wonderful price. Excellent for bullbaiting! As for what the woman was worth, he would have to wait and see.

He banged on the carriage door. "Help me out," he commanded testily.

The inquisitor general was neither old nor physically debilitated. He was simply lazy and overweight and took advantage of every comfort his position afforded. That he often chided his congregation for greed and covetousness never seemed inconsistent to him, however.

Stepping down amid a rustling of expensive dove-gray garments, the bishop fleetingly regretted soiling his new satin shoes. Yet the welfare of a new member of his flock—and one so much in need!—must take precedence over worldly goods.

Alana saw the bishop advancing regally toward her. The picture of a potbellied, hawk-nosed gull crossed her mind. But she ran to meet him and, kneeling at his feet, kissed the hem of his robe.

"Oh, Your Worship, fancy your being here to greet me! Surely it is a sign of His divine mercy."

The man beamed down on the woman who would hereafter haunt his dreams and caught his breath when black-fringed sea-green eyes raised to meet his. Salt-stained, disheveled, and fatigued though she was, Alana MacKenna fired his imagination.

"My dear, dear child." He took both hands and brought her to her feet.

Alana immediately put up her guard. Beneath the bishop's ecclesiastical garb and behind his unctuous manner, she sensed an adversary.

Late the next afternoon, the Irishwoman strode angrily out of the bishop's country house located on the outskirts of Santiago. Heartsick and furious, she put Conn into a canter, the wolfhound loping beside them without effort on the road into the city.

What a mess she'd got herself into! And what a simpleton she'd been in the first place, giving in to the wanderlust that had brought about many a MacKenna's downfall. Why had she left Ireland? Why hadn't she been satisfied with the profits from Seville? Or even sold her darlings to the English who lived in the Pale surrounding Dublin? Why? Why? She kicked the stallion into a furious gallop.

Alana had just been gulled by a master. The horses the bishop had stabled for her yesterday had disappeared—had been stolen, he said! Although she knew the man had them, there was no way to prove it, and she was not about to trade personal favors for her own property. To make matters worse, her money pouch had been lost, no doubt during the leap from ship. Now she was facing a hostile world without a single coin. Alana thanked God she at least spoke Spanish well. Otherwise, she might be in even more difficult straits.

Pulling rein, she hesitated, then dismounted. Where was she going anyway? What had she intended to do? She had no money. She knew no one. The nuns in Santiago who'd fed and clothed her yesterday were gentle and submissive. They would hardly flout the will of their superior once the inquisitor general, insulted by Alana's rejection of him, forbade them to help her a second time.

Alana scolded herself as she headed despondently toward a nearby beach. She should have known what was going to happen. On the other hand, when she had been snug in the bishop's carriage, munching on succulent meat pasties and sipping ruby-red wine, nothing had alarmed her. Were they not all alive and well and in the hands of a good Samaritan?

The avid black eyes had devoured her when she arrived after resting overnight at the convent. She wore a simple gray gown that took on sensual grace draped over her figure. Her silken hair was pinned on top of her head in shining braids. Her white throat and face contrasted with the gown's severity, giving her the aura of an exotic flower. Though Alana had long been aware of her beauty, the impact on men of her silver-blond hair, emerald-green eyes, and coral-rose mouth had become so familiar she seldom noticed it.

Invited to a midday meal, Alana had been eager to look in on the four horses so graciously stabled by her host. Not wishing to appear impolite, however, she ate and chatted with him as the hours wore on. But she began to feel apprehensive alone with him in the shadowy room so far from the foyer into which she'd been welcomed.

As the man drank more and more wine, her fears increased. His eyes glistened with lust, and his pallid skin became flushed and moist. He had edged closer and put ring-laden hands on hers. That she had suffered, but when a well-clad thigh nudged hers, her faith in the protection of the church had collapsed.

Alana now realized ruefully that diplomacy and cunning would have served ten times better than her loss of temper. Striking a bargain she had no intention of honoring, she might have succeeded in drinking the lecher under the table. Then she could have taken the horses, which were probably hidden nearby, back to the Santiago livestock market. There she would have had her money in half an hour, so exceptional was the breed she had dared bring to this remote outpost of empire.

Suddenly the enormity of the dilemma overwhelmed Alana. "Oh, Finn, Finn!" she sobbed. "What's to become of us? 'Tis a great fool I've been, and that's God's truth." Slumping to the sand, she rocked back and forth, weeping bitterly.

After a while she dried her eyes on a petticoat and sat gazing out to sea. Hers seemed like an insurmountable problem—lack of funds, no family or friends, and no salable goods. To sell the stallion or the wolfhound was unthinkable. They were friends.

They need not go hungry as might be the case in parts of Ireland or Spain during the winter. Fruits and fish were plentiful here. She could build a crude shelter and easily make money racing Conn against local horses. Alana grimaced. None of that would do, no matter how she rationalized it.

Besides, the three of them needed food and shelter within twenty-four hours. As far as employment was concerned, she could hardly displace a slave. And getting money from elder relatives might take six months, counting sailing time. *If* she had coins to pay for the message!

Alana began to skip rocks, gloomily watching the ripples spread in the sunset-tinted water. Gradually she allowed a thought to surface, one suppressed and hated. She actually possessed a rare piece of merchandise for which any jaded lord would pay handsomely.

When the deep voice addressed her over the dog's warnings only minutes later, it came as no surprise, and as beggars could not be choosers, she crossed her fingers. He just might be a decent man in whom she could confide.

The stranger's honeyed tones had followed on the grim realization that she must sell herself. Alana swallowed hard, tossed her head back proudly, and turned to face the future.

II

Count Gilberto de Salvatierra of the House of Altamira, with a lineage older than that of his king, studied his guest over the rim of his silver goblet. Gossip about this adventuress had spread swiftly over the scandal-starved island. The galleon's captain had embellished her reputation considerably once he came ashore, and the count had expected a coarse weed sprouted from stable dung. Instead, he found an elegant flower on the verge of full bloom.

Like most wealthy landowners in Cuba, Gilberto de Salvatierra kept a harem of lovely women. Some lived here in the capital, and others at his inland sugar plantations. He bought the best, and they had been very satisfactory—hot-blooded, willing, and inventive. Naturally, they usually slipped his mind after intercourse.

But this Venus with her hip-length, moonglow hair, and eyes that changed from a flash of emerald to the green of a moody sea—clearly, she was an enchantress who would be hard to forget.

They sat together in the central courtyard of his hacienda. It was open to the ebony velvet of the Caribbean sky, and stars blazed like the diamonds in his gold satin doublet. Somewhere in the sumptuous residence a singer sighed about the inconstancy of woman. The lute throbbed softly almost like a pulsebeat. Jasmine and gardenias intoxicated the senses with their fragrances.

"More wine, dear lady?" The nobleman leaned forward solicitously. He wanted her to be comfortable and contented.

"It is the finest Malaga." Not waiting for an answer, he refilled their goblets. "From my vineyards in southern Andalusia. You can taste the Mediterranean sun, can you not?"

Alana smiled politely and shook her head, toying with a dish that held sweetmeats. She felt so high-strung tonight just a little more might undo her. As it was, her head spun alarmingly.

"No more, *gracias*. It makes me sleepy."

He placed a lean brown hand on her forearm and squeezed ever so gently. "A state devoutly to be wished for at times."

Gilberto was amused by the blush that colored her alabaster skin. The Irishwoman had to be in her mid-twenties at least. Could it be possible she was innocent? Nonsense. Someone like her had undoubtedly known many men and she would not be traveling alone unless she were very experienced. Besides, she had been very frank about her need for a protector.

When Gilberto had arrived at the inquisitor general's for their weekly chess game, he'd witnessed Alana's stormy departure. Fascinated by anyone who quarreled with such a powerful man and intrigued by her loveliness, he had followed her to the beach. Long a voluptuary where the opposite sex was concerned, he had a sixth sense when it came to conquest. This time it had promised an interesting chase, although he'd never dreamed of winning such a prize. If she were a prize. Physical beauty did not signal passion any more than a blossom's prettiness meant perfume.

He took his hand away, amazed to see it tremble. By God, the Spaniard thought as he drank more wine, he admired her courage and spirit of adventure. Such qualities appealed to his warlike nature, and they would certainly add spice to lovemaking.

His women were trained to be obedient, even servile to his needs and demands. But when he bedded this one, he anticipated savagery and tenderness, wildness and sweetness. What was there about this Alana MacKenna to inspire such emotions? Wasn't it his way to take women without care or thought?

The candle's flame wavered in a breath of air and created shadows in the hollow of her throat, beneath her breasts and in her lap. Desire kindled, and the nobleman drew in his breath at its intensity. He rose abruptly only to fall back into the chair with a grunt of pain.

"What is it?" Alana jumped up and bent over Gilberto. He gritted his teeth, making light of injuries he had not mentioned.

"Nada, nada." Sweat beaded his forehead, but he winked gaily, hazel eyes warm and friendly. Alana unbent and returned the flashing smile, which had been calculated to melt her defenses.

"Nothing! You're suffering!" Hope burned that what the night had been going to bring might be postponed. "Here, drink this. You look as if you need it." She handed him his wine goblet.

Downing the liquid, Gilberto slowly relaxed as the spasms of pain faded. He cursed silently. Tonight would be one to remember. It was no time to be laid up with old injuries.

Taking Alana's hand, the man raised it to his lips. She shivered when the glossy black beard touched her skin.

"I am touched, *preciosa."*

"How were you hurt?" She withdrew her hand.

"Oh, I went with a friend of mine on one of his expeditions last year. With Juan de Grijalva. We sailed past Yucatán and went ashore in a region called Tabasco. We were friendly but—" Gilberto shrugged and stood up. "The natives insisted on fighting, so we obliged them. I was wounded several times, and my shoulder still hasn't mended. Those heathen are expert at cutting their enemies to pieces, you know. They practice human sacrifice and cannibalism."

"The Good Lord save us!" Alana crossed herself, eyes wide with horror. "What kind of savage beasts are they?"

Gilberto said, "I'll tell you more tomorrow. If it doesn't turn your stomach, that is. Now, if you'll forgive me, I want to go to my room and rest. I keep my medicine there."

Bowing with effort, he snapped his fingers, and a Negro manservant materialized. "Show the lady to her room, and tell the old woman to see to her every comfort." He turned to his guest. *"Hasta luego,* beautiful one."

Alana replied, *"Buenas noches, señor."* Following the servant through the dimly lit mansion and down a corridor, she breathed a sigh of relief. Thank God for *that* reprieve.

Her quarters were tasteful and luxurious. On one wall a full-length mirror with an ornate silver frame reflected furniture of pale wood. This lent an airiness to the room, emphasized by light-blue gauze draperies suspended over the bed. Cotton rugs in subtle greens, yellows, and blues were scattered over a red tile floor, and huge cushions in the same colors nestled by a casement window. A tiny taboret of inlaid woods and mother-of-pearl held silver goblets and a bottle of wine. Outside a fountain burbled, and moonlight streamed in the window, silvering bouquets of flowers that graced a dresser and bedside table. On the dresser Alana found perfumes, unguents, oils—and a magnificent pearl necklace.

Suddenly an old Indian woman appeared at the door to direct the positioning of a hip tub carried by two boys. She put towels and scented soap on a chair and a garment on the bed.

"Tap on the door when you are finished, *señorita.*" The crone vanished without a glance at her master's newest acquisition.

Alana eyed the tub warily but finally undressed and sank with a sigh into the hot water. It would have been soothing to soak until it cooled, but she was nervous about being caught naked.

She kept looking at the door, expecting the cat-eyed nobleman to enter unannounced. But there were no interruptions and after wrapping herself in a towel, Alana tapped on the door. The trio trudged in, eyes downcast, and within seconds the tub and her clothes were gone.

That was disconcerting! Heaven knows her only apparel had been in sad need of laundering. Dug out of a trunk in which worldly clothing was stored for emergencies, it had had a musty smell. Yet it was better than nothing. She could have used a petticoat for a bedgown.

Then Alana saw what had been laid so reverently on the bed. The robe of pale-green diaphanous silk was trimmed lavishly with cream-colored lace, and when she put it on, the folds flowed over her body like water. She gasped at the hundreds of seed pearls sewn into the lace's design. A garment for a princess—or a woman about to be seduced. Who else had worn it? Alana swirled girlishly, letting the sleek softness settle about her legs.

How fortunate to have met Gilberto de Salvatierra. The man appeared to be cultured and immensely rich; his breath had been sweet, and his fingernails clean. She could only hope he was kind.

A night bird caroled in the garden, and Alana leaned against the window watching the fountain make crystalline patterns in the moonlight. When the door opened, she turned sharply, putting a hand to her throat. She had slept a little but restlessly, very much aware of her vulnerability. These were disquieting feelings for a person accustomed to controlling her own destiny. But then she had never faced starvation and poverty before or been stranded in an alien land thousands of miles from home.

The Spaniard entered, and she was reminded of a great feline, treading stealthily, stalking his prey. He wore a black robe of a rich fabric threaded with gold, matching slippers of fine leather, and a golden cross set with emeralds that glittered dully against a mat of chest hair. An aura of heavy musk surrounded him.

"Did I spoil your dream?" Gilberto limped slightly, crossing the room. Standing in front of her, he examined her from head to toe. His tawny eyes smoldered, and his face flushed.

"No, it must surely be the other way around. Men dreaming of you!" He pulled the robe down about her shoulders and kissed the white flesh. "The way I have since the second we met." His mouth swept ardently across the swell of her bosom and up her long throat.

"Please. You don't understand—" Shyness, embarrassment, and modesty combined in Alana's protest as she tried to push his head away.

He chuckled and pulled her to him. This stunning piece knew very well that feigned innocence only fueled a man's passion.

When she backed away from his swollen manhood upthrust between them, he clapped a hard hand to the small of her back. Then he kissed her, and his tongue entered her mouth. Alana jerked her head away, startled.

"None of that," he murmured disapprovingly. "Kiss me. Kiss me, lovely witch, as only you know how to do."

"You're mistaken. I—" Words failed her.

She had had her share of fumbles in the past, of hasty fondlings and narrow escapes, but old wives' tales and memories of stallions rutting frightened her. Suppose he liked to hurt women or was one of those who could never get enough? She stiffened with fear.

"Kiss me!" Cruelty edged the impatient tone. "Don't fight me. We have a bargain, don't we? Do what I tell you."

Gilberto tore open their robes and swore with delight when their bare bodies met. She looked up at him, her wide eyes jade and quicksilver pools in the moonlight.

Drowning in their mystery and promise like an untried swain, the Spaniard experienced the same giddiness of desire he had known earlier in the evening when the shadows had touched her so provocatively.

He bent again to kiss Alana's inviting mouth, and her tongue met his tentatively. He was pleased she did not withdraw as his mouth grew more possessive, as he cupped and tasted the pearly breasts resting so heavily and deliciously in his palm.

One hand had been caressing her flanks and buttocks and now moved to more sensitive areas. Alana exclaimed in muffled alarm against Gilberto's lips and tried to evade the clever fingers that had found her private parts, the inviolate, guarded, unsullied parts. But her young body betrayed her, and all the feelings he so skillfully evoked lessened her resistance. She closed her eyes and bowed her head, shivering slightly. Like a gorgeous mare ready to be tamed, he thought, and lifting her, half-fainting, he carried her to the bed.

Quickly he stripped them both and eased himself down, taking care to rest on his uninjured side. *Por Dios,* what a treasure! How luminously her silvery hair trailed over her skin.

When her thighs resisted his knee, he spoke harshly. "Open the gates to paradise, woman." His voice hardened as he felt himself losing control. "Open them, or you'll be sorry." Her legs parted reluctantly, muscles quivering with strain.

He fell upon Alana and partially entered her. Gilberto moaned with surprise and pleasure. "Your *are* virgin. I *am* the first, by God!" And he bore mercilessly through her maidenhead, ignoring her cries, no longer able to contain himself and racked by almost agonizing ecstasy.

She struggled, but the Spaniard grasped her so tightly in paroxysm it was useless. His victory and the shock of penetration stunned her. She was changed. For now and forever. A sense of desolation flooded her.

"Preciosa, preciosa," Gilberto murmured against her passive mouth. "Of all the times, of all the women . . . " He would never be the same. In a certain way, he'd claimed her body and soul.

Studying shadows on the ceiling, Alana listened to the unfamiliar snoring. Now and then her lover—strange new intimate word!—moved restlessly. Once his hand brushed her hip, and she rolled away. His liberties had shaken her to the foundations of her being, and she needed time to absorb what had happened.

She was no longer a girl. At a time when only hardy individuals celebrated their fortieth year, she was already growing old at twenty-five. Alana fully realized she could have lost her virginity long ago far more brutally and under sordid or even bestial conditions. Rape by one or more men was not that rare.

Yet bitterness corroded her spirit at being bested by circumstances, and Alana hated the Spaniard for taking advantage of the situation. Increasingly aware of invisible little injuries on her body and a bleak sense of having been used, she wept with frustration and rage and sadness, touching her tender, abused flesh gingerly. Finally fatigue overwhelmed her, and sleep came, deep and healing.

Alana awoke to Gilberto's frank, satisfied appraisal. Still naked, his battle scars angry in the predawn gloom, he leaned over and dangled the rope of pearls in front of her.

"I meant to give you these, but I fell asleep."

He lifted her head off the pillow to clasp them around her neck, and Alana saw he was ready to make love again.

She looked away. He was the only man she had ever seen without clothes. Then Alana looked back shyly. Why was she hot with embarrassment, yet so strangely stirred?

Gilberto laughed softly. "I want you. Do you want me?" He laughed again when the pale face flamed.

Gathering her to him, he whispered, "You make me a young man again, do you know that?" It took their breath away to find they both shook so.

"Love me, silver woman," the proud Spaniard asked in a strangled voice, "for Christ's sake, love me."

And as his mouth and body melted into hers, the captive became the conqueror.

III

When Alana awoke the second time, it was to sunshine and a sense of unreality. She sat up and swung long legs over the side of the bed. The tissues and muscles of her naked body reminded her forcefully of what had happened.

Had she been impregnated with the seed of the Spaniard? Pray God she was not! Alana buried her face in her hands. Well, at least she was alive, and he had not abused her. It was a blow to realize how irrevocably committed she now was to a completely different life.

The Indian crone entered the room like a wraith, carrying a wrapper, clean clothing, toilet articles, and a basin of warm water. Slipping into the wrapper, Alana tried without success to ignore the servant, who changed the bloodstained linen and tidied the room. She saw calloused feet that spoke poignantly of years of hard labor, a withered arm, and the brand of a cruel master on one cheek.

When the servant had finished, Alana touched the useless arm lightly. "Thank you, grandmother." The gaze flicked upward, off guard, and the woman quickly curtsied and disappeared.

Standing in front of the silver-framed mirror, Alana brushed and braided her hair, deftly arranging it atop her head. After washing, she dressed in practical undergarments, the gray dress, and boots of cordovan leather. The dagger, which had been under the pillow, went back into its sheath. Now where was the brooch?

Someone knocked. "Are you awake, *señorita!* My master requests your presence at table." After a slight pause the voice asked if there was anything Alana needed. The words vibrated with the envy and obvious dislike of the ebony-haired girl who had served them the evening before.

There was the brooch, under a handkerchief. "No," Alana called, "but tell him I will join him shortly. And *gracias.*"

Fastening the ornament at her throat, Alana patted it lovingly. Like the face of an ancient sun-god, it was. The blessed grandmother who gave it to her had said it was very old. Not even from the time before the Norsemen, but from the age when Ireland had furnished gold to Crete. Alana had always thought it marvelous that Cretan artists made jewelry for the pharaohs of Egypt with Irish gold. She treated the brooch with awe, and as a lucky piece that linked her to the past.

On a chest near the window the pearls glowed against a scarlet silk shawl. Distastefully, yet appreciative of their value, she rippled them through her fingers. They were a symbol. If she wore them today, she would have become the Spaniard's property.

Alana walked to the window and gazed down on the busy port of Santiago de Cuba. She'd been told the city had been founded only five years ago when the slave supply on neighboring Hispaniola had begun to decline. From here explorers and would-be conquerors sailed away to discover exotic kingdoms for the glory of Spain and Almighty God. The famous navigator Christopher Columbus had called the peoples in these islands *indios*—Indians—because he insisted he'd discovered the gateway to India.

Church bells startled birds resting in the palm trees. They sprayed into the balmy air like droplets from a crashing surf. Alana crossed herself and whispered a prayer, asking forgiveness for her sins. Then she left the room. It was time.

The nobleman's home reflected his taste and his position—deep blue polished tile floors with a caramel and white design, dark wood furniture, wrought iron fixtures, fur rugs, tapestries, the heavy opulence of gold, silver, and copper. The brilliance and fragrance of tropical flowers accented each room.

Walking briskly along the corridor, Alana glimpsed Gilberto de Salvatierra lounging at a table under a shiny-leaved tree in the courtyard. Her heart skipped a beat. Her lover. The man on whom she must depend for her very existence.

She paused to catch her breath and study him in the harsh morning light. After all, they had seen each other only at dusk on the beach and at dinner, where candlelight cast a deceitfully youthful glow.

He reminded her of a blade of Toledo steel, slender, hard, polished, and menacing, an instrument of dangerous beauty and authority. Like the fine weapon he resembled, Gilberto was sheathed in a costly scabbard: a Moorish garment of exquisite silk which rippled with liquid highlights when he moved. On most men the long, open sleeves and loose ankle-length robe might have appeared effeminate. On him it only accentuated his masculinity. Intricately embroidered with dark green at throat and sleeve, the wine-red silk complemented the Spaniard's olive skin. Pearls glimmered in his earlobes, and golden chains shone on a chest partially bared to the mid-morning sun.

As if her thoughts had alerted him, he turned to stare at Alana MacKenna. A warm smile softened his natural hauteur. Favoring the injured leg, he labored to his feet and held out a hand in welcome invitation.

But she stood rooted, unwilling to meet the honey-colored eyes that had seen her every secret. Remembering their lovemaking, Alana gripped the pearls she was carrying so tightly they hurt her palm. Sweet Saint Bridget had been watching over her, that was the truth. She could easily have had to take up with some unsavory benefactor. Nevertheless, her transformation grieved Alana. How glad she was her parents had not lived to see the day their daughter became a harlot!

Alana finally took a hesitant step. Sensing her distress, the Spaniard thrilled at the extent of his power over her. But on the heels of that intoxication crept a pity and a tenderness the hardened man of the world had never known.

"Come," he coaxed. "Come and breakfast with me."

Walking to her side, Gilberto put an arm around the slender waist. When she trembled at his touch, passion flared and he pulled her to him without meaning to. Alana flashed him a look of entreaty.

"Come," Gilberto repeated more firmly. "There's nothing to be afraid of. Surely you know that by now." He pulled out a chair.

"I'm not afraid," Alana protested in her husky voice. Shivers went down Gilberto's spine. There were few qualities his race admired more than gallantry.

She patted away tiny beads of perspiration on her upper lip. His eyes wandered to her slightly swollen mouth and the mole at its corner. He thought of kissing it and of her response. There was also a mole on her left breast. . . .

Gilberto had heard of the "wilde Irish," although he had never taken any of their women before. What a challenge for a lover of his talents and experience to kindle, and then tame, her fires. They burned in her, no doubt of that. His loins tightened.

"And how are your wounds today, my lord?" Alana asked, her voice lilting musically. "I hope they are less painful."

"They're much improved, *gracias*. The medicine helped, although my exertions did not." He chuckled at the pink flooding her cheeks and lazily motioned to servants in a nearby alcove.

Within minutes they had been served: melon with a sweet orange flesh, strong coffee in the Moorish style, omelets, slabs of crisp bacon, oranges, figs, coarse sugar, and thick cream.

"Eat," Gilberto ordered. "Stop sitting there as if you were perched on a clutch of eggs."

Alana looked sheepish but went on pleating the damask napkin on her lap. "There is one thing—"

"Eat, *preciosa*. You hardly touched your food at dinner." The aristocrat smiled. "You'll need all your strength this afternoon when the seam-stresses arrive. That heavy dress is ridiculous."

"The one I was wearing when the storm struck was ruined," she said defensively. "The nuns gave me this."

"I know, but you would have been much more comfortable in the lace-trimmed robe. And so much more attractive." His eyes travelled over her. "You may find Cuba very warm, you know. Next month we move into the mountains, where it's cooler, but right now you need a wardrobe."

And he expects to be paid for every stitch, Alana thought. Her eyes hardened and narrowed. "If that black-hearted. . . ."

"The Bishop Bartolomé de Zamora is a man of God," Gilberto chided her as he signaled for more coffee. In fact, he held certain reservations about that statement. The Indies seemed to be the dumping ground nowadays for dissolute clergy.

"He is also a thief," she said with quiet anger. "Why, I never dreamed so eminent a man couldn't be trusted! My horses should have paid me a high return for the gamble I took. Instead I let him pull the wool over my eyes like a boyeen fresh from the countryside. Faith! I could have bought my own wardrobe and been home in Dublin by now."

Their conversation alternated between English and Spanish, each falling back on his native tongue for emphasis. Because Alana's father had sold and traded horses in Spain and frequently took her with him, she had heard and spoken Spanish for years. The MacKennas also had relatives in Cork and Galway, Irish cities that had been important in the old Spanish wine trade.

Gilberto, who had come down a hair in social standing at the king's court, had once been ambassador to England. Interpreters were available, but he found ignorance of English an impediment to love affairs, gambling, and intrigue.

That he and his new bed partner communicated so well and in the nuances of both languages had been another plus in the probable success of their relationship. Alana did not understand Spanish gutter slang, however, and the foul things he whispered during the night had in a curious way contributed to his mastery over her.

"I doubt he would be amenable to being petitioned about the horses. Especially now that you and I have an—arrangement. Keep in mind he is a very formidable man. Don't you realize he's the inquisitor general of the Indies? Don't accuse him of theft unless you can *prove* beyond doubt that he stole your animals. You are, after all, a foreigner on His Majesty's soil. The Irish are welcome among Spaniards, but the bishop does have an uncertain temper when his gout is bad."

"Holy Saint Bridget, his men would have taken my personal mount, too, if it hadn't been for Finn!" Alana's eyes widened. "Where *is* Finn? Why haven't I seen him?" She stood up, alarmed and ashamed that her faithful wolfhound had been so far from her mind.

Amused at such concern over an animal, Gilberto told the manservant to fetch Pepe Ortega. The lady wanted to see her hound.

"You've not taken him to set against your fighting bulls?"

The Spaniard walked around the table. They were now face to face. Close up, her facial skin was paler than her hands but darker than her body. It was smooth, fine-grained, and without scars, the complexion of an outdoor woman who cherished her looks. He noticed delicate lines around the eyes as if she laughed a lot. Her teeth were even and white with no unsightly gaps or decay as was common, even among ladies of the court. He recalled his wife's bad breath with mild distaste. Fortunately, *gracias a Jesús*, she was far away in Madrid.

"No, no, my pet. But being far larger than the mastiffs we use, he would be superb! He is safe, though. Don't worry." Gilberto grasped her chin between thumb and forefinger and stared into those green eyes which so intrigued him.

Could it be possible he was actually falling in love after all these years? Black-fringed lids lowered to hide the tumult of her innermost being. What ardor she conceals, he exulted, but restrained himself and kissed her lips so gently her eyes flew open in surprise.

Pepe Ortega entered the courtyard, trying to give the impression he was bringing the wolfhound, whereas in reality it was the other way around. Exactly five feet tall, the merry Andalusian seemed dwarfed by the animal, which stood almost thirty-three inches at the shoulder. Despite the fact that Spaniards held little affection for dogs in general and Finn was devoted heart and soul to his mistress, the ill-assorted pair had taken to each other within minutes. It was to be a friendship only death could destroy.

"Finn, Finn!" Alana dropped to one knee as the big dog bounded toward her eagerly, dragging Pepe Ortega behind like a diminutive terrier on a leash. She ran her hands expertly over the wolfhound's head and body, petting him and confirming his good physical condition. The dog crooned to her in tones of love, relief, and joy.

Rubbing the rough black coat, Alana asked, "Did you give him a bath? The stickiness from the salt water is gone." She beamed with approval, and without warning the hearts of both men quickened.

Receiving the full impact of her gaze, Pepe placed two fingers on his heart and made a bow more worthy of a grandee than an orphaned bastard toughened in the slums of Seville.

"It was no trouble, *señorita*." That this was a woman of quality he had no doubt. "I could see he felt miserable, and no one else would approach him. That dried salt really had him scratching."

"That's what amazes me. Finn tolerates most people, and he's gentle by nature." She giggled. "But to give him a bath! He hates water!"

The wolfhound yawned, displaying the teeth and jaws with which his breed was able to break the backs of wild wolves and bring deer and elk to ground. The man stared with respect, and Finn contemplated him in return, his intelligent dark eyes half closed as if in amusement.

"The Blessed Virgin protect me!" Pepe put his hands on his hips. "You pretended you liked the soaping and rinsing and at any time you were ready to leap at my throat!" The dog's long, thin tail, so inappropriate to his bulk and majesty, whipped against the man's booted leg enthusiastically. "And beat me to death besides!"

Alana laughed. "*Muchas gracias, señor.* I appreciate your thoughtfulness more than I can say. Are you in charge of my stallion, too?"

Gilberto, who did not like any animal but the horse, sat down to take the weight off his injured leg. Let them chatter. It seemed to please her, and she sparkled as Ortega discussed the two things she loved best, dogs and horses. The nobleman watched them, irritated that he had not aroused such an animated response from Alana. Her hair gleamed in the sun like silver floss, and when she smiled and her eyes danced, he felt a twisting in his vitals and a longing unrelated to making love. Was he lonelier than he realized?

"Have you nothing better to do than stand around chewing your gums like an old woman?" He glowered at his man-at-arms who'd accompanied him to the Italian wars, the English court, and now the end of the known civilized world.

Pepe saw which way the wind blew. "A thousand pardons. You know how I like horse talk—" He bowed and picked up the wolfhound's leash. "I'll take him to my quarters if that's all right with you, *señorita.*"

"He's accustomed to being with me," Alana said hopefully. Gilberto paid no attention to her comment but lifted the rope of pearls from the table where she had left it and turned it back and forth in the light.

With a sigh she laid her cheek on Finn's huge head. "Go with him, boyo, and this evening we'll walk the beach and you can chase the birds."

As Pepe guided the hound out of the courtyard, he found himself pondering the fate of the woman who'd spoken so lovingly to her pet. Before he and the dog had been sent for, Pepe had been in the kitchen munching cheese and bread and listening to household gossip about blood on the sheets from Alana's seduction. The island girls scoffed at a female that age who'd never spread her legs for a man. Thinking the count had tired of his harem and broken in another young virgin, Pepe had been prepared for anything.

The moment he saw Alana MacKenna he knew she was not like any other. Though her outer beauty was breathtaking, his primitive nature had responded to inner qualities that had nothing to do with her sex. The flame of rebellion, pride verging on imperiousness, a reckless and spitfire courage—all these touched his own devil-may-care nature and bound him spiritually to the Irishwoman. It was as if she and this almost-human animal had cast a spell over him.

"I hope," he said to Finn, who ambled contentedly by his side, "that he never beats her as he has the other women." Pepe's brown Moorish face, sensual in contrast with his frank gray eyes, contorted with disgust. That would be an atrocity. "Then, *amigo*, even though I've served him half my life, I will be forced to kill him."

And the giant dog, who heard the threat, growled deep in his throat.

IV

Getting out of bed carefully so as not to disturb the sleeping man, Alana removed the pearls. She still harbored the feeling that the day she wore them openly her surrender would be complete.

She pulled a long silk garment over her head, the feminine counterpart of the Moorish ones Gilberto wore at leisure. They were graceful, elegant, and modest, even if he had told her an Arab named Mohammed said silk had been invented so women could go naked in clothes.

Gilberto moved and muttered, flinging an arm onto her pillow. Alana froze, leather sandals in one hand. Was he going to wake up and spoil the only part of the day that belonged to her?

During the summer as his wounds healed, his strength had increased here in the mountains, and his appetite for her as well. She had only to brush against him and he would take her to bed. There were faint circles under her eyes from being awakened in the middle of the night, and the musky scent he used so lavishly had transferred itself to her.

Head bowed, Alana slumped in the darkened room so far from home, feeling satiated, unworthy, and old. She was surfeited with being kissed and touched and made love to. And she suddenly had a terrible yearning for emerald-green hills and countrysides silvered by ocean mists, for glowing peat fires and cold buttermilk, horses with manes glistening with dew, for laughing Irish eyes and bagpipes and reels, and, most of all, for a sense of the soul's belonging.

Her throat constricted with loneliness and heartache. *Oh, my God, is this all there is for me? Is this the pattern of all the days and nights to come?*

Alana ran out of the room and down a hall to the kitchen, tiles cool and slippery beneath her bare feet. It was now a few minutes after daybreak, and the country house was still. The servants no longer rose early. Their master dallied with his mistress in the mornings, and they slept until his shouts woke them to frenzied activity. She was alone with the new day—and how much she had come to like being alone.

Pausing to fasten her sandals, Alana glanced out toward the stable. Finn, who often seemed to read her mind, sat waiting patiently. When she appeared, the wolfhound trotted to meet her, eyes shining, silent in his greeting as if he understood no one must know about their outing.

"Finn, dear, are you ready to go?" She gave him a piece of cold meat filched from the spit. "Come on, let's see if Conn feels like a run."

The horse had regained the flesh and vigor lost during those weeks at sea, and Pepe Ortega groomed him daily so his black coat gleamed dully in the stable's dusky interior. Among the horses her father had raised, Conn had been Alana's special darling. He was full of fire but gentle as a fawn with her. For now she was the only one permitted on his back, but Alana felt sure he would eventually allow Pepe the same privilege.

"When he makes up his mind, I will be honored!" Like any natural horseman, Pepe knew class when he saw it. In this animal he recognized the product of meticulous breeding and loving care brought to the peak of perfection.

"As you should be," Alana had replied, showing frank affection in her smile for this man her animals had taken to their hearts.

"When my father bought the best stock in Spain, he knew what to do with it. He agreed with the desert people that a horse should spend the first few years in the open, hardening itself and building up resistance to disease and illness. At five or six, he was ready to be trained, but tenderly and without being overworked. Conn can carry a quarter of his weight at a steady speed over long distances without food, water, or rest, if he has to."

Lost in admiration, they had taken stock of the black stallion. How the Arabian's blood burned in his speed, power, and fluidity of motion. How the Moorish Barb's wild glory blossomed in his endurance and agility. How the prehistoric Irish horse survived with its strength and tenacity. The arch of neck and flow of tail were visual music. And in the large, kind eyes glowing with innocence, intelligence, and goodness dwelled the splendor and spirit of the equine prince.

"Have you never heard any of *The Triads?*" Alana had asked incredulously, forgetting Pepe would have no knowledge of old Irish chants. "One of them says, 'Three glories of a gathering are a beautiful wife, a good horse, and a swift hound.' "

Were she married, Pepe had gallantly assured Alana, her husband would most certainly have all three.

But she was not, she had answered sadly, nor was she about to be. The misery masked with a smile and a toss of the head aroused fierce, protective instincts the little Spaniard had never known before.

Unnoticed by Alana this particular morning, Pepe lounged on the washhouse steps near the kitchen door. With no duties to attend to and satiated from his predawn lovemaking with the cooperative laundress who was preparing his breakfast, he watched Alana disappear into a wall of greenery as she rode the stallion bareback. The wolfhound followed, his bulk easily parting the dense undergrowth.

That horse was worth a king's ransom! Black with a white blaze on its forehead and one white foot on the mounting side—*perfecto!* Especially when Conn boasted such bloodlines. Horsemen of the East said such a blaze brought its rider glory and good fortune. Whorls between his ears and on neck and sides were also supposed to bring luck. If he, Pepe Ortega, were any judge, Conn's mistress was going to need all the luck she could get.

Alana looked about as she rode through the woods. Her lover had little interest in the brilliantly feathered macaw that screamed so raucously or in an unusual lizard that changed color according to background. Nor was he concerned with the amazing bird of iridescent hue which fed from flowers' hearts and whose tiny wings whirred so incredibly fast they created a steady hum.

"Ah, Finn, is it not lovely! A day of silver and azure." Morning breezes skittered over the leaves, doves cooed, and rabbits and rodents fled the thud of the horse's hooves. Primeval beauty, the animals' purity and delicacy, the spiritual peace of the surroundings—these provided the balm and solace Alana needed. She searched eagerly for her landmark, a grayish-barked tree with purple blooms and glossy foliage. Here the path turned, and a few minutes later she arrived at the waterfall and its circular pool.

With an exclamation of joy, Alana dismounted, freeing the horse to graze. Finn drank and proceeded to investigate odors among bushes and ferns. Confident of privacy here, Alana took off her gown and jumped into the water. It was cooler than usual, and she squealed with the shock.

Whenever possible, she came here to bathe, rest, and sun herself. The glade had become a refuge where Alana was able to escape Gilberto's seemingly insatiable demands.

It was obvious that her personality brightened his household with laughter and easygoing geniality. She sparkled against the Spanish somberness like a gem on dark velvet. But her affability and cheerfulness had only emerged recently after the initial pain of being owned had faded and Alana had learned to make the best of a bad situation.

There were still times when melancholy flooded her spirit, making her tense and moody, times when the emerald eyes brooded and mourned the past. Then her lover tried to hold the Irishwoman to him through delights of the flesh, though he did not often succeed.

Alana had been depressed earlier but grew more lighthearted as she splashed and sang. Her monthly flux was near, and once again the mental burden of unwanted pregnancy had been lifted. For reasons known only to herself, the old Indian servant had given Alana a red powder. This, she whispered, would prevent her from conceiving as long as she took it regularly. Now it was almost the end of September, and despite the many times Gilberto had taken her in the past five months, she remained without child.

Floating on her back, Alana watched the sunshine on the water, thinking back to that first night when Gilberto had pierced her maidenhead. How frightened she had been . . . and how passionate he had been! He teased her now, excellent horsewoman that she was, about riding together through fields of ecstasy and that try as he would, he had not yet succeeded in putting a bit between her teeth. Her lover joked about it, but it angered him that he never reached her innermost being, no matter how skillfully he brought her to physical climax. Burying his face in her long hair or between her breasts, Gilberto called her a silver filly that must be tamed and mastered.

It would not be hard to give in. Alana found her benefactor handsome and exciting—even maddening. His scarred body, its very mutilation suggestive of savagery and virility, was a seductive one. Tightening her lips, Alana vowed grimly that Gilberto de Salvatierra would neither bit nor bridle her. He would be easy to love—and should she love him, she would be lost.

Suddenly, rising above the waterfall's melody, there was a baying in the distance. Alana remembered what it meant and climbed out of the pool which had suddenly become more of a trap than a comfort. Dressing hurriedly, she called to both animals in an urgent voice.

The loud baying came from greyhounds trained by Spanish landowners to chase down slaves; they were purposely mistreated and starved in order to make them into man-eaters. Pepe said the dogs always went for the abdomen to tear out the entrails because they were so hungry.

Atop Conn Alana felt reasonably safe, his speed, courage, and sharp hooves between her and danger. After all, the dogs might mistake her for whatever wretch they hunted. She cast a worried eye at Finn, whose hackles had raised at the sound, but his self-confidence, size, and enormous jaws allayed her fears. Alana had seen him do battle before.

Pepe took the reins when she returned home and put the horse in his stall. "They're getting close."

"Too close to suit me." Alana shuddered as the racket increased. She had turned to enter the house, when she heard the soldier curse with excitement and wheeled to see a woman running desperately toward them. Only a few feet behind her the hounds howled with blood lust, and one had a shred of cloth in its mouth. Without another thought Alana stretched out a hand in succor.

The runaway collapsed, exhausted, eyes bulging with supreme physical effort. Her clothing hung in rags through which old and new scars from whip and club showed plainly. She laid her forehead humbly on Alana's foot, clutching at her skirts. Finn leaped in front of the women, snarling and growling so ferociously the half-crazed dogs braked to a stop, churning dust. Pepe drew his sword and laid about mercilessly, injuring the more aggressive animals that barked and leaped into the air, angry at being cheated of their quarry.

Alana, who loved dogs, watched the ravenous creatures with fear and pity. Why, the poor things, their ribs stuck out like slats in a fence! And the mangy hides were marked by vicious beatings. She'd like to give their owners a taste of the same!

Two men appeared with whips in hand, and the dogs cringed abjectly. The largest of the pack, however, a brindle whose spirit had not yet been utterly broken, threatened them. The kicks he received sent him flying across the yard. When he landed, strangling on his own blood, the others transferred their attention to him like sharks to a wounded fellow.

"What's the idea of driving your dogs here?" Pepe demanded. "Those curs might have attacked the *señorita* while she was riding. Can't you control them any better than this?"

Brutes of the lowest order, the men stared at Alana. It was not often anyone saw this woman that all Santiago buzzed about.

"Keep your eyes to yourselves," she snapped, looking at them with loathing. There were other homes in the area belonging to aristocrats and wealthy commoners who fled to the mountains in the summer. Most of them employed servants of this ilk who managed the Indian work corps.

These were made up of either chattel slaves or forced labor. The former were transferred for life like inanimate objects to the settler who received the land they lived on as an *encomienda*, a grant from the Spanish crown. The forced laborers, under an equally repressive arrangement called *repartimiento*, not only were worked to death but had to pay tribute to crown and church besides. The hapless natives died miserably under both systems, the burden of being worth nothing perhaps as intolerable as ruthless physical exploitation.

"And keep your thoughts to yourselves, too," Pepe cautioned. He wiped blood off his blade. A bantam in size, he emanated strength, swiftness, and deadly efficiency.

"No harm meant, *hombre*," the man with the crossed eyes said placatingly. "We just want that bitch there." He reached out for the girl, who now stood next to Alana. "Come here, you wildcat."

"No!" She fell to her knees, supplicating in broken Spanish the woman whose eyes alternately flashed with anger and softened with sympathy. "Don't let them take me back, my lady. Buy me! Buy me!" Black, wavy hair cascaded over a dirty, tear-streaked face. "Slaves say you are kind. *¡Por favor!* Buy me!"

Alana's insides grew tight with indignation. Slavery was vile and evil. Ireland had banned it hundreds of years ago, and until she'd visited Spain, she grew up unaware that human beings were bought and sold like cattle. Certainly this girl who had breeding, should not be a slave. Her bone structure was good, even if the nose was overly bold for a female, soaring from tip to forehead without a break. Her complexion was probably creamy-tan beneath the grime, and the slightly slanted dark eyes were bright and pretty. Coarse clothing had not diminished a certain noble presence Alana found impressive.

"What's your name?"

"Inmaculada, *señorita.*"

Her tormentors guffawed. "Immaculate as a dung heap, be sure to tell her!" The cross-eyed slavemaster winked at Pepe. "She's been passed around so many times she ought to know every trick in the book. Besides, I got her first." He chuckled obscenely. "But it's like bedding a stick with a hole in it. We have some new plans for her, though." The other man nodded in agreement, grinning hastily at the sobbing girl.

"They gave me to an idiot last night! Locked me in the room with him! Slobbering and mewling on me." Inmaculada retched.

"She killed him! Can you imagine? A big two-hundred pounder. We watched her run a knife right through the blubber to the heart. But she should have been more cooperative. Now she'll have to pay for destroying her master's property."

Alana shivered with repugnance. Thank the Merciful Lord she had not been raped by scum like these but instead seduced with musk in her nostrils and jewels at her throat. She turned to the men.

"Who is your master? I'll buy her from him."

"The inquisitor general. The Bishop Bartolomé de Zamora."

Pepe saw the light of battle flare in Alana's eyes, and an answering warmth surged in him. He knew how losing her horses to the churchman rankled. She spoke of it often. In fact, he had offered to help steal back the animals, but the household had left Santiago for the summer before they could complete their plans. He saw her swell almost imperceptibly with rage and determination.

Her husky voice grated with restrained emotion. "Oh, so 'tis His Worship, is it?"

"What's going on out here?" Gilberto strode into view, dressed in a long-sleeved white shirt, black breeches, trunk hose, and thigh-high boots. He threw a cloak at Alana. "Cover your nakedness, woman," he said softly. "I don't like your being exposed to the eyes of this filth."

Flushing at the public rebuke, she did as she was told but immediately put a peremptory hand on his arm. "This girl has been badly abused. I want her for a serving woman."

The slavemasters made humble obeisances. The one who had been silent whined, "The runaway belongs to the bishop, my lord. He'll punish us if we don't bring her back." He had to raise his voice over the noisy gluttony of the greyhounds, which feasted on their still-breathing companion.

"My God, Pepe. Kill the poor thing," Alana ordered aghast. She turned away as he put blade to throat and gripped Finn's sturdy shoulder as if to assure herself he was unharmed.

Gilberto studied the runaway. "I suppose she'll do. You need someone to dress your hair.

"I was thinking of that!"

"You could teach this one, I do believe." He reached out and jerked the girl to him by the hair. "You don't belong to any island tribe. Are you from the place called Yucatán?

Inmaculada's face lighted up. "Yucatán! Yes! The island of Cozumel, my lord!"

"How can you tell where she's from?"

"See the profile? The natives we saw along the coast had these distinctive noses. Their temple carvings showed them, too."

He released the girl, who was exotic and well shaped. He might add her to the harem just to freshen the supply. Still, there was an air of wildness, much like Alana's. Which probably attracted her, he decided ruefully.

"You want her, do you?" Gilberto stared into his mistress' eyes with a slight smile, having intended to give her what she wanted from the first.

"Yes. Please."

"Very well." He addressed the waiting men. "It seems a shame the girl was torn to pieces by the dogs before you reached her. You were only doing your duty by pursuing a murderess."

He reached into a pouch at his waist and tossed four coins in their direction. Catching them expertly, they knuckled low foreheads and backed away.

"Now get your hounds out of here. They annoy me." Gilberto pushed

Inmaculada toward a fascinated Pepe. "Clean her up and feed her. We'll let you know when we want her."

The Indian girl looked at her savior gratefully. Two strangers, two lost souls, two prisoners. Somehow she sensed that. "You will never regret this." She kissed Alana's hand.

"She had better not," the Spaniard muttered.

Alana murmured, "*Gracias, Gilberto. Muchísimas gracias.*"

He cocked an eyebrow and, putting his hand under her elbow, started toward the house. "Pleasing you pleases me. Does that work both ways?"

She glanced up at him archly, noting with amusement the light flush that stained his skin whenever he began to want her. "Sometimes. Sometimes not." Alana was just beginning to appreciate the power of her desirability.

He shook her arm impatiently. "Getting saucy, aren't you?"

Alana shrugged but smiled to take the sting out of the gesture. "Would you rather I acted humbly and let you walk on me? Which would you rather have—pap or red pepper?"

They entered the room he used as an office. A distant kin and business associate of Diego Velásquez, governor of Cuba, Gilberto maintained a constant correspondence with the capital. It had been as Diego's supporter and representative that he had planned to accompany Hernán Cortés on a voyage past Tabasco, where he had been injured with Grijalva last year.

His wounds had kept him from doing so, however, and Cortés, the arrogant opportunist, had sailed without Diego's permission in February. Gilberto itched to go where Cortés had gone. Weren't there rumors of a golden city, a pagan Venice? Perhaps El Dorado, the Golden Man, lived there!

It went without saying every Christian had a holy duty in the Name of the Father, the Son, and the Holy Ghost to destroy those gore-splattered idols the natives worshiped. The Spaniard crossed himself mentally. But such affairs could wait. After all, life was short. He closed and bolted the door. The windowless room was cool and dim.

Alana recognized the signs and stamped her foot. "No, not now. I'm hungry."

He removed her cloak, letting it fall to the floor. "I am, too. You shouldn't look at me that way, my love. When your eyes get stormy and that lower lip pouts, my blood boils."

"Your blood is always boiling." Alana headed for the door. "Anyway, there's no bed in here."

"We'll use the floor."

She whirled indignantly. "I'm no cheap drab to spread my wares on the ground."

Grabbing her roughly, he said, "It doesn't matter where we do it. I've spoiled you rotten instead of disciplining you. Now you have to be taught a lesson."

Forcing his mistress to her knees, the man pushed her onto her back and effected entrance with a ruthlessness he had not demonstrated before. She cried out in pain and fear as he took her cruelly and silently. When he had finished, Gilberto rose, casually straightened his clothing, and waited for her reaction.

"You—you—" He had treated her like a tart.

"Didn't like that, did you? But I was tender as a mother compared to those slavemasters. Suppose they had found you at the pool? You'd have been torn apart as if they had been their own dogs. Just remember this in the future. Don't go off alone, and above all, don't expose yourself to other men. I don't like it."

"I'll remember," Alana whispered. She would never forget. "You could have scolded me," she added plaintively, "instead of hurting me."

Her lover wrapped Alana in the cloak, arranging the marvelous hair so it fell in silken streams. Like moonbeams come to life, he thought, pressing them to his lips.

He helped her up and then, sitting down in a rattan chair, drew her onto his knees. "My dearest. How I shall miss you. In fact, I don't know how I can bear to leave you."

Alana's head rested wearily on his shoulder, but her heart thundered with horror.

"Leave me?"

"Diego is anxious for me to sail as soon as possible. The message came a little while ago. He wants Hernán Cortés brought back in irons."

"Why?" Alana really did not care, but his explanation would give her time to pull herself together. She was badly shaken.

"Oh, Diego has a suspicious nature, and his friends and close relatives are after him to stop Cortés and let them take over the expedition. Still, the man seemed like the right choice at the time. He was rich enough to buy and provision most of the ships—although I hear he's mortgaged to the hilt!—and he was very popular. A born leader, I'd say. But bad feelings die hard, and sailing without the governor's permission is going to come back and haunt Cortés, mark my words.''

Anxiety whipped Alana's mind to fever pitch. Would she be abandoned to the hated bishop and other lechers who might use her at will? Would she be forced to sleep with a physically repulsive protector or one who had a jealous wife?

No! By all that was holy, she'd rather brave that land of cannibals. And wasn't this a chance to see the wonders of that new world she had dreamed about?

"Why can't I come along? He has women with his expedition, I've heard. It can't be too bad.''

He held her away from him in order to see her face. Was she serious? Perhaps she really did love him. Underneath the cloak he ran a hand over the body for which he so often lusted.

"Don't. Please.'' Alana repeated her question. "Why can't I come along? I know horses, I can bleed and physic and bandage, and I have an ear for languages. I could be very useful.''

Gilberto considered the idea. "If I had you with me, I would be the envy of every Spaniard in the Indies. But these heathen, as I told you, practice human sacrifice. God knows what they would think when they saw your hair and eyes.''

"They will worship me as a daughter of the sun,'' she said facetiously, sensing she'd won her point.

"Or of the moon, silver temptress.'' He pressed her hand to his cheek. He had not intended to be so rough, but sometimes she infuriated him beyond reason.

Should he take Alana along? He remembered armless, legless torsos in the temples, racks of human skulls, boy prostitutes dressed like girls who hid behind sodomite priests with blood-matted hair.

But he also thought of willing lips, warm globular breasts, and the valley of rapture in which he had pleasured so many times. The decision was not difficult to make.

V

Returning from the dressmaker's one morning early in November, Alana told Pepe to drive the carriage along the waterfront. After weeks of semi-isolation in the mountains she reveled in the bustling capital.

When Gilberto became her protector, she had disappeared from view. His wounds and the unflagging desire he experienced for her kept them from the public eye. In addition, the journey to his summer retreat had been made soon after her arrival. But grist for the scandal mill had been eagerly furnished by passengers who had sailed on the galleon with her and by seamstresses who fitted her costly wardrobe in the privacy of her bedroom.

Little doubt remained in anyone's mind that the Irishwoman, Alana MacKenna, was a sorceress. Hadn't she and her animals flown off the ship in the wake of the storm? Any number of people would testify to that. And didn't she hold the sophisticated count in such thrall he could hardly bear to let her out of his sight? The woman had most certainly cast a spell.

Today the sensation-seeking islanders were finally getting to see her. Wait until his wife in Madrid got wind of this! Any man could understand his obsession. The woman was a raving beauty! Feathered velvet caps swept the ground as the carriage clattered slowly by.

46

"I am reminded of slavering wolves. In fact, I prefer the wolves. At least they're innocent of evil intent." Alana spoke to Inmaculada, who studied her hands in her lap to avoid looking at the townspeople. "Are the men of your country this rude?"

Her companion smiled faintly, and their eyes met with affection. Although Gilberto disapproved, not trusting the untamed streak in either of them, Alana treated the young woman as an equal. She considered Inmaculada an aristocrat, whatever her skin color or culture. Furthermore, she was a sympathetic companion in whom she could confide.

The runaway slave had bloomed with good food, kindness, and decent clothes, and her Spanish had improved. She was fastidious and decorous; she knew and understood her position in the household, and only when she and Alana were alone did she lose her grave demeanor. The dainty Indian performed every duty with pride, dignity, and courtesy.

Inmaculada replied thoughtfully. "There are always men who are mean and vicious and cannot or will not change. But our men—those the Spaniards call the Maya—are taught from childhood to exercise restraint and honor. 'Do not throw yourself at a woman as a dog does before the man who will give him food,' our poets said. ' . . . become polished and a perfect man . . . and bring forth tall sons, strong, agile and handsome. . . . '" She drew a ragged breath and turned to watch a caravel entering the harbor.

"You had a husband? And children?" Alana asked.

After the unpleasant interlude with Gilberto, she understood better what the girl must have undergone in the slave barracks. It was so unfair how easily women could be taken advantage of sexually.

"Oh, yes! Ah Tok. Flint Knife. We had not lived together yet when the Spaniards landed and took me away. Our tribe did not allow it until several months after marriage. Marriage is a new experience to be approached with care so the gods are not offended. Nevertheless, I had gone to the island of Cozumel to worship at the shrine of the goddess of pregnancy. To ask her blessings once he and I were finally one."

"There is no such goddess, Inmaculada. You should have prayed to our Lady." Alana's tone held only mild reproof.

"If she is so merciful, why didn't she help me? Why didn't she save me after I was baptized on shipboard and parceled out to the bearded beasts like a piece of meat? Do you know they're forbidden to bed a native unless she's been given a Christian name? Then the Spaniards will strip her naked and rape her. Because I was virgin, I was called Inmaculada. When they were through, I was sold to the bishop, and he consigned me to the barracks with pious prayer.''

"Try to forget it. That's all over now. You're safe with me." Alana grimaced. "That bishop is a toad! I saw my darling Rose pulling his coach yesterday. His stablehands aren't treating the horses well. Not well at all!" She hit the palm of a hand with a clenched fist. "By my father's sainted memory, I'm going to get them back and take them with me!"

Inmaculada's face tensed. "Pepe and I will help you."

"Good! The ship sails on the dawn tide of the twentieth. We could do it some time after midnight."

"But can you—"

"Yes, I can get away. I'll leave a message for Gilberto to meet me on the dock. He'll be furious, but I *have* to do it."

Alana fanned herself when Pepe halted the carriage. Barrels of salt pork and cassava bread for victualing ships were being carried across the road.

"This green satin is entirely too warm for this climate, I don't care what Gilberto says. Oh, look, here comes the governor. Getting fatter by the day, I would judge."

Diego Velásquez, conqueror and governor of Cuba, was accompanied by minor officials, a Negro servant holding a parasol over his master's head, and a freakish-looking jester with a tiny monkey and parrot. Diego bowed with hat in hand and two fingers over a heart well encased in black taffeta edged with silver cord.

"My dear lady, you are a sight to behold. A veritable breath of spring." Richly dressed and vainly corseted, he peered down his long nose at the rounded bosom. *¡Perdición!* No wonder Salvatierra was so besotted. "It is my fondest hope that you will honor our reception next week with your radiant presence."

You old poop, Alana thought as she smiled sweetly. "I wouldn't miss it for the world, Your Excellency. The count and I will be there. You may be sure of that."

Velásquez motioned to Finn with a languid handkerchief. "What an enormous creature. Is this the Irish wolfhound I have heard so much about?"

The dog stared him in the eye. He sniffed the perfume and powder and stale perspiration. He had no way of knowing that Spaniards believed bathing robbed a soldier of strength. He simply knew his sense of smell was offended.

"Indeed it is. Finn comes from a royal line. One of his ancestors was given as a gift to a Roman consul in the fifth century. Quintus Aurelius Symmachus wrote he was a dog 'all Rome viewed with wonder.' "

"She's no dunce, the green-stemmed flower. She'd read us history by the hour," a squeaky voice declaimed. Alana looked over the side of the carriage at the jester. He had one brown eye and one blue one, which was opaque, and they stared in different directions.

The poor mite! His world must forever be in chaos. "Thank you, *señor*. I am not as well read as you are, I am sure, but perhaps we could chat some morning about things of the past." Her tone was serious, and the fool's face grew red with joy.

"She's a real lady, there's no doubt. And that's a truth that soon will out." Misshapen face working pathetically, he handed her the monkey. "A gift for the lady." It was the only creature in the world that loved him.

The governor chortled. "You've made a conquest, such as it is. That is his dearest possession."

"Then it shall be mine," Alana said firmly, settling the tiny thing in her palm. Her heart went out to the strange little man. "Of course you know I am sailing for Vera Cruz soon with the count."

A murmur of respect traveled through the rapt group. To speak so offhandedly of a journey that had brought death and suffering to those who had gone before. A brave one, this. Or foolish—

"Therefore, I want to leave him in your care until I return. And here. . . . " Alana fumbled in her purse. "Here are funds for whatever he may need."

She bundled coins equivalent to a servant's annual income into a silken handerchief and wrapped the monkey's paws around it. When the governor grew weary of this fool's antics, he might buy a fruit stand or a fish stall with which to support himself.

Alana returned the animal. "Mind you take good care of him for me." A tear dropped from the brown eye, and she quickly turned away.

"Now, *señores*, I must go. The count is expecting me."

Diego kissed her hand, staring with hooded eyes into her bodice. "*Hasta la vista, señorita.*"

"*Hasta la vista*, Your Excellency. Pepe, home, if you please."

Silence fell in the carriage. Alana stroked Finn's head absently, thinking nostalgically of Ireland. Why, 'twas silly for a grown woman to yearn for it the way she did. Wasn't one place as good as another?

"You are truly kind. More worthy than any around you."

With Inmaculada's compliment, Alana wrenched herself back to the present—hot Cuban sun, palm fronds rustling overhead, and heavy floral scents. She exhaled through her nostrils inelegantly.

"Faith! You never saw me in a real temper!"

Though the Count of Altamira had a firm grip on the crystal goblet, the governor's servant still poured with the utmost care. Even a droplet would earn a cuff or kick. This guest was clearly in the mood to mete out either, judging from the sullen light in the amber eyes.

Gilberto was a mass of aches and pains. The injuries he suffered fighting the French at Ravenna in 1512 and the more recent ones dealt by the Indians all bothered him tonight. If it had not been insulting to his host, he would have gone home to bed. He hoped he was not coming down with that cursed quartan ague again. A great deal needed to be done before sailing.

Ordinarily Gilberto, being typical of the Spanish aristocrat who disdained soiling his hands, would have delegated most of the work. Knowing what he faced, however, he was meticulously careful of details that might mean the difference between life and death.

Two items concerned him: a lack of blooded horses with good bottom and enough men to make up a force capable of overcoming Cortés. Hernán was a wily devil. There should be no underestimating him or the adventurers under his command. They were soldiers of fortune for the most part with nothing to lose and everything to gain—and they would not take kindly to their popular leader's arrest.

The problem also remained that however much Diego wanted Cortés put in irons and exploration continued under the authority granted him by the crown, the miser was unwilling to invest much of his own capital. Those who joined had to buy their own horses and equipment and received no pay, only a share in the booty. Had it not been for golden objects Pedro de Alvarado had brought back from Grijalva's expedition—and which Gilberto had admired at the time they were found—he would have suggested a younger man to take the lead.

The Spaniard hated to admit it, but at thirty-seven the rigors of his military career were catching up with him. There for a while after Alana entered his life, he had enjoyed an ecstatic resurgence of vigor. She had only to look at him and he had an erection. But this evening his ego had suffered a shattering blow.

As a love token he had decided to give Alana an emerald and diamond necklace with earrings to match. Of course, she had the pearls, which were worth a fortune, but she stubbornly refused to wear them in public. A galleon loaded with silks, jewels, spices, and laces from Europe had put into port two days ago, and visiting a shop that sold such costly trifles, Gilberto found exactly what he wanted—a fabulous set of jewels ordered by a wealthy sugar planter who had since died and whose unfortunate widow had married a more parsimonious spouse.

Gilberto and Alana had bathed and were preparing to dress for the governor's reception. Alana sat before the mirror in her robe putting finishing touches on an elaborate coiffure Inmaculada had created. "Doesn't this look lovely?"

Standing in back of her, he nodded, eyes alight. "Yes, it's lovely." Gilberto kissed each shoulder in turn. "Most lovely." Their eyes met in the reflection. "You have brought me much joy. You know that, don't you?"

"I am glad."

"Shut your eyes."

"Why?"

"God's breath, Alana! Don't you ever do anything I tell you without question?"

Closing her eyes obediently, she could not resist opening them when she felt the weight of the necklace.

"I see for once you are struck speechless." Gilberto fastened the clasp and put the earrings on the dresser.

"Oh, they are glorious! Fit for a queen! You shouldn't have!"

Alana preened, awestruck, and overcome with joy and greed. How the jewels sparkled and glowed! They rested sensuously on her collarbone, and as they warmed from her skin, she glowed with excitement and pride.

"Oh, Gilberto, aren't they marvelous?" She tilted her head back, and he kissed the hollow of her throat and cupped her breasts.

"Marvelous, yes. Breathtaking. Divine." He began to harden and pressed against her suggestively.

When his mistress broke out of his grasp and went to the door, the man protested loudly. But Alana bolted it, removed her robe and reclined enticingly on the bed, a naked Venus decked with riches.

Gilberto's spine tingled. "What about your hair?"

"Never mind. I can fix it again." She leaned on one elbow, woman incarnate. "Hurry, dark darling."

He threw off his robe and positioned himself. They kissed and fondled each other. But when he probed to enter, the stiffness receded. In spite of her assistance, all efforts proved fruitless. She tried to comfort him.

"You're simply fatigued. You've been doing too much and not resting enough. And besides, the heat has lingered too long and saps your energy." Alana kissed his eyelids, nose, and mouth. "Let's try again tomorrow." She went back to the mirror and the happy business of dressing for island society.

Embarrassed and perturbed, Gilberto swore at length under his breath. Impotence was something that happened to other men. But Alana was right. He *had* been overly tired lately. This infernal bathing she had wheedled him into was what really sapped his strength, not the weather.

And to tell the truth, her taking the initiative—which she had never done before—had put him off. By usurping his role, she had unwittingly injured his vanity. That must not happen again. Responsiveness was one thing, but domination another.

Alana, who found the reception stiff as Spanish furniture, was ringed by gallants. Across the room, she watched Gilberto drinking more wine than usual. Surely he wasn't still brooding! Didn't he realize he was no longer a young man?

Finally, he became engaged in conversation with the governor and a group of soldiers. Now was her chance to get some fresh air. Excusing herself, Alana used facilities set aside for ladies and then escaped to the garden. An Irish party, she recalled wistfully, would be full of gaiety and chatter and harmless flirting to liven up the evening. But Spaniards were so dull, so circumscribed by etiquette and their endless formalities.

Alana stopped under a tree which scattered its flowers with every breath of wind. She was anxious to be gone from here, to be back on a horse, going *somewhere*, doing *something*. . . .

When the man embraced her, Alana nestled against his chest. "Do you feel better, my sweet?" She reached up to pat Gilberto's cheek but encountered a smoothly shaven face rather than his familiar beard.

"Who . . . ?"

She was turned around gently but firmly. Alana caught a flash of blue eyes, golden earrings, and long coppery hair before he bent his head. Then this bold stranger, so tall he blocked out the moon, kissed her as she had never been kissed before.

VI

Brian Phelps knew quite well whom he was kissing, because he had kissed Alana MacKenna before. He noticed then how she fitted into his arms, as if they'd been tailored for each other, exactly the right size for loving.

This time the Englishman held her with care. Things might explode at any second. Still, she had made no resistance so far to the brawny arm around her or to the one supporting her as she bent beneath the pressure of his lips.

Their first encounter had occurred the evening before she boarded ship at Cádiz. He had lodged at the same inn as she while completing negotiations for his father, a ship chandler in Seville whose best customer was the Spanish fleet. The Phelps family had let it be known Brian was sailing soon for the Indies in search of gold and Lady Luck. Just another footloose younger son, that was all. His father hoped he would find the fountain of youth, and his mother, Saint Ursula and her eleven thousand virgins!

His real mission was secret and more serious. In 1493, by papal bull, the corrupt and evil Spanish Borgia Pope Alexander VI had cavalierly divided the New World between Portugal and Spain, with the lion's share going to the latter. Other ambitious countries and men privately protested the Line of Demarcation. England's power behind the throne, Thomas Wolsey, Archbishop of York and minister-confidant of Henry VIII, was certainly not satisfied.

Someone had to keep an eye on those cunning Spaniards and report back to Wolsey and the king on what had been discovered, what was being colonized, and what precious metals had been located.

It was one thing to maintain diplomatic, social, and economic ties with Spain and another entirely to be shoved aside overseas. Such a monopoly would eventually lead to war. In the meantime, as a free agent, Brian Phelps was to keep a sharp eye out. Should his intentions be revealed, he understood Henry's government would deny any knowledge of him.

Such weighty matters were far from Brian's mind this balmy evening. He was amused instead at how much this beautiful blond woman had learned since that evening when he'd mistaken her cloaked and hooded figure for that of his trysting companion, a chambermaid of the inn, and had immediately found himself between a dagger and a wolfhound.

Now, months later, Brian thoroughly enjoyed the answering kiss. How soft and willing her lips were! Perhaps she was more willing than he'd expected. He picked her up and retreated into deeper shadow.

Alana had never responded as she was doing now to this sweet and authoritative mouth. This man was built to accommodate her body, which rested in his arms as if it had always been there. There was a clean, fresh smell about him like grass on sunny mornings, and his kisses left her so dreamy she didn't object to being taken to a corner of the garden.

Alana was living every woman's fantasy: to be so lovely and desirable a mysterious stranger would carry her into the night and make reckless, rapturous love that had no consequences and brought only bittersweet memory and longing.

The man put a questing hand into Alana's bodice. As his lips left hers and caressed her warm flesh, the spell evaporated. His touch was overwhelming, electric! Suddenly ashamed at herself and furious with this stranger, Alana turned and struck him with her clenched fist.

"You whoreson! Taking advantage of a helpless female!" She pushed his arms aside and turned her back. Leaning over to accommodate her breast within the snug gown, Alana shook herself down like an animal whose fur had been stroked backwards.

"Helpless, is it?" Brian Phelps rubbed his bruised jawbone and grinned

disarmingly. "You've quite a clout there, like a tomboy. Must be from un-
ruly horses you've pulled rein on." The deep baritone rumbled with
amusement. "And as to taking advantage—didn't you enjoy that as much
as I?" He caught the fist in its arc. "Maybe more?"

"Let . . . me . . . go." She swooped under her skirts with the other
hand, and the dagger gleamed dully.

He released her. "This kitten still has claws, I see. Do you know this
makes twice you've hit me? I may lose my temper next time and twist your
little blade into a horseshoe."

"There will not be a next time, believe me. And what do you mean,
twice?"

"You don't remember?"

"Are you so wonderful that I should?"

"In Cádiz. In the stable."

"Oh, that Englishman! You arrogant . . . conceited. . . . "

He bowed, a strong hand on the fluted satin of his doublet. "None other.
Brian Phelps. At your service—any place and any time."

Alana made a derogatory remark and stalked away, holding her skirts
above the wet grass. Brian whistled mischievously at a glimpse of elegant
ankles above small black satin shoes with diamond buckles.

Entering the ballroom, Alana tried to locate Gilberto. She felt frightened
and guilty and discouraged the admirers who clustered around her. Her
lover was sitting with the governor and his spouse, Cortés' wife, and other
distinguished guests. As she approached, Gilberto rose and limped toward
her.

"Where in the name of Mary have you been?" He scowled, noting her
high color. He couldn't say why, but she didn't look as stunning as she had
when they'd arrived.

"I don't feel good. I think the jellied eel disagreed with me."

"I thought it was high myself. Why don't we pay our respects and go?
My shoulder is driving me wild."

As Gilberto began the elaborate process of bidding good evening to one
and all, he noticed the striking Englishman on the other side of the room. A
company of Spaniards had arrived yesterday, and with them this foreigner.
Diego Velásquez said Brian Phelps was a son of the fleet's ship chandler.

Dios, what barbarous names the English had. This young cockerel—
what was he, twenty-eight or so?—looked typical of many a ne'er-do-well

amply supplied with charm, energy, brassy nerve, foolhardiness, and fatal weaknesses. A handsome man, the type who always appealed to women. A giant over six feet tall with a chest like a shield and shoulders like a bull. Blue eyes that flustered the ladies, to judge from the fanning and fluttering going on around him, and a big grin in a tanned face. His hair was a ruddy chestnut glinting with golden highlights. It reminded Gilberto of a horse he'd left behind in Madrid.

Despite his yellow and maroon satins and rosetted shoes, Brian Phelps was no dandy. He had the air of a fighting man about him. Of one who would not back off and probably swung a broadsword like the Grim Reaper himself. Gilberto was pleased that Alana's glance slid over the Englishman without a flicker of interest.

Once in their bedroom, Alana massaged the sore shoulder with warm olive oil, gave her lover an opiate for pain and to induce sleep, and let him rest his head between her breasts. As the drug took hold and his lips slackened around the nipple he had fastened on, she drew away.

Her blood grew cold at the thought of what might have happened if Gilberto had found the Englishman fondling her. Would he have killed her or thrown her out? At the very least she would have been beaten and given another unforgettable lesson.

This time, though, she deserved to be chastised. What in the name of all that was holy had come over her? Alana McKenna was no wanton. Though Gilberto had awakened passions she hadn't known existed, she would not surrender to another lightly. She'd grown fond of the Spaniard. He'd been good to her for the most part, and he *was* in love with her. His love furnished a weapon Alana had not had at the start of their relationship.

Alana rolled onto her side and pulled up the covers. That rascal. He not only knew how to kiss, but he also made her homesick with those cornflower-blue eyes and that bold grin. And the sound of her own tongue. Confound him! She smiled as she fell asleep.

Their dark clothing blended into the shrubbery which grew around the bishop's stables and carriage house. As soon as the bank of approaching clouds obscured the moon, Alana and Pepe were going to take her horses back and put them aboard the caravel that sailed on the dawn tide. Their own mounts were tethered a short distance away with Finn and Inmaculada standing guard. Her duty was to give warning in case of late partygoers or insomniacs who might thwart the scheme.

The Maya girl had adapted well to the animals. Like other Indians, she had never seen horses until white men came. Nor had she ever imagined a dog larger than a man! But Finn's defense on the day the greyhounds tracked her down had made him very dear.

Pepe shifted position uneasily. Only he really understood the enormity of their offense. A foreign concubine, an Indian servant, and himself, a brave soldier but not one to be missed if this adventure went awry, were preparing to steal from the powerful inquisitor general of the Indies.

Whether or not the bishop had actually cheated the lady out of her property, what they were about to do was punishable under inquisitorial law. Not that he hadn't committed a crime now and then—Pepe crossed himself—but this one was directed against the Sword of God, a man who answered to no other. A lecherous man who'd desired Alana from the moment he'd set eyes on her and been humiliated by her blatant rejection of him.

This bishop had authority to torture sinners and absolve himself by confession to a fellow priest; he could spirit her away to use and abuse to his heart's content before tossing her to secular authorities for punishment as a thief.

Alana crouched next to Pepe, acutely aware of their audacious plan and her enemy's implacability. She tensed. The stable doors were being closed by the Negro twins who always drove the carriage. Their master had attended a social gathering miles away which had lasted until well after midnight. Now, their duties finally done, they waited wearily until two stablehands came and then took separate paths to their huts.

"I wish you'd change your mind," Pepe whispered. He had no qualms about handling those two buffoons or about freeing the horses and getting them down to the dock. The consequences were what worried him.

"Never."

"Do you realize what he can do to us? And the count unable to raise a finger?" Pepe rolled his eyes. God, the man would be beside himself as it was when they showed up with stolen horses.

"My dear Pepe, I appreciate your offer to help," she whispered back. "But I didn't ask for it. You're under no obligation."

He fell silent, as determined to be at her side as she was to carry out the plan. Sweat broke out on his face and body just thinking about the terror of the dungeons—being stretched apart on the rack, flayed alive, impaled, roasted in a metal oven, burned, mutilated by strappado, having thumbscrews, red-hot pincers, or leg crushers applied.

Blessed Virgin and Beloved Mother, the soldier prayed, *forgive this sinner what he is about to do. Keep in mind if you will, Nuestra Señora, that this bishop with his slaves and a harem and worship of luxury is not a true apostle of your dear Son.*

Having covered all bets, Pepe Ortega crossed himself, kissed his thumb, spit quietly, and, after checking the knife in his belt, concentrated on what he and Alana were about to undertake.

Clouds began to scud over the face of the moon.

Brian Phelps paced back and forth on the dock, bored and impatient. It would soon be dawn, and they couldn't get under way until the count's mistress deigned to join them. Fancy a woman of quality going on an expedition like this! Either she loved the Spaniard, who sulked nearby muttering in his beard, or she was going for gold, too. Or maybe it was the lure of the unknown.

Brian's great-grandmother had been Irish, and her horsemanship, temper, and fearlessness were family legend. She had been a true lady with a heart easily touched to pity, a Christian who gave generously of herself and her goods. She died, he recalled, of a fever contracted while nursing the poor. For all that, she'd still been an adorable hellcat whose husband worshiped her. It was Brian's judgment that although Alana MacKenna lived with her lover, she was much like Brian's ancestress and her own woman. Brian's thoughts were interrupted suddenly by the sound of hooves drumming on cobblestones.

"¡*Finalmente!*" The caravel's captain, who had been diplomatically badgering Gilberto, hurried off to his many duties. The nobleman turned toward the street with an expression that promised trouble for his headstrong mistress.

Within seconds Alana galloped out of the dark into the torchlight, materializing in a cloud of silvery hair. Her eyes glowed with green fire. Four horses snorted and stamped behind her, Finn at their heels like followers of a priestess of animal worship. Or were they a witch's familiars, attendant demons on one of Satan's servants?

"Woman! What have you done?" Gilberto reached for Conn's bridle, taken aback for a moment by a superstitious dread. Had he been having sexual intercourse with a succubus after all? Were the gossips right? He would not be the first man or the last to couple with a devil in female form and not know it.

Then his love conquered such wild imaginings. It was true witches could restore virility. She certainly had! But he had also seen her weep, lie abed with fever, have headaches, and suffer pain. If she were a witch, surely she would not endure the troubles of a human being.

Overwrought with tension and excitement, Alana reined in too tightly. The stallion reared dangerously, pawing the air. Gilberto was forced to jump aside, swearing both at the horse and at the sling he wore to relieve the agony in his shoulder. Extending his long arms, Brian gripped the bridle, forcing the great horse's head down with strength and a firmness of purpose to which Conn responded.

"Do you think you're the Queen Boadicea returning from a raid on the Romans?" By God, a man could fall in love with her! She looked irresistible in her disheveled state and madcap mood.

"Aye, Englishman! And I've returned with what's rightfully mine!" Alana felt an unexpected camaraderie between them. She wondered about it later. Was it their common ancestry of tribal Celts and Gaels swooping down from the mountains for loot and plunder? Whatever it was, their eyes met companionably.

Jumping to the ground, Alana tried to pacify Gilberto. He was irritated with her for slipping away without telling him and horrified at her defiance of one of the most feared men in the Indies. Furthermore, she had kept the ship, its passengers and complement, waiting. Not to mention what he privately felt had been a loss of face in relinquishing her horse's discipline to Phelps.

"You've put me in an awkward position," he growled angrily, hustling Alana toward the gangplank. Pepe lifted Inmaculada out of the saddle and led his mount behind the couple as unobtrusively as possible. Alana could calm the waters better than he.

He heard Gilberto grumble, "Well, what's done is done. Let's get aboard and worry about it later. We can use the horses, god knows. But I wish you had got them some other way." Though the Spaniard was not mollified by any means, neither was he in the towering rage the trio had anticipated.

Alana glanced over her shoulder at Brian Phelps, her eyes dancing with glee. *Oh, you're a bonny poppet,* he thought, *and as hard to handle as a sleek ship with a bone in its teeth.* He threw back his head and laughed. By the balls of Old Horny, this expedition would be one to remember!

"Tell me again, Manuel," Alana demanded. "Tell me again about the gold Cortés sent to the king." Contrary to Gilberto's insistence she keep aloof, she sat cross-legged on the deck watching a sailor scrape woodwork. How could she avoid anyone on a ship less than a hundred feet long?

The man's eyes glazed a bit as they always did when he described the riches he had seen. "There was a wheel of solid gold, *señorita.* Ten hand-spans in diameter and covered with strange beasts and symbols."

"Big as a cartwheel then!"

"Oh, *sí.* And another of solid silver. The same size! The sun and the moon, you see. Each one worth tens of thousands of gold pieces! That's what Captain Pedro de Alvarado told us."

"Is he as handsome as they say?"

Manuel's gaze cleared, and he spit. "Depends on your point of view, I suppose."

"Did I hear a woman who was more interested in a man's good looks than in gold?" Brian stood smiling down at her, legs spread wide apart for balance on the moving deck. His hair shone in the sun, and his large, good-natured eyes were penetrating in the clear light. "Or maybe she's a little girl today?" he asked softly.

How this minx tantalized him! That silvery hair was braided with bright-green ribbon, and she had on a rose-red gown. Its sleeves were rolled up, and the tips of hempen shoes showed at the hem. She looked good enough to eat.

Alana MacKenna had so many personalities a man was hard pressed to keep track of them: a spitfire with a dagger, an imperious princess, a gambler and adventuress, a child-woman fascinated by tales of pagan opulence. Brian wished they were alone so he could sweep her up in his arms again and take her to a secret place. They'd laugh and sing and have a tumble for the sheer fun of it—and then get down to serious lovemaking. But then, she was not his.

The Englishman sat down on the other side of the busy sailor and with an engaging grin handed him a piece of cassava bread to gnaw on. Tearing at his own chunk of the tough loaf, he urged Manuel to continue.

"All right, *hombre*, what else was in the hold?"

"A hundred ounces of gold, *señor*, from the mines of the Indian king. They were brought to Cortés in a soldier's helmet. And they gave him golden ducks and little dogs and big cats and monkeys, all of gold. I can remember a bow and arrow worked in gold and collars of gold and a feathered fan—mostly green like your eyes, *señorita*—with thirty-seven rods plated with gold." He fell silent, thumbing the scraper's edge idly.

Alana had recovered her poise. The way that Englishman undressed her with his eyes! It was a frank, amiable invitation though. Had she been free and anywhere else—knowing what she knew now—he would have his hands full! Instinct told her that when it came to love, to surrendering his heart, he was as elusive as the hunted wolf hiding in his own forest. She liked that. When you gave your heart, it should be wholly given, not in bits and pieces to this person and that.

During the time they had been at sea, he had tanned deeply and his chestnut-colored hair had lightened at the temples. His grin flashed often, big and white in the bronzed face, and somehow she knew he bared his teeth in battle like a Norse *berserkr*. This morning he wore a white shirt open to the waist. It billowed in the breeze to reveal mighty chest muscles, and in the fashion of the day his snug hose and tights left little to the imagination. Gold earrings glittered as he tilted his head back to observe a flapping sail.

"There were many pretty things," Manuel went on, working more quickly as the caravel's captain came forward. "But most were worthless. Feathered fans, cloth woven with feathers, leather embroidered with feathers—they must have millions of birds! Very fine cotton and trifles for ladies, Indians fattened for sacrifice who were rescued from their cages, a funny animal that carries her young in a pocket on her stomach—and—and—"

His mind went blank. Manuel had never had so much attention and did not want to lose it, captain or no captain. "Ah, *sí*, and shields, *señor*! Some with precious stones and others plated with gold."

The ship's officer bowed to Alana. "I see he is boring you again with his stories, my lady." Her emerald gaze was like that of his mistress, the sea, when she was pleased with him.

"Oh, no!" She stood up, swaying with the caravel's motion, light on her feet as a born sailor. "I asked him to tell me. I can't get over it. There must be a magnificent city there past the mountains!" They had seen snow-capped peaks a few days ago when they sailed into a bay to fill water casks.

"Yes, that's true. But if it's like the others our men have seen, it reeks with the blood of innocents whose hearts have been ripped out and offered to their filthy gods." The captain's mouth tightened like tackle on a wind-driven sail. "It is Spain's holy duty to bring them to Christ."

The little group crossed itself. It was accepted doctrine, especially among Spaniards, whose country had recently ended centuries of religious war against the Moors, that those who were not Christians must believe in Satan. Those infidels must be either baptized or eliminated. Of course, it remained to be seen if the Indians were even capable of comprehending Christianity.

"What do you know about Hernán Cortés, Captain?" Brian asked, uncomfortable with the conversation's growing seriousness. Let fanatical Spaniards worry about souls. He wanted to know about the trailblazers like Cortés, what they were seeking and where they were apt to go, any scrap of intelligence that would be useful in reconnaissance. Information, for example, such as the sailor had given him about gold, its abundance and various forms. Had Cortés simply had a windfall, or was there a continuing supply? If so, why, indeed, should Spain get it all?

"That one! He can coax birds out of the trees. I am proud to say he and I are both from Estremadura. His father, Don Martín Cortés, is a fine man, and our families have known each other for many years."

"Didn't Cortés help Governor Velásquez settle Cuba, then marry and raise cattle for a while?" Alana thought he sounded fascinating.

"Yes, he did. Then, after Grijalva returned from Yucatán, and it looked as though there was much more land to be explored and taken for the king, the governor gave Cortés command of a new expedition. But they had quarreled over women and politics in the past." He smiled at Alana. "An explosive mixture. In any case Cortés went at the command like a hungry man attacks a full meal. At that point Velásquez had second thoughts, but Cortés outfoxed him and sailed to Trinidad and Havana to outfit and recruit before the governor could stop him.

"Cortés, of course, won hundreds to his standard, and this past February he sailed with eleven ships first to Cozumel, then north around the cape and along the coast as we've been doing. Have you heard how he and his men whipped the feathers off the Indians at Tabasco? And they were outnumbered three hundred to one!''

"*Incredible!*" Brian exclaimed. A veteran of many battles in Italy, in France, and on the Scottish border, he was completely sincere in his admiration.

"They were soldiers of Christ, *señor*. He strengthened their arms and their hearts."

"Naturally," the Englishman agreed heartily. All military men knew the Spanish soldier was considered the bravest and toughest in Europe.

The captain stared at him suspiciously. He was not at all sure he approved of these foreigners who were being permitted into the Indies. It was bad enough that a death sentence in Spain could be commuted to a two-year indenture in the islands. Entirely too much human garbage was being discarded in this promising region.

"I have nothing but the highest praise for such valor." Alana put a hand on the captain's sleeve. "As well as for men like yourself who risk your lives to take us to our destination."

Her voice lilted like that of a dainty seabird, and her eyes swam with golden specks of sunlight. The captain fought a rash impulse to touch the mole close to her lips.

Brian chuckled to see the fatherly Spaniard caught in the toils of Circe. Taking pity on him, he pointed at the coast, lined with sand dunes and dotted with the figures of curious natives.

"How soon will we raise—what's the name of that settlement again?"

"La Villa Rica de la Vera Cruz." The captain disengaged himself. "I'd say a day or two. And it is already a thriving community, *señor*."

"Is that so?" Brian stretched. "Well, I for one will be glad to set foot on land. It took two months to sail to Cuba from Spain and now another three weeks to get from Santiago to here." He glanced at Alana. She was waving at Pepe and Inmaculada, who were near the horses' stalls.

"Do you realize, Irish, that it will soon be Christ Mass at home? It's hard to believe it's mid-December. I'll miss being with my relatives for the holidays, won't you?"

"Oh!" Alana exclaimed and hurried away without a word, homesickness welling up in her throat and heart.

"Women! They have as many phases as the moon." The captain kicked

Manuel in the buttocks. "Flapping tongues lap up trouble. If you don't want to spend the return voyage cleaning out bilges, keep your trap shut."

To his passenger he said, "If all goes well, we should drop anchor the day after tomorrow."

With a wink at the chastened deckhand, Brian wandered across the deck with a tidbit of sugar for his stallion, Bayard. He was careful to give a wide berth to the area where Gilberto de Salvatierra sunned bare to the waist. But those amber eyes were slitted, watching him like a deadly leopard.

You high-nosed bastard, Brian Phelps thought with a spurt of cold anger. *I'd like to fight you for her. We'd soon see who was the better man.*

VII

The newcomers were enjoying the hospitality of the constable of Vera Cruz, the first Christian settlement in a strange, new, and rich land that would eventually be called Mexico.

He stuffed them with gustatory delights—tomato, pimento, sweet potato, peanut, pineapple, avocado, papaya, and turkey—as well as familiar foods like apples, berries, nuts, onions, mushrooms, fish, game birds, and animals. No one cared to try the winged ants or monkeys, tame dog or boiled grasshoppers, iguana, or agave worms. Those were bad enough, for God's sake. But could any Spaniard imagine these natives not knowing about citrus, sugar, olives, wheat, sheep, goats, pigs, or cattle? Not to mention horses!

Most were impressed with the bountiful array. Why, a person could dine like a lord! They grew fond of a drink made from the bean of cacao trees, a cold, frothy mixture thick enough to eat with a spoon, flavored with vanilla, honey, cinnamon, and powdered orchid seed pods. The Indian name *cacahuatl* soon became known as chocolate.

Weather was good, and along with the others, Alana exercised her horses by riding north to the town of Cempoala, Cortés' first Indian ally. They commented with surprise on its orchards, temples, and attractive folk in embroidered cottons and bright feathers, who wore ornaments of pure gold in their ears, lips, and nostrils.

The town constable, a Spanish soldier appointed by Cortés, laughed indulgently. This was *nothing* compared to the great city built on an island in a lagoon two hundred and fifty miles away where Cortés and the army were now, ensconced like a mailed fist in a flower's heart!

"I can't describe it. You'll have to see it. It's another world!" he exclaimed. "When we marched over the causeway on November eighth, many of us swore it was a dream. Bernal Díaz said it must be like the enchantments Amadis of Gaul saw during his adventures." His listeners murmured excitedly. The popular medieval fantasty-romance about hero-knights and their chivalrous deeds was read throughout Europe.

He continued. "Actually, *señores*—and *señorita*—you came at a propitious time. You wouldn't have dared set out a few weeks ago, but the countryside is quiet now."

The Spaniards bridled. Dare, did the young puppy say? Were Cortés and his followers superhuman and they children just from the teat? No, no, the young man hastened to explain.

"You'll recall our expedition landed nearby this past April. And it wasn't long before we had won over the tribes here along the coast with the sword, the honeyed word, and the holy cross. They gave up human sacrifice and —may God forgive them!—cannibalism, which was part of their barbarous religion.

"The natives were glad to supply us with food and labor once they saw we were not going to hurt them, and we also promised to protect them from their overlords in Tenochtitlán. That's the name of the great city I mentioned. Those tyrants not only demand continual tribute from hundreds of towns under their control, but also take the tribes' young men and women for sacrifice to their awful gods!"

"Tell us more about these overlords. And about what we'll find as we go inland." Under the table Pepe put a hand on Inmaculada's knee.

The constable was fresh from Tenochtitlán, where, he said, the army was housed in a palace of sorts right in the heart of the Indian metropolis. The island-city was astonishingly beautiful, extremely well fortified and had at least sixty-five thousand buildings housing from two hundred and fifty to five hundred thousand inhabitants, all devoted to a god of war.

What were these people called? *Nombre de Dios,* the natives in this land were not one people like the Spaniards, who might have regional differences but spoke one language and had one religion. Here there were many tribes who spoke many tongues and had many gods. Cortés had recorded the tribes of Toltecs, Olmecs, Mayas, Totonacs, Otomis, and Chichimecas, to name only a few. Still, there were only two major groups with which one had to be concerned.

The most important group—those who ruled this vast territory—belonged to a small tribe called the Mexica, which had come to the Valley of Mexico long ago as wretchedly poor, snake-eating, pugnacious immigrants from a place in the north called Aztlán. These Aztecs, as the Spanish called them, were the most powerful of all the Indian tribes both economically and militarily.

The other group was a war-like people from the city-state of Tlaxcala, about halfway to Tenochtitlán. The Tlaxcalans were a proud and handsome mountain race that bitterly hated the Aztecs. At first, thinking the Spaniards their confederates, they'd attacked the army. Now, however, the Tlaxcalans were firmly allied with Spain, and thousands of their warriors had voluntarily accompanied Cortés on his march into the heartland of their enemies.

"Who is king of this mighty empire?"

"He has several titles. Uei Tlatoani, He Who Speaks for the Gods, Courageous and Angry Lord. He's looked upon as demigod and chief of the Valley of Mexico and all it embraces. We address him as Moctezuma the Second."

This man was sovereign of an empire that, as far as Cortés could determine, stretched east to west from coast to coast, south to Guatemala, the Mayas' land, and north as far as he chose to invade and subjugate. Yet, this vast country had no name!

The constable's eyes gleamed. "But in spite of Moctezuma's enormous wealth and power, do you know Cortés took him prisoner within a week after arriving in the Aztec capital? A week, *compañeros*! Right under the noses of his subjects! And what did Cortés have to back him up in this move? About five hundred men, including thirty-two crossbowmen and thirteen musketeers, sixteen horses, four cannon with a two-inch bore, brass falconets—and nerves of steel."

What absolute gall! Every Spanish mouth smiled arrogantly, and even the haughtiest in the audience could not fail to be impressed.

"But why did Cortés take the king prisoner? And is that why we would not have *dared* go inland?"

The constable smiled and held up a hand placatingly. He ordered more wine in an effort to smooth any ruffled feathers.

Gripping his mug tightly to keep his hands from trembling, Gilberto encouraged him. "I assume there was an uprising of sorts or Cortés wouldn't have taken such a desperate risk."

He needed to know as much as possible in order to carry out his mission for Cuba's governor—that of bringing Cortés back for trial and punishment. Other supporters of Diego Velásquez accompanied Gilberto, but gold spoke the tongue of angels—and Cortés' tongue was famous for its blandishments. Gilberto had to step cautiously, yet his attention began to drift to another perilous subject.

Impatience and denial were driving him mad. Alana had not allowed him near her for days. Not since one night on shipboard when he'd brought her to the pinnacle of joy several times. It wasn't his fault the woman had cried out so loudly in her ecstasy! Gilberto unconsciously swelled his chest. Next time she'd know enough to yell into a pillow.

Women! Give them what they want even when they don't deserve it, and you get kicked in the teeth. There was only tonight and tomorrow night before they left on their journey. Who could tell when they would have quarters to themselves again? Look at her, sitting there demure and dressed in black, as if such clothing could dampen that allure.

Her modesty only made her beauty more provocative and set his blood racing in anticipation of the delights it concealed. Bah! Butter wouldn't melt in her mouth. But his heart fluttered with love when Alana turned her head and met his eyes.

"Gentlemen! Please! One at a time." The constable turned to the Count of Altamira. This was no one to trifle with.

"It was not an uprising, sir, as we would term it. Moctezuma had secretly ordered our allies here on the coast to destroy us and Vera Cruz—or he would destroy them. Naturally, this would have left the army with no place to go if it had to retreat."

"In a nutshell, *por favor*, in a nutshell," Gilberto requested.

"You see, we'd been thinking of taking Moctezuma prisoner for some time. Something was in the wind, and we knew if the army was trapped on the island, we were dead men unless we held the whip hand.

"At the time there was no way of knowing the king had already ordered the garrison at Vera Cruz killed. When we did learn about the death of seven of our men, Cortés immediately forced Moctezuma to leave his palace and come to ours as hostage. A horse was also killed during the fighting, which was a bad thing in its way."

"Why?"

"Aside from the fact they're worth their weight in gold, the Indians believed them to be gods. In fact, gentlemen, at the very beginning they thought *we*, too, were gods."

Guffaws exploded throughout the room of the small fort where the group dined. *Gods!* That would pump a man up! Their informant persisted with a grin, realizing his listeners had no conception of the barbaric civilization they would soon encounter.

"You see, they were all expecting a very important god—the Plumed Serpent, Quetzalcoatl—to return from exile. He sailed away centuries back, and according to their calendar, he was supposed to arrive on a certain day in April of this year. By a fantastic coincidence, we landed on that day—Good Friday, April twenty-first, in the year of our Lord 1519!

"This god originally came here many years ago in a one-masted craft with a dragon's head on the prow. Our ships amazed them, of course. But what really astonished them was the fact that so many of us had white skins and red or yellow hair as this god was supposed to have had."

Norsemen? Alana wondered. Those devils had sailed everywhere. Or even Irish monks who were known to have voyaged to a mysterious land to the west in coracles made from animal skins?

The young constable paused to take a sip of wine. "I can't fathom what the infidels will think of *your* hair and eyes, *señorita.*"

"Perhaps they'll think I came from the moon or the sun," she said with a laugh.

"A goddess certainly." He put two fingers on his heart.

"Get on with it, man. Why was the death of the horse so important?" Brian Phelps had drunk too much wine and eaten too many deer steaks and sweet potatoes. He could hardly wait to throw himself down on blankets and a pallet of sweet grass next to his stallion.

A boor, this Spanish-speaking Englishman, but he would not care to cross blades with him, the constable decided quickly. Not with those enormous shoulders, huge hands, and a metallic glint in his icy blue eyes that presaged no mercy.

"The Indians thought the horses were deities. Rider and horse seemed like one bizarre creature to them, and the sixteen cavalrymen were thought to be the god's ambassadors. We wanted to play on their fears and consternation, so when one was killed, it spoiled our plan. They saw the horse died like any living thing."

The speaker's teeth flashed in his brown-bearded face. "We never could have done what we did without the help of Almighty God and the brave horses. But they simply aren't immortal like us Spaniards!" Fighting with Cortés had added iron to his soul. Older men watching him felt unexpectedly flaccid and wanting.

"That's the truth, by God! There'll never be men like Cortés' crew again! A drink to our immortality!"

Wounded and battered by the Italian wars and left behind to help man the fort, an aged musketeer raised his cup in salute. There was a buzz of relieved laughter and conversation as others followed suit.

Alana rose, Finn yawning beside her. She wanted to see her own horses before retiring. Conn and the Englishman's stallion had kicked each other this morning and brought blood when that flirt of a mare teased them. If she didn't watch out, Rose would be in trouble.

Gilberto motioned to a servant for their cloaks, hoping the smile playing around her mouth was meant for him.

"Sounds as if you have things under control for the time being then, and it's safe to travel to Tenochtitlán," he said.

"There's no doubt in my mind. We've proved we mean business. The Indian lord who carried out the attack here has been made an example. He came to Tenochtitlán with his son and several others at Moctezuma's orders, confessed their guilt, and admitted his king had instigated the plot.

"They were burned at the stake right at the entrance to the palace." The constable drained his cup. "The Aztecs have been sweet as honey ever since. On the surface at least. And Moctezuma's still Cortés' prisoner."

Alana sympathized with the lord, who had only done his duty. What kind of vacillating coward was this Aztec king? With thousands at his beck and call, why did he allow himself to be taken by a tiny bunch of strangers? Or feel pressed to deliver up a faithful warrior for execution? She let Gilberto put the cloak around her shoulders. Perhaps it was more to the point to ask what kind of man was Hernán Cortés?

She and Gilberto strolled into the starry night, sniffing the fresh air with pleasure after breathing in garlic, wine, and onion fumes for hours. Had she punished him enough? Alana had just about decided she was tired of sleeping alone.

He was much too proud to beg for her favors, and she would have been contemptuous if he had. However, she did not want her lover getting a disease from Indian women. She put a hand on his chest. "I'm going to go look in on the horses. Then—you."

"*Jesús*, how I've missed my sweet!" He slipped an arm around her waist beneath the cloak, fingertips sinking into the flesh of her breast. His hazel eyes glittered.

"Restrain yourself." Her tone was cool but friendly, and he dropped his arm. Wanted to keep him humble, did she? Just wait.

"I'll come with you if you like. There are a lot of ruffians here." Her stallion hated him for some reason but the nobleman still considered him a magnificent beast.

"No, Conn is too nervous. I have Finn here, and Pepe is staying with the horses. I'll be all right."

"Come back by the beach. It's easier walking." And hurry, woman, hurry. . . .

She smiled in answer and walked toward the livestock pens, carrying a lantern. Men played cards around campfires, while the more wealthy and influential lounged at the doors of crude huts. Bearded faces lit up as Alana went by. She passed a stone church, storehouse, slaughterhouse, empty marketplace, granary, and government buildings before reaching the picket line.

The horses whickered in welcome and tossed their sleek heads. Each stallion pulled at his rope, anxious for affection and a soft word. Rose called, too, from a distance where she stood with other mares.

Pepe Ortega arrived with an armload of grass to supplement their corn, the staple of the Indian diet and grown everywhere. "You needn't have bothered, *señorita*. He's much better."

"I wanted to say good-night to them anyway." She lifted the lantern. They peered at the gash in Conn's broad chest which the Englishman's mount had inflicted. "You didn't bleed him, did you?"

"No, I agree with you on that. What works for a man might work for a horse. I swear too many people who've been bled die from weakness. Surgeons and apothecaries may swear by the leech, but I've come to the conclusion they're wrong most of the time. We need all our blood to get well. And so does a horse."

She touched the lips of the wound gently. "Why, it's healing already!"

"Inmaculada applied a salve. It's made from barks and roots that are supposed to reduce inflammation and swelling."

"Then let her go on with it by all means. These races appear to be very advanced in the use of herbs." There was the red powder the old servant had given her to ward off pregnancy, for instance. Whatever it was, it worked wonderfully well. But her supply was running low.

"Speaking of Inmaculada, Pepe—"

"I know, I know," he interrupted laughingly. "She is dear to you, and you want to know my intentions."

"She is no slut to be laid at your whim," she flared protectively.

"She is a princess. When I asked the constable about a priest, he said there are two ecclesiastics with Cortés. A licentiate named Juan Díaz and Fray Bartolomé de Olmedo, who is a great favorite with the army. They have a chapel in the palace where we'll be married as soon as we arrive." He beamed, gray eyes luminous in his dark face. "You needn't worry, my lady. I never thought it would happen, but I am deeply in love with her."

"You've said that to many women, if I'm any judge, from Italy to England to Spain to Cuba!"

"But I never meant it before!"

"What a smooth-tongued rascal!"

They laughed, and Finn gazed up at them, panting as if he were laughing too. These were those he loved, and he was content. With the one who disliked him and never touched his fur, the wolfhound was constantly on guard, while the new one that smelled much like his mistress . . . she had been easy to like. Her voice was like wind in the bushes, and her hands on him were those of a friend. There was also another he had taken to recently. One with comforting, familiar odors about him, one who was kind and trustworthy.

Alana petted each horse and passed out a little sugar on her palm. "I'll look them over more carefully in the daylight, Pepe. Oh, they're anxious to get new ground under their hooves and the wind in their manes! Aren't you, my darlings?" She kissed Conn's nose, loving its warm velvet texture.

Smells in the livestock area triggered childhood memories, and she left the area reluctantly. A kinship had always existed between her and animals because she found it easy to see life through their eyes.

There was no need to put on airs with them or try to be something you were not. Asking nothing but care and affection, they gave their hearts in return. They felt emotion. They defended mates and offspring, had shy and gentle natures for the most part, and were more attuned to human minds than people knew or dared admit. It would not surprise her if an animal had a soul of sorts.

What Alana was mulling over would have brought a death sentence for witchcraft. Yet she was as sure as rain fell in Kildare that Finn sometimes read her mind. Take yesterday—

"For the love of God! Can't you see where you're going?" The roar of outrage was in English.

"And what in the name of Saint Bridget are you doing there where anyone walking by the horses could step on you?"

"Well, now, Irish." The voice became silky at the same time as a hand imprisoned her ankle. "I'd have dressed more appropriately if I had known you were coming to call." The great bare chest gleamed with a film of light perspiration in the lantern's glow.

"You huge lout. Let go of my ankle. It'll be a cold night in Hades when I come to call on you, believe me."

Without warning he jerked the foot out from under her, catching her deftly so she would not hit the ground. The pale hair flew around her shoulders and tickled his skin as he pinioned her arms and held her close.

"Let me go! I'll scream!"

"That might solve one problem, but it most assuredly would create others."

"Finn! Get him, Finn!"

Brian laughed delightedly, and Alana felt the vibration against her chest. "You've been too busy to notice that we've become the best of friends." She looked. Sure enough, Finn sat beside them watching Alana's struggles with benign interest. The wolfhound wagged his tail. They were obviously playing.

"Blast you both! Let me go!" She was entirely too near that mouth and body that had disturbed her so in the governor's garden. This was a man to avoid like the plague.

Brian had positioned her like a life-size doll. "How you do fit in my arms, Irish. Everything is in exactly the right place." He kissed her teasingly. "But I'm too tired tonight."

"You're too tired! Why, you arrogant ass! It wouldn't matter to me—"

He stopped the hot words with another kiss, more lingering than the first. "Listen, my bonny poppet," he murmured against her lips, "you sang a note or two on shipboard the other night. . . ." She kicked him hard in the shins. "Ouch! I just wanted you to know that some night *I'm* going to make you sing like a nightingale." He slapped her on the rump and released her. "Now off you go. Don't be keeping a man from his sleep, dear."

When he deliberately turned over and presented his back, Alana's fury reached such a peak she could hardly breathe. "You conceited ox! You ill-begotten bastard! You whoreson!"

"Such language from a lady," he said.

"I wouldn't lie with you if you were the last man on earth!"

The blue eyes sparkled at her over a superbly muscled shoulder. "It's the truth you're speaking. You'd have to wait in line too long."

After dousing him with a bucket of his horse's water, Alana strode down the beach, roundly berating Finn as she went. But it was not long before her sunny nature surfaced, and she began to giggle.

Oh, that big rogue. Heaven help the Indian women now. He wouldn't hesitate because they weren't baptized! And she would have to watch him herself. He had the charm of an Irishman, and that was the truth!

The hut she shared with Gilberto was the last one on the beach, close by a tiny cove. Peeking in, she found the Spaniard snoring and a sour stench of wine in the air. Wrinkling her nose with distaste, Alana decided to take a swim. The knee-deep water was fed by a stream that emptied into the sea so there was no undercurrent to worry about. It should be safe.

Floating lazily in the starlight, Alana was able to see the hulks of Cortés' fleet in the distance like ocean monsters stranded on the beach. How eager she was to cross the mountains as he and his army had done. To see that fabulous city and its ruler with his fifty-four feathered capes upon whose face his people were forbidden to look on pain of death.

"Is this a water nymph I see or a moon maiden?"

Alana turned over in the water. Gilberto stood on the shore, lithe and elegant even in nudity.

"I thought you were asleep. I'll come in shortly."

He waded toward her. "No need. I'll come to you."

Kneeling, he caressed his mistress and fastened an eager mouth on her nipples. As their bodies slid against each other enticingly, Gilberto pushed her to the shore so they lounged in the water, yet were supported by the sand.

"Have you forgiven me?" How gorgeous the woman was! Like an ancient goddess from the grottoes of the deep—or a siren luring him to eventual destruction.

Alana embraced him, stirred by their contact. "There was really nothing to forgive." She regretted that she could not give him the love he so desperately desired. Alana reached down into the water and put a hand around him.

"No, you're not a nymph. You are a witch from somewhere." The black-bearded face was pale, but the amber eyes glowed like jewels. "A snow-white witch with a glance of emerald fire and a mouth of flame."

"You endanger your soul, Spaniard, making love to a witch."

"Then I will forfeit my soul and go to hell on the wings of desire, locked into you forever."

He pulled her to him, and with those words that he half believed he entered her. Water rippled over their flesh, and the tropical sky trembled into a million pieces before their blinded eyes—and if there were cries on the wind, only the seabirds knew.

VIII

The company proceeded gloomily in the direction of the city-state of Tlaxcala. It had been an instructive trip since setting forth from Vera Cruz, but the constant evidence of human sacrifice had inspired deep fear, anger, and disgust in the stoutest heart.

Like Gilberto, many of the men had seen carnage at Ravenna and other battlefields, seen bodies blown to bits or mutilated in the heat of conflict. They had contributed their share of anguish and death to the enemy, too; blood and guts did not spoil their digestion.

But by all the saints! There was work here for the church that no one had anticipated. Human skulls by the thousands so neatly arranged they could be counted. Huge piles of thighbones. Children deliberately being pampered and fattened like baby lambs for the slaughter.

The travelers thought of their own families and relatives. How could parents countenance this evildoing even in the name of their religion? Why, multiply these practices by the number of Indian towns, and you had a monstrosity!

Gilberto leaned forward in the saddle to see Alana's face, white as the rabbit fur hood that framed it. Her eyes were closed. As he often did when

77

she slept, he absorbed the loveliness of her long black lashes, so striking beneath blond brows.

"Are you feeling better? Did the mulled wine help?" When Alana smiled weakly in assent, Gilberto cautioned, "We'll see more of this. At present there's nothing we can do about it, so try to steel yourself."

Passing a fortified hilltop town with its path to the summit cut into rock, Gilberto's mind took another turn. He had not told her about the letter which had been delivered by special courier yesterday shortly before dark. The contents, which oozed with veiled threats, had been written on cream-colored parchment of finest quality and sealed with red wax in which the imprint of an ecclesiastical ring was plain.

My beloved friend in Christ, Gilberto de Salvatierra, Count of Altamira: greetings and blessings! As the matter at hand is so vital, I will get right to the point. I have been saying prayers for your soul ever since you set sail. I simply do not believe you are aware of the mortal peril of hell fire to which your soul is being exposed by your relationship with the woman Alana MacKenna. I am deeply worried, my son, and am anxious to root out the evil which has so subtly and cleverly, like the Old Serpent in the Garden of Eden, insinuated itself into your life.

I, I, I! You vain beribboned lecher. It had hardly been necessary to read on. Gilberto knew perfectly well that the Bishop de Zamora wanted the Irishwoman.

As you know by now, she stole four horses, which I had recently acquired, on the night you departed from Cuba. I am sure this crime must have gone unnoticed at the time by so noble and Christian a gentleman as yourself.

What nonsense. How could he overlook four horses, each weighing almost half a ton, whinnying, sidling, and blowing as if they were possessed? The man had a tongue like the Old Serpent himself. Why didn't he come right out with it?

Such a brazen theft could be forgiven, even though it has made me the laughingstock of the island.

Ah, there's the rub, my sly friend. That and the fact that her rejection of your charity was bandied about all over the island.

* * *

She is after all a foreigner and unstable as females tend to be. But what really alarms me is that I am now positive—brace yourself, my dear Gilberto!—that this person is a witch! Oh, Merciful God, that I were there to protect you!

My stablehands swore on the holy cross that when she spoke to the horses, they obeyed her bidding by untying the ropes, opening their stalls, and running out into the night to join her! You will also remember those aboard the galleon who witnessed her flight to shore with her animals. A witch's familiars are usually cats and dogs, sometimes goats and toads. However, since Ireland is a land where horses have lived since the beginning of time, who knows what strange deviations may. . . .

Gilberto's attention wandered. He was glad Alana had suggested wearing a cloth cap under his morion so his head would not ache from cold. The constable had warned them of the chill here thousands of feet above the coast, and they'd ordered warm clothing from weavers in Cempoala. Combining heavy cotton from Indian looms and woolen fabric shipped to Vera Cruz by mistake, these garments had spared them the discomfort and illness Cortés and his followers had suffered.

The nobleman returned to the prelate's accusation. In a manner of speaking, by being Alana's lover he defied inquisitorial authorities. No one in his right mind did that, even a patrician like himself with influence and connections. Still, who was to say he was in his right mind when it came to her?

Alana *might* be a witch, that was true. The signs were right. She had come in the form of a seductive female who'd brought his virility to its peak, the most important of a witch's accomplishments and the main reason men risked everything for her. She was skilled in herb lore and had a large dog which acted overly intelligent for a dumb beast. Ivory and silver in coloration, Alana conceivably could draw her strength from Selene, the moon goddess.

What had she been doing the night he found her floating in the cove, bare body luminous and mysterious beneath the water, nipples upthrust like unopened buds drinking in strength from the sun? What a night that had been! He had never made love in the water before, and he might never again. But he would always remember it.

Gilberto pondered the words he'd said when they had joined so thrillingly. That he would forfeit his soul and go to hell on the wings of desire, sheathed forever in her valley of delight. He grinned reminiscently. Rather melodramatic for an old gamecock . . . but tremendously effective!

"What are you thinking about so evilly over there?" Alana made an effort to be frivolous.

He rolled his eyes. "I was reliving that night in the cove. The memory keeps me warm."

Her face grew scarlet. "Sweet Saint Bridget, is making love all you think about?"

Alana flashed him a flirtatious look. This was a different man from the one she met in Cuba, the languorous hedonist who reveled in material possessions and bodily pleasures. This was a conqueror, a warrior. The armor became him, and he sat atop his stallion like a paladin.

She was glad they had found each other—for whatever time fate allowed them. Alana was no seeress, as a few of her ancestors were reputed to have been, but she had an intuition that this savage land would someday tear them apart.

IX

Bayard raced easily alongside Conn. The stallion was descended from the mighty destriers, bred to bear the weight of his own armor as well as that of a rider clad in plate almost as heavy as himself. Larger and bulkier than the Irish horse, he had a peculiar buoyancy like that of a fleshy man who was a graceful dancer.

Manes and tails streamed in the wind like banners, and dark proud eyes glistened in the sun. Muscles bunched, flattened, and rippled under satiny hides, and the thunder of their feet intoxicated the equine princes. A flood of primitive exultation pumped such energy through the horses' systems the man and woman had difficulty restraining their mounts once they were finally reined in.

"If we don't stop them, they'll be in Moctezuma's palace by nightfall!" Alana yelled breathlessly.

"We'll be somewhere far away, that's for certain!" Brian Phelps slapped his horse lightly, laughing as Bayard sidestepped and snorted, shaking his splendid head in response. "Where were you headed, you handsome boy? You'll get me in trouble, taking this lady away from her lover's eye."

Conn nipped at the other horse. He had not forgotten their recent argument.

"Stop that, you bully." Alana reined her mount in the opposite direction, heading back toward the expedition. "We'd best get back. But I enjoyed that."

Brian smiled broadly. "We all did." He pointed. "Look. Isn't that Ortega?"

Pepe had not tried to keep up with these two fine animals. It would be good for Alana to take a run, get the cobwebs out of her mind. They would be seeing more bloody temples and pitiful captives in cages waiting to have their breasts torn open. He had not mentioned it to anyone, but he awoke many a night in a cold sweat from the terror of such a death.

"That was a romp," he observed, falling in between them.

Alana's hood had fallen back, and her hair had come loose. The ruddy glow in her cheeks was echoed in the soft rosy mouth, and her eyes danced and roved about. They took in mauve-tinted mountains and brilliant blue sky, snowcapped peaks that guarded the way to the Valley of Mexico and timber-mantled hillsides. "Oh, this is lovely country," she cried in sheer exhilaration, and the men smiled good-naturedly.

Brian said, "You remind me of something I heard once about an Irishwoman with silver-blond hair and green eyes. Deidre, was it?"

"And where would an Englishman be reading an old Irish love tale about poor Deidre of Ulster?"

He let the suspense build. They passed white-clad Indians with baskets slung from their necks who scurried from the horses. The bells on Conn's bridle pleased him, and he shook his head frequently to make them jingle. Pepe blew his nose, sniffling from a cold he had caught during the two-week ascent from tropics to highlands.

"From my adorable great-grandmother, Fionnuala of the O'Neills of Tyrone, descendant of Niall Og O'Neill, one of the Four Kings. You remind me of her, too. And I might add that I'm named for one of her seven sons."

"The line of Niall of the Nine Hostages! You've Irish blood then!" Alana's voice rose in astonishment.

The salt is in the sugar now, Pepe decided. The Englishman had changed from a vexation to a symbol of home. Nothing had ever been said, of course, but the attraction between these two, prickly as brambles, had not gone unnoticed.

Pepe was positive, however, she had never betrayed the count. She was fond of him and held her position with dignity and honor. Pepe and Inmaculada had discussed the problem privately, and she believed the Englishman had made up his mind to have Alana. Sooner stop a landslide, she had said.

How she knew this, Pepe had no idea, but then women were strange and wonderful creatures. His mind swam with visions of the Maya girl: lustrous black hair glinting in the sun, deep unfathomable brown eyes, a rare and beautiful smile. Brian's and Alana's conversation grew nostalgic and familiar, of who had married whom, castles they had visited as children, people and places familiar to them both. But Pepe rode dreaming of Inmaculada who would soon be his wife, his very own to smooth and stroke and love every night of their lives.

What the slave barracks had done to her proud spirit he had tried to erase with gentleness, patience, and understanding never tendered to another woman. What she had learned there she put into practice to please him. Pepe shivered with expectation. It would be a good marriage in many ways.

Gilberto watched the returning riders. When Phelps had asked Alana to race, the Spaniard had raised no objection. A hard ride would cheer her up, and if the Englishman knew what was good for him, he wouldn't try anything.

With Pepe following them, Gilberto had paid scant attention to their absence. There were too many other things on his mind. A number of men had remained at Vera Cruz, put off by eyewitness accounts of vicious warfare waged by armies of barbarians under shrewd leadership. Warriors armed with obsidian-edged hardwood sword-clubs, lances, bows and arrows, slings that hurled egg-sized stones, and spears propelled by throwing sticks which lent astounding penetrating force to the thrust. To make matters more frightening, an Indian's goal on the battlefield was not to kill his foe but to capture him for sacrifice.

Gilberto did not blame the men who'd stayed behind. In the first place they were volunteers. In the second, they were paying their own way. If he had not recognized this as his last campaign, he might have gone back to Santiago himself. It seemed a petty thing after years of campaigning, but he missed his own bed.

Getting old, he decided bleakly. Soon there would be nothing left. Court and church. A wife that twittered and was overly powdered, corseted, and mustached. Grandchildren. Memories to stab the heart on evenings scented with orange blossoms. A cold slab in the Salvatierra crypt. He groaned inaudibly.

Here, brighten up. She's coming now. See her long hair blowing in the sun like—what was it he had said once? Like moonbeams come to life. That was it! Gilberto waved, poignantly aware of life slipping by, enormously relieved that Alana waved back gaily.

Poor bastard, Brian thought cheerfully as he rode past the Spaniard. *He's really crazy about her* . . . which was just too bad. Because *he* planned to become Alana's lover as soon as the opportunity presented itself. If Salvatierra protested, it wouldn't be the first time a woman had been won with steel.

Anyone could see the man was getting along in years. It was obvious from the way he suffered with the cold and had occasional difficulty mounting a horse mornings. He was probably slowing down on his delivery in bed, too. But if he couldn't keep her . . . to the victor belonged the spoils.

Alana still bubbled with enjoyment over the ride and conversation. Imagine the Englishman having Irish blood! And how good it had been—really good!—to hear the names of home.

Cuffing Gilberto on the forearm, she demanded, "Why so glum? News from Velásquez? Affairs of state? The letter that was delivered last evening?" She had been nervous about that letter, wondering if it had come from the bishop.

Refreshed by her presence, he laughed. "You'll never believe it, but I was thinking about a nice soft bed."

She frowned. "For the love of God, you should have one as a tombstone."

Her girlish euphoria evaporated. Alana had become more and more sensitive to an awakening within her, of enlarging horizons, of her spirit growing and opening to new stimuli and challenges. Sex was not everything.

"I didn't mean it in that sense. But I'm flattered that going to bed with me leaps to your mind." How charming she was when she was angry. "It's just that my bones creak from sleeping on what passes for beds in this country."

"Oh." Placated, Alana agreed with him.

Here even the most important personage slept on a raised platform of earth covered with a grass mat. She had complained about it when Gilberto made love to her. At Tlaxcala they planned to ask for animal skins and cotton fabric with which to make a crude mattress. Among other things, this demonstrated to the nobleman just how primitive a culture this was. Not only did these people lack beds, but they lacked chairs as well.

"Let's hope we can arrange for better conveniences tonight," she said, reining the horse a bit to the right to avoid Finn, who'd dashed after a rabbit. Then she added, "I think I'll see how Inmaculada is doing. She's learning to ride, you know."

As she trotted off, Gilberto cast his experienced eye over the train of men behind him. Not bad, considering the lack of time in putting it together, but not strong enough by any measure to capture Cortés. Not this formidable commander from Medellín who talked and fought his way across two hundred and fifty miles of enemy territory, boldly marching into what could be one of the world's biggest cities, taking its ruler prisoner, burning his warriors at the stake right before his eyes, and somehow managing not to get killed by the thousands of Aztecs who surrounded him.

Naturally, one expected deeds like that from Spaniards. It was in the tradition. But Gilberto had begun to wonder if he might not be on the wrong side this time. He was not likely to get much from Velásquez for this effort. And who was to say Cortés had been wrong in striking out for Savior and sovereign? Hadn't he been successful so far?

In the meantime, perhaps Gilberto could kill two birds with one stone by trimming his sails to whichever way the wind blew. Better to join Cortés now for whatever loot and excitement was to be had and later—if the royal thumb pointed downward—claim circumstances, distance, communications breakdown, and the army's attachment to its leader as reasons for not discharging his mission.

That quandary resolved to his satisfaction, the nobleman studied his forces in more detail. In the vanguard ten gentlemen-adventurers rode Barbs. They were clad in standard equipment: steel morions, breastplates, shirts of mail, armpieces, and greaves. All carried the famous Toledo swords.

Behind them marched seventy-five foot soldiers clothed in quilted cotton Indian armor which had been soaked in brine. The men-at-arms also had Toledo blades with solid hilts and wood and leather shields; crossbowmen wearing plumed helmets carried their weapons and quivers; musketeers slanted the twenty-pound guns back on their shoulders. Steel points of long, heavy ashwood lances gleamed in the sun.

These were veterans of wars against the Moors and of European hostilities. Riffraff, really, not worth the powder to blow them to smithereens. Nevertheless, they were the best soldiers of their time. The armies of civilized nations trembled when they faced the death-defying Spaniards. Frenchmen complained that they were mad and valued a little honor more than their lives.

Sturdy native porters bent under their loads stretched out to the column's rear. Each carried fifty pounds and traveled twelve to fifteen miles a day. It seemed unbelievable that there were no draft animals in this country, only these stolid, enormously strong human carriers. One had trotted by yesterday with a fellow porter asleep on his back.

Armorers who doubled as blacksmiths, carpenters, and clerks shouted to Alana, who'd found Inmaculada up on Rose and managing well. The women's laughter drifted on the wind, and the mouths of white men quirked in answer to the sweet sound.

Spreading out on either side of the procession like colorful designs on the dun earth, coastal tribesmen strode purposefully beside fighting men from plain and mountain. Each was painted, befeathered, well armed, and dangerous.

Most of the thirty-eight provinces dominated by the Aztecs hated their ruthless overlords, despised the burdensome tribute and the forced labor, and bewailed the painful loss of their young adults snatched away for sacrifice to the Aztecs' hungry tribal god—Huitzilopochtli, the Left-Handed Hummingbird.

But a fresh wind was blowing, and the Great Lord Moctezuma now languished in the hands of the fearless invaders. So said rumors which flew over the snow-filled passes like arrows. Booty, women, food, and power would be waiting for the taking when the Aztecs' stranglehold was finally broken. And no one wanted to be left out.

X

Xicotencatl the Younger lounged morosely against a wall of the council chamber. It had been converted into a banquet hall and draped with garlands of pink tuberoses and aromatic pine branches. Dramatic feather banners flanked the stalwart warrior chief.

The insignia of his clan displayed a white heron on a rock against a red ground, while that of the city-state of Tlaxcala boasted a golden eagle with outspread wings on a white ground, the whole of which was richly ornamented with emeralds and silver.

He was watching his old, blind father touch the face of a big man with dark red-hair and eyes like blue morning glories. Although the stranger had the coloring of many of the Spaniards who now ruled precariously in the Aztec capital, Xicotencatl rather took to him. This man seemed different, more open, than the others. Perhaps he came from a different tribe. The Indian liked the engaging grin and his air of honesty and courage.

Standing erect, the brooding chieftain smiled at his wife on the other side of the room. If only the elders had let him destroy the Spaniards! He had had the invaders on the brink of defeat. That they did not turn out to be allies of the Aztecs made no difference to him. They were the enemy. He felt it in his bones.

The white men were not gods as many had believed. No more than he was! He'd seen them piss and heard them fart and knew they threw themselves on women like starving dogs. Nor were the huge animals they rode the deities they claimed. His men had killed a female by hacking her head off, and her feet hung this very minute in one of the temples overlooking the city.

When his father ordered him to the Spaniards' camp to offer Tlaxcala's hospitality, he had refused. With only a little more effort they could have been wiped out. They all had been starved, wounded, without salt or medicine, fatigued, and discouraged by the thousands ranged against them. They were superb fighting men, brave beyond reckoning and careless of death. Yet by all the gods of his forefathers, there had been only about four hundred of them!

They might even have retreated if it hadn't been for Cortés. You had only to enter camp to feel the mettle of his personality. Whatever else Xicotencatl thought, he saluted Cortés as a leader. But for those who resisted him, the man was inexorable.

When the Four Speakers of the Council finally ordered his warriors not to obey him unless he bowed to Cortés, Xicotencatl at last acquiesced to what he felt had been a tragically mistaken decision. He fully realized it had been made in the hope of bringing the Aztecs, an ancient, hated foe, to their knees by enlisting the aid of those who just might be the emissaries of the divine Quetzalcoatl. Yet the astute young leader was appalled. Didn't others see the peril facing them?

At times he felt like a hawk bound to its nest in the upper branches of a lofty pine tree. In the distance he saw a forest fire consuming everything in its path, but none heeded his frantic warnings, thinking they saw the rosy glow of sunrise. He was a patriot. He loved his people, who had resisted the oppressors of Tenochtitlán for a hundred years, and would gladly die for them, but now he was unable to help them.

A slave offered him chocolate in a polished horn container, and he sipped the honey-sweet liquid slowly in order to savor its taste. It was one of the few luxuries he had desired, and the visitors had been most generous with gifts of cacao as well as salt, bright red cloth, and glass beads.

Tlaxcala had lacked the chocolate bean, salt, and cotton for at least fifty years because the Aztecs attacked the merchants whenever they tried to leave the mountains. The women of Tlaxcala had risen to the challenge and learned to weave cloth from fibers of the maguey plant, often with enough delicacy to make veils.

Xicotencatl studied the women seated with his wife, each quite lovely in her own right. He compared the one dressed in light green with startling jade eyes to the white orchid of the vanilla plant. The girl from the coast with the Maya profile who wore an orange skirt and a cream-white over-dress adorned with blue embroidery reminded him of the dahlias he raised so successfully. His wife wearing pale yellow with fireflies in that blue-black hair and the full mouth like velvety petals–there was a beautiful rose!

With the intuitive sense which always surprised him, Corn Flower looked at her husband that very moment. They'd tied the edges of their cloaks in the knot which symbolized marriage almost five years ago. Yet he still felt his insides flare with desire at the thought of making love to her. Of burying his face in that wonderful hair perfumed with wild roses. Of kissing those golden-brown breasts whose nipples had suckled his sons. Of planting other seeds in her silken garden.

As if every word had been spoken aloud, a flush rose from her collar-bone. Lowering her eyes modestly, Xicotencatl's spouse once more attended to her guests. Inmaculada, attuned to the Indian face, felt gently amused and rather sad. She loved Pepe Ortega but would never forget Ah Tok, her young husband who was lost forever. Her clever ear continued to absorb nuances of her hostess' speech. While the city-state's language had been affected by isolation, it was still basically the same Nahuatl dialect enforced by the Aztecs and spoken by millions.

Pepe called his sweetheart a prettier version of Malinche, Cortés' interpreter and mistress, because Inmaculada had already proved very useful to the entire expedition and would undoubtedly be invaluable in Tenochtitlán. Alana's recognition of her aristocratic origins had been on the mark. Inmaculada's father was a Chontal Maya, a lord of the sea. There was a choking sensation in the Maya's throat when she thought about her family. Better they believed her dead than to know about the treatment she'd received aboard the ship and in the slave barracks.

Inmaculada herself harbored no particular grudge against the faceless men who had used her. They'd been nothing to each other, and they could have watched each other die with no more emotion than seeing a chicken's neck wrung. But the girl had sworn bitter revenge on the sanctimonious bishop who'd given her to the slavemasters with prayers for the salvation of her soul. And then watched through a peephole from the next room as she was abused. *Oh, yes, unholy holy man. Your blood will flow under the blade of my knife. Because as surely as I sit in this pine-scented room, I know you cannot resist her—that you will come from Cuba and cross this land to have her. Either in your bed or at the stake. And I will be nearby, waiting. . . .*

As the three women stood together, Alana recognized the symptoms of her friend's mental sufferings and hastened to help her. She turned to Inmaculada. "Did you tell Corn Flower where you came from?"

"Do you know of Xicalango?"

"I have never been away from Tlaxcala. My knowledge of the world is small."

"That may be true, but your kindness to strangers surely cannot be surpassed elsewhere." The Indian women smiled warmly. Inmaculada continued. "Xicalango is a town far to the southeast on the sandy shores of the sea. Here the Mayas have traded with the Aztecs for generations. My father had a fleet of canoes and many slaves."

"I have heard of the canoe fleets on the lakes surrounding Tenochtitlán."

Disdain showed on Inmaculada's features. "*Ours* were carved from a single tree trunk, and I have often seen them twice as long as this room."

"What else are you telling her?" Alana asked. When her friend repeated the claim in Spanish, she gasped, "Why, that's all of eighty feet!"

She took the cup of chocolate Corn Flower held out and bowed slightly in place of words she did not know. The Irishwoman was enchanted with the manners of this rustic people. Their gravity, self-control, and calm pleased her, as did their soft voices.

They ate delicately, using only the three fingers of the right hand. There was no coughing, spitting, or stuffing of the mouth such as Spanish soldiers excelled in. Before and after the meal a cloth and bowl of water were provided for each diner to cleanse his hands. Laughter and muted conversation sang in the room, and black eyes and dusky skins gleamed in the glow of pinewood torches.

Alana had a strange feeling of having been here before. Or if not here, at least in a gray stone place that was very similar, where warming fires blazed in big tripods, where bear, deer, and puma skins hung on the walls, echoing the wildness of savages that guarded the frontiers. Yes, here she might have been in the hall of an Irish mountain king.

She admired these people who had not shown fear of horses or gunfire when the conquistadors first appeared. They demonstrated an indomitable spirit, willingness to forgo luxuries in order to keep their freedom, pride in their independent accomplishments, readiness to die for what they believed in. Alana was deeply drawn to these qualities.

Xicotencatl noticed fatigue on the face of the black-bearded Spaniard. Reluctantly the Indian aristocrat moved to extend his hospitality. It would shame his whole community if he were not a genial host. He assisted the three women to their feet from the low wooden platform where they'd been sitting. As they stood around him, the orchid, the dahlia, and the rose, he said, "Truly, I am standing in a bower of loveliness."

Gilberto yawned, full from turkey soup, rabbit stew, grilled venison, maize cakes, sweet potatoes, squash, and a dish of cherrylike fruit. The meal had been good even if it had had too many spices and not enough salt. Surreptitiously, he loosened his clothing when Alana was not looking.

Dios, it had been a long day. He was ready for bed. Walking toward the handsome quartet and feeling the slightest bit ignored, Gilberto wondered what they found to talk about with such animation.

"I think it's time to retire, my love. There's a great deal to do tomorrow before we ride on."

"But we'll spend Christ Mass here, won't we? You don't plan to be on the road, do you?"

"No, we'll be here. Are you curious about your present?"

"Oh, yes!" She clasped her hands in front of her with a touching gesture. "I can hardly wait!"

After thanking their hosts, Alana and Gilberto went to their quarters, which had been strewn with fresh flowers and warmed by wood-burning braziers. On the way they saw Brian Phelps kissing the hand of a tall, comely woman of middle age whose black eyes smoldered above high cheekbones.

Inmaculada said she was no virgin but a wealthy widow who had itched for the Englishman since the hour he arrived. Of course, anyone could tell she was no maiden such as were usually offered to white men in hopes their godlike qualities would take root in untried wombs. Brian winked at Alana behind the Spaniard's back, and she tossed her head with irritation.

"This is better." Gilberto sighed, naked body motionless under the fur coverlet. "By God, this is better." How he loved Alana's breasts pressing into his back and her body nestling around his buttocks.

Alana kissed the nape of her lover's neck, sniffing the musk he still affected, regardless of travel. "Sleepy?" She put an arm around him and played with the hair on his chest.

A snore was her only answer. She withdrew and lay on her back, thinking. Now and then a faint tinkle of bells sounded. Someone had entered a room, brushing aside bell-fringed cloth which served both as door and as warning of entry.

Suddenly there was a commotion followed by smothered laughter. A Spaniard called out in alarm and rattled his sword. It was nothing, the Englishman assured him. He and his partner had rolled off the platform that passed for a bed. Anyone with as lively a piece as he had would do better on the floor, take his word for it! Chuckles rumbled through the large guesthouse.

Gilberto turned over, having come awake like a cat, and grabbed a weapon. "Are you a lively piece?" he asked, blowing in her ear.

"I thought you were sleepy." She rolled onto her side, facing away from him, unaccountably cross and edgy.

"I was, but even though I hate to admit it, I think Phelps has a better idea." He pulled her against him. "Turn over."

"Who cares what he thinks?" She obeyed slowly.

"You'd better not." Gilberto squeezed her tightly, ignoring her resistance and the hands pushing at his chest. "You'd better not," he repeated. "The only riding you'd better do with him is on horseback."

Wouldn't he ever shut up? For some reason she couldn't help thinking about what was going on in that other room. Memories of that rapturous kiss in the garden, his big iron-hard body and her excited reaction to Brian's fondling made Alana move nervously.

"Don't be so vulgar, Gilberto, nor so silly."

Her lover nudged her tongue with his. "Don't you like me to be vulgar now and then?"

He ducked under the furs and greedily kissed the nipples waiting for him. When he touched the smooth belly, the pale hair, and the jewels it guarded, his mistress moved impatiently. A love fragrance surrounded him there in the warm blackness and made him dizzy, and he wanted to drown in its source.

Without waiting another instant Gilberto slid into that glorious body he knew so well, yet would never know at all. Putting an arm beneath Alana's lower back, he penetrated as deeply as possible. If only he could own her completely just once, and make the woman he loved pregnant with his child!

"Oh, darling." She moved to accommodate him.

Then it happened again. Alana felt Gilberto tense with humiliation, fear, and anger. He growled like an animal, "Help me." But nothing helped. Finally, he said something foul, shoved her away roughly, and turned his back.

Witches could steal your virility just as easily as they could restore it. Especially when they wanted to have intercourse with another man. Suppose it had been that blue-eyed bastard, for instance . . . oh, God's blood, why did he have to love her so much?

What was it the Bible said? "Jealousy is cruel as the grave: the coals thereof are coals of fire, which hath a most vehement flame." He had been crazy to bring her along.

"You're tired. It's the altitude and the cold."

"Last time you said it was the summer and the heat."

"And you ate too much." Exhausted and upset, Alana tried to comfort the unhappy man. "Mornings are always better. You'll see."

The next day it was better, but the magic was no longer there.

XI

Alana positioned a candle on a tripod at the chapel's entrance and lighted it. It was one of many which had been packed with wafers and consecrated wine being sent inland to Fray Olmedo. She felt certain he would not mind.

The Christian sanctuary at Tlaxcala had been set up in a small temple during Cortés' visit and was kept whitewashed, clean, and perfumed in deference to him. To date, the simplicity of the services and the reverence of white worshipers had made no dent in Indian attitudes. Gods to whom they had bowed down for as long as the tribe existed still performed admirably.

"Why are you doing that?" Corn Flower was fascinated by the candles. In the absence of sheep and cattle, no tallow existed from which to make them.

"This is a custom in my country. There we put a candle in the window to light the Christ Child's way. But your buildings have no windows, so I am doing this instead."

The explanation led to Alana's asking why good people like the Tlaxca- lans made obeisance to ugly statues sprinkled with human blood. She was unable to talk about the ceremonial cannibalism, however, having been so appalled by it. Why not look to the Blessed Virgin whose likeness stood right here on the altar? she urged Corn Flower. It was she who lived in heaven and who had borne the Holy Babe in Bethlehem even while Virgin.

Inmaculada translated impassively as Alana went on. Because Corn Flower was a friend, she had to be frank. Long ago in Ireland—that was the country Alana came from—there had been priests called Druids. They had been much like priests here in that they were philosophers, historians, seers, poets, and theologians. For all she knew, they may even have had comparable calendrical knowledge. These Druids, Alana was sorry to say, had also practiced human sacrifice in the belief it propitiated the gods. But they came to see the Light, and that was what the Tlaxcalans must do.

Xicotencatl's wife was frightened. "Our priests are good men who lead pure and physically difficult lives. They fast, sleep little, and do not have women. They are hallowed vessels through which the gods speak and send the Word. If sacrifice is not made and custom not followed, the gods will destroy us with famine, plague, and war."

Her sensuous mouth trembled. "And if he does not have blood, the Lord of the Sun will not have strength to rise. I love my husband and children with all my heart! What would we do without the sun?"

Alana gradually realized there was no easy way to breach the chasm between the two faiths. Furthermore, she did not wish to distress her hostess, so they smiled and patted each other's hands. Inmaculada sighed with relief.

After Christ Mass services the Europeans settled down to a merry time: eating, drinking, gossiping, dancing, and relaxing. They'd been told there was a hard march ahead over an icy pass.

Gilberto's gift to his mistress was a saddle he had had made in Cuba especially for this occasion. Of the finest black leather and workmanship, it was padded on cantle and seat with brocaded skirts of bright yellow lined with woolskin. The silver-plated pommel front and cantle back were engraved with biblical scenes. Openwork in the bronze stirrups was executed in a hearts-and-flowers design.

The gratitude and delight Alana expressed—how grand it looked on Conn!—melted most of the ice around his heart. Later, seeing her astride his gift, he was doubly charmed. Her usual riding costume consisted of russet colored boots and full, ankle-length pants in the same color, designed to look like a skirt. A heavy linen shirt was topped either by a colorful Indian blanket with a center slit for her head or by a jacket of white rabbit fur with a hood. She was delectable. She rode like a Spaniard, and every white man was her slave.

Inmaculada gave Alana a crucifix made from exquisitely minute shells, and Pepe surprised her with saddlebags of untanned deerskin. Alana immediately put on the cross and stuffed her new saddlebags with other gifts: a shawl, gloves, golden hairpins, hair ribbons, and other pretty trinkets.

Thanks to the sale of her three stallions in Vera Cruz, Alana had had money of her own to spend. Gilberto liked nothing better than gold. She had bought him a magnificent chain with a pearl pendant from an Indian goldsmith. He swore it was worthy of being worn at court.

The Maya girl's eyes sparkled over a bolt of shrimp-pink velvet and tortoiseshell combs inlaid with silver. Pepe insisted the joy of his betrothed was gift enough for him, but Alana insisted he take a little bag of gold pieces. The green eyes and the gray sought each other with a love as pure as childhood prayer.

When Tlaxcalans saw the exchange of gifts, their usual custom at banquets, they wanted to participate. Xicotencatl the Elder asked what would please Alana. She considered furs, jewels, or featherwork and then asked for release of all those being held for sacrifice. There had been an uproar, but her wish was granted.

One unsettling thing had happened, however. Somewhere in the woods Brian Phelps had found mistletoe. As kissing did not appear to be an Indian rite, he had had a gay time initiating willing victims.

His hosts were tolerant. They liked the great red-hair. He was a lord of honor and would not take advantage of their women. If they were overcome with desire and gave themselves willingly, no one would mind. Besides, the children adored him, and what better mark of a man was there?

Alana excused herself late in the day to change her dress and freshen up before the evening meal. The upper classes here liked their good times, generally feasting and enjoying entertainment until well after midnight. As she neared her quarters, the Englishman appeared and pulled her into his room.

"Are you crazy?" Her heart thudded madly with apprehension and excitement. In his present state of mind Gilberto would beat her black and blue if he found them like this.

"Yes, I'm crazy about you." He dangled the mistletoe. "Bet you kissed a lot of boys at home."

She tried to move away, but Brian trapped her in a corner. "Let's pretend we're at home, Alana, with a Yule log in the fireplace and wreaths everywhere. Mulled cider on the board and an ox on the big spit. Carols and snow and reels and plum pudding—" He leaned down to kiss her.

"Stop it!" Her eyes filled with tears.

"Oh, now, Irish, I didn't mean to make you cry." He put his arms around her in a friendly way and kissed her eyelids, brow, and nose. When their mouths met, it seemed so sweet and tender she started to cry in earnest.

"Now, poppet, now, now. Is it close to your time of month?" She nodded, her face buried against his chest.

"Ay, our womenfolk often got into a tizzy then, too." He smoothed her hair. "You're hurting my reputation, you know. Females don't usually cry when I kiss them. On the contrary."

"Oh, go on with you," Alana said, half laughing and half weeping.

Brian held up the mistletoe again. "One kiss, Irish, and you can go."

"All right, all right! You'll get us killed if I don't." She took his chin in her hand, gave him a sisterly peck, and fled. Faith! Being alone with him meant trouble.

The column departed from Tlaxcala in a cloud of dust. Corn Flower watched sadly as her husband and his men marched out of the city to escort the travelers to the Valley of Mexico. Then she gestured to Alana, who'd been thinking they would be in Tenochtitlán before the New Year began. The Irishwoman wondered what the coming year would bring.

She saw Brian on a prancing Bayard, throwing kisses to the rich widow like a Crusader going off to do battle with the Saracens. Gave her a bedding she'll never forget, Alana mused, and accidentally caught his eye as the thought crossed her mind. Laughing aloud, he bowed from the waist, and she turned her head so Gilberto would not wonder at her smile. He had been much too suspicious of her every move, and that was rapidly becoming an irritant between them.

They rode past orchards and fields and towns with neat stone houses, gardens, marketplaces, and steam baths. Tlaxcala itself disappeared from view, but the great walls of stonework marking the city-state's boundaries were plainly visible in the distance. These walls seemed to grow out of mountains on either side of the open country through which the column was marching. They did not meet, however, but extended past one another far enough to create a narrow entry and exit commanded from the parapet above.

Alana waited impatiently for everyone to funnel through the single-file passageway—foot soldiers, cavalrymen, extra mounts, the Tlaxcalan forces, warriors from other provinces, porters bent beneath packs, swine the Spaniards had brought, women to make tortillas, the prisoners released from their cages, and the hangers-on any expedition attracted. Conn was champing at his bit.

Even the veteran soldiers who'd seen many battlements in Europe grudgingly acknowledged the impressive engineering of this wall, which was twenty feet thick, nine feet high, and five miles long! One would never expect such a thing from these heathens. But then Cortés had not expected the stubborn resistance and caliber of fighting man he encountered here either.

Gilberto had decided to follow the route Cortés took in November as it avoided hostile regions about which he had no dependable information. The path was adequate but narrow and led through a high defile between volcanoes barring the way to the Aztec heartland: Popocatepetl, "The Hill that Smokes," and Ixacishuatl, "The White Woman." Those who'd seen mountains in France, Italy, and northwest Africa swore in awe, and the women were wide-eyed with fright. That one spouting sparks and red-tinged smoke must rise almost eighteen thousand feet above the sea, and the pass itself twelve thousand!

No wonder it was so cold, and you had such difficulty breathing. And the horses! Alana worried about Conn and Rose, even though they were blanketed heavily against the numbing wind and sleet.

"Thank God!" she gasped to Pepe. "Look! Places to stay overnight. I was afraid we'd have to sleep in the open."

Inmaculada, bundled up to her eyes, explained, "These are rest houses for merchants and travelers. You'll find them throughout the Maya and Aztec territories."

The party was packed into the houses as tightly as olives in a cask, but there it was possible to heat food, change snow-wet clothing, and sleep fitfully.

Alana fretted over Gilberto's cough and slight fever. He could easily develop a chest cold—or worse—after being exposed to severe weather so soon after the balmy seashore. If only she had poultices—!

"Stop fluttering about. I'm not a child."

Yet he reveled in the fuss she made over him, having his cloak adjusted and his wine warmed. On the other hand, might it be a guilty conscience? When they made love the night before leaving Tlaxcala, she had done everything to please him. Was this another Christ Mass gift, he had asked dryly? They both knew that certain spark, that breathlessness, was fading.

Cuerpo de Dios, he ached in every joint. But look at her! Cheeks red, nose, too, tired but impervious to illness, ignoring the cold. She ate the coarse stew—rabbit and sweet potatoes in an onion gravy—chewed on those leathery tortillas, slept with her head on a saddle, and bloomed like a rose in the snow.

The entire column was relieved to drop down to a lower altitude the next day. They all stared in wonder at the passing towns and settlements. Simple but elegant houses of polished stucco and fine wood rested on pilings in flower-edged lakes. Manicured gardens and orchards filled the air with perfumes, and lagoons teemed with waterfowl.

Exotically garbed and coiffed Indians watched from canopied litters and decorated canoes. Groups eddied about the foot of a *teocalli,* the god's house, typical of the Aztec temple-pyramid with its bright paint, feathered banners, steep steps, smoking altars, and stone sculptures—architecturally harmonious temples of death.

The Irishwoman's appearance aroused equal interest and curiosity among the spectators as did that of the huge and powerful Finn in a spiked iron collar and the sleek, muscular Conn with his proud head and glossy mane and hide.

The men with Alana were carefully inspected, though the Aztecs were by now all too well acquainted with this type. They noted the dark, elegant soldier with eyes like the Spotted Lord of the Jungle casting a proprietary glance toward his woman. And the other man nearby, a mighty warrior who had doffed his helmet to reveal hair the color of trees in autumn. Was he a descendant of Quetzalcoatl, Our Precious Feather from the sunrise? Did his smile not shine like the sun?

It was now the last day of 1519. Alana MacKenna, descendant of Ireland's High Kings who had walked in Tara's halls and been crowned on the hallowed Hill, approached her destiny. The city called Mexico-Tenochtitlán floated lotuslike on the surface of the lake called Texcoco. Spell-binding as a fairyland, the island capital glowed in the sun its people worshiped.

Lofty pyramids crowned with brilliantly adorned temples, palaces coated with silvery stucco or built of ruby-red stone, smoke rising from innumerable shrines and braziers into a turquoise sky—it was a vision of paradise—incredible, astonishing, and mysterious. A network of canals bound the metropolis together in a latticework of shimmering ribbons, like fillets in a woman's hair. It was an embroidery of engineering genius fashioned with incense, feathers, gems, and gold.

That her fate was interwoven with this pagan Venice Alana knew as surely as she made out its trees swaying in the fragrant wind. Whether this presaged life or death, happiness or tragedy, there was no way to know.

But she did know her whole existence had been directed toward this moment, this heartbeat in time, when she arrived in Mexico-Tenochtitlán. Where the eagle on a cactus had devoured a serpent long ago. Where the feared Mexica-Aztecs held sway over their world.

BOOK TWO

The Monk's Temptation

XII

January, 1520: at the palace of Moctezuma's father
in Mexico-Tenochtitlán

The woman who slept with Cortés sat quietly at his side, hands limp in her lap. They had made love before coming to the hall for dinner and Malinche—also known as Doña Marina and sometimes the Tongue—was drowsy and content. She had known both Indian and Spaniard, and one man was much like another. But Cortés wielded his manhood with irresistible authority and calculation.

Closing her eyes, she pictured him lying naked on the sleeping mat, pale and passionate and vulnerable as no one else saw him. The army thought he kept himself under iron control and had followed him from Cuba, toying with death at every step. Some men idolized him; others despised him. But each knew that Cortés was the Man.

However, only Malinche had put a hand on his bare chest and felt the beat of that bold, cruel, and kind heart against her palm. She exulted in the power to make his heart pound with desire and she wondered at his body's fragility and mightiness. If she wanted to, Malinche could kill the Man more easily than a thousand Aztec warriors.

103

"What are you thinking, my splendid turtledove?" The large dark eyes of the conquistador glowed with interest. He had sampled many women in his thirty-five years, but her secret places constantly titillated and excited him.

Her haughty mouth softened at his use of the Indian endearment. "Of murdering you, my lord."

Cortés rubbed the scar on his lower lip that was concealed by a carefully groomed beard. "That was not the answer I expected." He smiled that seductive, magnetic smile which weakened almost any will not made of the same well-tempered iron as his.

"Is not hunger sharpened by danger?" Malinche asked.

"You pick up proverbs as a bird does seed." Cortés leaned toward her, breath spicy with cloves, voice slumbrous with promise. "Tonight, then, you must satisfy my dangerous appetite."

Dusky rose tinted her handsome face, and he chuckled softly. His mistress' composure was seldom ruffled. Neither by the stigma of having been a slave nor by the challenge of diplomacy. Not by seeing the slaughter at Cholula or being surrounded by cannibalistic enemies. Not by battle or blood . . . but by a certain way they made love. One that tore down her imperturbable facade to reveal the untamed savage beneath.

Still, the evening was young, many duties awaited him, and it was not his nature to stay in one place. Furthermore, since Hernán Cortés was forever on the lookout for new and superior weapons, whether of metal, flesh, or thought, he might become distracted before he exacted his demand. He rose abruptly from the gem-studded golden chair Moctezuma had given him. Smoothing it lovingly, Cortés looked around the room. He wanted to find Gilberto de Salvatierra again and talk to him about contacts at court.

Cortés walked away on sturdy legs bowed from years in the saddle, but his Indian consort did not stir. One might have mistaken her for a tawny-skinned idol whose hair flooded over its breasts like glossy raven's feathers.

Alana watched the exchange between Cortés and Malinche with curiosity. She knew the woman came from the coast and had been given into slavery by her mother. The slavers sold her to Tabascans, who presented her to the Spaniards after having been vanquished by them in March of last year.

Along with nineteen other girls, Malinche was immediately christened and given to the woman-hungry strangers. Four months later her master went to Spain as Cortés' representative to spread the booty of this new land at the king's feet.

By the time the sails disappeared on the horizon Malinche had been transferred to Cortés' bed; she had now been at his side almost a year. In fact, they were so inseparable he was often referred to by her name among the tribes.

It was easy to see the woman loved and respected Cortés, who was approaching the crude table where Alana and her party nibbled at maize cakes and spooned up chocolate.

"Keep your eyes off this one, Alana. You might meet a knife in the dark otherwise." Gilberto squeezed her thigh with unncessary force.

Since their arrival, his jealousy had mushroomed out of control because of their proximity to the army. Everyone was housed together in one structure; Moctezuma had quartered them in his father's palace and furnished them with whatever they wanted.

A huge complex of buildings encompassed by a wall with towers and buttresses, the palace was spacious and luxurious. Cortés and his officers enjoyed individual apartments complete with baths and servants. The floors were polished wood accented with jaguar skins; colorful cotton and feathered draperies brightened up the walls; aromatic barks burned, scenting the air. Thousands of Tlaxcalan allies camped in open courtyards under awnings while men-at-arms were distributed indoors throughout halls large enough to accommodate more than a hundred apiece. The evening meal had been served in one of these.

"Don't be ridiculous, Gilberto. I'm not interested in him! Or any other man, for that matter." But she knew she could have answered in Nahuatl for all the impact her denial made upon him.

The continuous lovemaking that went on kept him on tenterhooks. Immense as the palace was, it seemed as if somewhere at any time of the day or night men coupled with women and clothing rustled amid whispers, moans, laughter, and occasional whimpers of pain. Alana was reminded of a stable of stallions. Yet she understood. These Spaniards and a few Greeks, Italians, and Portuguese, some of whom were tough prison dregs and others unlucky adventurers, lived on the edge of the blade. Not to mention one Englishman who kept no concubine but attracted willing candidates as pollen did bees.

The army honored Alana's relationship with the Count of Altamira, but there was one man who drifted around her like a piece of flotsam. He was always present when she happened to be alone, and absent when she wanted to call him to Gilberto's attention. Since the day they'd settled in, this captain of crossbowmen had annoyed her. Taut and vicious as his weapon, he remained at a distance. She felt his eyes, nevertheless, hot with lust, examining parts of her anatomy with the same proficiency with which he fired the iron-tipped quarrel.

Men called him *El Baboso*, the Slobberer. When he was lost in thought, saliva shone on his lips and oozed down his chin. Alana soon grew to loathe the sight of him . . . and to fear him.

For the first time in her life Alana was afraid to be alone in the dark; now when she went to the courtyard reserved for the horses, Pepe accompanied her. Sometimes his friend, amiable Bernal Díaz del Castillo, the army's raconteur, came along. This only made her lover's suspicions worse, and their nights became a mixture of heaven and hell.

"Compañeros." Cortés gripped Gilberto's shoulder and stood smiling at Alana, Pepe, and Inmaculada.

He prided himself on an almost uncanny ability to read character. True, he made mistakes, but only because mankind was so paradoxical, overly emotional, and unreasonable, harder to handle on occasion than a slave being branded. In each gaze turned up to him, the conquistador glimpsed the fire and ice and silk and steel of the human soul that continually fascinated him.

In the remarkable green eyes of Salvatierra's woman—no, she was her own woman—a gay and ardent spirit shone. A searcher lived behind those emerald seas, a defier of convention, a reckless wanderer. She was a companion worthy of a Spaniard, this one. No doubt Alana MacKenna would be divine in bed, but he was the first to recognize forbidden territory. He bowed over her hand, oddly exultant at the admiration in her face.

Salvatierra himself had responded tensely to his touch. His golden eyes followed every movement his mistress made: he was a battle-tested veteran and gallant cavalier but a silly fool in love. Indeed, what man was not? Yet jealousy created problems Cortés could not permit at this difficult point in time.

Across the table the frank regard of Pepe Ortega met his probing gaze without flinching. Loyal and trustworthy, here was a man who'd watch your back. It spoke well of the nobleman that this man was in his service.

The Maya girl beside Ortega returned his look with the same opaque blankness he encountered in Malinche from time to time. He simply could not penetrate it. Whether it held hate or fear or love—or even worse, indifference—he could not determine.

Both these women symbolized the future. For from their wombs, as from those of all Indian women brought to God's mercy by baptism, would spring children with both bloods. A new race! And he, Hernán Cortés, had struck the mold!

In the next letter-report to His Majesty, he must suggest this territory be named New Spain of the Ocean Sea. He and many others were strongly reminded of home by its fertility, size, climate, rugged mountains, valleys, and plains. And by God's grace and the king's, he would become governor, captain general, and chief justice of this lovely treasure-house.

But that was in the future. Cortés turned on the charm. "When is the happy day, *señorita*?"

Inmaculada's reserve thawed, and glancing shyly at Pepe, she replied, "We will be married the day after tomorrow." She was impressed that despite the hundreds of details he handled, Cortés had made the effort to learn about their nuptials.

"I would consider it an honor to give the bride away, Ortega."

Pepe flushed slightly at the compliment. "What a story to tell our children and grandchildren!"

"Fray Olmedo will be pleased to preside over a more elaborate ceremony than usual. Most of his services have been rather hurried affairs," Cortés commented dryly. He shook Pepe's hand vigorously. "Congratulations, *hombre*. May you have many sons."

Having disposed of amenities and laid the groundwork for attracting new supporters against the faction in the army that was faithful to Diego Velásquez, Cortés spoke to Alana.

"I've been told the Aztecs supplying the horses' fodder are bringing roses for your animals to sleep on. They must think you're a goddess."

"Is that why they're doing it? It seems a shame to have them trampled to pulp. My mare eats them, the precious ninny."

"Don't worry about the flowers. They grow by the thousands at Xochimilco. You know," he said reminiscently, "when we first came, roses were brought for all the horses. There were fewer than twenty then." His mouth grew tender, and his eyes warm.

"Did you know the natives saw them as fantastic gods and thought the horses ate their bits? That they were so ferocious we bridled them to keep them from eating people?" Cortés laughed. "Of course, we never did anything to dispel that notion, and we tried to bury any that died in order to keep the god theory alive. Eventually, though, a few were killed and dissected."

Cortés' meal arrived on golden plates, a service Moctezuma had used in religious ceremonies and which his jailer had appropriated. He speared a flaky piece of fish nestled in delicate tomato sauce.

"What I'd give for an honest rack of lamb! And olives! How I miss them." He pointed a finger at Alana as he swallowed. "I almost forgot. Moctezuma wants to meet you in the morning. Not only that, he's invited you to go sailing with him."

Gilberto wiped his mouth on his sleeve. Alana reminded herself to speak to him about that. He had not been careful of his toilet lately, and he was usually immaculate and vain of his appearance. Was it to nettle her? She felt at a loss to explain what had happened between them.

"What do you mean, sailing? I thought he was a prisoner," the count demanded abrasively.

Gilberto noticed Alana's tiny frown and wiped his mouth on his sleeve a second time. He knew it irritated her, but by the wounds of Christ, she could take him as he came! He'd taken her in when she was between the sword and the wall, fed, clothed, and housed her, given her jewels, and loved her. Son of a bitch, how he loved her! And now here she sat, after all he'd done for her, flirting with Cortés and every other cock in sight. The nobleman belched involuntarily.

Alana groaned inwardly. Was it going to be one of those nights? To keep up appearances, she coaxed, "Try this delicious quail, Gilberto." She then repeated his question while cutting the offering into bite-size pieces on his plate.

"I was under the impression he was a prisoner, too. And what do we go sailing *in*?"

"Our boatbuilders have constructed two sloops," Pepe said. "Didn't Inmaculada tell you I went with the woodcutting party to an oak grove about twelve miles away? Those Indian carpenters are really skillful. Just show them what you want done and they do it."

"Where did you get the rigging?" she wondered.

Cortés rubbed his scar with a knuckle. "There was plenty of salvage from the fleet we had to, ah, condemn before we left Vera Cruz. One of my best officers, Gonzalo de Sandoval, who's down there now, sent me the anchors, sails, cable, rudders, and iron that were needed."

Alana stared at him with awe. The constable had told her and the others what Cortés had done last August and of the control he exerted over his roughneck crew through sheer force of his personality. For the deeds they were about to perform, he had declared in one of his frequent and persuasive orations, they would be remembered like the ancient Romans!

First, he cajoled the army into surrendering all the gold it had accumulated over a four-month period and sending it to the king as a gift; then he wrecked and scuttled the fleet to cut off any avenue of escape. *He* was determined to go to Tenochtitlán, and the men had followed him. Into the lion's mouth, gambling on one cast of the dice.

"The sloops are a good emergency measure," Pepe stated, mashing a sweet potato vigorously. "You've mounted the cannon on them, too, I see."

"Moctezuma likes to have them fired while the sloop tacks back and forth." Cortés' face was now impassive. "He's as much a prisoner of himself as he is of ours, of course. Why, Andrés de Tapia goes everywhere with him, gaming, womanizing, hunting. Moctezuma is free to do what he wants. Including making those cursed sacrifices."

Alana asked about the Aztec ruler's submission to the Spanish crown and how cooperative his chieftains had been. Most of them had capitulated, Cortés replied. After all, they considered him their divine ruler. It was too bad Moctezuma's nephew, a young firebrand named Cacama, had been so stubborn and tried to foment a rebellion in the Valley of Mexico against the Spaniards. But he and his accomplices soon learned their lesson.

The ceremony in which the pagan king ceded his sovereignty and treasures, which poured in constantly from three hundred and seventy-one towns, had been duly recorded. Diego de Godoy, royal notary and the expedition's official recorder and collector of the king's fifth, had documented the entire procedure. That was the Spanish way.

A knot of men crossed the hall, talking, guffawing, and picking their teeth. Leading them was Pedro de Alvarado, a big gorgeous figure of a man with blond beard and hair glinting in the torchlight. The Indians called him Tonatiuh, the sun god, saying the sky shone in his eyes. He could have any woman he wanted, and he was currently enamored of Luisa, the regal daughter of Xicotencatl the Elder of Tlaxcala, who had been given to him. Alana did not envy her. His eyes seldom smiled, even though he was forever laughing, and the sensual mouth had a cruel twist.

He possessed the manners of a prince, nonetheless, making sure the newcomers made the acquaintance of the conquistadors present: wild Cristóbal de Olid, intense Francisco de Montejo, high-voiced Juan Velásquez de León, madcap Diego de Ordaz, who had climbed Popocatepetl while it erupted, elegant Francisco de Saucedo.

Others crowded around, including the gawky youngster Luis Alonso Orteguilla, the appealing page who attended Moctezuma, eager Corral, Cortés' ensign bearer, two of the five big Alvarado brothers, gentle Lares, called the "good horseman," and Aguilar, the nervous interpreter, who'd been a prisoner of the Mayas in Yucatán for eight years.

And these, Alana thought, were only a few of the immortals toasted by the aged musketeer in Vera Cruz. Which names would ring down through history with the swish of a sword and the thunder of a cannon? Ah, these were *men!*

Conscious of Gilberto's slit-eyed scrutiny, she excused herself, and followed by a chorus of chivalrous objections, she and Inmaculada left the group just as the page complained to Cortés. It seemed that a coarse sailor had pissed twice in full view of Moctezuma while on sentry duty outside the king's apartments.

Alana shook her head. "Faith! Aren't some men pigs? Imagine making water in front of a man whose subjects don't dare see his face!"

Her friend sniffed. "The Great Lord made a mistake. Just as he did in sending gifts to Cortés and then telling him he mustn't come here. After the sailor pissed the first time, Moctezuma gave him a gift and asked him not to do it again. The man is not a complete simpleton, so he repeated the act in hopes of another gift."

The women separated, each taking a different direction to her own apartment. Many people were passing back and forth: servants with flowers and foodstuffs, Botello, the army's astrologer, ringed by several anxious Spanish women, Aztec courtesans chewing a gummy substance called chicle, soldiers at leisure, a few of Moctezuma's clowns and stilt walkers . . . and the crossbowman.

Alana's heart skipped a beat, and she turned into a doorway immediately beside her. A steep stairway descended into the depths beneath the place. She turned uncertainly and saw him crouched in the doorway like a predator. Panic-stricken, Alana hurried down the steps. There was torchlight not far away. Someone would help her.

Cold air struck her face, restoring a measure of common sense. What an idiot she was! He'd terrified her so she'd put herself in a vulnerable position, and was probably doing exactly what he wanted.

As she came around a large pillar, she stopped, startled by a dramatic tableau. Four Indian men clad in breechclouts were shackled to a heavy anchor chain which had been welded into a ring. Their black eyes snapping with malice, they leaped to their feet and snarled in Nahuatl. Cacama and his rebel companions had no love for the white race.

Her pursuer burst into the dungeon, his erection plainly visible within his breeches. Panting like a mad dog, he hardly seemed to notice the Aztecs, who shouted and hooted, egging him on. Their loins quickened. Maybe he would give her to them when he was finished.

"Get away from me!" Alana drew her dagger, but in semidarkness and among the strong, lusty men, it seemed frail and useless. The crossbowman fingered his breeches, and his swollen penis popped into sight. The Aztecs yelled, and Alana, trapped between them and her attacker, screamed.

Brian Phelps leaped down the steps, sword in hand. He had given the woman credit for more brains than this, for Christ's sake! Instead of running back to the hall or simply yelling her head off, she went down into this warren where anything could happen. It was a good thing he'd been nearby. As he hit the floor, there was a scream. Then another. He raced toward the sounds.

The crossbowman had Alana's arms pinned to her sides and a hand over her mouth. He grunted and sweated as they struggled. The Aztecs were silent now, intent on the outcome. No one saw the Englishman until the last second when he yanked the soldier backward by the scruff of his neck.

"See this, you bastard?" He jammed the sword point into the man's midriff hard enough to make him yelp with pain.

"You bother her again, and *after* I slice that pitiful thing off, I'll gut you!" Brian lifted the man off the floor. "Understand?"

Brian's enormous strength and the deadly promise in his chill blue eyes impressed the soldier as much as the sword point. He growled a surrender and hurried away, fastening his breeches. Her lovers couldn't be around every minute. He'd catch her yet and show her what it was like to have a real man.

Brian put an arm around Alana, who looked dazed. "I don't have to shake you, too, do I?" A few tears of delayed shock fell, and he shook his leonine head. "There you go, ruining my reputation again."

Alana pulled away and straightened her clothing. "They encouraged him." Her voice shook.

"And why not? 'Tis the oldest game in the world, surely. Nationality has nothing to do with it. A nice piece of—" He paused. She was in no mood for masculine philosophy.

"Can't say I blame them for wanting to see one of us humiliated. The only reason they're charms on that bracelet is that they tried to put starch in Moctezuma's backbone so he'd drive us out of their valley. No shame in that." He touched the visor of his morion in salute before escorting Alana back to the staircase. Only a few servants were in the torchlit corridor when Brian and Alana stepped out of the dark doorway.

"Thank you for helping me." She was reluctant to leave his comforting presence.

"Get along with you now. And stay out of trouble." He slapped her behind and headed for the dining hall, whistling a cheerful English air.

Knees still trembling, Alana reached the apartment without incident, undressed, and went to bed, stiff and awkward as an old woman. If Finn had been along, that would not have happened. She felt a twinge of guilt. Shouldn't she go see how he was feeling? He had eaten a whole turkey carcass yesterday, and the gluttony had laid him low. Lares, expert with dogs as well as horses, was on guard for any threat of bones piercing the bowels.

But she was too tired. Confident Lares would care for the wolfhound as if he were his own, Alana fell into a troubled sleep. She dreamed of the crossbowman leering and slobbering and fingering her private parts.

"No! No! Sweet Jesus, leave me alone!"

Gilberto rolled away and muttered, "If that's the way you feel about it, plenty of other women would be interested."

"Oh, darling, forgive me. I was having a bad dream." Alana leaned over him and ran palms along each side of his head. "Am I giving you these white hairs I see?" she asked teasingly.

"God, yes." The nobleman kissed her breasts and held them to his cheeks. "There are moments when I wish I'd never met you." He smoothed her body nervously.

After they made love, he slept, but Alana did not. Had age crept upon her lover without her noticing? The deep lines scoring his hawklike face could have been drawn with a dagger's point. Her dagger! It was still in the dungeon! In the commotion she had forgotten to pick it up.

The Irishwoman was wide awake now. It had been her father's and his father's before him and was not a possession to be shrugged aside. Their family coat of arms was embossed on the handle; when she had a son the dagger would be his. Besides, if it had fallen close to the prisoners, one of them could have swooped it up and hidden it.

Should she tell anyone? Cortés would flog the crossbowman—he was very stern about discipline—and punishment would make him even more revengeful and determined. Furthermore, the rogue might twist the situation to his advantage by lying. She could hardly go to Brian's room and ask for help, and Pepe was on guard duty. She would have to go herself.

Alana slipped out of bed, put on a skirt and loose overblouse, wrapped herself in Gilberto's black cloak and hurried out of the apartment. There was a surprising amount of traffic, but no one paid attention to her, just another woman who might be on her way to a rendezvous. It took only moments to descend the steps and reach the dungeon, where the four prisoners slept heavily, snoring and groaning. Noiselessly Alana retrieved the dagger and ran.

Gilberto was waiting for her. He struck Alana on the side of the head with a fist, sending her sprawling. He leaned down, grabbed a handful of hair, and pulled his mistress to her feet.

"Where have you been, whore?"

Alana opened her lips to answer, but shock left her momentarily speechless.

"That's right. Why answer? It'll only be a lie like the others." Gilberto was breathing rapidly, his eyes flaming, his pupils dilated.

"You're hurting me."

He slapped her. "I'll hurt you so you'll remember it." With his free hand he pulled off the cloak. "Whose bed were you in, you ungrateful slut?"

"No one's, I swear by the Virgin Mary. I lost my dagger and was afraid to wait until morning for fear someone else would find *it*." The last word exploded between gritted teeth as he slapped her again. The skin of her lip cracked.

The overblouse came off next, torn from her shoulders. He jerked the drawstring in the skirt. It fell. The provocative curves and hollows of her bare body taunted him, and with a groan of despair Gilberto fell to his knees and buried his face in her flesh. He kissed her, and her lilylike fragrance made his senses reel.

"Forgive me, *preciosa*. Please! It's just that I can't bear to think of anyone touching you but me." He got to his feet and wrapped his arms around her. "Let me love you," he begged. "Let me make it up to you."

He carried her to the bed, and she was silent while he caressed and then took her. But when his climax came, he was caught unawares by an agonizing pain. Blood oozed from the hollow of his throat into the chest hair.

"What—?"

The Irishwoman studied his face coldly. The point of her weapon pressed steadily into the vulnerable spot.

"That was the last time, Spaniard. The last time. Unless I say so."

XIII

Moctezuma puffed glumly on a red clay pipe incised with silver and studded with turquoise. Thanks be to the gods, it contained precisely the right amounts of tobacco, marijuana, and liquidambar. He refused to put up with mistakes today. Nothing suited him, in fact, not even his dwarfs, dancers, clowns, or jugglers. The Supreme Aztec wriggled well-manicured toes in new jaguar-skin sandals. At least they fit. But everything else was out of joint and had been for some time.

His guards heard exclamations of frustrated rage and the crash of a vase. They stiffened, listening intently. Recently he'd lost his temper with dancers from the city of Texcoco who made a misstep in front of him. Unable to execute them for the error because they were subjects of another king, Moctezuma had ordered the secret militia to search out those in Tenochtitlán with the same names as the dancers. These innocents had been sacrificed instead. The guards held their arms tightly to their sides so the sweat of terror could not stain their tunics.

The man they feared slumped down heavily into a high-backed, legless wickerwork chair which sat on the floor. Dropping the pipe in a golden dish, Moctezuma covered his eyes with a long, slender hand. Nothing had gone right since Cortés arrived last year. Ancient prophecies which forecast calamity, destruction, slavery, and darkness were gaining more and more credence in his mind. Was he himself not a captive?

It was mortifying how bitterly he had been censored for not annihilating the strangers. But what would his critics have done? After all, *they* had not been in the unenviable position of marking time until the man-god, Quetzalcoatl, returned to reestablish his rule. Or wondering if Cortés were that god.

When Quetzalcoatl had been exiled long ago, the royal house of Mexica-Aztecs had been charged with governing the land in his absence. But when he came back, this stewardship was to terminate. Relinquishing this control would end Moctezuma's power and lessen his prestige.

Had his detractors been faced with that distinctly unattractive contingency? They had *not*. Nor had they borne the burden of ascertaining whether the newcomers were gods or mortals. Why was he accused of weakness and cowardice? Had everyone forgotten the successful military campaigns he led? That he had extended the tribe's domination farther than any other ruler? And what about the twelve thousand prisoners of war captured and sacrificed to Huitzilopochtli?

Had anyone helped him deal with this stunning problem? No, he'd been forced to call upon common village magicians to pronounce spells. Astrologists, necromancers, mediums, warlocks—they all had given him conflicting information, and he'd had them killed. Then Cortés and his men marched across the causeway, spears glinting in the sun, pennons fluttering like bats, coats of mail rattling and clashing. They were gods perhaps, but not at all what he'd expected. Quetzalcoatl's emissaries possibly, but profoundly changed from the form of that Light of the World.

Was it true he had been unworthy of his heritage? As Cacama had said, maybe he was an old hen. He should not have been so uncertain, and he could have set a better example.

Yet there had been terrible and inexplicable catastrophes visited on the tribes for years before the Spaniards came. Fear lived with everyone, not only with him. Could he help it if he was inordinately affected by such things? Could he help it if surrendering Tenochtitlán had been the will of the gods?

"Lord. My Lord. My Great Lord." It was the usual salutation.

Moctezuma caught a whiff of magnolias. Only his favorite concubine,

Yellow Plume, wore that scent. Without moving, he growled softly, "How dare you disturb me when I am sad? Do you want to be sent to the House of the Joy of Women?" He had no intention whatsoever of putting her in the young warriors' brothel, but a man couldn't let his harem get out of hand.

"If thou art sad, Lord, let me lighten thy heart with love."

Yellow Plume was the only person who dared enter his quarters when he fell into a black mood. The threat was real enough, however. The tiniest hint of royal displeasure could mean slavery, prostitution, or sacrifice. Yet she loved him more than his other hundred and fifty women, even his two legal wives, and she loved without thought of self or reward.

Like a boy, he peeked through his fingers, suddenly cheered by the ravishing young morsel kneeling at his feet. She was his most talented and versatile mistress. But he held her in rare regard principally because she cared for him as an individual, not as a source of riches or position. Almighty gods on high, a man surely deserved one such woman in his lifetime!

"Is it indeed Yellow Plume? The feathered flower that perfumes my bed?"

She inched forward until her breasts touched his knees. Sleek black hair pouring over her shoulders tickled his bare legs and sent shivers down his spine. Hazel eyes caressed Moctezuma's longish face with its short, silky black beard and straight hair sweeping gracefully over his ears. The couple smiled at each other tenderly.

Moctezuma had made his own rule about people not being allowed to look him in the face on pain of death. But that was ridiculous during intercourse, so he had been tolerant with women, especially in private. His brooding, intelligent eyes lingered on the luscious dark-red mouth. He slipped a hand inside the neck of her gown, fondling her breast and rubbing the nipple gently between thumb and forefinger. "Is it she?"

"It is she," Yellow Plume finally answered in a strangled voice, caught up in the passion he always evoked. "It is she."

Moctezuma rose, lifting her by one elbow, his hand still firmly cupped around her breast. She was ready. He was ready. He would lose his sorrow in her hot, sweet body. "What did you come to tell me?" he asked, nuzzling her throat and ear.

"The white one with eyes of jade, Lord. She is here."

They had reached Moctezuma's bed, adorned with fine furs beneath a magnificent canopy of multihued feathers. Incense smoked beside it, and the room was warm and dim. He seldom took women here; it was a distinct honor for him to do so. But the man didn't much care today. He had never wanted her so intensely. This was one thing Cortés could not take from him!

Dispensing with the usual ritual, he pulled the girl down on top of him, pushing their clothing aside. They gasped with joy as their bodies joined. He removed the rest of her clothes so he could look at her.

"She is waiting. . . . " Dark lashes swept down.

Moctezuma was on fire. He was a volcano, ready to erupt. "Let her wait. Let them all wait. Let the world wait—while the great Moctezuma makes love!"

Alana did not mind waiting. She and Inmaculada, who would interpret for her, wandered through the anteroom. Ceramic vases, stone sculptures, feathered wall hangings, and other decorative objects had been transferred from Moctezuma's new palace a short distance away, where he'd lived until Cortés had brought him to the complex where the Spaniards were now lodged.

Actually, Alana had almost decided against coming. She'd felt terrible after the beating Gilberto had given her. Not only that, the bruises on her face showed plainly and her lip hurt where it had split. But Inmaculada had borrowed cosmetics from royal concubines, some of whom were as pale of skin as Europeans, adroitly applied the beauty preparations, and insisted Alana keep the engagement. It would be a fascinating experience and take her mind off her troubles.

When Moctezuma emerged from his private apartments, Alana thought he seemed younger than his forty years. His eyes shone, the rather sallow complexion had a healthy flush, and he greeted them warmly. A fragrance of magnolias wafted from him, and Alana recalled with a pang of regret the musk Gilberto had affected. She would always associate that scent with the first man she had known.

The Aztec and the Irishwoman gazed into each other's eyes. His so black and hers so green, monarch and exile. Each knew a special melancholy the other recognized.

Alana understood Cortés and his officers were fond of Moctezuma, although the less perceptive made him sound like a blooded horse they had
caught and tamed. She sensed he had given in instead.

Moctezuma now motioned the women toward elaborately carved stools
directly in front of him and settled down to enjoy a favorite pastime—
admiring female beauty. The stranger's coloring enchanted him.

Inmaculada said respectfully, "I speak the tongue of your people, Great
Lord, and will translate for you both. My mistress is anxious to talk with
you."

He frowned, and she knew instinctively the question that flew across his
mind. Was she another self-assured, lovely, deadly harbinger of the future? Another Malinche? She wanted to put his mind at rest.

"I come from a town near Xicalango. My father was a Chontal Maya
who traded with your merchants for many years. White men kidnapped me
and took me to Cuba, where I was put in slave barracks. Later my mistress
saved me from being eaten by dogs. I would give my life for her."

So they all hated the Spaniard. Moctezuma knew, of course, about the
beating Alana had received, just as he knew everything that went on. He
nodded. Misery loves company, the sages said. He felt better and signaled
the chamberlain to bring a golden casket. For Alana Moctezuma chose a
necklace of opals set in gold, their milky depths flickering with iridescent
fires. She had never seen them before and was openly enthralled. He placed
Inmaculada's amethyst bracelet on her wrist with his own hands, a high
compliment. Feathered capes and bolts of fine cotton, as well as other gifts,
would be delivered to their apartments later, he assured them.

"What do you give a man who has everything?" Alana had asked in despair the night before. "He'll give us presents. He's forever giving someone something. I must take a gift with me!" Pepe happened to notice a soldier plaiting horsehair to pass the time. After Alana described the gold and
feathered flychasers Aztec nobles carried, the man made a handsome repli-
ca from black, white, and sorrel horsehair, and this Alana brought as a gift
for the Aztec warrior.

"Ah," Moctezuma exclaimed with delight, swishing it back and forth
like a whip. "From the mighty horses!"

Suddenly Cortés and his men appeared. He and Pedro de Alvarado, Velásquez de León, and Gilberto wore full armor, as the Spaniards always did

in the ruler's presence. Bernal Díaz, who usually managed to be in on anything that promised to be interesting, escorted Cortés' mistress.

"I am glad you have come," Moctezuma said gaily. "I would like to show White Willow my own palace instead of going sailing. She will appreciate the birds, the fountains, and the gardens." The curious affection existing between him and Cortés warmed his words.

Malinche started and glanced at Alana. "White Willow! He speaks of the miracle his tribe found when it ended its wanderings here two centuries ago. When they found a place where everything was white that the elders had said was of the utmost purity." She inclined her head an inch or so. "Moctezuma has seen into your heart and found it so."

"Blessed be the pure in heart," Alvarado murmured mischievously to Gilberto, who was trying to catch Alana's eye.

Cortés inspected her carefully. She wore Indian clothing—a cotton blouse and skirt the shade of new leaves embroidered with white flamingos and exotic flowers topped by a vibrant blue mantle edged with snowy fur. Sandals of ocelot skin graced her feet and the opal necklace her breast. Her pale hair was braided with blue wool. He could see why Indians might wonder if she were a goddess.

Was this woman the wedge he needed in his firm commitment to halt the human sacrifice tainting this land and brutalizing its people? If Moctezuma regarded her so highly, perhaps she might persuade him to stop the practice. He must discuss this matter with her as soon as possible.

When the conquistador did not answer immediately, his prisoner rose swiftly and angrily. Those present saw once again, if only for a moment, the despotic potentate of a territory as large as Spain. The commander who had led huge armies to victory after victory. The royal priest who tore out still-beating hearts for sacrifice to his gods.

"But of course!" Cortés gestured magnanimously as if there had never been any question. "My men will naturally want to accompany you. As you know, they never get enough of the wonders of Tenochtitlán."

The Aztec's glower faded. He shrugged imperceptibly. A little freedom at this point was better than none.

As long as she lived, Alana would always remember what she saw that day. She walked in a dream, shaded by a feathered canopy that was supported by gold-plated poles and carried by lords of the realm. Women scattered orange dahlias and marigolds in a carpet for them to walk upon, and attendants swung censers of incense that rose in fragrant clouds.

They left the older structure housing the army and headed for Moctezuma's newest and largest palace to which the aviary-zoo was attached. The enormous two-story pile contained his living quarters and harem, hundreds of guest rooms, tribute storage areas with lodging for those who recorded it in books of fine paper, archives, housing for hundreds of guards and servants. The edifice was also the administrative center of the Aztec empire, complete with council chambers, tribunals, and accommodations for judges and clerks. It was a miniature city, covering acres of ground.

Passing along the serpent-headed wall which enclosed Tenochtitlán's sacred center, a stone-paved plaza five hundred and twenty by six hundred feet, Alana gaped with astonishment. At lofty pyramids whose flat summits supported elaborate temples. At thousands of dark-robed priests who tended the precincts and assisted supplicants and participants in daily ceremonies. At a circular *teocalli* where Quetzalcoatl was worshiped as the wind god. At grisly racks of human skulls displayed by the tens of thousands. At a ball court, seminaries, granaries, arsenals, buildings for pilgrims, a twenty-ton calendar stone, and a platform for gladiatorial combat.

Vivid memories suddenly rushed back to her of priests near Vera Cruz who had taken the travelers on a tour of gore-coated chapels and a butchering area. She stumbled and crossed herself.

Moctezuma inquired with concern, "Are you ill, White Willow?"

Cortés had noticed the growing horror on his companion's face. He said tightly, "If I'm not mistaken, she is comparing the marvels of your civilization with what she knows is going on up there."

He pointed with anger at the Great Pyramid that dominated the island. Its temples soaring sixty feet high housed chapels so sacred only Moctezuma and the supreme high priests could enter. The one painted white and crimson was dedicated to the war god who was also the sun god: Huitzilopochtli, Left-Handed Hummingbird. The blue and white temple was sacred to Tlaloc, the god of rain. For who could live without war, sun, or rain?

"It is such a self-defeating bondage!" To Cortés and his men, as fanatical in their faith as in their quest for fame and fortune, cleansing this abomination from the sight of God had become a crusade; Christian compromise on idols, human sacrifice, cannibalism, and sodomy was unthinkable.

Serpent-skin drums boomed, punctuating his words. Alana shrank from the red smear which soiled many of the hundred steps leading up to the temples. After sacrifice, black-clad priests cooked the limbs of the corpse, prepared the skull for the rack, and sent the remaining meat to the aviary-zoo for birds of prey and predatory animals.

Moctezuma's eyes flashed. Of course, daily sacrifices continued. How else could the pantheon of gods be pacified? Why, there were sixty-five major deities alone! He knew Cortés would have destroyed the holy places as he had done on the coast and at Cholula, if he had had enough men. And he might have succeeded. In a land without iron or steel, Spanish swords, guns, and cannon were mighty weapons.

Perhaps there would come a time when Quetzalcoatl's will would be done, when the sun would not need fresh human hearts to give him strength to rise each dawn. In the meantime, Moctezuma could not—would not!—desert the gods who had brought his tribe to the pinnacle of glory.

"Please," Alana said, putting a shaky hand on the arm of each man, a gesture that horrified the Indians.

"You have touched a divine person," Alvarado told her, smiling coldly.

This cavalier would put Moctezuma to the sword without a qualm. His daredevil streak made him very popular with the men, but she wondered if that quality, as well as his impulsiveness, kept him from being the leader he might have been.

"Let your visit to my home be a pleasant one," the Aztec said. He saw Alana's black-lashed eyes open wide with childish awe and delight. The man idly envisioned her naked, her white flesh and silvery hair contrasted against his own light-brown body. She was a strangely pretty creature who attracted many lovers. He knew about all of them. He laughed to himself. The foreigners had no idea what an intricate and accurate spy network existed in their quarters. He took her hand and led her through the halls like a queen.

The palace was far too immense to be seen in one day. There were, Inmaculada breathed incredulously, hundreds of chambers with hundreds of bathrooms! Like the nobility, the king bathed two and three times a day; even common laborers bathed at least once. Alana giggled. No wonder Aztecs incensed the soldiers within an inch of their unwashed lives!

As soon as the party entered, they were served velvet-smooth chocolate redolent with vanilla, foaming in chased golden goblets which the guests were to keep. The women goggled at fountains, patios shaded with cotton awnings and ablaze with potted plants, walls of alabaster, porphyry, and marble, ceilings of cedar, pine, and sandalwood. Panels of exquisitely patterned featherwork hung from golden pegs.

As they walked toward the gardens, Alana saw Brian Phelps not far away in the midst of a cluster of young women. He towered over the froth of color and shiny black coiffures like a sturdy English yew ringed by a garland of tropical blossoms.

"That's picking up the language the best way possible," Bernal commented. He knew from experience. Moctezuma had recently given him a girl from his own harem, who was promptly christened Francisca and introduced to the valiant soldier's way of love. A muted wave of laughter sounded on the sweet-smelling air, confirming his observation.

Inmaculada chuckled. She liked the big Englishman and hoped he would bed her mistress soon, marry her, and keep her out of trouble. She hadn't decided whether Alana had a tendency to be in the wrong place at the wrong time or it was simply her thirst for knowledge and an eagerness to enjoy new experiences that was forever getting her into trouble. That Alana showed the tiniest bit of pique at Brian's gallantries was a good sign. How annoying to have Salvatierra tagging along, making calf's eyes! She should get away from that selfish voluptuary. He had held her long enough.

Gilberto hardly saw the pools and aquariums, the treelined canals interlacing the gardens, ducks and egrets, and masses of waterlilies and hyacinths. But he did spare a glance for golden replicas of birds unable to live at this altitude. Then he overheard Moctezuma say he was tired and wanted to return to his apartments to rest. Tomorrow he would see that White Willow was rowed about Tenochtitlán to see the markets, goldsmiths and featherworkers, nunneries, and libraries. Whatever her heart desired was hers for the asking.

Her lover wished Alana were his for the asking. He could have kicked himself back to Vera Cruz for beating her last night. Yet his jealousy had burst into an unmanageable tide. He had wanted desperately to make love this morning, but she would have no part of him.

Why, he hadn't had another woman since she first came to him. Alana had been everything he'd ever wanted. The witch! If she continued to refuse him, however, he'd have to go elsewhere. There were half-breed camp followers from Cuba, whom he heard were free of disease and looked interesting in a gypsylike way.

Yet suppose she really didn't care? The man's heart constricted. After all, she no longer faced the predicament that had brought them together. Plenty of attractive, potentially wealthy men would come running now to put their boots under her bed. A sullen light dulled the amber eyes. The bishop's letter might bring her to heel.

Alana knew Gilberto like the back of her hand. When the group broke up so Moctezuma could be escorted back to his gilded cage, she motioned frantically to Inmaculada. While her friend distracted the Spaniard with a shield of gold and mother-of-pearl on the wall, Alana darted into a nearby courtyard.

He wasn't going to take his pleasure with her today! By Sweet Saint Bridget, he wasn't! In fact, the arrogant count was in for a long, dry spell. He couldn't abuse her and hurt her pride like that and get away with it. Was she a trollop of the stews to be humiliated with a blow and a bedding? No, there would be no reconciliation until she felt like it!

She sat by a fountain with the sun warm on her back, more than content to be alone, to drowse and listen to birdsong and water splashing, to mull over Moctezuma's cordiality and the wondrous and horrendous sights of this city. Slowly Alana became aware of a whisper of garments, a sibilant sound like a snake twisting and slithering through the grass. She opened her eyes, startled and terrified.

Savage Serpent, the high priest, had made a special trip to look at this woman. Of them all, it had been rumored she really came from the Land of the Dawn where Quetzalcoatl had lived in exile. He had to admit he was sadly disappointed.

It was not unusual for gods and goddesses to be ugly, even hideous. Somehow, though, this woman's appearance seemed rather obscene: white skin like the belly of a fish, hair almost white as cotton, eyes of a weird changeable green. Her breasts were overly large, her feet huge, and that mole by her open mouth looked like a speck of dirt.

He had never possessed a woman. His vows forbade it, and the beautiful boys had always been sufficient for his needs. If he had been allowed one, she would have been in shades of brown and cream and black like a baby rabbit, succulent as a partridge and hot as *chilli*. Oh, he had pondered it in the long nights. A man could not strip and sacrifice them for years on end and not conjecture. One had to set an inviolable example for young priests rising in the church hierarchy, however. He shifted his feet as pain lanced through his knees. This arthritis was getting intolerable.

Alana shuddered visibly and closed her eyes in thanksgiving when Fray Olmedo, Brian, and several artillerymen entered. The two religious leaders nodded frostily. Each knew the other would not give an inch; each knew he was in the right.

"Father," Alana said breathlessly, "have you been enjoying the sights?"

The cleric's stern face relaxed. He liked the girl and sympathized with her problems. She came to confession regularly, voice soft and hesitant. This bunch of rascals over which he made the sign of the cross had described so many sins he was seldom surprised anymore.

"Indeed, I have! This is a glorious city, isn't it? A garden city, you might say. And I am more impressed than ever that it was built—like other towns—without the use of the wheel. A few toys have wheels, but for some reason the principle has eluded them when it comes to construction or transportation."

Brian commented, "Aye, you're right. And another thing I've noticed. They don't have iron tools. They've accomplished all this with stone, wood, bone, copper, and obsidian."

Fray Olmedo continued, "How much we have to offer each other. But I'm afraid the men in power, like Savage Serpent here, won't permit a peaceable exchange of information."

"You know him?" Alana's nostrils quivered at the stench of incense, dead flesh, and stale blood that hung like a miasma around the Aztec. Indian priests never cut, combed, or washed their hair. They let it descend in grisly disarray down their backs, heavy and matted with human and animal blood. They were a sight to make the heart pound and sweat break out on the palms.

Savage Serpent's body was painted black. It was mutilated and emaciated from fasting and self-inflicted torture, his ragged ears so serrated from penitential notching they no longer bore any resemblance to normal ears and his long fingernails encrusted with dried blood. Thorn-studded cords dangled from slits in his cheeks.

Sensing Alana's approaching hysteria, Fray Olmedo guided her protectively out of the courtyard. Brian stood studying Savage Serpent. Merciful

God! He'd turn a man's insides to ice with those eyes. Someone had told the Englishman that these priests took massive doses of potent narcotics. No wonder! You'd have to be out of your head to spend a lifetime cutting hearts out.

Disgusted and uncomfortable, Savage Serpent turned and limped out of the courtyard.

"Jesus!" Brian snorted. "He smells like the jakes on a hot day."

XIV

Alana did not move out of the apartment but had another mat and bedding brought in. Finn now slept at her feet. By unspoken agreement, she and Gilberto maintained a more or less normal routine in public.

Fortunately, his time was more and more taken up by Cortés, who valued his fighting ability and battlefield experience, as well as his bold spirit. The wolf pack could always use another set of fangs. Deprived of his mistress' sexual companionship, however, Gilberto lost weight, grew testy, and did not eat well. He had apologized until blue in the face, but Alana did not budge, nor did the wolfhound who guarded her, ruling out any nocturnal foray which might break down her defenses with soft words and kisses.

Surprised to discover she did not miss his attentions, Alana found it pleasant to stretch out after a busy day, sleep the night through and wake up, refreshed, alone. This was a time of mental, physical, and spiritual rest. Eventually pity replaced the anger she'd felt for her lover. To be so vulnerable—faith, that must hurt! But she was occupied with the world around her and made no move to forgive and forget.

Pepe and Inmaculada were married now and among other gifts had received gold bars from Moctezuma. They spent a short honeymoon at his palace in Chapultepec, wandering through the famous hanging gardens and his orchid, vanilla, cacao, and magnolia groves.

Alana rode her stallion north to Teotihuacán to visit monumental ruins around the Pyramids of the Sun and the Moon, remnants of a polished culture vanished centuries before the Aztecs came. Xicotencatl the Younger, Corn Flower's husband, and a squadron of Tlaxcalans accompanied her on the trip which took several days. She felt completely at ease in his fierce, soldierly company.

On the way back she toured elegant, urbane Texcoco, the most stylish and sophisticated city in the Valley of Mexico, and marveled at its literary academy, extensive archives, and magnificent gardens. Gardens! They were everywhere. The Nahuatl vocabulary even had words descriptive of different kinds of gardens, indicating they had long been part of Indian life.

Tenochtitlán's markets, shops, canals, streets, hospitals, parks, schools, botanical gardens, craft centers—these intrigued Alana. More and more she could be found studying, examining, learning, tasting, listening, and absorbing, for she had come to love these people. Inmaculada prophesied this woman would soon know more about the valley than Cortés and the rest of them put together.

The *totocalli*, Moctezuma's House of Birds, was Alana's favorite place. Here species from every part of his domain lived in pampered captivity in wooden and bamboo enclosures nine feet high and six feet across. Half of each structure was roofed, and the other half open so birds could take shelter or bask in the sun. Hundreds of servants worked tirelessly to clean cages, fix food, doctor the sick, gather feathers, and keep the grounds immaculate.

Alana had charmed the ancient keeper with honest praise. Her smile warmed his heart, and in his mind he paid her the ultimate compliment. She seemed much like a small waterfowl with white plumage, a coral beak, and eyes reflecting the water upon which she floated.

Because he had dedicated his life to his precious charges, the old keeper of the House of Birds had not been surprised when Alana visited often. He noticed she was especially dazzled by the sacred quetzal birds, the most splendid of them all. They were his loves as well. They came from remote cloud forests to the south; their bronze-green plumes, shimmering like fire in the lake, were reserved for nobility and brave warriors.

"Oh, the darling! Sweet Saint Bridget, but he's superb!" From the keeper's wizened claws Alana took a giant, an emperor among quetzal birds. The tail, fully four feet long, swept the ground. Chocolate-brown eyes, bright and healthy, peered at her warily.

Just then someone touched her hair which was loose to the hips, and the keeper took the quetzal from her grasp and disappeared. Tlacateotl, the high priest's nephew, was not one of his favorite people.

Adultery in Aztec society was punished by death. Transgressors' heads were crushed by a stone after the woman had been strangled. The crime had to be confirmed by impartial witnesses, however, because the husband's testimony could not be considered unprejudiced.

Tlacateotl, the warrior-prince posing in sun-dappled shade, had learned early to take advantage of this qualification. When women he chose to visit did not cooperate, a veiled threat regarding his close relationship with Savage Serpent usually broke the ice. The only son of his uncle's favorite sister, Tlacateotl took full advantage of his close blood relationship with the high priest.

In the House of Young Men where he'd received a general education and basic martial training, the young Aztec had received his introduction to sodomy. His handsome features—huge, melting black eyes, long, lush lashes, a sensuous mouth—and his virile, muscular body had made him a highly desirable partner, and he was much in demand. But in spite of his success with the men, he vastly preferred female companions.

He'd been studying the white woman carefully from a distance. He liked her large bosom and pure white skin.

He knew she lived with a man who was not her husband, and he assumed she must be like the women the Aztec system permitted warriors to enjoy. With utmost confidence he slipped an arm around the supple waist and pulled her close. Then an unprecedented thing happened. Her nipples pressed against the bare skin of his chest as if no material intervened. Their thighs gently touched. The lovely hair touched his skin, her emerald eyes gazed into his, and he was shaken to the very core of his being.

Tlacateotl had watched the Spaniards kiss, and he lowered his seductive mouth experimentally. One could always learn. Their breaths mingled; his muscles tightened expectantly; his loins sang. But then she broke away and ran as if demons were chasing her.

*   *   *

Alana found the army barracks in an uproar. Weapons were being cleaned and tested, armor donned and horses saddled. Extra sentinels had been stationed along the wall surrounding the palace complex, and gunners manned cannon with tense faces. Fray Olmedo was preparing to say mass, and Cortés stood talking loudly to Alvarado and Malinche.

"For God's sake, what's happened?" She managed to catch the arm of a soldier's wife.

"Oh, you remember the uproar it caused when Cortés insisted on taking one of the Aztec temples for our chapel?"

"Of course." It had been a stupendous concession on the part of the Indian priests, in deference to Moctezuma, to allow Christians to worship atop the main *teocalli*. She, for one, had never been at ease in the midst of its ceremonial ferocity.

"Now it seems their gods—" The woman spit. "At least according to Moctezuma, their gods are angry and want us thrown out of the city. Or better yet out of the country. There's a lot of unrest, and by the Blessed Mary of Seville, I think we should go." She crossed herself.

Alana shivered to think of Savage Serpent's rage, of the power he and his associates wielded. The entire social, economic, and military structure depended on the whims of fickle, cruel gods, as interpreted by those men!

After attending the hurried services on the fringe of an edgy congregation, Alana hurried to the apartment. If hostilities were imminent, she wanted to make her peace with Gilberto.

He was buckling his cuirass while Finn watched sleepily. She moved to help him.

"Don't bother."

"Gilberto." She bit her lip. "Gilberto, I don't want you to get hurt."

"That's nice of you." He smoothed his thick hair and put on his helmet. "Why so worried all of a sudden?"

This was not the man she knew or the contrite lover who'd tagged her footsteps for the past month. Had she waited too long? Did he have someone else? She felt a wave of the old fear. She didn't want to be alone.

"Why shouldn't I be, after all we've meant to each other?"

"You've treated me like a leper." Spanish pride cooled every word. He loomed in front of her, eyes narrowed and unfriendly beneath the visor. "You've made it plain my love was no longer welcome and made me a laughingstock besides."

"Faith, man! If you hadn't hit me in the first place—and for nothing!—none of this would have happened."

He groaned and grabbed her arms. "You're right and I'm sorry. I've told you and *told* you I'm sorry. You witch! I still dream of you every night after all this time."

They kissed desperately, both of them shaking with desire. It had been a long drought. Alana had discovered just how long when she had almost let the Aztec warrior's mouth meet hers. Touching Gilberto's cheek, she felt herself melting before his armored masculinity.

"Stay here," he whispered. "I'll be back as soon as I can."

Councils of war and the emergency situation kept him, and it was close to midnight when things calmed down. No attack of enraged Aztecs seemed forthcoming, and those off duty relaxed. A reckless few went so far as to indulge in Indian narcotics well away from Cortés' stern eye.

Searching for Gilberto, Alana finally found him hunched in an out-of-the-way alcove of one of the halls where infantrymen were quartered. She put a hand on his arm. "You had better come eat and then rest. We'll be up early, I'm sure."

He glanced at the three men sitting with him. "My little *madre.*" They chuckled and as if by signal rose to hide her from view.

He spoke slurringly to two girls sitting at his feet, women Alana recognized as the camp prostitutes from Cuba. "Have you met my little mother?" Sloe eyes swiveled toward her.

Gilberto pulled Alana down on his lap. She smelled a sickly sweet odor on his breath. Was he experimenting with drugs? How foolish! And how dangerous! The pupils of his eyes were dilated, as were those of his companions; he obviously was not himself.

"Sit still, my dear. I want you to see how I've passed the days and nights since you left me alone. My friends here have introduced me to new pleasures. Tricks they learned in Tangier."

The girls giggled, and one of them smoothed Alana's leg with a hot hand. She drew back in horror when they rose on their knees and ran their fingers under her skirts. Striking the nearest one across the face, the Irishwoman tried in vain to get up.

Gilberto suddenly covered her mouth with a firm hand. "Where are your quarters?" The girls pointed, eyes glittering, and someone threw him a cloak which he wrapped around Alana. Unnoticed in the turmoil, the group hurried out of the hall.

Alana had descended into hell. Her only hope was Finn, who had been eating near the horses' courtyard. One shrill whistle would bring him, and she tried to bite Gilberto's hand, but he only laughed.

They entered a small room where Alana was stripped naked and held so she could be fondled. The girls began to undress with feverish haste while the men stared lustfully. Sickened and terrified, she knew what was in store.

An argument arose over who was to have her first, and without thinking Gilberto gestured angrily with both hands. It was the break his captive had been waiting for. Swooping up the cloak, as well as her dagger, which had fallen on the floor, Alana leaped over the bed mat and raced out of the room, covering herself as she went. Once in the open she put two fingers in her mouth and blew a piercing whistle. The wolfhound galloped in from the hall where he'd been following her scent.

Panic-stricken, Alana went out the first door she saw, pushing aside the soldier who tried to stop her. As Pepe Ortega walked by minutes later, the guard told him about it. Wasn't the good-looking blonde a friend of his and his wife's?

Holy Mother in heaven! She shouldn't be out there alone tonight! Especially in view of the powder keg they were sitting on right now. The Andalusian was puzzled by such foolhardiness. Regardless of her popularity or Moctezuma's protection, Tenochtitlán after dark was no place to be alone.

"Of all the!" What was going on here? Gilberto stood not far away, disheveled and bleary-eyed. Pepe ran to catch the nobleman as he collapsed, his sword clattering on the floor. Idiot! Cortés would execute him if he heard about this.

Inmaculada stared down at the Spaniard with disdain. The white race would never learn to handle narcotics. They would prove as catastrophic for them as alcohol was for the Indians.

"All right, I'll put him on his feet, but you get the Englishman and go after her. Now! If that high priest finds out she's by herself!"

Inmaculada made the sign of the cross reverently and then supplicated old Maya deities, too. Whoever fell into Aztec hands tonight was as good as dead . . . might all the gods protect Alana MacKenna!

XV

If there was one word Brian Phelps knew in Nahuatl, it was "woman," and as he prowled along the serpent-headed wall separating the religious precinct from Moctezuma's palaces, he heard it often. Somehow the devils knew she was out here tonight.

The voices rang with excitement. Hunting humans, especially a beautiful female valued by the enemy, was tremendously stimulating. High on the Great Pyramid stood Savage Serpent, his scarlet garments like blood in the light of the altar fires.

Brian ducked into the aviary, hoping Alana had gone there to hide. Huge as he was, the Englishman sped among the latticed enclosures so swiftly and quietly only a few birds awoke, then quickly settled down again.

Where could she be? Cortés estimated Tenochtitlán had more than sixty-five thousand buildings. Brian listened uneasily to the eerie wail of conch-shell horns saluting the moon. Gooseflesh rose on his arms. This was a magnificent place, and he was glad to have seen it. But how it fed on death, agony, and terror! Any hapless Indian who got drunk, wore a garment below the knee if not authorized to do so, or walked accidentally into a forbidden room of the palace, musicians who blew a wrong note, commoners wearing feathers—each courted a swift trip to the Land of the Fleshless.

Brian swore fervently. She could be anywhere!

This whole mess had become too rough and tough for his poppet, despite her reckless nature and her love of adventure. Too many men were on the prowl. Anyone with half an eye could see her relationship with the Spaniard had deteriorated, and whatever happened tonight must have been very serious to have driven her out of the palace.

Just then Brian heard a hair-raising snarl in the direction of Moctezuma's newer palace. Sounds of a scuffle were clear, and a cry of masculine pain broke off in midair. The Englishman grinned as he ran that way, his broadsword ready in one big paw. She'd nailed one of them, the little wildcat!

Without warning, two men tackled him, flying out of the dark like javelins. Fierce, fanatical, dedicated, the Aztecs grappled with him but were no match for the big blade and their antagonist's brute strength. Brian concealed the bodies on the shadowy side of the wall where the struggle had taken place.

Within seconds he crouched near Moctezuma's palace entrance behind the stylized statue of a jaguar, eyes darting here and there. Warriors stood at attention beneath the coat of arms, an eagle gripping an ocelot in its talons. This side of the plaza appeared to be tranquil. The guard changed. Torches flickered. The stone structure was silent.

Did they have her yet? Brian gritted his teeth, sick to his stomach to think of her spread-eagled on a sacrificial stone.

Oh, Irish, sweet Irish! Why didn't I tell you I loved you when I had the chance? The word trilled through his mind again. Loved? Yes, loved and wanted for his own. Forever. Now, when it was too late, he finally knew.

Maybe Moctezuma could save Alana. The Englishman decided to return to the barracks, get Inmaculada, and wake him. He crept away from the statue and along the wall, taking care to keep his head down. When he approached the area where he had been attacked, Brian swerved and trotted toward the botanical gardens.

These were five miles in circumference, an incredible collection of thousands of plants from every part of the empire and beyond used for medicines, research, religious rites, and experimentation. No one frequented them at night, and he could reach the palace faster and with less danger by traveling along their perimeter. The zoo was not far away, and the animals spoke to one another, sullen and restless, sensitive to the city's wrath and rancor. Brian had visited the menagerie and its reptile house. God's blood, he didn't want to fall into one of those pits in the dark!

Bushes rustled to his right. Instinctively he fell into fighting stance. Brian deliberately had not worn a helmet in order to avoid its gleaming in the light but had protected himself with a steel mesh skullcap covered with a dark quilted material. A black cloak fastened across his chest concealed the cuirass. He balanced on tiptoe, sword in one hand and a lethal smashing club he had taken from the dead Aztecs in the other.

Alana tore a long strip off the bottom of her cloak and wrapped it around the wolfhound's midriff. She could not be sure without a light, but it felt as if the Indian's lance had only grazed his ribs. She held the rough-furred head to her chest and patted it. Bless his heart! He wouldn't let anything hurt her if he could help it.

But she shivered with fear. There had been only one man and not a very strong one at that. Otherwise, she wouldn't have been able to kill him. *Kill him!* She couldn't believe it. The sensation of the dagger sinking into his flesh . . . she couldn't shake it. God forgive her!

When they'd collided, Alana had been frantic and defensive. She remembered swearing at him and then stabbing hard. Her language facility had improved to the point where she understood the shouts of the other pursuers very well. Capture, multiple rape, and delivery to Savage Serpent for sacrifice at dawn. Alana had had no choice—kill or be killed.

The hunters had spotted her shortly after her hurried departure from the barracks, having been called for duty in case of trouble. Any Spaniard who poked his long nose out of the palace tonight would wind up under the knife. But a woman! And the one with silver hair and green eyes at that! Moctezuma might give her special privileges, but his influence was weakening. They'd give her something, all right!

Alana sank onto the ground. Finn stood next to her, sniffing the air. What a nightmare! Where was she, for the love of Jesus? She couldn't decide whether to remain here until dawn or try to get back to the palace and hope she met no one on the way. Wherever she'd run after her encounter, it was black as a tomb. Even the remarkable glow from the temples did not penetrate here.

Tears trickled down her cheeks. Everything had gone wrong. How could Gilberto have done the things he did? Didn't he love her anymore? She wished she had never, ever left Ireland. Had stayed put and married some nice old poop who'd have been kind and kept her safe. Alana wiped her nose.

Finn tensed. The ghost of a growl vibrated in his chest. Alana put a warning hand on his muzzle. Whoever walked out there trod like the big cats in the zoo, padding along with spring, violence, stealth. Her eyes started from their sockets in an attempt to pierce the gloom. Sweat gathered in the folds of her body and on her palms and face. The dagger she gripped was poised, sharp as death.

Then her dog bounded away. Alana clapped a hand over her mouth in consternation. *Oh, dear God, deliver me from the Philistines!*

"Why is it I'm the only one you cry on? No wonder my doublets shrink." Brian sat on the ground with his back to a tree trunk. His broadsword rested by one leg, his club by the other. Finn sat alert at his right hand, close to the touch, and Alana curled up in his lap, weeping quietly.

"You always seem to be so handy," she whispered brokenly.

He smelled the sweat of fear, and his heart contracted with tenderness and compassion. Poor darling, so brave and alone. "Why did you leave the barracks? You know better than that." He spoke softly in her ear, brushing her cheek with his lips as he did so.

Alana told him the sordid story, and Brian snorted in disgust and amazement. He thought Salvatierra loved Alana. Lousy bastard. He didn't deserve a nice girl like this. Then he returned to a certain part of the story.

"Do you mean to tell me, Irish, that you're naked as a little jaybird under that cloak of yours?"

Alana jerked as if stung. Oh, no! Not him, too. . . .

Sinewy arms drew her back and wrapped around her more securely. Brian laughed deep in his throat. Why, he was literally tucking her under his wings, trying to keep her warm. The big tease.

"Na, na, ma pet," he said, unconsciously parroting an old childhood nurse. "Na, na. Brian'll let naught harm thee." He gathered her close as the cuirass permitted, burying his lips in her hair, rocking her gently, making sure she was covered against the cold. "Try to sleep. When it's light, we'll decide what to do."

When Brian knew she slept, he drowsed, comforted by the wolfhound's vigilance and the total absence of sound in the gardens. But one mental eye remained fully awake, ready to trigger a grab for weapons. When first light brought the surroundings into focus, he saw they were in luck. Not ten feet away was a small shed probably used for tool storage and gardeners' supplies.

He shook Alana. "Let's get out of the dew. Otherwise, we'll be chilled through before the sun's up."

She uncurled stiffly and followed him. At the doorway she stopped. "I have to—"

Brian saw nothing but trees, shrubs, plants, and grass around them. "All right, but hurry." He relieved himself out of her sight and smiled to see the wolfhound lift a leg in company.

They found water to drink in the two-room shed and a dish of leftover maize porridge sweetened with honey. Thick and stiff, it was easily divided into three portions. Alana was relieved to have her stomach stop complaining.

"What shall we do, Brian?"

He propped the sword against the wall and hooked thumbs in his belt. "Do you have any idea where we are? I thought I did when I left the precinct wall, but my mental compass has gone haywire." Tired, tousled, and dirty, she was still the most alluring woman!

"We must be near the zoo, but the animals' voices are deceptive. They seem to come from different directions."

"I think I'll make a quick inspection. It's not quite dawn but there's enough light to see what's in the immediate vicinity."

"Don't leave me, please."

"I'll be close by."

Alana looked up at him, woebegone and defenseless, her mind full of the events of the past night. "I'd feel better if you'd stay here. Then we'll go together."

"If you feel that strongly. . . ." Brian glanced into the other part of the shed. "Why don't you come in here and rest? There's a pallet and a few cotton blankets. Finn and I will stand guard."

Rubbing her eyes, Alana trudged into the dim room and stepped on the

tines of a wooden rake carelessly left pointed upward. The handle flipped
up, banging her forehead.

"Oh, blast it!" Her hands flew up to rub the bruised area.

"What did you do?" Brian hurried in and came to a dead halt. In her
momentary pain, she had released her firm grip on the black cloak. Snowy
flesh glimmered in the semidark like an ivory carving. Her body was more
beautiful than he'd ever imagined.

It seemed so natural he never even thought about it . . . although he
could no more have kept from touching her than stop breathing. He slipped
his arms under the cape. Alana stepped away and then was still.

"Irish, darling." The handsome face moved close to hers. "I love you.
Did you know that? And I want to make love to you." He kissed her lips
sweetly. "But I want it to be right." His mouth touched her eyelids, her
throat, and the mole by her mouth.

"We're meant for each other. You know that, don't you? I knew it when
I held you in the garden months ago. My flesh, my bones, my nerves and
muscles—my heart—they knew the moment we touched."

Alana moved slightly, not resisting him but not accepting him either.
His hands dropped to her hipbones, obedient, patient—and powerful
enough to make her do anything he wanted.

"I'll wait if you say so. I don't want to force you just because we're
alone."

With Gilberto there had always been an apartness, he the aggressor, she
the conquered. She'd known only him. Suppose it was always like that?
Somehow she couldn't bear that.

But the Englishman was different, special. At this moment, denying
himself and not taking her as he could so easily do, he grew in her estima-
tion, and her heart opened even wider to him. Had she always loved him
and never realized it?

Bartering her body to the Spaniard had affected their entire relationship,
yet what she learned in his bed had been preparation for this morning. For
this dewy, quiet young day when for the first time she was to give herself
entirely, willingly, like a bride. Suddenly Brian cupped her face and kissed
her with breathtaking passion. Did he know her so well? She lowered herself to the pallet, frightened, yet insanely glad, eager, though shy as an innocent colleen.

"You're not afraid to take off the cuirass? Suppose someone surprised us and you were without. . . . " Alana turned.

Immediately her eyes and mind were filled with him. He stood naked beside her, a god of the ancients come to earth. His superbly sculpted torso flowed out of long, athletic legs and strong loins. His chest and arms bulged with muscles. How effortlessly he could have forced her! Dark-red hair against which golden earrings glinted grew in paler echoes on his breastbone which tapered down to a flat belly. He was Eros, Apollo, and Hercules in one. Overwhelmed by such manly grace, Alana felt desire consume her like a heat wave. His skin was as white as her own where clothing had protected it from the sun, and in the center of that milky expanse, framed by golden-russet hair, his manhood stood erect.

Brian knelt and untied the strings of her cloak. He threw it back so she reclined ivory and silver, coral and green on the dark background.

" 'Behold, thou art fair, my love . . . thy two breasts are like two young roes that are twins, which feed among the lilies.' " Brian fondled her nipples and found them already raised and sensitive to his ardent caresses. Grasping her breasts, he kissed her abdomen and then her thighs.

" 'My beloved is gone down into his garden . . . to feed in the gardens and to gather lilies.' " Her voice faded away.

Brian drew himself up to lie beside her. They gazed at each other, each aglow with the particular glory of his sex, and it seemed they were once more virgin. As if first ecstasy and first love yet awaited them.

They kissed. " 'His mouth is most sweet: yea, he is altogether lovely . . . his legs are as pillars of marble, set upon sockets of fine gold.' " Alana smoothed the insides of his thighs. This was the man she had waited for.

"Take me, Brian," she whispered. "Take me now and forever."

The dark blue eyes burned with exultation. When he went into her, the lovers shivered with excitement as if they were very cold. "How we fit, Irish! How we fit, for God's sake! Like a sword in a scabbard." He crushed her mouth beneath his. "Do you know how rare that is?"

Alana shook her head, wanting only to be aware of that marvelous kiss, of his body joined to hers. She had waited so long for this. Without warning Brian lost control and took her. Alana murmured in dismay.

"Don't fret, my love, there's plenty more." Brian laughed tenderly and nuzzled her breasts. "It was just my pent-up longing from the months I couldn't have you. But Lord save us if that's a sample!"

The Englishman looked down into her face. "Oh, woman, you were made for me! I will never let thee go now. . . . 'Thou hast ravished my heart.' "

Alana's cheeks stained with red. Her emerald eyes smoldered like opals. "How beautiful you've made the Song of Solomon to me. I shall remember this morning until the day I die."

"That mustn't be for years and years. For I will never have enough of thee."

He entered her again so vigorously she clutched him forcefully with her nails and cried out. Afraid his great weight would hurt or distress her, Brian rolled onto his back, taking her with him, the two still firmly joined.

"Oh, yes, I'm made for you! I am thy scabbard, Sword of Love!" She was on the verge of fainting. Her heart pounded tumultuously.

"I feel thy womb, Irish. I am touching thy innermost treasure." He pressed down on her shoulders as she sat on him like a naked goddess. "I am going to give thee a son," he promised. "Then you can belong to no one but me."

She studied the face staring up at her, aglow with love and desire, felt the hands possessing her, and the brawny torso between her knees. Happiness surged through her being. "Then give him to me! Give him to me!"

Within seconds their time neared and Brian quickly laid her under him again. He enveloped her mouth with his, and as she began to moan against his lips, he carried her with him . . . and they spun out into nothingness, revolving on a bolt of lightning pulsating with rapture.

Alana's eyes gradually focused on the man by her side. Any son from that union would be as virile and handsome as the man who made him. She had never known such ecstasy. Nor such a sense of oneness and belonging.

She kissed him lingeringly. " 'He brought me to the banqueting house, and his banner over me was love.' "

He sat up, leaning on one elbow. " 'Oh, prince's daughter! the joints of thy thighs are like jewels . . . thy neck is a tower of ivory.' " He caressed her, catching his breath with delight.

Dawn was breaking. In the distance shell trumpets blared to awake the "Venice of the West." Alana tenderly caressed her lover's mighty chest and abdomen. "I suppose we must go."

"Soon."

Her fingertips stroked him and she watched with awe as his manhood bloomed within her gentle grip. "Do you want me again so soon?" Alana's senses tingled in answer.

The man reached out and took her, and their consummation, and the next ones, reached into worlds and distances they never dreamed existed.

During those hours of intoxication none came to the gardens, and only a few were aware of the feast of love being devoured in the small room.

Malinche lounged by a door, wishing things were settled enough to take a walk to the street of the goldsmiths. She grew weary of these males with their constant chatter, arguments, gambling, and copulation. She even grew weary of Cortés. But not often.

The almond-shaped jet-black eyes roamed through the hall, which was the largest in the palace. None of the Spaniards would have dreamed of vying with their captain for her attentions. Nonetheless, they were not immune to her scrutiny. A few posed the better to show a good leg.

Aye, she thought, but Cortés had knocked down a hornets' nest. The Indian woman admired his bold insistence on a place of Christian worship right in the soul-heart of empire. In a room of the main *teocalli* itself, elbow to elbow with the bloody idol of the Aztec tribal god. Cortés was like a white-hot iron that seared the mind with daring and indifference to death in the name of the holy cross. She could not have served a cowardly man and hoped they would soon make a son blessed with the same courage. At the rate he was going, her lover might not be around for long.

Inmaculada approached Cortés' mistress. "Have you seen them yet? I've looked everywhere, and no one's seen them." She was sick with worry, and so was Pepe.

"Don't fret. White Willow has Moctezuma's seal on her wrist. Even the dissidents out there wouldn't harm them. Yet." Malinche smiled gently and spoke softly. "Has it occurred to you that they are finally alone? The simplest fool can see they belong together. When they get tired of making love, they'll be here."

"That's occurred to me, of course. And I would be glad to see it happen. It's past time for her to start a family and be bedded by a man who can handle her." Inmaculada frowned, fingering an amethyst necklace Moctezuma had given Pepe to match her bracelet. "But Gilberto de Salvatierra won't have it."

Her companion put a hand on her shoulder. "Whether he will or won't, he had better resign himself to the inevitable."

When Brian and Alana entered the hall, silence fell. Only two among hundreds, they were nevertheless well known. Their disappearance had titillated the army's imagination and fired its gossipmongers. A few moments later Cortés and his officers, including Gilberto, anguished but still coping, returned from the chamber where Moctezuma's treasure was kept.

Alana had made a dress of sorts from her cloak by wrapping it around her body under the armpits and belting it with a rope she'd found. Brian's cloak worn over her bare shoulders completed a most modest costume. Yet the pale hair falling in disarray gave it a wild, exciting effect. The radiance of a pure love and sexual fulfillment shone on her face, making her complexion sparkle, brightening her eyes, and softening her mouth. A similar glow made Brian more youthful. He walked with a bounce in his step and a swagger in his gait.

Spectators knew the couple had achieved that unnamable, infinitely precious oneness for which so many had searched in vain. To have loved like that—once in a lifetime—would make the whole cursed game worthwhile.

Cortés had been arguing—yet again!—about how equitably he had parceled out Moctezuma's riches. He didn't need any more trouble. But when he saw the lovers, so fair and beautiful, he realized an explosive situation had fallen into his lap whether he wanted it or not. He rubbed the familiar scar on his chin meditatively.

A verse from the Song of Solomon came back to him:

> Who is she that looketh forth as the morning,
> fair as the moon, clear as the sun, and
> terrible as an army with banners?

He'd bet his fifth of the loot there wasn't a man here who did not wish the blonde had chosen him for her night of nights. Cortés himself envied Phelps. His manhood stirred, and he glanced at his mistress. She smiled cryptically and walked away with that feline Indian step he could never quite duplicate. Too bad it would be nightfall before he could join her.

Chatting with his lieutenants, reluctant to draw any more attention to the couple than was necessary, he waved casually. Out of the corner of his eye, Cortés saw Salvatierra blanch at the sight of Alana MacKenna. He aged imperceptibly in that instant. Savage hearts that had envied him in the past melted in sympathy. When the nobleman grabbed his sword hilt, their hearts hardened once more. That was the only answer.

Brian saw the Spaniard coming and pushed Alana aside. Good! He had wanted to run this arrogant son of a bitch through for months. The great broadsword blazed in the light as he drew it forth. He laughed aloud with the sheer joy of being alive.

"Are you ready to fight this pretty morning?" The Englishman flicked his blade up and down.

The Spaniard's mouth tasted as if a herd of swine had tramped through it. What an idiot he'd been to play around with narcotics! Their bodily effects were devastating, and indirectly, his experiment had driven Alana into this man's arms.

Gilberto looked at Phelps with respect. The Englishman crouched on the balls of his feet, weaving back and forth, his dark-blue eyes gleaming as wickedly as the steel of his weapon. He showed a mouthful of good teeth in a predatory grin and ran a thumb mockingly along the edge of the blade.

Alana prayed Cortés would step in. Knowing the men as she did, she couldn't stop them. In fact, they wouldn't even hear anything she said. Soldiers nearby bet on the outcome. The *inglés* was bigger, heavier, and stronger. But Salvatierra was a Spaniard. Coins and golden objects changed hands.

The conquistador walked toward the men with no hint of haste in his suave manner. He came between them and spoke too softly for the rest to hear.

"Gentlemen, gentlemen. I would be the first to admit that a pair of breasts has more pulling power than a pair of oxen. But they are not worth dying for."

His compatriot stared at Brian with honey-colored eyes. "I consider this situation *un pundonor.*"

"A point of honor? Possibly. But you should be glad she hasn't planted the horn on your forehead long before now." Cortés grasped Gilberto's sword arm. "Let the woman choose. Don't be an ass. I'll get you one of Moctezuma's own daughters if you like. There's plenty of lusty—"

"No."

The would-be mediator sighed. "Very well. Let me make it very plain then. This must be a fight to the death—"

Alana protested. "No! For God's sake!"

"—and I will hang the winner."

That put a different light on the matter. Cortés was a man of his word. Brian sheathed his broadsword. No honor involved as far as he was concerned. There'd be another time.

Gilberto glanced at Alana's face. Yes, she'd been worried about him, too. Perhaps? He had braced the Englishman, shown he had no fear. Cortés' threat brought a reprieve, and he could afford to wait for a future opportunity.

The crowd dispersed. Too bad. That would have been a fight! Cortés returned to his discussion, and Alana fled to her room. She was shaking. How horrible if either of them had been killed!

Inmaculada hurried in with fresh clothing and directed slaves with hot bath water. She helped wash her mistress' long hair and noted love marks on the alabaster skin with silent interest.

"Pepe and I were so frightened. We thought the high priest had caught and sacrificed you."

Alana told her why she had run out of the palace, how she had stabbed a man to death, and how she and Finn had gotten lost in the dark.

"But then Brian found you?"

The green eyes closed. "Oh, how he found me!" She sat in the tub, wet, soapy, and resplendent. "He said he gave me a son, Inmaculada. I'm glad I can tell you. I don't think I could keep such joy to myself."

Alerted by noises in the apartment, her friend whispered, "He's back. Better get dressed so he doesn't see those marks." She smiled. "Wouldn't it be nice—to have the Englishman's son?"

Speaking in a normal tone of voice, Inmaculada said, "I'll return these cloaks after they've been cleaned and get this sandal mended, too."

"Thank you. So much."

Gilberto turned his back as the Maya walked through the room. He didn't care to think of her unkind ministrations last night when she brought him out of his drugged stupor. Nor of Pepe's face.

When Alana came out of the bathroom, hair wrapped and body concealed in a voluminous robe, his heart skipped a beat. Why, how small and delicate she was! He had forgotten. He had come to take her for granted, and she had strayed.

"There's chocolate, cold meats, and bread on the tray. I thought you might be hungry."

"That was sweet of you."

He watched her eat heartily. Yes, he had forgotten. Where had those hours of abandon gone? The night he pierced her maidenhead, the love-making at his summer place and aboard ship, those divine hours in the cove at Vera Cruz. . . . He had had to face the truth when he saw her with Phelps, the light of true love shining in her eyes. Alana had come to him as the door to old age yawned wide. She had postponed his aging for a while with her youthful gaiety and loveliness. But now the door was opening again—Gilberto could feel it in his bones.

And how could he keep her if she wanted to go? She was no longer dependent on him financially. In fact, Alana didn't need him anymore for anything. A wave of loss and loneliness washed over Gilberto, knotting his insides. How much he had loved her!

Clearing his throat, he asked, "Do you want to move out?"

Alana hesitated and then nodded, suddenly finding it hard to swallow. They had shared so much, and he had been good to her, except for the last few weeks when he had not been himself.

"You have brought me much joy."

She remembered the night he said that and then presented her with the fabulous diamond and emerald necklace and earrings. "I will be glad to give the jewels back."

Gilberto sat on the edge of the bed, cutting his nails. The scent of musk clung to the air. His silvering hair was glossy with oil, and his black beard immaculately groomed. Gilberto de Salvatierra would always be a very attractive man. He brushed the clippings off his lap.

"No, I want you to have them. But just once I'd like to see you wear those pearls in the daylight."

Alana reached under her pillow. "Here they are."

He rose and put them around her neck. "They've always been a symbol, haven't they? You'd wear them in the dark but never in public. It took me a long time to understand why. You were saying only your body was mine."

Tipping her chin up, he murmured, "Pity me, fair witch. Love me one last time to show I'm forgiven. I'm sorry for what I did to you. Surely you know that." He kissed her throat.

"You have a lot of nerve." She walked away, toweling her hair.

The Spaniard followed, reaching around to cup her breasts. A violent resentment seized him to think they now belonged to Phelps. "Pity me, Alana. One last time."

"No."

He parted the damp hair and kissed the nape of her neck. "I'm not asking you, my dear, I'm begging. Don't you know how it hurts to let you go forever? Please." He turned her around in the circle of his arms, holding her gently, looking charming and disconsolate.

Alana experienced a strange sense of power. Begging her! This proud, vain man was throwing himself on her mercy. It made up in a twisted way for the beating and the bizarre tryst he'd arranged to humiliate her.

Gilberto sank to one knee, pressing his forehead to her thighs. "Do you remember, *preciosa*? The green silk gown edged with lace and pearls, the bird singing in the moonlight, the fountain splashing. . . . Oh, Jesus, how glad I was to be the first man inside you! I felt like a god that night!"

He looked up at her, eyes like topaz in the half-light. "And do you remember what I begged you even then? I said, 'Love me, silver woman, love me.' " The words vibrated with emotion and his voice almost broke.

"I did," Alana said huskily. "I did."

"Then just once more. For old times' sake. No one will ever know."

She weakened. This was the man who had taught her to love. Who had truly loved her. Who had been cruel only because he loved so possessively. If it hadn't been for him, she might have wound up the tart of some loathsome creature.

Alana held her hands out to him. "All right. This once. In memory of the past."

Entering his valley of rapture for the last time, the Spaniard heard the tinkle of bell-fringed cloth at the apartment entrance. Brian Phelps was poised there, a smile dying on his face. Because the head of the pallet turned that way, Alana did not see him. But Gilberto did. *Now we're even, Englishman. How do you like it when the shoe is on the other foot?*

The nobleman laughed as he bent to the woman's upraised arms.

Alana sped happily along the corridor with the wolfhound padding beside her. At last she was free! Free! Gilberto hadn't put up the fuss she'd expected, and they were parting on friendly, even affectionate terms. She did feel guilty about giving in to him after the near sanctification of Brian's lovemaking. Yet it had been the only kind of farewell possible. After spending a year at Gilberto's side, being as close as or perhaps closer than a wife, words would not have been enough. Anyway, it was all over now.

She had to ask where Brian's room was located. In the excitement she must have misunderstood him. He was supposed to come for her. Alana's heart pounded. What difference did it make! She would seek him out anywhere.

The Spaniard who shared the Englishman's quarters came from León and had brown hair and blue eyes like some of the "wilde Irish" his people resembled. He commiserated with the beautiful woman who asked for Phelps. He didn't know what she'd done—he'd been afraid to ask—but if it were up to him, he would forgive her. How appealing she looked, huge green eyes sparkling, slender hands hugging a bag of personal things like a child come to a birthday party.

"He's not here, *señorita*."

"Oh, he must be!" Alana laughed merrily. "What I mean is, if he's not, he's not, but he won't be long, I know." She started into the apartment, anxious to see and touch the possessions with which Brian surrounded himself. When the man barred the way, she frowned.

"He won't be back tonight. But he gave me a message for you."

Her face cleared. Of course! Cortés must have needed him. Brian was a brave and resourceful fighter, after all. As the soldier's wife said yesterday, the gods were grossly offended by the violation of their sanctuary, and the Aztecs were perturbed. The palace was for all intents and purposes in a state of siege, with men sleeping in armor with weapons to hand and horses saddled in readiness.

The man from León had begun to recite a message from Brian. Her smile faded as he spoke.

" 'I opened to my beloved; but my beloved had withdrawn himself, and was gone . . . I sought him, but I could not find him; I called him, but he gave me no answer.' "

Alana mulled the quotation over and over. What did he mean?

The Spaniard was puzzled, too. Maybe this wasn't the right woman. But he was also sleepy and tired. Bowing slightly, he left the lady to her thoughts. *Dios mío*, he could hardly invite her in to wait! Then remembering something else, he poked his head out.

"I forgot to tell you. He went to someone's apartment earlier tonight. When he came back, he told me the girl he was searching for wasn't there anymore."

XVI

Ever since Cortés had rushed to Vera Cruz on May fourth to deal with the punitive expedition sent by the governor of Cuba to arrest him, Pedro de Alvarado's disposition had worsened. His personality was slash and thrust, not watch and wait, and he would much rather have ridden at his good friend's right hand than have stewed here in tense Tenochtitlán. Even though he was in command.

Furthermore, Cortés did not have more than two hundred and fifty men with whom to face more than a thousand. Such odds had become commonplace to the conquistadors, but these were Spaniards, not Indians! Alvarado wished with all his heart he was there to lend a hand.

Consequently, when the Irishwoman said she planned to take ship for home, he was relieved to be rid of one more problem. Now that no one was responsible for her, it was only a matter of time before she caused further trouble.

He had to admit she kept to herself though, helped tend the horses— there she had an angel's touch!—and spent hours with Moctezuma's favorite courtesan learning Nahuatl, a confusing language in his opinion. But why bother if she was heading for Ireland?

"I thought I might stop in Tlaxcala awhile. I rather like it there, and I'm interested in the women's spinning techniques."

Alana finished her meal and excused herself from the table. Alvarado had been very gallant, insisting she dine with him and Luisa each evening since Cortés' departure. In an offhand way he had kept her under his protection. Yet she didn't really care for him, and the Indian woman had never been friendly, although she smiled coolly at mention of her city. Of course, she'd never been unfriendly either, Alana reminded herself honestly. Being given away, even to a blond god, couldn't have been the easiest thing to handle. Perhaps the doe-eyed Luisa had loved a man of her own race and pined privately for him.

If this were the case, Alana knew exactly how she felt.

"When are you leaving?"

Alvarado rinsed his hands in a pearl-studded jade bowl. He liked to live well, on the edge of danger or not.

"In two or three days. I want to do some shopping before I go, and Moctezuma is giving a farewell banquet."

"You think you'll be safe in the marketplace? That old priest would love to get his bloody hands on one of us."

Alana held up the seal she wore on a ribbon.

Alvarado raised his eyebrows in surprise. A heart held up in a hand, insignia of the dreaded secret police. Since Moctezuma had threatened the Spaniards with extinction if the Christian chapel were not removed from the temple, and after he'd learned of those nineteen ships and fourteen hundred men come to capture Cortés, he had reverted to his old, haughty self. That seal should keep any priest at bay. The stinking bastards didn't want *their* hearts torn out!

Alana had remained in the same apartment while Gilberto had moved in with a fellow nobleman from Madrid. She'd returned there after failing to find Brian and found her old lover already gone. She'd wondered about his abrupt departure; it did not seem logical. Why desert such luxurious quarters when he thought she had gone to another man? Surely he would have welcomed her back once he learned of her rejection. Alana could not put her finger on what was wrong.

And another thing . . . María de Estrada, one of the unmarried Spanish women, had asked to share Alana's apartment that very next morning. She had heard there was a vacancy and wanted a little more privacy. Where did she get that information? Had Gilberto guessed what was going to happen? And if so, why? María could not recall who told her—barracks rumor, that was all.

Inmaculada was furious with both men—and Pepe, too, simply on general principles. He was a man, wasn't he? Blast them, playing fast and loose with people's feelings! She noticed Salvatierra's smug expression. There was no doubt in her mind that he had engineered Alana's humiliation, but her friend flatly refused to discuss it.

Cortés had left two-thirds of his force in Tenochtitlán to guard Moctezuma and the treasure and to keep the uneasy peace until he came back. It was inevitable that Brian, Gilberto, and Alana saw one another now and then in the midst of the reduced force of fewer than two hundred men.

The soldiers gossiped lazily when they were not on duty. About Phelps who stamped around, black as a thundercloud, Salvatierra who looked as if he'd won a fortune in gold, the blonde who was peaked and wan and distant, too. Time was when she was good for a joke or a laugh or a soft hand with your wound or mount. But now, by God, you'd think she hated men!

Alana had decided to ride Conn to the great marketplace in the northern part of the island instead of being carried in a litter. The stallion not only needed the exercise, but provided a margin of security as well. Not, she mused bitterly, that it mattered anymore.

She had felt miserable lately, weepy and nervous and moody. If this was being in love, faith, she'd rather have the ague! Oh, damn Brian Phelps for being a cruel, handsome rogue! Leading her on that night and day with a tongue oiled with guile. . . . *Thou hast ravished my heart.* Ravished, indeed! Killing was too good for him.

Sweet Saint Bridget, he had said he loved her, and she'd believed him! The liar! It was almost more than she could bear to know his coming after her had not been to rescue her but to satisfy a long-frustrated physical urge. She need not have been so grateful for his daring the perils of the night. What was danger to him but food and drink? And flaunting her in front of the army like a prize heifer and then ignoring her after she'd served his purpose—might he burn in hell!

Putting a knee in the horse's side unexpectedly, Alana scolded, "Stop puffing up like a big toad. The cinch has to be tighter than *that.*" Conn's beautiful head swung around, ears perked. Long-lashed eyes fluttered with injured innocence.

"Get along with you. I'm on to your ways." Despite her gloom, Alana had to smile when the horse snorted and pranced to show he was glad she'd come for him.

Riding out from the palace, Alana began to look forward to the shopping trip. Tenochtitlán bloomed like an immense multicolored water lily floating on a pad, clinging to the mainland with its tendrils—the three causeways reaching across Lake Texcoco's brackish waters to Tepeyac on the north, Chapultepec and Tacuba on the west, and Coyoacán and Ixtapalapa on the south. The main thoroughfares bisecting the island-city from top to bottom and side to side were continuations of the causeways; no land link sprouted from the east, however, because a canoe port was located there for discharging passengers and cargoes. Travelers and trade goods then arrived at their destination either on hard-packed dirt streets or by canoe. Alana thought the arrangement charming and had been delighted not long ago to be rowed right into the gardens of Moctezuma's palace.

Militarily, the Aztecs had done a clever job of planning their own defense or an enemy's entrapment. Heavy wooden bridges spanning the multitudinous canals were portable and could be removed at a moment's notice. Thus a foe could be isolated on a water-locked islet in the center of the city and disposed of at leisure.

Causeways, the capital's first line of defense, had been provided with similar safeguards; openings were cut into them that could be breached only by movable footbridges. The water lily's splendor had been well secured against invasion.

Moctezuma's seal was fastened to the bridle above Conn's white blaze. Here it could be seen quickly in case of trouble, although Alana anticipated none in this district, away from Savage Serpent's influence. In the months since her arrival—it was already mid-May, 1520!—she had become a famous figure. The Indians had begun to welcome her almost everywhere as they sensed her genuine interest in them.

They had seen her eat honeyed sweetmeats at open-air stands and make fun of herself when spiced dishes brought tears. Once over their initial fear, mothers allowed her to hold and cosset ebony-eyed babies. A number of slaves owed her their freedom. She bought birds and released them and gave clothing to the poor. She had even sent rare flowers and fine paper up to priests who supervised the nearby temples, politely refusing to offer live quail, snakes, or butterflies.

As she proceeded through the arcade-bordered marketplace, many of the tens of thousands of marketgoers watched her discreetly. White Willow, as she was now known to them all, dressed in black like their own holy men and wore the face of the sun god at her throat. Her hair was a wondrous hue, as were the sparkling eyes which gave you an odd feeling when they gazed into yours. She bore an air of sadness, too, of being among strangers, and that withdrawn look spoke of hurt and rejection. Who did not know these things? And here among them, who would turn away such a warmhearted person? She was not, after all, a cold-blooded Spaniard.

Alana dismounted and led her horse so she could make a few purchases. Conn stepped with care, and Finn paced beside her, nervous among so many strangers, even though they were quiet in manner and speech. The gigantic wolfhound need not have worried. His huge, heavy frame was enough to intimidate a race whose only dogs were mute, hairless, and tiny enough to carry.

Alana's linguistic ability in Nahuatl had graduated to that of a ten-year-old, and merchants chuckled and encouraged her to try new words. She bought plain leather sandals for travel, tanned jaguar and puma skins, and wheeled ceramic toys for Corn Flower's youngsters. For Corn Flower herself she chose a mantle of incredibly soft rabbit fur that was dyed yellow and edged with black, and on an impulse a fine obsidian knife for Xicotencatl.

If only there were more time to wander through the enormous market once again. To see the extraordinary variety of merchandise which funneled in from the entire country to this well-policed, clean, and colorful square. Surely, as Bernal Díaz had rhapsodized, no such place existed anywhere else in the world. From gold to tamales, animals to slaves, turkeys to jewels, indigo to copper, cotton cloth to glazed pottery—it was a sight Alana would never forget.

"Alana!" Yellow Plume, Moctezuma's darling, was dressed in shades of coral and brown, bedecked with white feathers, pearls, and gold, and accompanied by lesser courtesans and servants. They wafted through the crowd like a flock of brilliantly plumaged birds.

"You are shopping, too." Alana grasped her friend's hands. "How do I sound?"

"Very good! You are doing well." Yellow Plume laughed softly.

"What are you going to buy?"

"A little dog. One I can teach to do tricks."

"Would you like mine?" Alana asked in jest.

At the girl's mock horror, everyone stared at Finn who'd become mesmerized by the pens filled with plump canines. They were raised for food and pets and were often slaughtered to accompany the dead as soul companions.

"He wants that one!" A courtesan pointed at a pen. That did not seem unreasonable. Man ate man. Why shouldn't dog eat dog?

Alana watched her dog nose a cage with only one occupant, a black puppy with a comical white ring around his right eye. She knew the wolfhound to be gentle. It wasn't what the Indians thought. What was it then? Did he want it for a friend? Could he be lonely? She had never thought of that! The Spaniards' mastiffs and greyhounds were mean and vicious, and Finn had never fraternized with them.

"I'll buy him for you." At least that way the puppy would not be eaten. Alana paid for the dog in cacao beans as she had paid for the other purchases. Then she tucked him into a saddlebag, closing it securely around the animal's neck so only the droll face showed. Onlookers smiled, and Finn reared up on his hind legs to lick the diminutive head.

"What are they called?"

The dog seller grinned at the trouble White Willow would have with this word. "They are called *xoloitzcuintli*. He-who-snatches-his-food-with-teeth-as-sharp-as-obsidian."

Alana threw up her hands in despair, thanked the man, and turned to Yellow Plume. "I must go now. I will see you at the feast tomorrow." She mounted, and those watching remarked a skirt cunningly split in the middle and boots like the ones the white men wore.

As she settled herself in the saddle, the music of drums and clay flutes grew louder. Alana looked with interest at a colorful procession escorting four miniature litters toward the northern causeway. "What is going on there?"

Her friend studied the ground. "The spring rains have not been good. The children are to be given to Tlaloc."

"What do you mean, given?"

"Do not look," Yellow Plume warned softly.

"*What do you mean, given?*"

"They are being taken to the mountains."

"What for?"

The girl sighed deeply. She didn't want anything to happen to her new friend. "They are crying a lot."

"I hear them," Alana said, tightly reining the horse so he stamped and frightened those around him. "Why?"

"They are afraid. The more they cry, the more it will rain."

Alana gestured impatiently and compressed her lips. "What is going to happen to them?"

"The priests will wall them up in a cave."

"Alive?"

"Yes."

"To die of hunger and thirst?"

"Yes," Yellow Plume reached out a futile hand as Alana moved away. *Ah, White Willow, you do what so many of us under the Aztecs' thumb would like to do. It is fear that keeps us from it. You must understand that.*

For if we do not watch child sacrifice when ordered to do so, or should the parents refuse, we are then declared despicable, unworthy of public office, and cast outside the law. She fanned herself, her beautiful face expressionless, and craned her neck, as did the others, to see the drama which was about to unfold.

Moctezuma had canceled the farewell banquet, and Inmaculada was beside herself. What had Alana been thinking of! To snatch a child marked for sacrifice away from the priests! They must have been livid with anger. No wonder they had complained so to their king. What did she intend to do with the youngster? And why do such a thing now?

"Por Dios, I've never seen her act this way before." Perplexed, Pepe smoothed the mustache he had been cultivating.

"She's in love." The Maya sat with arms folded, part of her mind on her husband's words and part on what to wear to the audience with Moctezuma after the midday meal.

"Then she should be happy. As I am." The Andalusian's gray eyes sought the velvety brown of his wife's, seeking, always seeking some new facet of this woman he had not yet discovered.

"Ah." Inmaculada smiled. "I am happy, too, then."

"It is the Englishman, isn't it?"

"Yes. It would have touched your heart, really. When she took her bath that afternoon after they'd been together, she glowed like a bride. I swear a radiance surrounded her. Now Brian won't even look at her, and she's plunged into the depths of depression. A lover's quarrel, obviously, but she simply won't talk to me about it." Inmaculada's mouth pursed. "I'm convinced Salvatierra had his finger in that pot. He's entirely too pleased with himself to suit me."

Pepe's thoughts had wandered away from the conversation. Lord, but she was pretty! Like any recent bridegroom he could not get enough of her. All that copper and darkness with soft pink places that gave a man the shivers.

"Stop it."

"What?"

"Thinking what you're thinking. I have to get dressed and make sure the little girl is fed."

He put his arms around her and nuzzled her playfully under an ear. How he loved that silky black hair! "What makes you think you know what I'm thinking?" His voice was muffled.

"I'm a mind reader." Inmaculada closed her eyes, savoring the touch of his lips and the muscled firmness of his chest against her bosom. "Didn't I ever tell you my grandfather was a famous sorcerer?"

"Didn't I ever tell you his granddaughter was an enchantress?"

"You're silly." She giggled as his mustache brushed her throat. "That tickles."

Pepe suddenly swooped her up in his arms and deposited her in the middle of their bed. "I'll tickle you," he threatened, lying down next to her.

"We don't have time," she protested.

He kissed her again, and there was all the time in the world.

When the women met to go to Moctezuma's apartments, Alana sensed her friend had just come from lovemaking. She appeared somehow rounder, smoother, sleeker. A pang of envy sharpened Alana's tongue, but the Maya murmured placatingly, apologizing for being a few minutes late.

As Inmaculada translated Moctezuma's impassioned Nahuatl into Spanish and Alana's defiant Spanish back into the Indian tongue, Alana regretted having lashed out. Inmaculada was frightened, but because Alana's vocabulary and comprehension were in no way adequate to the argument, she interpreted for her friend as calmly as possible.

"Do you realize exactly what you have done?" The angry lord scowled at the white woman sitting before his throne. Black made her skin and hair too pale. He preferred her in colors.

"I saved a child from being walled up in a cave! From dying of hunger, thirst, and horror!" Alana sprang to her feet. The green eyes flashed. "And if I could have saved the other three, I would have done that, too!"

He was taken aback by her ferocity, almost like that of a mother. Why should one child matter so much? The rain its sacrifice would have brought was of much greater significance.

"When I said you could have anything your heart desired, White Willow, I did not mean you could interfere with our religion. How would *you* feel if I came to *your* land and told you how to worship, how to dress your sanctuaries, and what you could and could not do?"

Moctezuma wrapped his cape of red parrot feathers more closely about him. He could not get warm of late. It was as if his blood had grown cold.

Alana admitted she would be angry and annoyed.

"Yet you have meddled. Who are you to say we are wrong or that the way we praise the gods is not good? The sacrifice which so revolts you has been practiced in our land since man hunted the mammoth animals with curving tusks. Ask the Maya girl. Her tribes have sent messengers to the gods for many years by throwing them into the waters of their sacred wells."

Inmaculada nodded, studying the polished stone floor.

The Spanish soldier who guarded Moctezuma's apartments and had been watching with fascination exclaimed, "Whew! Hold your noses, *señoras*. Here comes a stinking dog that walks like a man."

Savage Serpent wore the human skin of a sacrificial victim next to his own. He glared through eye holes in the facial skin, and his lips were drawn back wolfishly over filed teeth inside the gaping mouth. The high priest bowed slightly to Moctezuma; he seldom bothered with the obsequious formality required of others. He was answerable only to his gods. When he turned away from the women, they were able to see how strips of skin tied in knots at the back of the skull and down the spine held the macabre garment together.

"He honors Xipe Totec, the Flayed One," Inmaculada replied in a low voice. "The deity of spring rain, new vegetation, and the growth of young plants."

"He needs to be dunked in a couple of tubs of spring rain, if you ask me!'' The soldier spoke flippantly, but even his stout heart had quailed momentarily when the priest stalked by. At home they'd have locked him in a madhouse! He wished Cortés would get back. Pedro de Alvarado was as brave as they came. But seeing the captain would make the soldier feel not only safer but a bigger man to boot. He gripped the lance tightly and settled his broadsword. If the chance came to slit this bird's gullet, he'd be ready.

Moctezuma exclaimed in dismay while Savage Serpent talked to him intensely at length. A terrible odor crept through the elegant room, a stench that assailed the nostrils and choked one's throat. Alana began to feel ill.

The ruler's fine dark eyes glittered as he waved the other man aside. His thin beard seemed drawn in ink on a skin grown sallow with vexation and repugnance for the head of his church.

''I did not know until now that the child came from Tula. The priests of Tlaloc had reserved her for three years for this particular rain festival. Now you've ruined everything! The sacrifices are tainted and can't be used.''

Savage Serpent added venomously, ''The child was most rare, my Lord. Hair almost as golden as yellow poppies and eyes bluer than a morning glory.''

Moctezuma drew in his breath. His mother had been a Toltec from the legendary temple city of Tula, and he knew all the stories and myths about Quetzalcoatl, the Feathered Serpent. The god had ruled there for many years before sailing into the east to become the morning star.

Scholars assured Moctezuma that Feathered Serpent had taken women carnally as lesser men did; a child with hair and eyes like that meant it had to be one of his descendants. He understood the priest's indignation. An offering like this and of such holiness might not be seen again for generations.

His mind wandered from the problem at hand. The fact that Quetzalcoatl had ancestral roots in Tula just as he did had been one of the reasons he'd accepted the white men as the god's emissaries. They were kindred! Yet he had also had to wrestle with his duty as war chief of the Aztecs to repulse invaders and capture them for the altars.

But how could one deny the presence of gods? Most of the Christians were fair-skinned with red or yellow hair, and many had blue eyes. They'd sailed in stupendous canoes, coming from the east and stepped ashore on the exact day Quetzalcoatl's return had been forecast.

Cortés had worn a flat-brimmed, low-crowned hat similar to the god's, as pictured in sacred records. The newcomers brought magical weapons and terrible beasts as befitted gods, despised human sacrifice, and, above all, were invincible in battle. Some had died, true, but Cortés and a majority of others led charmed lives.

But it no longer mattered. Moctezuma had a feeling nothing mattered any longer. Savage Serpent's harsh words penetrated his revery.

"Sacrifice White Willow?" The king stood up, startled. "No, no, Cortés wouldn't like that." No, indeed!

"Her eyes are the color of water in certain pools and lakes," the high priest persisted. "She would make a reasonable substitute. We need something, Great Lord, and we need it now. As you know, the rains have been insufficent, and the municipal granaries are practically exhausted. If the corn crop is not good, our people will go hungry. It is our punishment for accepting these poisonous snakes into our nest."

The priest started toward Alana. "Without sacrifice it will not rain. *It will not rain!*" Savage Serpent wanted her ugly albino breast beneath his knife. He hissed with frustration.

Alana stood rooted. If he touched her, she'd scream! The man personified Death—implacable, remorseless, ruthless. Her heart fluttered and then thundered; alarmed, she pressed a hand to it. As she did so, her fingers brushed the shell crucifix Inmaculada had given her.

Her friend saw Alana's face suddenly blaze with a life and light which had been missing. "Yes, it *will* rain! *It will!*" She walked to meet Savage Serpent's advance, knees shaking.

"Can't you understand? You're both intelligent men. You don't need to kill anybody to *make* it rain. God in heaven will send rain down to make the corn grow. Send it down with love for all His children."

Moctezuma bit his lip. Cortés and his holy men had been telling him things like that for months. There was even a ceremony in which they ate the flesh and drank the blood of their man-god. It seemed similar to that of the Aztecs except no human being was actually offered up as a pure and perfect sacrifice. He could not deny the miracles and wonders of battle, the conquest and victory the Spaniards attributed to their god and his archangels. Suppose White Willow was right? What an idea! It would shake the very foundations of the great *teocalli*!

"I am tired." That was a lie. He felt completely exhausted. He wanted nothing but a pipe and Yellow Plume's breast under his head.

"But—" The priest may have scowled, but Alana could see nothing behind the bland mindlessness of the flayed face.

Moctezuma's voice became feather-soft. "The festival is marred. Consult your auguries. If you need new sacrifices, get them."

"What about the child this woman stole?"

"She may keep her—"

Alana glanced at the priest with triumph.

"But she must leave Tenochtitlán and never return on pain of death." Moctezuma motioned sharply. "I have spoken."

Savage Serpent paused in front of Alana on his way out, standing so close she was able to make out pores in the victim's skin.

"Our paths will cross again. Depend on it. And when they do—" He made a vicious stabbing gesture, barely missing her as he did so.

Hate vibrated between the Aztec priest and the Irish Christian, but she stood her ground, and finally, her adversary swept out of the room.

Alana said, "Thank you for the child." Her voice was husky and shaky with strain and fatigue.

Wearily, her host chose a silver tube from a tray of pipes offered by a slave. "Don't bother. Just take her and go." She had disappointed him, as all the foreigners had. The slave held a red-hot coal to the tip of his pipe.

She persisted. "And thank you for the many favors and gifts you have granted me and my friends." Alana hesitated, distressed at such an awkward parting.

"Wait." Drugs in the tobacco had already soothed him. He must be bone-tired for them to travel through his system so quickly. "You say I have done you many favors. I want one in return."

"If it is in my power."

He sucked on the pipe. Ah, that was good! "We will never see each other again. I will be going to the Land of the Fleshless—soon." He shook his head at her exclamation. "Not long after Cortés returns from the coast. And once I am gone, the land will disintegrate into chaos.

"As you know, there is a certain woman who is very dear to me. Those I can depend upon have promised to take her out of Tenochtitlán at my death. But I want your promise that she will be treated with dignity and honor and be cared for. She is fragile and must not be torn to pieces among wolves and foxes."

"I will be in Tlaxcala for a while." When his eyes narrowed, she added,

"They are your enemy, I know, but I trust them. Besides, Yellow Plume is not an Aztec."

Only recently had Alana understood why Cortés had been able to penetrate to the center of the heavily populated country so swiftly with such a small force. The Quetzalcoatl legend had contributed to his success, of course. And Bernal Díaz maintained it had been Spanish courage and cunning fortified by the hand of God. Horses, cannon, muskets, swords, and crossbows were other factors, as was Malinche's ability to translate and convey linguistic subtleties that had enabled Cortés to exploit and channel long-established resentments and animosities. But the most vital element had been the hatred of oppressed tribes for their Aztec masters, a hatred that united them in an alliance with the Spanish and ensured the Aztecs' downfall.

Moctezuma's golden sandal weighed heavily on each province: garrisons of warriors, overseers, tax collectors, constant tribute, random rape ensuring a perpetual reign of terror. Yet even these were bearable next to the loss of the flower of the tribes' youth for sacrifice each year. To be an ally of Cortés meant a step toward revenge and retribution.

You are hemmed in by enemies, Great Lord. No wonder death seems near. Alana repeated, "I trust them. Send her to me there." Impulsively she leaned forward and touched his bejeweled hand. "But surely—"

His long face brightened. Yellow Plume came from the sleeping quarters, gorgeous as a jungle moth in shades of lilac. She stopped beside the throne. Long-lashed hazel eyes glimmered with unshed tears.

"Did you take the child because it has blue eyes like those of your lover?" Moctezuma had almost forgotten to ask that question.

Alana started and flushed painfully. Had that been the reason? "It was something I had to do."

"He will come back to you. He will never forget that night and that morning in the gardens." Moctezuma laughed tolerantly. "Didn't you wonder why you weren't disturbed? My guards kept your trysting place safe. No, you didn't notice. You were each deaf to all but the other's love."

He stared longingly at the face of his courtesan. "When heart calls to heart and flesh to flesh—commoner or king, man or woman, white or brown—it is like the mushroom that brings delightful oblivion." Yellow Plume knelt at his knee, and he put a hand on her head.

Gradually his black eyes became opaque, inscrutable. Somewhere his soul sailed the lakes of the Valley of Mexico for the last time beneath a canopy of gold-encrusted quetzal plumes. Then, for an instant, anguish and grief ruffled the ghostly waters. Not for himself, not even for the woman Moctezuma loved best . . . but for what might have been.

XVII

The little girl sighed contentedly and snuggled closer to the woman. The faint scent of roses, the soft breasts and protective arm comforted her, but it was still hard to fall asleep.

So much had happened so quickly. One day she had been the beloved child of doting parents, and the next day she'd been whisked away to the city of the dreaded Aztecs. On the way she'd heard her mother weep, and now and then her father's melancholy face came into view, but the wrinkled old priests refused to let her talk to them. The nunnery where she was housed was cold and unfriendly, although attendants treated her like royalty.

Not long after her arrival three holy men appeared. They'd painted her with a sticky gray substance mixed with seeds, fastened a paper headdress on her blond hair, and tied her to one of four litters. She and the three other children had begun to cry, frightened and lonely for their parents. The men smiled mysteriously, searching the crowns of the childrens' heads. Curls and whorls in imitation of whirlpools were choice offerings to Tlaloc, god of rain and watery places.

Blue Butterfly stared into the dark. There had been one priest in particular, a big man who had a mouth like two stones clamped together. And he smelled. That was the last thing she remembered before he blew powder up her nose: the stink of the man. He stunk like the reed shelters along the road where one moved one's bowels.

She had continued crying, even though everything had turned hazy. Then she got the hiccups, and her stomach ached. About that time someone cut the cords and snatched her off the litter into the air amid a hullaboo of sound.

"Are you warm enough, little dove?" Alana murmured in Nahuatl, tucking a fur around the child's neck.

"Yes, thank you." When Blue Butterfly first awoke in the palace where the strangers lived, she'd been frightened by their red and yellow hair, blue eyes, and white skins. But her mother came in the middle of the night to comfort and love her.

While her mother washed away the paint and seeds and dressed her in ordinary clothes, a woman with silver hair, green eyes, and a rueful expression waited nearby. Blue Butterfly peered into those eyes and liked what she saw, and the woman and child had smiled shyly at each other.

She reached out of the covers and put a hand toward the floor. A big tongue and a tiny one licked her, and she giggled. When Blue Butterfly first saw Finn, she had fallen deeply in love. Never had she seen such a huge, gloriously ugly animal! He had immediately offered a paw, which was a huge compliment, the white woman had assured her.

His constant companion was a delicate black *sholo* with a funny white eye ring, a rascal if there ever was one. As a special favor, although the girl surmised it was simply to make her feel good, she had been allowed to name the hairless mite. He was now Yaotl, the Warrior, because he bossed the good-natured hound without mercy and often led him into needless trouble.

She heard a muted sob. This had happened before. Awash with sympathy, Blue Butterfly turned over and put her arms around the woman's neck. It seemed a small thing to do.

"Ah, you sweet child!" Alana lapsed into English as she often did when moved. "Here you are in a strange city with strange people. You'll probably never see your parents again because they're in disgrace—and you're comforting me!"

She smoothed the girl's hair back from her forehead and hugged her. "No wonder your mother and father said they'd rather never see you again than have you dead. You're an angel, that's the truth. I should be ashamed.''

Alana reverted to the Indian tongue. "Go to sleep, my priceless jewel.''

The girl burrowed into the furs. It was nice to be loved, even by those you didn't know too well. But she missed her neatly whitewashed room, her wardrobe and personal treasures in the wickerwork chest. And she missed the wall hanging her aunt had embroidered with pink rabbits when she was small. In fact, she missed everything—and everybody. Tears welled up and dampened her little pillow. She had to be brave. They all had told her that. But they didn't understand. She was a nobody now. Blue Butterfly did not belong to anyone anymore.

While a slave brushed her hip-length hair, Alana drowsed and thought about Corn Flower's pleasant patio. Bees buzzing in the daisies, minute hummingbirds sipping from a flowering vine called cup of gold, children laughing, aromatic herbs in the garden perfuming the air. She could hardly wait.

It would be good to be in Tlaxcala again and out of the Aztec capital, removed from heartbreak and memories, separated from the two men she had loved who had hurt her so. In a way, Alana was thankful Moctezuma had ordered her to leave; tomorrow morning both she and Blue Butterfly would be gone forever.

"What is the music and chanting I hear?" she asked idly.

The slave replied, "It is the yearly festival in honor of Huitzilopochtli, my lady. Last night they made his statue from chicalote seeds, and today they dance and sing and praise him.''

"A statue out of seeds?''

"They are ground into paste by women who have fasted for an entire year. Then—''

Alana began having hunger pangs. "A year!''

"Oh, yes. Then they form the paste over a wooden framework in the shape of a man. When that is done, others paint and dress the god in his holy garments and jewelry.''

The slave, who came from a fierce northern tribe that took scalps, let the woman's hair slide through her fingers. What a lance ornament this would make!

The gray and white bird that had been the old aviary keeper's farewell present to Alana tried to get their attention. It burst into song, warbled melodiously, paused, and then squawked exactly like a duck. Alana chuckled, her thoughts straying to the hundreds of birds in Moctezuma's *totocalli*. What a riotous rainbow of plumage they provided!

She had visited a family of featherworkers at the palace and been awed by their dexterity and artistic sensibility. Men prepared, cut, and mounted stencils; women graded, sorted, and dyed feathers; children made glue from orchids, bat excrement, and pulverized roots. Their products were exquisite. Alana had bought fans, wall hangings, a waist-length cape, bracelets, a few exotic birds and animals and some dramatic hairpieces. All these items would be a sensation in Ireland.

Blue Butterfly's mother insisted her daughter had talent for this kind of work. The child had even been pledged to the featherworkers' god in the hope she might develop skills to embroider and dye cloth, tint rabbit fur, and judge colors. This, of course, had been before she was chosen for sacrifice. Alana only hoped Corn Flower could find foster parents willing to develop this gift. Indian girls handled a spindle at six and the loom by ten. They were as strictly disciplined as the boys. Blue Butterfly was now almost ten and would be expected to help with weaving and other household tasks. Unless Alana decided to adopt her.

It was no use! She could not forget her narrow escape earlier in the day when she'd gone to say good-bye to the keeper of the aviary and exchange gifts as was the custom. Though buying slaves went against her principles, Alana had bought him one—a plump, modest, middle-aged woman who'd sold herself into bondage because of poverty and childlessness. When Alana saw the old man's face, she knew she'd done the right thing. This slave would receive good treatment and protection, and the keeper, who had lived for so long only for his birds, would at last enjoy a warm bed partner and wifely care.

Taking one last leisurely tour of the great aviary, Alana paused longest at the quetzal enclosure. Thinking she recognized the large male she had been privileged to hold, she called to it.

A deep and silky voice responded in Nahuatl. "You seek the quetzal. An eagle comes in its stead."

Tlacateotl had been elated by his progress in the military hierarchy. Young as he was, he had quickly become one of the elite. He was initiated

into the order of Eagle Warriors, and in a recent War of the Flowers between Tenochtitlán and Michoacán he had captured the commander of a
thousand men single-handedly.

The armies in this peculiar war had agreed to fight with an equal number
of combatants and to capture a stipulated quota of prisoners for ceremonial
dispatch. When that was accomplished, they went home. Tlacateotl supposed such an arrangement had merit, for it saved lives for future warfare
and sacrifices. But he loved the sensation of a weapon sinking into flesh,
the smell of fresh blood, and the terror on a dying man's face. Even more
than that, he adored the intoxication of womankind, and this one had been
on his mind continually.

Since Brian had made love to her, Alana had forgotten about the warrior-prince. Now, as he unleashed the full power of that lazy, slumbrous
black gaze, she backed away from the sexual magnetism radiating from
him.

"You speak my language now, I hear." The Aztec spoke quietly. The
doe had been flushed. She must not be frightened. He glanced about,
pleased with his cunning. He had waited to appear until she'd entered a
dead end—the only way out was past him. His slaves, strategically placed
around the corner and out of sight, were under threat of death to bar the
way to intruders.

"Yes, though I speak much like a child."

"I have heard you are going away."

"You hear much about me. I go in the morning."

The sensual mouth pouted. "I will never see you again."

"I— No, you won't." *And a good thing it is, too.* She folded her arms
to keep from being undressed by those gloriously lashed eyes. *How unjust
that a man had such lashes,* Alana mused. *They should adorn a woman.*

"What is this material?" Tlacateotl ran a fingertip along her wrist. "I've
never seen it."

"Your people have no word for it. Silk is made from a covering a certain
type of worm spins around itself."

"As you spin a web of desire around me," he said plaintively. He circled her waist with one bare arm, his eyes wary. She made no move to flee.
Women were all alike, weren't they?

Tlacateotl felt his manhood swell and a fire center in his belly. This one had to be very experienced. A friend in Moctezuma's guards had told him the giant red-hair had made love to her for hours in the gardens. It was getting harder for him to breathe.

He put his other arm around her. Drawing Alana close, he kissed her. He'd been experimenting with this Spanish innovation, and so far he'd met with great success.

"No, no. Don't. Let me go."

Each one said that. They knew they shouldn't but wanted to anyway. Oh, her body was lovely! In his dreams he'd entered it a thousand times. He'd often pretended women in the House of Joy were she, and now he actually held her in his arms. She was so different, so exciting and unusual. He kissed her again and forced his tongue into her mouth. She pushed against his chest frantically, surprising the warrior with her strength.

"Why do you resist? You want me." Tlacateotl touched the nipples pushing against the silk of her shirt. "I won't hurt you. I'm trained to give you enormous pleasure." He buried his face in the cleft between her breasts and ran a hand over her body.

"You have plenty of women, a man like you. Let me go."

"But I want *you*." He bit through the silk and deftly moved his loincloth aside at the same time. He heard her gasp as he poked into her private parts. This time Tlacateotl kissed her savagely. Women liked tenderness, but they responded to lust.

"Let me go, you Indian dog!"

The Aztec bridled at the epithet. "Dog, is it? Are you not a tease and a bitch who sleeps with one man and then another like the cheapest whore?" Her face reddened, and those haunting eyes sparkled with rage. Excellent! That would make the battle more tantalizing.

"If I am a dog, then here is my bone!"

Tlacateotl acted with the brutal swiftness for which he was famous. Pinning her against the latticed bamboo wall he silenced her mouth with his, flipped her skirts up and lifted her off the ground with an arm like a steel band. He tried to enter her, but she fought back like a puma.

Suddenly they crashed to the ground as Alana threw herself violently to one side. He glimpsed pale hair when her skirts bunched up, and he swore with delight. This was even better.

"Come here," the Aztec gasped, reaching for her leg.

But Alana had garnered more experience in rough-and-tumble than he knew. As the man rose to his hands and knees, she jumped to her feet and delivered a vicious kick to his jaw with the point of her boot. Tlacateotl's teeth crunched together, and he heard a crack. Too startled to move, he hesitated just long enough for her to get away.

Cursing, the young man got to his feet and yelled for one of his slaves. The husky, good-looking boy responded like an obedient dog. His master berated him for not stopping the woman and then motioned him closer. Sodomy was punishable by death unless one was a priest, but what one did in private was no one's business.

Tlacateotl relieved himself and then headed for the baths. He never forgot a woman who rejected him, and as the warrior strode haughtily through the spotless streets of Tenochtitlán, tonguing his broken tooth, he made a silent vow of vengeance.

Alana shivered. How those molten eyes had drained of passion and hardened to obsidian! A man like that who considered himself God's gift to the opposite sex took defeat hard. But he would forget; she had simply been a novelty.

"There's Alana!" Inmaculada entered the room with Blue Butterfly.

Alana gathered the girl onto her lap. "Hello, darling. What have you been doing?"

What a gorgeous creature she was going to be! Skin like darkest honey, hair yellow as butter, and eyes of a blue that splintered into turquoise in the sun. She might have been from northern Spain or Italy, and among Indian youngsters, enchanting in their black-accented tawniness, she stood out, a spring flower among autumn leaves.

"You have developed a very special relationship," Inmaculada observed.

Alana hugged her charge. "Oh, yes. We are both exiles far from home."

A sudden and bitter pang struck at the Maya's heart. *Do you think you are the only one who has suffered? Am I not an exile, too?* She closed her eyes to conceal her agitation. Alana MacKenna had been good to her, had treated her like a sister. Why did she sometimes feel this urge to strike out?

"And another thing—we are alone, the two of us. We don't belong to anyone but each other." Alana was surprised by Blue Butterfly's keen look. She must remember the child was more sensitive than she appeared. Indian impassivity was often deceptive.

"We were watching the festival," the child volunteered.

Collecting her poise, Inmaculada smiled. "It's thrilling. You should come enjoy it. There must be close to a thousand warriors dancing in the sacred precinct. The flower of Aztec nobility, I imagine. And I saw some very handsome men!"

The women laughed, and Blue Butterfly nestled the crown of her head under her sponsor's chin. Why were they laughing? She had thought the Aztecs fearsome, yelling, leaping, howling, urinating as they danced, clapping palms to their mouths. She did not like them at all.

The distant chants and drumming, which had been growing in volume, stopped abruptly. Screams and shouts began to echo through the palace.

"What in God's name—" Alana made the sign of the cross and held the child more closely. Something terrible must have happened. Men were rushing past the doorway noisily, fastening armor and securing helmets, calling and questioning excitedly.

"Inmaculada? Are you in here?" Pepe ran into the room, sword in hand. "¡*Gracias a Dios!*" His wife grunted involuntarily when he clasped her against his cuirass.

"I was afraid you were out there watching the dancers!"

She tried to free herself. "I was. But the child wanted to be with Alana. Why? What *is* the matter?"

An outcry from hundreds of throats answered her, a roar that reverberated through the palace in billowing waves of sound, chilling the heart with its grief and anger.

"Alvarado and about a hundred men have massacred the dancers! Chopped them up like kindling! And they were unarmed! We're in for it now with Cortés gone!"

"The Blessed Virgin save us, we'll never get to Tlaxcala!"

The three adults stared at one another, moistening their lips and trying to maintain their composure for the child's sake. The Spaniard thought of being sacrificed, and terror rippled through his intestines. The Maya thought of her husband and then, to her amazement, of the sweet taste of revenge. The Irishwoman thought of the man she loved and mourned their estrangement, and the Indian child, bred to be brave, thought of the big, old Aztec priest with a mouth like two stones clamped together.

Cannon boomed, and they all jumped. "I have to go!" Pepe kissed his wife hastily and raced out of the apartment, pulling on his gauntlets.

"Be careful!" the women chorused.

Alana kicked a straw mat, sending it flying into the air. "That arrogant, cold-eyed, hot-tempered fool! What did he do that for?"

"Because Cortés is in Vera Cruz. Maybe he had a suspicion the dancers were going to attack the palace and try to rescue Moctezuma while there was only a small garrison on hand."

"Whatever the reason, we'd better see if we can be of any help." Alana was changing into old clothing. No use getting blood on her good things. "Now, darling, you are to stay here and not leave the room. Do you understand?"

In a hushed voice Blue Butterfly said she did and clutched Yaotl, the tiny *sholo*, who had scurried in to avoid the racket and the rude feet that kicked him aside.

"You take care of the dog and the bird, and I will come back for you. I promise." Alana kissed the girl and patted her cheek. "Don't worry. I would never break my promise."

When the women were gone, Blue Butterfly wept. It was so hard to be brave when you were alone.

Brian Phelps could have wrung Alvarado's neck. The stupid son of a bitch, why antagonize the whole city? Chances of getting out of this alive were very slim. If the Spaniard had been worried about the dancers working themselves into a battle frenzy, why hadn't he just sat tight? Beating off an attack would have been touch and go, but nothing this tough outfit could not have handled. Brian suspected the Tlaxcalans of putting a bee in Alvarado's bonnet about an attack's being imminent.

He ducked a shower of arrows as he relieved the man from León on the wall. "How goes it?"

"Bad business," his friend said solemnly.

"You can say that again," Brian agreed sourly. Slapping the man lightly in the shoulder, he warned, "Take care of yourself."

"You, too, *amigo*. May God be with us all."

As night fell no further assault was launched against the white men; that was planned for first light. The city was alive with torches and voices; drums throbbed ceaselessly, and altar fires flared. Every able-bodied man in Tenochtitlán was a warrior, consecrated at birth to the war god, and tonight he checked his weapons: sling, bow and arrow, dart, lance or spear, sword-club, and knife. Rope specialists, who bound the stunned and the wounded, examined their lines with care.

Inside the palace other warriors scrutinized the tools of their trade with grim concentration: crossbows, iron-tipped quarrels, muskets and ball, harquebuses, Toledo blades, and cannon. Horses were lovingly tended and then bridled, saddled, and armored for the coming fray. Some animals slept, one hip higher than the other, an iron-shod hoof resting delicately on its front edge.

Brian found time for contemplation after midnight. This was a pretty kettle of fish! He had decided to return to England as soon as Cortés was back and gave him permission to take ship, but now he'd be lucky to be alive the day after tomorrow. Realist that he was, Brian knew Henry VIII and his minister, Thomas Wolsey, both engrossed in personal concerns, would spare only a passing regret for the disappearance of their secret agent.

What he regretted most was his inability to advise the king of the rich, productive, potentially profitable investment these new territories represented. To urge haste in mounting expeditions to compete with Spain in discovering, exploring, and colonizing the New World. And to hell with the Line of Demarcation!

The conquistadors had battered down the golden gates of a new continent, a glittering empire that would fill their monarch's coffers and extend the sway of their church over millions. If England did not act soon, Spain—an ancient foe—would have sealed off its acquisitions from foreign influences much as it had done with its own nation over the centuries.

Brian slammed a mailed fist against the parapet. Because of Alvarado's rashness and cupidity, there was no way to get the information to London. He, for one, looked forward to the dressing down Alvarado was sure to get from Cortés.

Coming off guard duty at two in the morning, Brian saw Spanish and Indian women working over wounded and dying men. But the one for whom his eyes always searched was not in sight.

Alana. Brian's heart lurched at the name. Those hours together had been magic. He had fallen in love with her long ago, and finally making love with her had been white-hot ecstasy one minute and the tenderest devotion the next! Then he had gone to her room like a swooning boy and found the Spaniard on top of her and her arms reaching up to him. They never guessed how close they came to death that day.

Brian had gone over it and over it. Surely she knew how he felt. Hadn't he vowed he loved only her? What else did she want? She seemed so *different* now, ignoring or snubbing him whenever they passed or he glanced hopefully in her direction.

Was the Irishwoman only a whore after all, worth nothing more than the cheapest slattern? Or was she the kind who had to have every tomcat who flicked his whiskers and, after enjoying him, cast him aside? If there was anything Brian hated, it was a female who used him physically.

God's bones! He wasn't the first bucko to be made a fool of by fragrant flesh and a hungry mouth, and he'd no doubt fall for the same story again in the future. Flexing cramped muscles, he felt a seam give in his doublet. She had missed her calling, that was the truth. The woman was a superb actress.

But the emptiness would not go away, and he worried. What would happen to Alana if the garrison were overrun and annihilated? It was an oath that made his heart ache, but the Englishman vowed he would kill her himself rather than let the Aztecs mutilate her.

Gilberto de Salvatierra was beside himself. Why in the name of the Sainted Mary hadn't he gone with Cortés? Once at Vera Cruz he could have slipped over to the governor's camp and informed Pánfilo de Narváez, the commander and Cortés' longtime enemy, of the ticklish situation in the Aztec capital.

Instead, here he was, caught between a sharp sword and a stone wall. And he could blame Alvarado's bloodthirsty, rapacious action for that! To cut down unsuspecting, unarmed men, as well as a number of women and children, was savage and brutal, but to strip their corpses of golden ornaments and jewels was adding insult to injury.

Alana had mentioned the Indians' contempt for the Spanish attitude toward gold. They said white men lusted for the "excrement of the gods," hungered for gold like pigs, fingered it like monkeys. When they found treasure, they grinned like little beasts and patted each other with delight.

And why hadn't he gone on the expedition? The reason was blond, green-eyed, and beautiful. The nobleman thought he had gotten Alana Mackenna out of his system, but she was still there, the breath he drew and the blood that nourished him.

Tonight, as he listened to the groans of the wounded, Gilberto longed for his former mistress. He imagined her laughing with Ortega about the wolfhound's bath, picking flowers for coiffure and bodice, and he remembered her face lighting up at the sight of the diamond and emerald jewelry, and how she had looked on shipboard, her eyes guiless and disarmingly childlike. He thought of how she'd bloomed like a rose in the freezing mountain pass and how this strange, harsh kingdom had burnished her loveliness.

Although their relationship was now completely changed, Gilberto experienced pangs of guilt about what he had done. Not that he cared if Phelps' balls burned to a cinder with frustration, but he did regret having hurt Alana—this warm, generous human being who had meant more to him than any other. In her lived the last of his youth. Gilberto moodily caressed the elaborately chased sword hilt as he pondered the most difficult decision of his life.

Dios, that sweet, wild Irish heart! How it grieved him to think of its stopping. But when the Aztecs broke into the palace, Alana would die by his hand.

The first week of siege was hell. Attacks at dawn, war parties trying to scale the walls, grisly priests screaming chants, hand-to-hand combat on the parapets, fires crackling, iron balls cutting swaths through brown flesh, the stench of gunpowder, cannon shot, blood, sweat, horse manure, human waste, and fear.

Women set up a dispensary for the wounded which soon included nearly all the palace occupants. It was not necessary to participate in battle; arrows and slingshot stones poured over the walls like hail, almost always finding a target.

Food and water were rationed, and Malinche and Inmaculada put slaves to work arranging a communal kitchen where meals could be served quickly and continuously. Supplies were scarce: chickens, tortillas, eggs, beans, dried fruit, and whatever else Moctezuma's larder could spare.

Horses grew restive and irritable, burdened day and night with high-peaked Moorish style saddles, heavy bronze stirrups, and iron breastplates. Alana and Pepe took the lion's share of responsibility for their care while cavalrymen fought on the parapets.

"These horses may be our only salvation . . . if we manage to break out of here," Pepe commented drily.

"But Cortés sent word he's coming." Alana was as nervous as a leaf in the wind. "He's not afraid of anything. He'll know what to do."

"Do you realize how many Aztecs are waiting out there?" Her friend's face was pale even in the sunshine. "Suppose they wipe him out before he gets anywhere near us? What then?"

"Oh, how should I know?" she snapped. "Am I supposed to tell the future in horse turds? Ask Botello, the astrologer!"

The Spaniard rolled his eyes as she walked away. What a temper! No wonder she had trouble with her men.

As she left Pepe, Alana noticed a flurry of activity surrounding Pedro de Alvarado. The group broke apart, revealing Moctezuma's elegant figure. His intelligent face was drawn, and neither his magnificent headdress nor his finely woven garments concealed the dejection in his bearing. His ankles were chained.

He had just appealed to his people to withdraw and discontinue the assault for his sake. They had shouted insults and battle cries, and a few even fired arrows at him. Moctezuma wanted to die. He watched without expression while a soldier removed the shackles. Then he and his sorrowful retinue ascended the stairs to his apartments and disappeared.

Alana felt very sorry for him. But he was not the only one with problems. She went wearily to her rooms, grateful to find them empty. Faith, how she needed peace and quiet! Sprawled out on the bed mat—no one dared undress in case of emergency—Alana stared into space. Aye, she had a problem. She was pregnant.

But who was the father? The baby had been conceived either during those magic hours with Brian or when she'd given herself to Gilberto. That had been in April. It was now the beginning of June, and she was caught tight as a drum.

Instinct said it was Brian. Or was that because she'd loved him? How many times had she relived that delirious moment when he touched her womb! *I am going to give thee a son. Then you can belong to no one but me.* The memory of their lovemaking had made her moan in the dark more than once.

Yet common sense insisted it could also have been Gilberto's seed, taking root in what the Englishman called her innermost treasure, one he had softened and made ripe for fertilization. Restless, Alana sat up. What did it matter? She and the child would be dead soon.

It must be close to dusk, and Blue Butterfly's supper had to be attended to. Her appetite had failed since the siege began, and Alana blamed herself for not getting the girl to safety. In the end, her death would only be delayed, not prevented.

She brushed her hair and tied it at the nape of her neck, wiped her face with a moist cloth, and changed shirts. At the doorway Alana stooped to retrieve a scarf of a lovely blue, the shade of Brian's eyes. She dropped it and stomped on it with her dirty boots.

At the kitchen area Alana helped supervise meals for those coming off duty while she kept an eye on Blue Butterfly, who munched on bean-filled tortillas. A furtive bite was going now and then to Yaotl, whose comic face peeked out of the shawl in which he had been wrapped.

"By the bones of Saint James, *señorita,* is this food for a hungry man?" An armorer with a bandaged arm looked at his half-filled plate in disbelief.

"Complain to Pedro de Alvarado, *hombre,* not to me," she replied tartly. "Who's next?" Her face flushed when the Englishman stepped up, and she shoved a plate at him.

This was the closest they had been in weeks. When their fingers accidentally touched, each let go of the dish as if it had turned red-hot. The crash drew little notice amid the constant, deafening clamor, and Finn gobbled the spilled food in seconds.

"I'm . . . sorry. I'll have another plate fixed for you." She motioned to a slave, who dipped into a huge container of beans.

Brian waved it aside. Before he could help himself, he blurted, "There's only one thing in the world I'm hungry for!" He saw her recoil. *Oh, Phelps, you ass, why did you phrase it that way?* "I mean—"

"I'm quite aware of what you mean, you whoreson bastard," Alana hissed, her green eyes igniting with anger. "And I wouldn't furnish you that meal if my life depended on it!"

He saw red. What was she so up in the air about? *He* was the one who had the grievance. *He* was the one who had been ribbed so unmercifully about not being able to plow the field but once. *He* was the one whose trust and love had been violated!

A cold voice asked, "Is he bothering you, Alana?"

Gilberto had seen her blush and start at the touch of the Englishman's hand. He had been startled by a flash of jealousy so hot he found his fists clenched and his abdominal muscles tensed in a tight knot. That she should care so much—

"Yes, he is." Alana wanted to strike out, to hurt, to make Brian pay. The Spaniard could do it for her.

The men glared at each other like stiff-legged hounds on the verge of a dogfight. "Let her alone or you'll regret it." Gilberto spoke in strongly ac-cented English so there would be no mistake about his warning.

Brian answered in Spanish which he had spoken most of his life. He wanted no misunderstanding either. "I already regret the whole matter. From start to finish."

He turned to Alana to impress on her what he had said. Her great eyes shimmered like woodland pools with unshed tears. "Ah, the devil take you both," he grunted and stalked away. She and Salvatierra deserved each other.

The Spaniard laughed and leaned forward confidentially. "So much for him, my love. Why don't you, ah, ask your roommate to sleep elsewhere tonight?" His honey-colored eyes glowed at the thought.

Alana said in a firm voice, audible to the men arriving to be fed, "Now *you* are bothering me, *señor*."

Men! *That* was what they always wanted. Nothing else. Always the body, never the brain. Always the flesh, never the spirit. She, for one, was through with men, and that was the truth!

News of Cortés' unexpected victory over Narváez and Moctezuma's plea for cessation of hostilities seemed to have put an end to the fighting. It had lasted seven days. The Aztecs now settled down to starve the besieged garrison. The Spaniards were going to pay down to the last living soul for their treacherous murder of the dancing lords.

Sentinels on the towers reported that footbridges across nearby canals had been taken up. The western causeway to the rear of the palace had been closed off and its portable bridges removed. Barricades were visible in the streets, as were gaps that had been made in the pavement to hinder cavalry.

Food and fodder deliveries ceased. Porters or servants trying to enter the palace were stoned to death or had their necks broken. Arrests and execu-tions of those suspected of being in sympathy with the white men became frequent. Soon no one even made the effort. Too many innocents were dy-ing. Alvarado's couriers passed through the net, however. Every message of distress served to lure Cortés back into Tenochtitlán—and the Aztecs wanted him most of all.

The days dragged. Alana kept Blue Butterfly at her Spanish lessons, and Yaotl learned to do somersaults. Pepe taught Inmaculada to play cards and took his turn on the parapets. They suffered hunger pangs and thirst as stoically as possible, sharing rations with the child, the two dogs, and two horses.

From time to time Alana saw Gilberto and Brian from a distance. They were strangers to her. Like the other men's, their armor was dulled, rusted, and dented, and their clothing stained and wrinkled, but like those of fellow conquistadors, their Toledo swords remained bright and keen.

That most famous sword in the world was created from veneers of steel welded onto an iron core called the soul. Made on moonless nights, the better to see the weld, and only when the warm south winds blew, it was repeatedly tempered in river water, each immersion accompanied by a blessing. Smeared with fat from a he-goat's kidney, darkened by cooling, sharpened, polished, engraved, basket hilt affixed, master maker's device punched in the blade near the guard, each Toledo blade now waited, poised for action in mid-June, 1520.

Cortés would be here soon. Then the swords would be immersed in blood. No one tried to fool anyone else. It was doubtful if even their wily leader could wrest victory from the chaos Alvarado's deed had wrought.

Alana was embroidering an altar cloth when Gilberto stopped to watch.

"How are you?" He yawned, worn out from meager meals and almost uninterrupted duty.

"Oh, all right, I guess." She severed a thread with her teeth. "How are you?"

"Tired. Tired of waiting. Tired of beans and no wine and soiled linens and sleeping in armor. And awfully tired of not being with you." The last words were more wistful than he intended.

"Everyone is tired."

He touched her hair where it flowed over her shoulders. When she pulled away, Gilberto's mouth twisted. "Am I so repulsive? I can remember—"

"You remember the past. This is the present, and there may be no future." Alana rose, folding the cloth neatly.

Seizing her hands, Gilberto pleaded, "Not to go to bed. Only to hold you close and know you still care a little."

Alana laughed cynically. "You couldn't hold any female close without getting into bed. No, Gilberto, you aren't going to talk me into anything this time.'' She still wondered if he had not had a hand in Brian's humiliation and rejection of her.

As if the thought conjured him up, the Englishman strode by, helmet under an arm, chestnut hair curling around his big head. He glanced at the couple frostily, a flaring of the nostrils his only sign of agitation. But Alana shrank from his contempt and jerked her hands out of Gilberto's grasp.

''Are you afraid of his seeing us together?''

''I don't want to talk about it. I just want to be left alone.''

''But—''

''Gilberto, I don't want to talk about it!''

Then they all heard it. A clear, shrill bugle call blaring in the distance. Artillery in the palace crashed and boomed in joyful answer. Cortés! Cortés was coming with reinforcements, horses, food, weapons, and hope!

¡ *Bueno, hombres, bueno!*

¡ *Gracias a la Virgen Santísima!*

¡ *Muy bien!* ¡ *Salvación!*

¡ *Gracias a nuestro Señor Jesucristo!* Cortés! Cortés!

He rode in white with anger and fatigue, plumed cap and velvet cape covered with dust. After him streamed a thousand foot soldiers, ninety-six horsemen, nearly a hundred crossbowmen, harquebusiers, and two thousand warriors from Tlaxcala, who swelled the Indian allied forces to eight thousand. It was June twenty-fourth, Saint John the Baptist's Day.

The conquistador was flanked by dear friends: Juan Velásquez de León, relative of Cuba's governor, but Cortés' man from the beginning; Gonzalo de Sandoval, the army's favorite officer and its finest horseman, who'd been managing affairs at Vera Cruz. He was riding Motilla, a dark bay with white star and forefoot, considered the best and fastest horse in the Indies. Pedro de Alvarado, another close and dear friend, was seen to lick his lips with some misgivings. He, too, was enormously popular with the common infantry, for the most part penniless adventurers, criminals, fugitives, and reckless veterans of European action. They understood one another and gathered around the officer as he faced his superior.

Cortés was bone-tired. He and his small army had marched two hundred and fifty miles to the coast, defeated a force four times their size, contended with an outbreak of smallpox, and marched back to Tenochtitlán—all in one month. And then! He'd found the work of the past year undone by one rash, impulsive act!

Alana saw the confrontation on the other side of the hall but was so relieved by the reassuring presence of the new troops she paid little attention. Then she heard Cortés exclaim in anger. This was rare. He seldom raised his voice.

Ordinarily Alvarado could get away with anything. Like a spoiled younger son, he depended a great deal on looks and charm, although no one denied his extraordinary courage and martial skill. But this time he could not escape his commander's wrath or his own public humiliation.

"That was a bad thing you did! A great mistake! And I wish to God I'd never heard of this business!" Cortés wheeled impatiently to go to his apartments, Malinche hovering at his elbow. Two of Moctezuma's chieftains approached, speaking respectfully but urgently, their feathered headdresses bobbing up and down.

"Visit him? Why, the dog doesn't even keep a market open for us or see they send us food to eat!" His dark eyes flashed angrily. Everyone heard him, and the chieftains covered their faces with horror. They didn't want to tell their master that! Several of Cortés' officers remonstrated with him, arguing that Moctezuma had personally intervened to save the garrison, that he'd been kind and generous, that he'd given the Spaniards his daughters. After all, Alvarado *had* massacred hundreds of his young noblemen without cause.

Their leader swelled with fury. "And did you know the dog was double-dealing behind our backs? He'd secretly negotiated with Narváez and sent gold, information, and provisions to the fleet with which Diego Velásquez intended to destroy us." He barked at the chieftains. "Tell your master to open the markets or I won't answer for the consequences!"

As the Aztecs sullenly retired, Alana spoke to a brown-bearded man-at-arms with a newly healed scar on the bridge of his nose. "We're so glad you're here."

He spit in disgust, narrowly missing her boot. "We're not glad to be here, I can tell you."

Another disgruntled Narváez volunteer chimed in. "We've walked into a trap. We were fools to listen to Cortés' golden tongue."

His companion swore. "From the looks of it, that's all the gold we're likely to get, *amigo*. The countryside is empty. The city is silent and deserted—and a huge city it is, too. There's no food—" He slammed his sword in and out of its scabbard. "We should have stayed in Cuba."

She nodded, having said the same thing again and again about Ireland.

Sweet Saint Bridget, how many times had she wished she were home. Sighing, Alana returned to her quarters to rest before the evening work. Now that Cortés was here, things would be all right.

But things were not all right. Enough was enough. The Aztecs declared war.

XVIII

Bernal Díaz sprawled against the wall like an armored doll that had lost its stuffing. Fighting day after day with only a small ration of bread to sustain him had felled the young soldier temporarily. It had not diminished his storytelling ability, however, and Alana and the other women listened, enthralled.

"Oh, what a fight! What a battle we had! It was something to see us covered with wounds and dripping blood. And here Cortés showed himself the brave man he was!"

The foray to the top of the great *teocalli*—to rescue the image of Virgin and Child from the Christian chapel and rid the area of snipers—had been a stunning *tour de force*. Three hundred Spaniards and a few thousand allies had vanquished thousands of Aztecs in mortal combat in full view of the city. Cortés had then told the enemy chieftains to look upon their dead, their broken idols and charred sanctuaries. He would do the same to Tenochtitlán if the Aztecs did not lay down their arms.

Such a glorious bluff! Almost every man and horse had been injured. Dozens of soldiers were dead. Food and water were scarce. The palace, under continuous attack, was badly damaged. Ammunition and powder were running out, and the Narváez forces picked at him day and night to flee.

181

The conquistador's ploy did not work. Moctezuma's brother had been appointed by tribal electors to replace the ailing leader, and this man hated Cortés for having chained him in the dungeon like an animal. No, he vowed, if it took twenty-five thousand Aztecs to get every Spaniard, so it would have to be. His men were behind him all the way.

Moctezuma died at the end of June. He'd suffered wounds to his head, arm, and leg from stones his own people had thrown when he'd appealed to them to lift the siege and let the Spaniards go. But the injuries to his primitive soul were the gravest of all. Moctezuma was spiritually and emotionally spent. He refused to eat or allow medical treatment, and the great leader soon departed for the Land of the Fleshless, a lonely, disappointed man.

It was rumored the Spaniards had stabbed him to death, but Alana thought this unlikely. As a hostage he would have been their safe-conduct through dangerous territory. Then, too, lesser dignitaries who'd been taken prisoner had not been killed. Cortés would not have done away with so valuable a personage.

"Alana! *Alana!*" The noise was deafening, and Inmaculada had to yell over crackling flames, banging muskets, screams from within and without the walls, and the continual roar from the thirteen brass falconets.

"Can you get away? Yellow Plume is in your room. She's afraid to come any farther, and I don't blame her."

Alana handed the Maya a basin of bloodied water. Speaking right into her ear, she said, "Nothing much we can do but rinse the wounds and bind them with clean cloth." Those who required care were grouped around the makeshift hospital. So many had been injured in the streets or canals. Cortés had been trying to break out of the city for almost a week.

What a relief to get away! Alana retched, overcome by gruesome sights and stinking smoke and a growing fear. But the courtesan and Blue Butterfly must not know. It was essential there be no panic.

Yellow Plume looked haggard, yet still lovely in her mourning. She was surrounded by servants and baggage. The two women embraced fervently before sitting down. "Are you all right?" Alana asked.

Tears trickling down her cheeks, the courtesan shook her head, describing her lover's last moments. "He said you must remember your promise."

Yellow Plume made a helpless gesture. Jewels glittered on her slim fingers. "You have your problems, and I don't want to add to them, but what shall I do?'' Pampered, shielded from the world, she was a tropical macaw torn out of her bower and thrown fluttering into the whirlwind.

"Stay with me. You will be safe. Something will happen, and we'll get out.''

The huge topaz eyes widened. "Don't you know what they're saying out there? The gods have delivered you into their hands! The stone of sacrifice is ready; the knives sharpened; the wild beasts roar for their offal; the cages wait for those to be fattened,'' she lamented. The servants started to wail.

"Now, now, shhhh, shhhh.'' Signaling to her friend's personal attendant, Alana ordered a sedative and warm covers for Yellow Plume; then she sat holding her hand until the courtesan fell asleep. This *was* a problem. Moctezuma had assured her those he trusted would take Yellow Plume to Tlaxcala if he died. Events probably happened so quickly he'd been unable to arrange her escape, and now no one wanted to be identified with his household. His servants had even removed their obsidian lip plugs in an attempt to conceal any connection with the despised ruler.

How tired she was. Yet every hand was needed, to fix food, nurse the wounded, draw water from holes that had been dug, even keep watch so soldiers could rest. Watching the Spanish and Indian women working like slaves, frightened as they were, had been an inspiration to Alana.

Rubbing her forehead, she walked slowly toward the main hall where the hottest fighting raged. Surely hell itself wasn't much different! The Irishwoman crossed herself, asking Christ's mercy on the dying tended earlier and His help in meeting the fate that almost certainly awaited the besieged. She waved wearily at Pepe some distance away, and Finn trotted forward to greet him.

Without warning there was a calloused palm over her mouth. Her arms were pinioned, and Alana was lifted off her feet and rushed into the doorway and down the stairs below the palace where she had gone the night the crossbowman tried to rape her.

The crossbowman! She'd seen him from time to time, firing his bolts with speed and accuracy, his wolfish grimace revealing rotten teeth. Not him, please, God, not him! Alana struggled, eyes wide with horror, as her abductor turned at the foot of the stairs and stopped in an alcove. The man put her gently on her feet.

"You!" Alana almost sobbed with relief.

"Did I scare you?" Brian asked.

"Scare me? Of course not."

Laughing, he placed his helmet on the floor, unbuckled the dented cuirass, and took off his sword belt. "You are the most maddening woman on earth. Come here." He yanked her to him.

"Let me go! What's the idea of carrying me down here as if I were a side of meat? I don't want anything to do with you."

Brian kissed her lightly. "Shut up, Irish. We may die tonight, tomorrow—who knows? I've decided to let bygones be bygones." He untied the scarf holding her hair. "I'm going to make love to you once more before the Aztecs get us."

Wrestling loose, she backhanded him across the face so hard the Englishman staggered. His face grew pale and grim with anger, red marks showing plainly where she had struck him. He grabbed her wrist and shouted, "Lie down!"

"I won't!" Looking wildly about, Alana noticed he had made a bed of grass covered with a blanket. There was a rather wilted bouquet and a small bottle of wine. Had a party planned, did he? She kicked the bottle over, breaking it, and stamped on the flowers.

"*That's* what I think of your making love to me. And as far as bygones are concerned, you can stick them—"

"You're getting a tongue like a cavalryman, Alana, and you know, I've put up with just about enough from you."

"You've put up with enough from *me?* And haven't I put up with enough from you?"

The dark-blue eyes smoldered with rage and irritation, and his hand tightened brutally on her wrist.

"You're hurting me."

"I'm going to do worse than that if you don't behave. What's the matter with you anyhow?"

Goaded by pain and fright, fighting the desire to surrender, Alana drew her dagger and slashed at him. It tore his shirt and brought blood where it glanced off the collarbone.

"You wildcat! Give me that!" They struggled hand to hand, and she felt his swollen masculinity brush against her. An irrational fury lent her strength, and the Englishman had all he could do to subdue her without injury.

Panting and cursing, Brian finally dragged her down onto the blanket.

"By the rood—ouch!—there was a time when you'd jump between the sheets with me."

"And sorry I was, too!" She bit his hand hard enough to leave marks.

He swore and slammed both her arms out to either side, holding her wrists to the floor. She tried unsuccessfully to knee him in the groin.

"If you want to play rough. . . ." Brian lowered himself onto her without hesitation, releasing the hand without the dagger. Burying his face in her bosom to avoid being scratched, he opened his breeches and pulled up her skirts.

"Let me go!" Her voice rose in a scream. "I won't be—" The words died in a sharp gasp of pleasure. He had entered, and her body closed around him.

Brian groaned, "Oh, my poppet, my bonny poppet. You're ready . . . you do want me . . . oh, sweetheart, I love you, I love you, I love you!"

The dagger clattered to the floor.

The lovers stood caressing each other, fully dressed now, but reluctant to face reality. Fired by anger, continence, and desire, their climax had been volcanic, the lava of ecstasy barely cooling before passions erupted again—and again. But now it was time to go.

"Once more," Brian whispered and kissed Alana lingeringly. She strained up to him, holding his hand on her breast. "Ah, woman, I could take you to bed for days and we would never tire."

"You silly goose," she murmured against his soft lips, "I'd wear you down to a shadow."

He chuckled and his teeth gleamed in the dim light. "Aye, I believe you would at that."

"Brian, I must tell you something." In case they did not get out alive, he had to know about the child.

"I don't want to hear about it. When I saw the two of you together, God, it really rocked me on my heels. But now that's not important."

"When you saw what?"

"When—" Brian drew his sword and shoved Alana behind him. Men were running down the stairs, arguing as they came. Their voices echoed in the passageways.

"If we go tonight, we won't be able to see to defend ourselves."

"*Nombre de Dios, burro,* if we go during the day, the whole city will be upon us. The dogs don't fight at night, haven't you noticed that?"

Brian called out, "What's going on, *señores*?"

The soldiers barely paused. "Cortés wants Cacama unchained and brought upstairs. We're getting ready to evacuate at midnight."

"What's the date, Alana?"

"I'm not sure. Either June thirtieth or July first. Why?"

The Englishman held her close. His words were solemn. "It's a date we should know. Something tells me this is going to be a sad night for a lot of us."

"Oh, Brian!" She clung tightly to him.

He held her away from him, drinking in the beautiful green eyes, the luscious mouth, and the long, silvery hair. "Now listen. Get the horses and Finn and the little girl and meet me outside your room. I'll get Bayard and find out what's happening." They kissed, hard. "Hurry!"

Brian ran to the main hall, where the horses were tethered, saddled, and ready for action. But he came to a halt, drawn by the spectacle of most of the army ringing Cortés, his officers and the officials charged with preserving the king's fifth. Nearby an enormous pile of loot glittered and shone: gold ingots and wedges, golden objects of every description, pearls, emeralds, jade, opals, garnets, silver—Moctezuma's treasure trove.

Cortés spoke to his secretary and the royal notary. "Bear witness, gentlemen, that there is no way to transport the rest of this gold under our present circumstances. Before the king's share and my own were taken out, there was more than seven hundred thousand pesos' worth. I now give the balance to any man who cares to take it." He chewed his lower lip with frustration at not being able to save that for which he and his army had sacrificed so much.

Pepe appeared at Brian's elbow. "It weighed up to eight tons before the fifths were removed." The two men pursed their mouths. What a temptation to dive in like the others and pack their pockets full.

"*¡Soldados! ¡Compañeros!*" Cortés was perturbed by the senseless greed his forces were demonstrating. "He travels safest in the dark night who travels lightest." The conquistador fingered Moctezuma's gift from their first meeting, a splendid golden chain strung with brilliantly executed golden shrimp.

But the men paid no attention to his words of caution. The Narváez contingent in particular had never seen such wealth before, and was it not for this that they had followed Cortés into the maw of death?

Brian noticed Bernal Díaz carefully choosing four excellent *chalchihuites,* the jade Indians prized above gold for their rarity. Only the nobility were allowed to own or wear them.

"Bernal is taking pieces of jade, Pepe. He's an old campaigner who knows what he's doing. Looks like a good idea to me."

The Spaniard eyed the treasure with regret. Inmaculada had sent the gold Moctezuma had given them at their wedding to Tlaxcala for safekeeping. Better to follow Cortés' advice and Bernal's example, he supposed. Later if they needed help, shelter, or food, the natives were more likely to accept jade than gold, which was not used as a medium of exchange.

"Where's your wife?"

"She's gone to get our baggage. I told her to meet me at Alana's rooms."

Brian tucked the jades and a big pearl he could not resist under his armor. "Good. We'll rendezvous there as soon as possible and then get back here so we can fit into the order of march." Leading Bayard, he hurried off.

A soldier with an eye patch and one arm held the reins of Alana's two horses. He grinned. "It's a good thing you're here, Phelps."

"Why? What's going on?"

The place was in turmoil—women chattering and crying, dogs barking, a bird screeching, clothes flying in all directions. Despite the urgency of the situation, Brian began to laugh and could not stop. When he did, he found a battery of eyes focused on him—black, amber, green, and blue, each glistening with tears.

"Ladies." Brian made a sweeping bow and stepped in. The clamor began again as they begged for instructions, comfort, and assistance.

"Quiet!" he bellowed. Silence fell. There were stifled giggles. "That's better. If I'm to be nursemaid to a bunch of females, you're to do as I tell you." Excited murmurs rippled through the group. Who could doubt such strength, power, and manliness?

Close to midnight, the garrison gathered to hear Fray Olmedo perform mass and invoke the protection of the Almighty against the perils of the night. Hundreds of unkempt, unwashed heads bowed and then promptly disappeared beneath steel headpieces or brass-studded leather caps.

Blue Butterfly hugged the tiny dog close to her chest, still upset at deserting the gray and white bird she had grown to love. She blinked up at Alana tearfully.

"Don't worry, my precious," the woman whispered. "The slave has promised to take him back to the keeper at the aviary. The bird will be safe there, and I'll get you another later." God willing.

"Is Yaotl asleep?" They pushed the shawl aside and smiled wanly to hear him snore. Brian had insisted the dog be drugged to avoid his barking and giving a premature alarm.

Alana glanced around, making certain for the tenth time that all was in order. She and the child were riding Conn, Inmaculada and Yellow Plume the mare; Pepe led a wounded horse loaded with baggage; the courtesan's servants were on their own. She was terribly concerned for Finn, who limped badly from a stone bruise in the thigh, but there was no way to make things easier for him.

She smoothed the wolfhound's head and hugged him. "Take care, dear friend." These last tense moments were emotionally charged for everyone.

Malinche kissed Cortés' hand as if he were her god, and he openly pressed her to him. He and fellow officers embraced, and many of the men did the same. Alvarado wrapped a cloak solicitously around Luisa. Spanish and Indian wives and women of both races waited patiently with their lovers.

Cavalrymen petted their horses, some kissing and stroking them, all murmuring and crooning to their four-footed comrades who'd helped them achieve victory and would now accompany their masters in defeat.

Finally, the moment came. Torches were extinguished. Brian reached out in the semidarkness, and like Malinche, Alana kissed her man's hand in respect and love. He squeezed her fingers.

Suddenly with a pang of guilt, she thought of Gilberto de Salvatierra. Where was he? Had he been killed earlier today and she not informed? Was he one of the motionless figures in that corner?

Then there was no more time for thinking. The signal to march had been given.

Sandoval and Diego de Ordaz, supported by other distinguished horsemen, rode in the vanguard at the head of two hundred crack infantry. The rearguard, including most of the Narváez greenhorns, was under the command of Alvarado and Velásquez de León. Cortés, Olid, and select officers took charge of the column's center—noble prisoners for use as pawns, the king's fifth and Cortés' fifth, baggage, and heavy guns. A hundred carefully selected veterans surrounded them, and the Indian allies were equally divided among the three divisions. Francisco de Morla and Francisco de Saucedo, the Elegant, whose plumes flew jauntily from his helmet, were assigned a hundred Spanish elite to deal with trouble spots that might develop.

Malinche and Luisa, the latter a chieftain's daughter from Tlaxcala, were escorted by several hundred Tlaxcalan warriors dedicated to the women's safety. Brian and Pepe managed to push in behind them, having decided this was the safest position for their women should either or both of them go down.

Alana pulled the cloak more securely about Blue Butterfly and her own head, covering them against a steady drizzle that added to the misery of the night. Clouds obscured the moon, and the great water lily of a metropolis slept, its petals folded, its inhabitants exhausted.

Sounds magnified in the silence as the column moved through the streets. Alana imagined hundreds of thousands of ears listening, hands reaching for weapons and quilted armor, curses of hate and vengeance being uttered. She shuddered, visions of sacrificial altars and Savage Serpent tumbling through her mind. Then hope leaped in her heart. She could see the causeway ahead!

This western link with the mainland led to Tacuba and had been chosen as the shortest route to safety. Two miles long and wide enough for eight horsemen or fifteen pedestrians to cross abreast, the stone embankment was built high enough above the water to act as a dike, its secondary function. Once on dry land, Cortés planned to travel north around the head of the lake, then southeast to Tlaxcala, where he was certain of a friendly reception.

The Spaniards and Aztecs had fought over possession of this causeway for the past two days, the latter finally winning out by sheer weight of numbers. But at this hour it was unguarded and stretched ghostlike across the lagoon's surface, an extension of the street over which the fugitives hurried as noiselessly as possible.

Here at the shore where causeway and street were normally joined by a removable wooden bridge, only black water met the eye. The gap was the first of three openings built into the causeway for defense and irrigation. Cortés had anticipated the problem by having a portable bridge constructed. Unfortunately there had been no time to build more than one; after the column crossed, the bridge would have to be carried to the other two openings which lay ahead.

The sudden blare of conch-shell horns blasted the night apart. An artilleryman near Alana swore shakily, and she heard men urinating in their fright. Her mouth tasted bitter with fear. The city was now alerted by the priests on the pyramids who'd been warned by spies of the enemy's exodus.

Then another terrible sound began to reverberate through the Valley of Mexico. The huge, cylindrical snakeskin drum in the temple of the war god was beaten only on extraordinary occasions. Its solemn thunder could be heard for miles, and it beat in every frightened pulse a promise of doom.

"*¡Adelante! ¡Adelante! ¡Por el amor de Dios!*" Cortés motioned frantically to the officer in charge of four hundred Indians and more than a hundred Spaniards fitting the portable bridge into place. There was not a second to lose.

As soon as it was fast, Sandoval tested it. Motilla's hooves thudded loudly on the planks, an urgent counterpoint to the rhythm of the drum. "*¡Vamos! ¡Vamos!*" The vanguard surged forward, the remainder of the column on its heels.

Brian said sharply, "What's that?" A sibilant rustling like the hissing of snakes was growing louder and louder.

"Wind?" Pepe suggested. He walked at Inmaculada's stirrup, immediately to the rear of Alana's horse.

Before anyone could answer, the wind came, but it was a wind of death. Of stones and arrows and spears from Aztec warriors rushing to the attack in canoes, paddling the water into foam.

"I thought they didn't fight at night!" a woman screamed. . . .

Alana heard canoes crashing into the sides of the causeway. *My God, they're eager to get at us!* She heard Yellow Plume shriek and tried to look back, but a painted face appeared right beside her, and Alana struck awkwardly with the sword Brian had insisted she carry.

The razor-sharp blade sliced the man's shoulder away from his body.

She felt the impact vibrate up her arm as it chopped through bone. Her gorge rose, and Alana almost dropped the weapon in repugnance. Blood darkened the Aztec's white tunic, and he stared up at her. Then he vanished, and Conn trampled the body, snorting as the dying man thrashed beneath his hooves.

"He's trying to get me!" Blue Butterfly leaned back, kicking at a man in feathered headdress who was pulling her leg. Alana did not pause a moment. This was no time for niceties or moralizing. Life, or death on the sacrificial altar—that was the choice.

Brian rode the Aztec down as he fell. "Irish, you make a good soldier! You're a warrior's woman, all right!" She barely heard him.

"I didn't want to do that," she shouted.

"Do what you have to . . . stay alive!" He backed into the press to help Pepe. Alana heard Yellow Plume sobbing steadily in hysterical cadence. There were so many yells and screams and moans her voice was that of a small, weak bird.

Couldn't they move any faster? They were inching forward at a snail's pace. Word traveled back that the vanguard had reached the second gap and was being badly harassed by a fleet of war canoes that had been lying in wait. Where was the bridge? *Sweet Jesus, where was the bridge?*

Word was sent from the rear. The bridge was immovable. Pressed into stones and mud by the tremendous weight they had borne, the timbers could not be dislodged, even by the more than five hundred men. They, too, were being attacked, many were being slain, and every survivor was wounded. It was no use.

The bridge could not be moved!

News sped from mouth to mouth. The column was marooned on the causeway section as if it were a giant centipede clinging to a branch in the middle of the lagoon. A great groan of despair arose from the trapped refugees. The primitive sound came out of Alana's mouth just as she sensed the pressure from behind. Discipline and order had deteriorated. The retreat turned into a rout. They had been ambushed—everyone for himself and the devil take the hindmost!

She turned in the saddle, keeping a tight arm around the girl's waist. Her small group was intact so far, protected by the Indians around Malinche and Luisa. But it was too dark to see the wolfhound.

"Finn! Oh, my God, where is Finn?" Her mount might kick him to death or force him over the causeway edge into the water, where the Aztecs would kill him.

"Never . . . damn . . . jump. . . ." Brian's reply was broken and jumbled, but the last word caught her attention. She was amazed to find they were close to the second breach. She reined Conn in, dismayed at the necessity of crossing over those who'd fallen into the watery gap. A ghastly bridge had been created by the headlong flight—corpses, dead animals, baggage, cannon, chests of gold, ammunition wagons, provisions . . . and the dying, who raised their arms in pitiful appeal.

An arrow thunked into Conn's side. Rearing and wheeling in pain, he launched himself across the debris, heedless of bit or rein. Alana felt the horse's hooves sink down into the soft flesh, and she burst into tears, on the brink of hysteria.

What a nightmare! *Oh, Holy Infant so precious and mild, save thy children.* That cursed drum never paused for a second, fraying the nerves, filling the brain, pouring through the veins, constricting the stomach with terror. *Oh, save us, save us on this sorrowful night, this noche triste!*

Blue Butterfly pulled at her sleeve. "See? Over there!"

Her keen young eyes had noticed Cortés and Sandoval gesturing and no doubt shouting, although their voices were drowned in the uproar. Water came only up to their saddle girths; they'd found a path to the shore through a shallow channel. The lake was seldom more than six feet deep, and they had located an easy escape route. But most of the people, like Alana, were caught in the crush and unable to join Cortés.

The column swayed and contorted around her as hand-to-hand fighting erupted between Aztec and Spaniard, Aztec and Indian ally, Aztec and woman. Muskets and crossbows had been discarded at the second breach. They were useless in the crush and the dark; only cold steel and brute strength would save them now.

The moon peeked from behind a cloud, and Alana glimpsed María de Estrada, who'd picked up a broadsword and shield to defend herself and two wounded Spanish women. She hacked at the Aztecs climbing out of the water, back and forth, in and out, with the fervor of desperation. Dead men were heaped around her, drenched in blood and soaked by the drizzling rain. Her mouth was stretched wide as she battled relentlessly.

A few of Cortés' officers worked their way through the press on horseback, trying to whip the column into order, the better to withstand the hordes of canoe-borne assailants. One of them saw María.

"*¡Soldadera!* By the bones of Saint James, here's a woman to make your heart sing! Aye, *soldadera,* marry me after this is over!''

"Be careful what you say, *caballero!* I make love the way I fight!''

"What a way to die, *señorita!*'' He saluted her, sword hilt to his brow, teeth shining in his dirty, bearded face.

Wild laughter rippled through the crowd. Those were *Spaniards* for you! The gallant exchange gave heart to many, including Alana, and the struggle intensified as they approached the third and last breach in the causeway. Horsemen jumped into the water, swinging blades at fanatical Aztecs who clung to them like leeches. Wounded and dying men grabbed the manes and tails of the struggling animals, hoping against hope that they would be pulled to shore.

A faint light silvered the water. Dawn. Alana gasped. Had this been going on since midnight? Time had stopped. They had been under attack for an eternity. She looked around, almost afraid of what she would see.

A flotilla of canoes darkened the water on both sides of the causeway like a horde of deadly water bugs, although the majority were concentrated near the city. She saw Cortés and his elite heading back from shore to help the rear guard, where most of the action was taking place. Unable to contend with the stream of reinforcements pouring out of Tenochtitlán, those forces were about to go under. Velásquez de León had fallen at the first breach, and Alvarado was unhorsed. Tonatiuh. Son of the sun. Instigator and perpetrator of the massacre of the dancing lords. Ah, the Aztecs had plans for him!

Brian appeared at Alana's elbow, cuirass and helmet battered as if they had been hammered and gashes oozing blood in his thigh and neck. A big grin flashed. "Not so bad right here, darling. More nuisance than danger.'' He pointed at Malinche and Luisa, being pulled through the water of the last breach. "Get to shore as soon as you can. And make Conn behave.''

"Are you all right?'' She took hold of his wrist, warm and dear to her grip.

"Yes. Everybody else is, too, Finn included, bless him. They're not far behind you. We've been damned lucky so far, all of us.'' Brian leaned forward to look into the child's face. "How are you?''

Blue Butterfly smiled weakly, and he said, "That's a girl.''

"Cortés was already safely on the mainland, but he rode back in there—'' Alana tried to see to the rear, where masses of soldiers still engaged in deadly combat.

"Cortés would never desert his men. A Spanish gentleman and man of honor? Never! Besides, he's a soldier's soldier. He's always done whatever he's asked them to do."

Bayard shook his head and fought the bit, trembling and exhausted from hours of activity. Brian soothed him. "Good fellow. I'm glad you didn't die under me like some of the others."

"Watch out!" Alana cried.

An Aztec crawled up the slanted side of the causeway to fling himself on the man from León who had fought side by side with Brian throughout the night. The man ran the Indian through and kicked him wearily back into the lagoon. "Dog."

The refugees had now reached the edge of the last gap which was full of people and horses, swimming, splashing, struggling, some of them drowning despite their efforts.

"It's your turn, Alana. Go on. Hurry! Swim the gap and then ride for the mainland as fast as Conn will go." The Englishman's eyes measured the distance.

"Aren't you coming?"

"Pepe needs help, so my friend will go with you." The man from León took Conn's bridle, his face old with fatigue and strain.

"One kiss." Alana reached impulsively for her lover, and their lips touched.

Bayard screamed, poised spraddle-legged for a moment, and then fell heavily sideways into the water. Alana's horrified eyes saw the spears that had penetrated his vitals and released the blood which spouted from the large veins in the belly. The horse's eyes were already closing when his carcass hit the surface, making waves that upset several canoes.

Caught off guard by his mount's death throes and hampered by armor, Brian struggled to the surface. Dozens of warriors leaped in after him with shouts of triumph, dragging him into a large canoe. As they bound him, Alana heard him calling her name over and over.

Stunned by the tragedy when they were so close to escape, his kiss still on her mouth, Alana stared as the canoe became smaller and smaller and finally vanished into the multitude that milled around captives and discarded booty being unloaded on the island.

Brian, Brian. Holy Mother of God. My dearest love. She hardly knew the stallion had eased into the last breach, swum across, climbed onto the causeway, and trotted slowly to the mainland. When the man from León lifted her down from the saddle, Alana fainted.

The survivors' ordeal was by no means over. They took refuge in a suburb of Tacuba, defending themselves as best they could until Cortés and his men joined them. As if in a dream Alana saw tireless warriors like Bernal Díaz continue to answer darts, arrows, and stones with swordplay and spear thrusts.

"Won't it ever stop?" Inmaculada was practically lame from riding horseback for so many hours. She held Yellow Plume around the waist; the courtesan had become speechless with shock.

"Not until they catch us or kill us," Malinche answered, watching anxiously for Cortés. "If we can just get to Tlaxcala!" Luisa's eyes brimmed with tears. How she longed for home.

The conquistador finally arrived, grim and ready to drop from exhaustion, accompanied by the sadly decimated remnants of army, cavalry, and allied forces. Pedro de Alvarado limped in, his blond head a sunflower among the black-haired Indians. He had eluded the Aztecs by pole-vaulting the breach, amazing those who'd witnessed the feat. He embraced Luisa, mourning his fine sorrel mare.

Hostile action had now ceased, and Cortés called a halt in front of a small *teocalli*. Dismounting like an elderly man, he sat on the steps and dismally reviewed the survivors.

There was no one who was not bloodied, injured, famished, thirsty, and dead tired. Only twenty-three horses had come through alive; forty-five of their fellows had died. Muskets, cannon, and powder were gone. Many personal friends, good officers, and infantry had perished or been taken for sacrifice. But Alvarado, Fray Olmedo, Sandoval and his Motilla, Olid, Ordaz, and Ávila, as well as Martín López, the shipbuilder, had made it. And, of course, his beloved Malinche, the girl from Tlaxcala, and the interpreter, Aguilar. The noble prisoners, including Moctezuma's small son and two little daughters, had been slaughtered in the carnage. His baggage, the precious diaries, and the marvelous treasure were gone forever.

Hernán Cortés covered his face with his hands and wept.

He was not the only one. Alana rocked back and forth in mindless grief. She could not bear to think of Brian spread-eagled on an altar in the taloned claws of cruel priests his muscled chest bared to Savage Serpent's knife.

Oh! She pressed both forearms to her abdomen protectively. She had never told him about the baby.

Blue Butterfly came toward her, and Alana managed a smile. The child had shown remarkable courage; she deserved love and attention after such terrifying experience.

"Look," the Indian girl said, kneeling beside Alana. She unwrapped her shawl to reveal the little dog, Yaotl, who'd been drugged to keep him from barking during the retreat. His white eye ring as comical as ever, the *sholo* reclined on his back, fat stomach smooth and pink, stubby front legs comfortably folded. A faint sound whistled in and out as he breathed. The Irishwoman did not know whether to laugh or cry. He'd slept through it all.

XIX

That particular day in mid-July, 1520, proved to be lovely. Clouds tumbled across a lapis lazuli sky. Maize and maguey fields rippled in the breeze, and in the distance snow-covered mountains glittered under the bright sun. Tlaxcala nestled in its hollow like a woods fox in its lair, each *teocalli* on the surrounding hilltops gleaming white, red, and blue.

Houses in the city were decorated with garlands of flowers, and arches made of roses and honeysuckle sweetened the air. Priests hurried through sacrifices, freshening the blood in their hair. Other citizens rushed to prepare for the return of the white men and their own warriors. Cortés' welcome was to be as warm and cordial as it had been that first time almost ten months ago.

After all, though he was abruptly kicked out of Tenochtitlán, he had already proved two things: The Spaniards were the bravest soldiers of all, beside whom the proud mountain people were happy to fight, and the Mexica-Aztecs were neither as awesome nor as valiant as the tribes who'd always feared them had thought.

The Spaniards marched into the Indian town as if they owned it. They'd escaped from the capital, fought their way through the countryside for more than a week, and defeated an unexpected enemy horde in a daylong

197

battle at Otumba. Their clothing hung in tatters, and their armor was a wreck, but their spirits were high.

To the women with them, especially Alana, their arrival was nothing short of miraculous. At Otumba it had looked as if the tiny force of fewer than five hundred Spaniards, twenty horsemen, the civilians, and a few thousand Tlaxcalans would not survive, for Moctezuma's successor had gathered together an immense army with which to destroy the white men and their allies for good.

But the Christian force commended itself to God, the Virgin, and Saint James and then plunged into the fray. Cortés and his men had been engulfed by the enemy, so Alana saw only an occasional flash of sword or helmet which marked their positions. The valiant, half-starved horses mustered strength and stamina, running, galloping, and striking out with their hooves. Cortés' and Juan de Salamanca's mounts took them right to the litter of the barbarians' chieftain, whom they killed, claiming his golden banner as their spoil.

Their symbol of authority and command gone, the Aztecs fled the field. They had been defeated by horses of iron and men of steel and their own inherent weakness—the umbilical bond to the tribal body which made individual thought or action inconceivable.

Alana shook herself. The bad dream was over. They were now entering Tlaxcala's central square, and she saw Corn Flower and her husband coming forward. The women and the sick and wounded, including Gilberto who'd fallen at Otumba, were in the center of the formation; able-bodied soldiers marched on four sides. Spectators cheered and threw flowers, although many faces in the crowd remained somber. Thousands of families had lost relatives in the hostilities.

A tall, slim Spanish priest towered over the throng, telling his beads, his eyes inspecting the newcomers as they broke ranks. Fray Mateo de Aldana was searching for a special person. No, two persons—a nobleman, Gilberto de Salvatierra, Count of Altamira, for whom he had a letter, and a silverhaired woman.

Fray Mateo examined the veterans critically, including the tired man who led them. They were tough, tough as saddle leather between the teeth. Listening to their confessions would undoubtedly curl his hair. The sinful, lustful satyrs. Yet, paradoxically, he knew the Spanish soldier to be the most devout Christian.

He did not notice some of the army cross themselves surreptitiously.

They recognized him from Cuba. No one else had eyes like the Soul Seeker! This was no jovial monk who looked the other way now and then like good, old Father Olmedo who'd been along since the start and understood things.

Young as he was, Fray Mateo had already built a reputation on dealing with cases of demonic possession. Why, he could even tell you how many demons existed . . . more then seven million, *hombre!* In any case, the witches responsible for such possession in others, after roasting awhile in a hot iron chair, had admitted guilt and were beheaded and burned.

It was rumored that his black hair had turned prematurely gray as a result of confessing these witches. The soldiers studied his eyes and concluded they were not much different from those of the Indian priests who presided over sacrifices. But no one voiced such a blasphemous idea. Each was weary beyond description and very hungry, and it had been a trick of the light, surely, that gave such an impression.

Life soon returned to normal, and the summer deepened as wounds mended, strengths revived, and plans were made. It seemed as if the Spaniards and their friends had always been in Tlaxcala, so close were their ties of war and suffering.

Cortés awoke near dawn one day with severe pain. Those two missing fingers throbbed like the cord of a crossbow that had released its missile.

His mistress stirred unwillingly. "What is wrong now?"

"My left hand—" He swung his legs over the edge of the bed and sat up groggily.

He did not want to admit Moctezuma's dying face haunted him. That he, Cortés, had been fonder of him than he'd realized. Nor did he want to mention the nightmares which were unbecoming to a man of his considerable accomplishments.

The conquest of Moctezuma's empire was not complete, and Cortés was not yet finished. He had no intention of relinquishing this fabulous prize. Once he laid the land before the king like an enormous jewel, it would bring him his heart's desires.

"Drink this, Hernán, while I put ointment on those stubs."

Whenever Malinche addressed him by his first name, Cortés knew he had better not argue. The liquid tasted nasty and clung to his tongue.

"What in Christ's name is that?"

She snorted. "Never mind. But you'll feel better shortly. And I wish you would have those head injuries looked at again in the morning. There's actually a dent in the bone of your skull."

Cortés got to his feet, feeling all his years, relieved himself in an earthenware pot, rinsed his mouth with wine, spit, and barely made it back to bed before the narcotic began to take effect.

The woman snuggled up to him. What a man this was! Life would be nothing without him. She felt him run the flat of his hand over her naked body. His fingers probed gently between her legs, cupping the pelvic mound.

"I'm even too tired to make love," he complained.

"Relax, relax," she whispered soothingly. Making love was the farthest thing from her mind.

"Hate to . . . see good men and horses . . . dying. . . ." He dropped off to sleep and his fingers twisted cruelly as if gripping the hilt of a sword.

Malinche moved away to the other side of the bed. Her eyes stared into the dark. Once awake, she always found it difficult to go back to sleep. It was the noise—that awful racket—that obsessed her. It was impossible to forget. She could still hear those ferocious cries out on that causeway in the blackness and bone-chilling rain.

Alala! Alala! Alala! Jaguar Warriors yelling, *Now is when! Now is when!* Conch-shell horns braying, drums booming, horses shrilling as they toppled into the water, groans of agony, shouts for help, vain pleas to God, women shrieking. . . .

Of all the women, only a few remained. Herself, thanks to whatever gods had kept her safe. Luisa, the elder Xicotencatl's daughter, whose homecoming had ensured their reception as well as their stay. María de Estrada, the only Spanish woman left in the whole country, who had many suitors after her brave performance on the causeway. There was the Irishwoman, Alana MacKenna, her Maya friend, Inmaculada, and the child from Tula named Blue Butterfly. And she must not forget the courtesan Yellow Plume, who, if events continued to progress the way they had been of late, was about to cause a lot of trouble.

In a handsome residence not far away, Luisa's brother Xicotencatl the Younger was dressing for the day while his wife reclined against pillows and watched. Corn Flower had grown increasingly unwieldy in pregnancy, but what bothered her more than anything else was not being able to make

love. Her husband was thoughtful and kind—she had always been his favorite. Yet she knew perfectly well he was now visiting the other wives as
he had done in the past when she was expecting. Polygamy was permitted
if a man could afford it, and Xicotencatl was rich.

"What about the woman?" Jealousy stabbed at her like cactus spines.

"What woman?"

His wife made an impatient gesture. "What's-her-name."

Xicotencatl fell into the trap. "Yellow Plume." He paused in fastening
a cuirass of thin silver plate over a quilted cotton tunic. She had made it
herself to fit close to his powerful body and protect the shoulders and
thighs. "You knew her name."

"Maybe I did. What do you plan to do about her?"

"What makes you think I plan to do anything?"

"I've seen the expression on your face." Corn Flower stared stonily at
the man she loved. This might be a good reason to become a Christian.
They were allowed only one wife!

She thought seriously of Yellow Plume. No one, least of all herself,
could deny the woman was stunning with those topaz eyes and magnificent
hair. As Moctezuma's prize concubine she must know how to make divine
love. Her life had depended on it.

"I have fewer wives than most wealthy men." His fiery temper warmed.
"If I should decide to take another, it doesn't diminish what I feel for
you." He put a conciliatory hand on her swollen abdomen. "It's just—"

Her eyes filled with tears, and she turned away from him.

Xicotencatl swore silently as he walked out. Woman could be so in-
furiating. *I've spoiled her rotten! She chooses to forget how the wife before
her must have felt.* He passed Alana's room and collided with Yellow
Plume as she came out. He smelled magnolias, a remarkably unsettling fragrance.

"Forgive me," she murmured, her long lashes dropping to hide confusion and intense interest. She was hardly a welcome guest here, being in
the city on sufferance solely because of her friendship with the white woman. She had to watch her step.

The warrior's attention riveted on her moist, seductive mouth. The girl
raised her eyes to the stern face and found herself shy and awkward. It was
the most appealing transformation she could have made from her role as
elegant whore. Because it had been sincere, its impact was devastating.

His smile was like a warm wind. "There is nothing to forgive. Let me assure you that you are welcome here, and if there is anything I can ever do to make your stay with us more comfortable and pleasant—''

Tracing the outline of his mouth with her wonderful eyes, she replied, ''Oh, there is.''

Alana left her quarters on the way to the stables, greeting the couple as she passed. The courtesan's blush and a glitter in the warrior's eyes perturbed her. A love affair would make Corn Flower unhappy. But if it had not been Yellow Plume, it would have been another woman; moreover, the courtesan had to make a liaison before her beauty faded.

After feeding her horses and examining Rose, the mare, who was pregnant by the dead Bayard, Alana headed for the chapel. She wanted to unburden her heart to God, ask Him once again what she should do about Blue Butterfly's future, whether she herself should become Gilberto's mistress again or go back to Ireland. It was so hard to know what to do. If only—if only Brian were here.

An Indian who'd been recently baptized met her outside the chapel. ''I'm glad to find you here,'' he said. ''I was on my way to tell you that your dogs have gone into the sanctuary over there.'' He pointed. ''It would be most unfortunate if they did any damage.''

''Oh, of course! I'll go after them at once.'' Alana descended the steps of the converted *teocalli* and hurried to the foot of the near sanctuary.

''Finn! Yaotl! Are you up there?''

Thank goodness the priests were not here! What were those dogs doing? She had never known Finn to be so naughty as he had been the past few weeks. She might have to give Yaotl away if this kept up. He was the one who led Finn into trouble, the little mischief.

She had not been in a pagan temple for a long time and was shocked and sickened to find two fresh human hearts in a dish on the altar. At the back of the room the dogs were rummaging energetically through mounds of skulls and thighbones.

Alana backed out of the entrance. She couldn't stay in there another second! ''Finn!'' she called weakly. He was not only desecrating her hosts' house of worship but upsetting his mistress as well. When he did not respond, Alana raised her arms skyward in a fit of anger and indignation. ''Finn, if you don't come out of there, I swear by all that's holy, I'm going to beat the stuffing out of you!''

*   *   *

As the woman lost her balance and fell, bouncing down fifty feet of steps, Fray Mateo watched grimly. He praised God he'd surprised the witch practicing her sorcery and been able to stop the unholy rites.

She had startled him with her beauty when she whirled around to see who was shouting. That cloud of moonbeam hair, her oval face, eyes like green fire and the devil's mark by her mouth clearly identified her. He had tried to catch her when she fell, not out of compassion but because she had to be kept in good condition for trial. This was the woman for whom he was searching. There could hardly be two females like her.

Unfortunately for him, one hand had momentarily grasped her breasts. His skin burned as if raked with nettles. Obviously only a witch could cause such an acute reaction. The bishop, Bartolomé de Zamora, had warned him—very discreetly, of course—of Alana MacKenna's fatal charm and held up the infatuation of the count as an example.

"Don't let her allure cloud your vision, my boy. White flesh, full bosom, tempting loins—no, be careful or she will turn you into a weakling, even as Circe turned the men of Odysseus into swine!"

When the woman groaned and rolled her head back and forth, the priest came down the staircase, lifting his robe in order not to trip. As he did so, an immense animal rushed past to nose his mistress anxiously and watch the approaching man with suspicion. Fray Mateo felt the slightest chill at the baleful glare. This was one of her familiars, of course.

"Get away," the man ordered as firmly as possible, realizing that the hellhound was bigger than he. The dog retreated a few steps, wary but willing to permit assistance.

The monk squatted next to the prostrate figure, his large silver crucifix at hand should those eyes try to do him harm. In spite of his good intentions, he was fascinated by the enchantress lying before him. The line of her long throat, the parted lips, that globular swell, the sweep of hip—

He flushed and pulled the hair shirt tighter around his male parts. For shame. Oh, Lord, for shame! *Why dost Thou send me this affliction of wicked lust? Oh, debased, abandoned sinner that I am! Thou puttest temptations before me to test Thy humble servant, and I fail Thee.*

He had had this problem once before in France, where he'd been assigned for a time. An epidemic there had felled many older priests and created a drastic shortage. Ordinarily a man of such tender years—though such travail was good for the soul!—would never have been made father confessor in a convent. And as ill luck would have it, he arrived at the height of a wave of hysteria. Demons were driving the women out of their minds!

Profane ravings and cursings were bad enough, and erotic dreams which involved him had been even worse, but what almost did him in was the nude dancing and gyrating. Crazed creatures! Except for his infant sister he had never seen a female unclothed. And certainly not cavorting around with bosoms bouncing, bottoms trembling, and bodies thrust forward as if to— Fray Mateo agonized over how long it had taken to get transferred. In penance he had flogged himself nightly until he lost so much blood his superiors ordered the practice abandoned. Since then the young man had had no trouble.

With the aid of Our Father in heaven, who surely understood this weakness, the priest did not anticipate trouble now either. Having girded his mental loins sufficiently to withstand any magic, he was able to present a serene front when Alana finally regained consciousness.

The first thing she saw was the silver cross shining in the sun. Had it dazzled her, and caused her to lose her balance? No, it had been more than that. Those pale metallic eyes had blazed behind the crucifix and mingled with it into a single shining flame which struck like lightning.

"Father." Her husky voice broke. "God must have sent you to me."

Fray Mateo rejoiced. She was his to command.

Alana heard a woman weeping bitterly. Was she dying? Oh, no! Then the baby would die, too, and that mustn't happen! She forced her eyes open. Torches were burning. It must be night.

Friends hovered around. Inmaculada and Pepe, mussed and anxious, Corn Flower, plaiting and unplaiting one braid, Xicotencatl wearing nothing but a breechclout and oddly vulnerable without regalia, a tearful Blue Butterfly with her arms around Finn's neck. In a far corner Alana thought she glimpsed the robes of a Spanish priest, but her vision still had not cleared completely. There had been one, hadn't there?

"Good! Her soul has returned!" A Tlaxcalan physician sat next to her, a dish of burning copal in his palm. He had been holding it under her nose as a restorative. When Alana smiled feebly in response to his statement, there was a murmur of relief and thanksgiving.

"You've been gone for two days," the physician said. "I was afraid we would have to expose the brain to relieve the pressure from the skull fracture." Frankly, he was glad it had not come to that. Operating on a white woman could have been ticklish.

He handed the dish to Inmaculada and rose to his feet. "I'll be back in the morning, but send a messenger if you need me. See that she takes the medication regularly and sleeps a great deal." Wise old eyes swept over Alana. "You were both lucky and unlucky."

After he had gone, warning against too much excitement, the child came to sit beside her and have her tears kissed away. She laid her head on Alana's shoulder. "You aren't angry with Finn, are you? Or with Yaotl? They didn't mean to do anything wrong."

The wolfhound rested a giant head on the bedcovers and studied them sadly. Alana pulled his ear. "No, I'm not angry anymore."

Inmaculada sat down heavily and rubbed her eyes. "*Gracias a Dios*, you're going to be all right. It was touch and go for a while."

"I must have taken a very bad fall."

"I'll say you did," Xicotencatl agreed heartily. "I just happened to look over from the Communal House and saw you tumbling down the steps like a disjointed doll. You could have been killed."

Corn Flower had stopped plaiting her hair. "Now that we know you're awake and resting, we can get a good night's sleep." She gathered up both husbands and the little girl and shepherded them out of the room. "We'll come back tomorrow," she called over her shoulder.

When they were gone, Alana whispered, "Did I lose Brian's baby?"

"I'm afraid so."

"That's what the physician meant. Lucky and unlucky. Oh, better that I had died, too!" Grief-stricken, the Irishwoman lapsed into her native tongue, praying and lamenting. She beat feeble fists on the bed, and Finn whimpered.

"Stop it now. Stop it. This isn't good for you after that crack on the head." The Maya leaned down and kissed her friend's forehead. "Don't, Alana. Conceiving a child is easy. Replacing you is impossible."

Inmaculada was right. There was no way in the world to replace someone you loved after they had gone.

XX

The Soul Seeker made a point of being on hand when the witch and her Indian companion visited the sick, wounded, and maimed. Now and then he was called upon to give last rites, and he frowned to see a dying soldier's frowzy head cradled on her bosom. It was only Christian charity, after all. Why should it bother him?

Although the hazel-eyed nobleman who had been her lover found it difficult to hide his irritation, the monk congratulated himself. He had made considerable progress in dampening the satanic influences at work in Alana MacKenna's soul. She had confessed her adultery, but only after being brusquely urged to do so. Naturally, he had to know all the details in order to help her save herself.

He pounded at her. Fornication! Lust and carnal knowledge! Nakedness and wantonness! These were loathsome in the eyes of the Lord. She must quench the fires of her ardent nature before it was too late. Repent, woman, repent! Salvation! Salvation! The eternal soul must be cleansed. Confession every day. Penances. Listen to him! His pale eyes, neither blue nor gray, burned with passion. They had a hypnotic effect, especially when one was very tired.

The monk often pondered his instructions. Although the revered bishop had warned him to bring her back to Cuba quickly, he felt strongly of the opinion that he should first try to exorcise the evil spirits in this female by himself. Besides, these heathen appeared to be fond of her. Taking her away without their consent, should she object, might create problems. It would be best to bide his time, then strike without warning like the flick of a lash.

It was significant whether or not this silver-haired, green-eyed person actually was a succubus, a female demon who had sexual relations with men while they slept. Did they exist? *Naturalmente.* He had battled with succubi himself! Discovering one in the act, however, would not only provide evidence needed for the trial but give him future lecture material as well. Fray Mateo fully expected to be made abbot of a monastery after his arrest of this woman who was known as the famous New World witch.

"Why is he always skulking around at night? Doesn't he ever sleep?" Gilberto was distrustful, as well as fretful from pain. His right arm had been disabled by injuries from clubbings and slashings. He suffered headaches from a blow over the left eye, and worst of all, his testicles and penis had been brutally bruised when Indians had yanked him out of the saddle at the Battle of Otumba.

Alana had refused to live with him, saying she had to keep the child with her now. She had changed. Who had not? Yet, she spent a lot of time in his room during his recuperation, sitting demurely with sewing or embroidery in her lap, feet side by side, dress modest and dull. The Spaniard loved having her near.

He worried about the Soul Seeker. For Alana to have survived what she had and then fall prey to this injustice! Name of God, he was as devout as the next man, but he could not go along with the charges lodged against her in the letter the monk had brought him.

It was similar to the first one, an expensive cream-colored parchment sealed with a blob of wax as red as congealed blood. The contents went over the same old ground. The prelate had been saying prayers for his friend's soul. Alana MacKenna had stolen the horses. She was a witch, and her horses and dog were familiars.

Even worse, however, was the rest of the complaint. Gilberto read it aloud.

> As I have received no reply to my letter of last year, I am sure you have been occupied in the work of the Lord, bringing the heathen under control so we may soon bring them the Word.

Nevertheless, I must repeat that when the witch's horses slipped their tethers, they kicked over a lantern. My stables burned to the ground, and the fire badly damaged other property as well.

Now, for the worst news of all. Unknown to me, my nephew, a rapscallion but a member of my noble family, was sleeping in the hay and perished in the flames!

Gilberto groaned every time he read that.

Murder, my Illustrious Count! Murder! There is no question in my mind of her guilt or of inquisitorial responsibility for her punishment. Therefore, realizing how helpless you are in the grip of her spell, I am sending a young priest in my name. He came to me from Calahorra in Spain, where his esteemed uncle was instrumental in the burning of thirty witches in 1507.

Mateo will not fall prey to this succubus! He will bring her back to me to be put to the question. Trial and punishment will be swift, I promise you.

You have been a victim of—

Alana interrupted, "Why, there was no lighted lantern. And no fire either, or we'd have seen it from the dock. He's making that up!"

The nobleman settled back tiredly. "We have to face facts, regardless. Not only have you made him the laughingstock of Cuba and rejected him as a—protector—shall we say?—you've committed a number of crimes punishable under inquisitorial law."

"Crimes?" The Irish fire flashed indignantly.

He was glad to see her temper flare. Alana had been quiet and melancholic for too long. "Would you like me to list them? Theft—"

"Of my own horses!"

"—murder, destruction of property, wearing male clothing, blasphemy, adultery." He shook his head. "What a terrible woman you are!"

They laughed, but Gilberto soon sobered. "I really am concerned, my sweet. This monk cannot be bought, swayed, or threatened. He is determined to take you back for trial, and I don't understand why he hasn't done it."

The Spaniard rubbed his arm. "We must think of a way to get you to Vera Cruz without his knowing and then on to Spain before the authorities in Seville are made aware of the bishop's intentions. I have friends there who could arrange for your transportation north to Ireland." He kissed the inside of her wrist and noticed with interest that she flushed and jerked it away. "I could set you up with your own household in Madrid, but you would always be in danger. I will give you up rather than have anything happen to hurt you."

Tentatively, he held out the uninjured arm, and almost pathetically, the man thought, she nestled next to him. Poor little kitten, she needed shelter and security. How *good* it was to have Alana back!

When Fray Mateo spied on them later, a treacherous tenderness overcame him and melted his insides. He never forgot the witch as he saw her that night curled up in a ball like a little girl with one pretty foot showing from under the covers, nails rosy-pink and skin snowy-white.

Such a lovely thing, that foot. He'd never thought about feet before, but the arch of this one curved delicately, almost innocently, and he wanted to fondle it and smooth the slim ankle. Finding himself suppressing an insane wish to kiss her instep, he ran back to his room. Fool! Her magic worked around the clock. It was to have been expected that temptation would rear its head. But he knew how to deal with that!

From a small travel chest, the monk withdrew an object carefully wrapped in spare garments. The fine red leather whip had been a gift from his devout uncle. Red because blood would not be so obvious and the heart would not grow faint. Tiny hooks barbed its tip. Hooks that embedded in one's flesh and gouged out tiny pieces with every blow.

The unhappy young man stripped to the waist and knelt before a small statue of his Lord. As his penance proceeded into the morning hours, his senses reeled, and he heard a voice crying out, "Forgive me! Forgive me!"

XXI

Holding the bridle in one hand, Alana washed her stallion's face. Conn squinted and tried to avoid the wet cloth.

"Ah, you're worse than any little boy I ever saw. Stand still." She smiled broadly at the beautiful, restless animal, whose hide shone in the sun. "Anyone would think you were my darling, the way you act." Alana gave the soft muzzle an extra swipe and released the bridle.

"When you're dry, I'll brush you," she promised. "In the meantime I'll work on Rose." Alana stepped over Finn and his shadow, Yaotl, playing among baskets of maize and grass stacked for fodder.

The mare whickered, pleased with the attentions of this creature who petted and pampered her. Alana ran an expert hand over the slightly swollen side. "And how is Bayard's foal today, *mavourneen*? Ah, do you remember how handsome he was and how we raced that day?"

She wiped away a tear. "Here now, we'll have none of that. 'Tis over and done with." Alana began to groom Rose's mane.

"It still doesn't seem possible the men and horses we knew are dead. Velásquez de León and his silver-gray mare with the docked tail and pretty neck. Francisco de Morla and that fast, dark chestnut he was so proud of. And Lares and his sweet bay with her sunny disposition. It was a shame to lose so many. The soldiers say that after God, the victories, before the retreat, belonged to the horses. Did you know that?''

"Are you talking to yourself?" Gilberto came toward her, his arm in a sling.

"Heavens, no, I'm talking to my friend here." Rose turned her head and nudged Alana's shoulder.

"I wish you'd be more careful about saying things like that. Pretending to converse with animals can only make things worse."

He had come to the conclusion long ago that she simply had an unusual rapport with animals, but it was what the monk thought and reported that was crucial to her safety.

Her former lover was looking much better, Alana decided, thanks in part to her nursing. His hair and beard were as black and glossy as Finn's hide except for the white accents that had appeared since the debacle at Tenochtitlán. His doublet, breeches, and trunk hose were the shades of red and amber most flattering to him. The emerald crucifix he affected and pearls on his ears were his only ornaments.

Gilberto de Salvatierra, Count of Altamira, scented and exquisitely dressed, studied the Irishwoman tolerantly. "You smell like manure." The long aristocratic nose crinkled.

"It's a good, honest smell."

"I suppose, but hardly a perfume for a lovely lady."

She swung around and began brushing the horse vigorously. The Spaniard watched skirts swinging and full breasts swaying. "Why won't you make love to me, then, if I'm such a lovely lady?"

Gilberto looked at her longingly. Pale blond hair pulled back with a ribbon but charmingly disheveled. Dirt smudged on cheek and nose. Dark-lashed green eyes, serene and questioning. Skin faintly moist with perspiration and shirt open to the cleft. Utterly adorable. The sun-warmed fragrance of forage imprinted itself on his memory. The nobleman would see her in his mind's eye whenever he smelled it again.

Dios, if she only knew how he dreamed of taking her! If he just weren't so afraid. He could face French cannon, Spanish swords, or Aztec lances, but he could not face the possibility of failing to please her.

Tipping her chin, he kissed her apologetically and had to restrain a response when the delicious mouth answered his so warmly. "Perhaps on the way home. On shipboard—" They smiled reminiscently at the suggestion.

When there was no answer, he frowned. "You *are* coming with me at the end of the week, aren't you?"

It was mid-November. He had to go. Like an old war-horse, he yearned to stay and participate in Cortés' new campaign to bring the Aztecs to heel; he gloried in having fought with the conquistador. It had been the adventure of a lifetime! Cortés' deeds would resound through the ages like a broadsword clanging on a shield!

But common sense prevailed. He would soon be forty. His wounds, both old and new, caused him discomfort every waking moment. The estates in Cuba and Spain undoubtedly needed attention after a year's absence, and if his wife had produced another daughter, a son must be conceived to carry on the family's ancient line before she passed childbearing age.

"Only one thing stops me, Gilberto. Smallpox! I'm terrified of it!"

He ran a fingertip down her flawless cheek. "I understand. It has killed a number of people right here in Tlaxcala, though, and you haven't been affected. Not everyone gets it, you know."

"I realize that, but I couldn't stand it. I couldn't!" The disease had arrived with the Narváez ships in April and had raged throughout the country since the end of September. The Indians had died like flies. Moctezuma's successor had died from it, and the late king's nephew, Cuauhtémoc, had been chosen and elevated to rule the Aztec dominions. She had not cared about that; she had been concerned about Blue Butterfly's well-being and her own.

"Isn't it possible the smallpox is even more virulent down in Vera Cruz, where it's so hot and humid?"

"I suppose so, but from what I hear the epidemic seems to be abating. And I'm afraid for you, Alana. This Soul Seeker wants glory, and you're his means of getting it."

She smiled tenderly. "Never mind that now. Inmaculada and I have made plans. But I do want you to know something. I was pregnant in July before I fell and had that miscarriage."

His eyes blazed. "Why didn't you tell me?"

"You were wounded and ill. I didn't want to add to your woes. So you see, you have nothing to worry about."

"That was before." Humbled pride showed in his face.

Alana pressed against him and put an arm around his neck. In her own way she had loved this man—still did. Gilberto had provided her with the best in exchange for what any man would have demanded.

Expensive clothes, jewels, good times, kindness and faithfulness within the scope of his nature, a chance to see a whole new world—he had given her all that. The least she could do before they parted for the rest of their lives was help restore his self-confidence.

"I promise it will be the same as before." One hand gently caressed those parts of him that had given her joy, shame, and pain. She murmured against his lips, "Tonight?"

"What a terrible woman you are," he whispered, but his heart leaped with happiness.

The moon shone on the sleeping City of the Eagle. It was a balmy night, redolent with scent of pine from nearby mountains. Her Indian friends said this sometimes happened, this pleasant respite before winter.

She had waited for Gilberto eagerly in her room, hair washed, body powdered and oiled, senses aroused. Alana felt excited and almost unsure. No one had made love to her for several months.

Thinking about that, she deliberately blotted out the hours with Brian. Life was so short. She had to go on. Yet she found herself turning often to the sensuous verses of the Song of Solomon, recalling each glorious moment the words re-created.

"Where *is* he?" Gilberto must have lost his nerve. But he would come later. She must be patient. He could not resist and would be waiting when she returned from her walk.

She continued her stroll toward the orchards, a trifle edgy and nervous. Finn flushed a rabbit and ran into the darkness, yipping excitedly. Alana always felt safe with him at her side, even though no danger existed at present from the rougher elements of the army.

Cortés had moved his forces to the southeast near the volcano called Orizaba. Here he trained Narváez's men who had escaped what had come to be known as the *Noche Triste,* the sad night, and integrated them with his veterans. Tens of thousands of Indians from different tribes flocked to the banner proclaiming his motto: FRIENDS, LET US FOLLOW THE CROSS; AND UNDER THIS SIGN, IF WE HAVE FAITH, WE SHALL CONQUER. His allies liked the last part. They craved revenge.

The conquistador also had unexpected windfalls of men and supplies. Diego Velásquez, the jealous and spiteful governor of Cuba, had dispatched more powerful, well-equipped expeditions than those of ill-fated

Narváez. No news had trickled out of the hinterlands, but by now Cortés' star was surely on the wane. Still, the men he and Jamaica's governor sent fell over their swords to serve such a bold and gallant leader.

Using a combination of new and seasoned troops and fresh cavalry, Cortés had now brought Aztec garrisons in subjugated towns and populations in the region sympathetic to Tenochtitlán under his control. The blade with which Cortés planned to win the Valley of Mexico was being forged.

Thinking of the soldiers, Alana was ashamed of the fury that had possessed her when she treated the crossbowman shortly after the *Noche Triste*. At first she had not recognized him beneath the blood and dirt. Then, while cleaning a savage chest wound, she had glanced up into the hot, hard eyes of the creature who had tried to rape her. She kicked a pebble, unable to accept the fact that good men had died while such depraved brutes survived. Seriously injured as he was, the man had gasped a vulgar invitation. If Inmaculada had not prevented her, Alana would have struck him.

A cool wind murmured through the cherry and apple trees, caressing her skin. The orchards smelled of fallen leaves and a delicious bouquet of fruits to come. As she stood waiting, a man put his arm around her waist, and the odor of musk mingled with the scents of the night.

"You're here," she breathed with satisfaction, placing one of his hands on her breast. "I've waited so long." When he cupped the other breast, she sighed contentedly.

His beard slid smoothly along her throat and across the nape of her neck. The lips nibbled and sent little thrills down her spine. Alana stretched, and the man gripped her harder. His breath quickened as her nipples rose beneath his fingertips.

"Kiss me, Gilberto." Alana tried to turn around.

"No," he whispered hoarsely, "not yet. Let me remember you first, each and every part of you." He put a palm flat on her abdomen, holding her to him while his free hand searched and fumbled beneath her gown.

She laughed throatily. "Easily, for goodness sakes. Have you lost your touch?"

"It's been forever."

"Aye, it's been that."

Alana reached in back of her. He was small but hard as wood. Different. Injuries, uncertainty, and the strain of trying too hard would account for the change. Once they started to make love, he'd revert to normal. Then he'd be all right.

Suddenly he grew frenzied, shaking and pushing himself against her. He ripped her gown down the back. "Oh, God!" His voice sounded strange. "Oh, God."

If that was the way he wanted it—if that would help—Alana let the gown drop and pivoted slowly to face him. Her nude body glimmered, and hair flowed like moon-silvered water past her hips. Shadows hovered beneath her voluptuous bosom.

"You're a witch. A witch!"

Alana nodded, smiling, eyes closed. She had heard that before. "If being a witch will help, then that's what I am. I admit it." Her arms reached out to the dark figure. "Come to Circe, my love."

He groaned, and for a moment she thought he'd conceded defeat. Without warning he pounced on her and half pushed, half pulled her to the ground like a puma bringing down a deer. Twigs and stones bruised her flesh, but her protests died against his ravenous mouth.

Taken aback, Alana wondered at Gilberto's behavior. Hands worked painfully on parts of her body and a peremptory knee slammed between her legs.

Was this her skilled Spanish lover? The size, the beard, the long, slender hands and knowing ways . . . it had to be! As his mouth parted from hers and pounced on a nipple, Alana grabbed the man's hair and brought his face up close to hers. Free of her own dreamlike state, she saw only too clearly who it was. Disbelief, revulsion, and fear warred in her mind, mixed with an almost hysterical amusement.

"You!" She tried to move out from under him.

The man panted, "I am going to enter the enchantress and break her spell over me!"

They began to struggle in earnest. It took all her strength to keep him away from her. "Let me go," she demanded, "or I'll scream loud enough to wake the dead! I'll let everyone know what a hypocrite you are!"

He laughed. "And who would believe you with your flagrant nakedness? I can say you were trying to tempt me. To buy me off from returning you for trial." The man buried his mouth in the hollow of her throat. "Damn you for the gorgeous harlot you are. I've wanted you since the first moment I saw you."

In his wildest dreams he'd never imagined the softness and silkiness of the Irishwoman's white skin. Her jugular vein throbbed against his lips, her heart pounding furiously. Her breasts spread to the sides of his chest under his weight as he pinned her down. Her great eyes, startling even in the dim light, widened with panic above the edge of the hand he'd clamped over her mouth. Alana's assailant probed and almost made entrance. She moaned and fought, but reason had deserted him. The heat of that secret place against the tip of his organ flooded him with insane vigor. In a final burst of desperation, Alana tried to get away, kicking and pummeling. He pulled her back and shoved her under him. Ramming a fist between her teeth, completely unconscious of the bite, he concentrated on the forbidden treasure that was so near.

Alana's strength was ebbing. Good God, where was Finn? As if summoned by her agony, the wolfhound silently closed viselike jaws around the rapist's left shoulder and dragged him several feet away. Bones crunched when he bit, and the man screamed.

"That's enough, Finn! That's enough!" Alana tried to get up but could not. The dog mustn't kill him! She crawled to where the dog shook his quarry viciously. "Stop! Finn!"

The man was dropped to the ground in anguish and shock, mumbling to himself. For some reason the only objects he saw were two snow-white breasts moving back and forth. How repulsive they were with their large, dark tips. Females must always be covered! He stared at the woman on her hands and knees next to him. She was absolutely *naked* all over! Had the witch been trying to seduce him? He grabbed at his private parts. Yes, she had bewitched him!

What horrified him almost as much were the eyes of her hellhound. They gleamed with yellow flames from Satan's caverns! When the creature snarled, saliva dripped from its fangs onto his cheek, and he wet himself in terror.

"Don't—don't let him kill me, for the love of God!"

"I should, but I won't." Alana felt as if every inch of her had been beaten. Now that Finn was under control, she staggered to her feet, found the torn gown, and wrapped it around her.

"Get out of here. If you know what's good for you, you'll get out of Tlaxcala."

"No one will believe *you*. They will believe me instead!" He had inched to a tree and propped himself up. "You're in league with the devil. They told me, but I wasn't sure. Now I have proof." The voice soared into a scream as a broken bone shifted.

"You make me sick," Alana spat. "You and your prattle about repenting. How many times did you tell me to prostrate myself before the altar and repent? A fine one to be talking, *you* are."

"You are a witch. You admitted it! You tempted me. The devil's handmaiden, that's what you are." He managed to stand, leaning against the tree trunk. As he hugged the damaged arm, she heard him strangle another scream.

"I promise you one thing, you evil slut." His ghostly face and hair floated disembodied in the gloom, and the half-crazed eyes bore into hers.

"Wherever you go, whatever you do, I will find you. And when I do, I will personally bring you before the tribunal and see you put to the question. Witches always confess by the time the Soul Seeker's through with them." He coughed up phlegm. "I'll shave off your hair and use red-hot pincers on your white body. I'll stretch you on the rack until you tell me who your accomplices are. I'll hang the Hades dog from the ceiling with twenty-pound stones dangling from his feet."

"Get away from me. You're mad!"

He started back on the path to the city. Finn growled, and the man whimpered and stumbled, holding the injured arm protectively. "*Incantatrix, incantatrix,* knowest thou not the law laid down in Exodus? 'Thou shalt not suffer a witch to live.' "

He turned, and the words struck through pine-pungent air like hailstones, hard and stinging. "You will burn at the stake, Alana MacKenna, and your familiars with you. Bound with chains as the flames rise from your pretty feet. Your milky flesh will char and fall off the bones. You will never tempt another poor human being again. *You will burn,* I swear it!"

The malediction branded itself on Alana's mind as it faded into the night. Should she have noticed what was happening? How was she to know that in turning to him for succor, peace of mind, and forgiveness, she had encountered one who had none to give, because he had discovered none himself? Faced with a celibate's torment, he had found life unbearable. Until now. Now, when her death would free him forever.

BOOK THREE

The Englishman's Sweetheart

> *. . . but I found him whom
> my soul loveth: I held him
> and would not let him go. . . .*
> —The Song of Solomon, 3:4

XXII

December, 1520: on the outskirts of the city of Tlaxcala

The Indian battalions passed in review before Cortés. Dust kicked up by thousands of feet sifted into the air. Conch-shell horns sounded exuberantly, bone whistles shrilled, and drums kept cadence.

"*¡España!*" they shouted. "*¡España! Tlaxcala! Tlaxcala!*"

Faces framed in plumed and bejeweled headgear turned in the Spaniard's direction. This was the Man. The one who promised to lead them to final victory over the hated foe.

Cortés sat regally astride his mount. A full suit of new armor glittered in the winter sunshine, and a scarlet cape fell from his broad shoulders onto the haunches of his war-horse. Beside him his ensign bearer proudly held aloft the conquistador's gold-embroidered banner embellished with a red cross and blue and white flames.

Cortés raised a velvet cap with grave courtesy as the allies marched by, waving battle standards worked in glowing feathers. Instinctively his mind ticked off their weapons, and he was glad that this time they were not to be used against him and his men.

His real attention was riveted on an officer at the other side of the parade ground. That young man might be a favorite of his and the army's darling,

221

but Gonzalo de Sandoval was entirely too softhearted when it came to women. Take the green-eyed blonde, for instance, whose protector had returned to Spain in November. It was common barracks knowledge that Sandoval considered her enchanting.

Not that Cortés blamed him. Even from a distance she tugged at a man, and the siren's song would prove even more seductive now that she was alone in the world. A pity her Englishman had died on the causeway at Tenochtitlán. They had belonged together, those two. She'd returned to Tlaxcala only minutes ago, after having spent almost a month in the mountains hiding from a monk called the Soul Seeker. Fortunately he'd sailed for Cuba in the meantime.

"She's going to cause trouble," Pedro de Alvarado spoke to Cortés over the din. His cold blue eyes were fastened on Alana's small figure. When she stopped to watch the display, Sandoval had ridden up beside her and was now pointing out the insignia of the bristling array of warriors.

"You ought to get rid of her," he suggested.

His commander nodded and saluted a smartly turned out unit under the banner of Xicotencatl the Younger. "A good idea," he agreed.

The conquistadors looked at each other. It was too noisy to continue the conversation, but each knew what the other thought. She might as well have the devil's mark somewhere on that white flesh. As far as Fray Mateo de Aldana and the Inquisition he represented were concerned, she was a sorceress. The devil's handmaiden.

Not that Cortés believed it. He had had ample opportunity to observe the woman, and he did not miss much. She might cause a lot of mischief, but he doubted the witch theory. Yet to see her today, dressed in black with that sun god pin at her throat, astride a black stallion and guarded by a black hound as large as a man, one might wonder. . . . Certainly Sandoval must be warned to avoid her like the plague. An order for her arrest might come from the Holy Office at any time. By God, he must be getting softhearted himself because he would hate to give her over to those vultures. She was a gallant harlot.

Alana buried her chin in the collar of her fur jacket. She was tired of being cold, although Finn and the two horses had thrived in the crisp air of the higher altitudes.

She had ridden down from her hiding place among the savage Otomis who patrolled Tlaxcala's borders only because Pepe had come to tell her the Soul Seeker was gone. As Alana smiled at the handsome Sandoval and watched the review, she relived the period of her capture and escape from the crazed monk.

After the scuffle in the orchard, Alana had returned to her quarters, badly shaken. When Gilberto arrived, skittish as a boy who'd never possessed a woman before, Alana had clasped him to her breast, anxious for the safety of his arms. Her touch proved to be a smoldering match put to the priming pan, and they had made love as vigorously as they had in the old days.

But within the week he had reluctantly gone back to his wife, children, and estates. The night he took her virginity, Gilberto de Salvatierra had known he would never be the same. He had been right.

The moment Gilberto rode out of sight the Soul Seeker had pounced. But Alana's captivity had been brief, mainly because she was held in such high regard by the older soldiers pressed into escort duty. Cortés preferred to employ these men as guards and on garrison details. Though they were tired and worn out, they'd not forgotten Alana's compassion and nursing care after the *Noche Triste*.

On the first night en route to Vera Cruz, they'd turned a blind eye to her escape under cover of early-morning darkness. When dawn broke, God-fearing sons of the church that they were, they swore the witch and her familiars had flown away while they'd slept. The monk had been beside himself with fury.

"Forgive me, *señorita*, but they want me to join them."

Alana saw Cortés and Alvarado signaling. "Don't let me keep you from your duties." She felt honored. Sandoval was a legendary soldier.

"*Hasta luego* then." His eyes caught and held Alana's.

"Until later, *señor*. My regards to both gentlemen." She, too, left the parade ground and rode slowly through the streets of Tlaxcala to the guesthouse. It was almost like coming home again. Not that the cave where she'd hidden had been uncomfortable. The Otomis, instructed by Xicotencatl the Younger and awed by her and her beasts, had furnished plenty of food, furs, and firewood.

No, the refuge had been more than adequate. Nevertheless, she had not been able to get warm. It was a mental cold, a gripping fear she could not escape as long as Fray de Aldana was on her trail.

Alana shuddered to think of his hate growing every second like some implacable cancer. Her physical rejection, Finn's attack, and the bishop's rage once he learned she'd slipped through his fingers—these would focus into white-hot religious zeal inseparable from personal revenge. And she was the target.

Perhaps she could appeal to Cortés for help. She suspected he'd be glad to get rid of her. He controlled the route to the coast, and no ship sailed without his permission. Alana was willing to risk the tropics now that the smallpox epidemic had more or less run its course. The sooner, the better—before her time ran out.

Fortunately she had ample funds. Not to offer Cortés, but to grease all the palms it would take to get Conn, Finn, and herself to Cuba and from there to a quiet cove in the Canaries. Rose would have to stay here; she was due to foal in three months or so, and an ocean voyage would kill her. Though she knew Pepe and Inmaculada would cherish her, Alana hated to leave the lovely mare behind. Yet she *had* to get to the Canaries and find transportation north to Ireland. Her life depended on it.

Ireland! It had been an eternity since she had walked its blessed soil. Alana smiled sadly while she unloaded baggage from Rose's glossy back. Would she ever see it again? Hadn't she been away long enough? Her wanderlust had been satisfied, and she'd seen many strange and wonderful things. She had gold and jewels to last a long while—Alana patted a bulky bundle—and had made the bittersweet discovery that life was much the same everywhere.

She'd lost two very dear men, and a wave of grief overcame her as she thought tenderly of her unborn child. Was there any tragedy worse than having each loved one blotted out and being left alone as she was now?

Alana now led her mare and Conn to the stables nearby and tied them in separate stalls. She unsaddled them, gave each a quick brushing, and checked the condition of their hooves. Someone had already strewn sweet grass for their beds, replenished the water buckets, and filled the mangers with dried maize.

"Courtesy of your friend, Pepe Ortega, I imagine," she told them.

For a few moments she stood listening to corn being crushed between powerful teeth. She stroked the stallion lightly, and his satiny skin twitched in response to her touch. How simple animals were, how uncomplicated. They were so good, so gentle, so pure.

"Are you in there, Alana?" It was Pepe's voice.

She sighed. "Yes."

He stopped at the doorway. Inmaculada had been piqued about his riding into the mountains. A messenger would have done just as well, she said sharply. Alana did not need him to act as nursemaid.

Devoted as they both were to the Irishwoman, her reaction had astonished him. When Alana came outside, he suddenly saw her through his wife's eyes. She was a stunning, desirable woman who made a man's blood run faster, even when it was broad daylight, and she was covered from chin to toe.

The silvery hair was severely coiffed at the nape of her neck. This and the black she affected lately emphasized the elegant bone structure of her pale face and made her big eyes seem larger and greener than usual. He always found it hard to believe they were so green! The faintest of lavender shadows marred the delicate skin beneath her eyes, and for some reason this moved him deeply.

Naturally, she would be divine to take to bed. Any man who did not think so was a liar or an idiot. In the count's service he had often seen her after lovemaking with her glorious hair loose, that coral mouth full and bruised from kissing. Yet he had never desired her in that manner. She was above him. A very special person. So whether she believed him or not, his wife had no cause for the tiniest breath of jealousy. Inmaculada was his one and only.

"You look tired," he said, embarrassed by his own silence.

"We were riding at daybreak, you know. I'm not made of iron like you Spaniards." Alana removed the fur jacket and rubbed her forehead. "I'm going to get a hot meal, take a bath, and go to bed for a quick nap."

Pepe hated to give her the bad news.

"There's something you'd better do first."

"What's that?" She touched Finn's head. "He needs to be fed, too."

"I'll take care of that. But there isn't much time. She's been asking for you."

"Who's been asking for me? Corn Flower? Is her baby due?" Her face lighted up.

"No, it's Yellow Plume." He knew how fond they were of each other.

"When I left, she and Xicotencatl were hand in glove." Alana laughed. "The pretty thing. She had him jumping through hoops." Alana smiled at a little girl walking by. "What does she want, do you know?"

Pepe answered softly, "Yellow Plume is dying."

* * *

Like other major Indian communities throughout the country, Tlaxcala operated a general hospital for civilians and a veterans' facility for disabled and overage soldiers. Alana had marveled over such concern. In the places she had known, veterans had no place to go but the gutter, no succor but death, no hope of sustenance but charity.

Beggars had been eliminated in this New World. Maize and clothing were distributed to the poor; deformed and handicapped persons were cared for. Alana had been in the Tlaxcalan hospital before and knew that Indian doctors in private practice occasionally referred patients to staff surgeons and physicians if they had special needs or required isolation. The wealthy and aristocratic were generally treated at home, however, and it disturbed Alana that Yellow Plume should even be here. She was relieved to see the competent doctor who'd attended her for the miscarriage.

"I'm glad you came. She may die at any moment." His dark, bloodshot eyes were weary and troubled. He hated to surrender, but Yellow Plume's affliction defied his knowledge and skills.

"Why is she in the hospital at all? Have her brought to my quarters, and I'll be glad to nurse her." Alana's personal problems faded away. Her friend needed help.

The man shook his head and urged her to follow him. "You must hurry. She is alive only because she set her mind on waiting for you." It never failed to fascinate him how a valiant will could hold death at bay.

He handed Alana a cotton rectangle soaked in pine oil that had twine ties at each corner. "Put this on."

"My God! Has she caught smallpox?" She thought of the girl's silken complexion. As Alana placed the mask over her nose and mouth, tying it in back of her head, they entered a large room lined with pallets. Braziers burned incense in a vain attempt to lessen the terrible odor.

"Oh!" Alana said weakly. Even the physician paled a trifle. She looked around fearfully. There was only one patient here, a shriveled old woman with a distended abdomen that humped up the bedding in obscene parody of pregnancy.

"We've come to the wrong room," she whispered.

His eyes were sad. "No. That is your friend."

Alana clapped both hands to her mouth. The doctor motioned to a nurse to be ready in case she fainted. They waited, motionless, as if rooted to the floor.

She turned to stare at him. Horror and pity mingled in the emerald eyes. She cleared her throat a few times before the words came out. "Is it contagious?"

"I don't believe so. She has been here two weeks, and I don't believe so," he repeated. Slender, deft fingers toyed nervously with a jade and silver necklace. "I've come to the conclusion it is poison."

It was a Nahuatl word unfamiliar to Alana. He had to explain what he meant.

Her eyes flashed with fury above the mask. Then she jerked it off, grimacing in dismay at the powerful stench. "If I'm in no danger, I want her to see my face."

Yellow Plume groaned and muttered. She'd lost almost all her hair and rolled her head back and forth restlessly.

"Then go to her! You *must* hurry." The man pushed Alana. To disappoint the courageous spirit still flickering in that ruined body was unthinkable. Sadly he remembered the victim's vivid beauty and he silently condemned the murderer to a slow and painful death.

"Come with me. Oh, please come with me!" Alana took his hand like a frightened child. "I . . . can't . . . do it alone. I thought I could. But I can't."

His humanity flowed out to meet the foreigner's need. Still clasping her hand, he led her to the pallet, where they knelt together.

Alana's throat tightened. Only the doctor's warning glance forced her to speak. "Yellow Plume, my darling, it's Alana."

Sunken lids, lashless and waxen, fluttered open. In the cadaverous skull the hazel eyes that had once captivated the ruler of millions lit up with recognition and affection. A gnarled hand reached out. Alana took it, careful not to touch the gangrenous fingertips.

"I . . . waited." The breathing was harsh, the breath foul. But Alana hovered over the girl, kissed her forehead, and caressed what remained of the once-magnificent coal-black hair.

"Don't talk, my sweet. Save your strength."

Yellow Plume gasped for air. "I . . . confessed. The priest came. . . ."

Alana asked the physician, "Praise God, has she become a Christian?"

He answered with faint mockery. "No. But before we—before a certain time, we, too, confess our sins. It is done only once in a lifetime." He gazed mournfully at the ruined loveliness. "Although what sins she committed I cannot imagine."

"Alana."

"Yes, my love. I'm right here with you."

"My *huipil* . . . the purple *huipil* is for you. Only . . . you."

Alana's voice broke. "I understand. The purple *huipil*. I will not forget."

The eyes closed. The skin began to darken. Soon the nose thinned, and the corpselike body seemed to shrink inward. Alana cried in earnest now, her tears falling on the pitiful hand she held.

Then the dying girl smiled. With what must have been superhuman effort she lifted her free hand and placed it on her swollen belly.

The concubine spoke in a strong natural voice filled with love. "Ah, there you are, Lord! Look what I have brought you. It is our babe!"

And then she was gone.

XXIII

The inquisitor general ran a critical hand over his shaven head. He hated the prickly feeling of stubble under a wig, but the pate was smooth as a woman's butt. His barber-slave had done a good job. He turned his thoughts back to the objects displayed in front of him.

The man chuckled evilly. Even though the monk had not succeeded in bringing Alana MacKenna back to Cuba, he had brought her belongings. How furious she must have been when she discovered she'd escaped with the wrong packhorse!

His clever black eyes gleamed with avarice. What she had collected was a drop in the bucket to judge from stories he'd heard. Take the opal necklace wrought in gold, for example. Look at the gems shimmering and burning in the dimness of the shuttered room. Unlike Czechoslovakian opals, these were rosy-red and flickered with yellow flames.

The featherwork had been beautifully executed, almost like a tapestry. He found it astounding that cannibalistic primitives were capable of such artistry. A shame it was worthless. The bishop tossed the exquisite wall hangings onto a chair and held up a cape.

How these iridescent green feathers matched those breathtaking eyes! As sure as his name was Bartolomé de Zamora, they were the same shade. He

229

had never forgotten the day Alana rode out of the sea, an ancient goddess risen from Poseidon's grottoes. Through dull days and restless nights the memory recurred to tantalize him. The hair had flowed like molten silver in the wind. Water streamed off full breasts and down to loins pressed to the horse's back. Marble-white flanks shone in the sun. . . .

A fan of blue parrot plumes crumpled in his grip. He would go to the land of the infidel himself and find her. Find her—and burn her. Then his torment would be over.

The bishop dropped the mangled fan on the floor and leaned reverently over his disk. Like a child, he had kept the best until last.

Gold.

The metal shone dully as he fondled these treasures from heathen kings and bloodstained temples. Perspiration broke out on his naked head; he hardly felt the gouty toe strike a footstool. Had the bishop seen himself, he would have been convinced Satan possessed him. Heavy features coarsened with greed, lips thin and tense with excitement. He did not differ from any other man under the spell of what Indians called "excrement of the gods."

Suddenly recovering his wits, the bishop sat back and folded his hands. Only his eyes continued to touch and covet the golden loot. A necklace set with a hundred and sixty-two garnets and one hundred small emeralds—he had counted them three times—turquoise and gold earrings several inches long, a mirror encrusted with mother-of-pearl and coral, a miniature shield with bizarre animals worked in silver, a toy crocodile with movable jaws and emerald eyes, large shells decorated with huge pearls and amethysts, a package of paper-thin sheets six inches high, a box of oyster-shaped slabs thick as his middle finger.

Almighty God, all this precious gold was his!

He reveled in fantastic daydreams. He would buy a see in a pleasant countryside and get out of this pestilential hole. Though he'd become inquisitor general of the Indies only four years ago, the lust for power which had catapulted him to the top had diminished. Hedonism and sloth had long since smothered any further ambitions.

When a Negro slave announced the arrival of Fray Mateo de Aldana, the bishop noticed the servant recoil from the monk. *Yes, you do well to flinch from him. This one is walking death.*

"My dear Mateo!"

Cold gray eyes ranged disapprovingly over the older man's casual attire. But the Soul Seeker's lifelong obedience was indelibly ingrained. He bowed with respect, hands hidden in the sleeves of his coarse habit.

"Your Excellency, may this day find you in good health and in the blessed hands of our beloved Lord."

"Thanks be to His divine mercy," the bishop intoned automatically. He found it hard to talk to Mateo. He had no interest in or patience for small talk and no talent for politics. The Soul Seeker's entire being was devoted to one goal—the rooting out and destruction of heresy. To him the church was a divine and immaculate mistress that must be protected and defended at all cost.

"Sit down," the bishop urged. "Sit down and have a glass of sherry. You're pale as parchment."

His visitor looked ghastly. That mangled shoulder had not healed, and he still suffered from fever. The wolfhound's massive jaws had rendered his arm entirely useless.

Fray Mateo lowered his bony frame onto a chair, his knees shaking with weakness. He almost refused the wine, but its fragrance and jewellike color assaulted the senses, and not even the unbending will which ruled him kept his hand from trembling as it closed about the glass.

"Have you been fasting?" His superior's tone mixed awe with choler.

"Yes. Until this morning." The sherry seared the monk's vitals, leaving a comforting warmth in its wake, and he relaxed as much as his painful shoulder would permit.

"Are you trying to kill yourself?" The bishop challenged his visitor angrily. He shouted to the slave to bring cold meats, bread, and fruit immediately. The bishop's fine clothes rustled as his big body moved in irritation.

"You are of no use to me in this condition, Mateo. If you wish to emulate Saint Simeon Stylites and sit upon a pillar sixty feet high preaching in the desert, by all means do so. But I'll have no anchorite practicing excessive austerities on my staff. I expect piety and self-sacrifice, but I forbid starvation and harm to the body. There is more work to be done here than there are men to do it. In this holy war the savages must be brought to the glory of God, but that can be done only by maintaining spiritual *and* physical strength."

The men crossed themselves as the servant placed a silver tray on a table next to Fray Mateo's chair. The bishop turned away, riffling through letters he had been composing until the hungry man had satisfied himself. Then he swung around, noting with satisfaction that the color had returned to his subordinate's face.

"Now! We have some old business to talk about." The bishop picked up a slab of gold and smoothed it sensuously between his palms.

"You mean the witch, Alana MacKenna."

"Of course."

The Soul Seeker started from the beginning. He told of finding the woman in Tlaxcala, where she was worshiping the devil in front of a hellish temple smeared with gore. Of her being so overcome by the great silver cross he brandished that she'd lost her balance and fallen down the steps to lie unconscious at his feet.

Fray Mateo conveniently omitted his accidental grasping of her breast. Although the sorceress haunted his nights, he'd been able to drive away her image during the daytime.

"Well, continue, continue," the inquisitor demanded.

Whore that she was, the monk went on, she suffered a miscarriage from the fall. He could only assume she'd been pregnant by one of the two men he'd been told she had lived with.

"Why didn't you bring her back here as I told you to do? We could have put her to the question." The bishop was very annoyed.

Mateo answered that many Indians believed her to be a goddess because she went around performing witchcraft. For instance, she had saved a child from being walled up to die in order to bring rain, and it had rained the very next morning. Then at Christ Mass last year, she had asked for and been granted the release of prisoners being held for sacrifice in the Tlaxcalan domains. This was an unheard-of concession undoubtedly inspired by magic. Those prisoners were no doubt followers of Lucifer by now!

His Excellency could easily see there would have been trouble if he'd tried to spirit her away. Consequently, it had not been until November that he'd felt it safe to act. The Indians had been preoccupied with preparations for war, and he'd waited for his chance, pressing a few crippled veterans into service as a military escort.

"Are Cortés' soldiers not God-fearing Christians that the devil's handmaiden could escape so easily? Perhaps he should be reprimanded!"

The monk assured his superior that if Cortés had done anything right since setting foot in what he called New Spain almost two years ago, it was trying to convert the stubborn idolators. Why, even the date his fleet landed had been a good omen—April 21, Good Friday, *anno Domini* 1519. No, a reprimand did not seem in order in Fray Mateo's humble opinion.

The Soul Seeker admired Cortés, a man after his own heart. Strike to the vein like an angry snake, and sink the fangs home so no mistake can be made about your purpose. That was the way to victory with cross or sword. He felt the conquistador employed more compassion and justice in dealing with people than he himself thought necessary, however. It never occurred to Fray Mateo that his lack of humor and understanding of human nature left him unhappy and incomplete.

"Getting back to the witch"—the older man licked his lips—"did she—did you get proof she is a succubus? We must have proof she is a female demon, one who has sexual intercourse with men while they sleep." He crossed himself. "After all, a man doesn't always know what happens, and temptation is a bitter cross."

The bishop was startled and displeased to see those chill eyes blaze and a dark flush rise to the roots of the prematurely gray hair. He remembered the monk's problems at the French convent where nuns had been possessed, dancing naked and gyrating in crazy positions.

"I am waiting, Fray de Aldana." The formal address and the suspicion inherent in it encouraged a quick reply.

"I have no proof," the man hurried to admit. The bishop's gaze from across the desk penetrated as sharply as the red-hot spikes the Soul Seeker often ordered driven through a heretic's limb.

His armpits dampened with terror. Priests, too, were subject to the ministrations of the Holy Office, and this particular primate enjoyed inflicting pain. That was not an unusual characteristic among inquisitors, but this one had subtle ways. . . .

"I am ashamed to say she—she did try to seduce me!" The words rushed out. Anything to satisfy those deadly eyes. "Of *course*, she didn't succeed! With the help of our Lord, I fought her tooth and nail. That's how I was bitten."

"The dog thought you were going to harm her."

"Exactly!" Sweat rolled down the pallid face. "Just thinking of that hellhound makes my shoulder throb."

His host poured more wine. A little pressure kept these fanatics in line.

"Don't worry. Even without that charge, we have plenty of crimes with which to convict her. Theft, arson, murder, wearing male clothing, adultery, blasphemy. . . . If that's not enough, I'll make something up.'' Inquisitorial methods included lying and trickery as long as they brought heretics to punishment and showed them the error of their ways.

The bishop's hand touched the green feather cape. ''It is easy to see how she became so potent a force. Alana MacKenna is a very beautiful woman.

''That is all for now, Mateo. Go with God and concentrate on getting well. Then we will go to the infidels' stronghold and make an example of the devil's strumpet by burning her at the stake.''

The monk rose painfully, made his farewells, and had almost reached the door when he remembered the letter. He had intercepted it after the witch's lover, the Count Gilberto de Salvatierra, had sailed for Spain. It had given her instructions on whom to contact in Cuba for assistance in secretly taking ship for home. Those mentioned by name had been arrested and thrown into the dungeons.

Then he decided discretion was the better part of valor. The letter could wait. Besides, the inquisitor general had already forgotten everything and was again greedily fingering his golden toys.

Finn whimpered with excitement in his sleep, and his long legs jerked involuntarily as he chased imaginary prey. Eyebrows and whiskers twitched comically, and Alana had to smile in spite of her melancholy and worry.

What was he after? Rabbits perhaps or wolves. They had seen plenty of them in the mountains, as well as bears and a tawny feline larger than Finn. Then again he might be reliving that day she and Brian had raced the horses on the way inland to Tenochtitlán. Did dogs remember?

Alana had no difficulty picturing the scene that had become one of her favorite memories. The stallions, joyous in their freedom, skimming the ground. Brisk winds scouring the air crystal-clean, mauve-tinted mountains and snow-covered volcanoes shining brightly against azure skies and pine-studded hills. The Englishman, chestnut hair glowing in the sun and sapphire eyes sparkling with life and love—

There was a hoarse bark of outrage. Finn sat up and looked at her sheepishly.

Alana chuckled. ''Didn't catch it, did you?'' She scratched his ear. ''That's the way with dreams, I'm afraid. And life, too, sometimes.''

The black hound fell back onto the floor with a thud, banging his tail. His eyes remained open, sweet and innocent, fixed on his beloved mistress. He listened as she began to talk to him. Speaking her thoughts out loud helped Alana sort them out.

They were in a fine pickle, and that was the Lord's truth, she told Finn. Her golden ornaments, as well as those sheets and slabs of gold, were gone and probably in the hands of the bishop. Yet there had been no way of knowing the bundle of tools and kitchen implements had been wrapped the same as her treasure.

It was fortunate the string of pearls and the diamond and emerald necklace Gilberto had given her had been around her neck. Had she not managed to conceal them, there would be no hope for her now. By portioning out a pearl here and a diamond there, she still had a fair chance of getting to Ireland. But she would arrive almost penniless, and the condition of her property and stock by now was anybody's guess.

Alana confessed to being deeply disappointed at receiving no word from Gilberto. After all the time they'd spent together—and what she'd put up with!—he could have sent one short letter.

A yellow thread snapped in the embroidery she was applying to a skirt hem. Yellow Plume. It would be a long while before she forgot the skeletal remains she'd dressed and surrendered to a priest for cremation. For a price he'd promised to store the ashes in a proper place. The dead woman had been born under an evil star, he said, destined for brief happiness and then disaster. But now she walked the gardens of paradise, where her soul was at rest.

Pepe said the courtesan had been poisoned by an enemy of Moctezuma's, but Alana disagreed. Pregnant women often acted strangely, and the jealousy and envy of Xicotencatl's possessive wife, Corn Flower, had been widely known. If she had been the murderess, punishment had come with a vengeance. Her child had been stillborn.

Alana felt a deep sadness; her suspicions cast a pall over her friendship with a family that had gathered her to its heart.

As far as a purple *huipil* was concerned, none had been found among the dead girl's belongings. It had evidently been the vagary of a deteriorating mind. Yellow Plume had remembered a blouse to which she'd attached great sentimental importance. Purple had been her favorite color, and the last time Alana saw the courtesan with Moctezuma she'd been dressed in shades of lilac.

The Irishwoman threw the embroidery down and paced back and forth nervously. Finn stood and stretched. His simple nature reacted instinctively to her emotions.

The tremor of distress he sensed had been caused by an encounter Alana had had the day before. It would be Christ Mass soon, and there was much bustling about in the city. Important chieftains had embraced Christianity, and Cortés had recently knighted the son of a deceased Tlaxcalan nobleman, the first instance of European chivalry to be conferred on an Indian. The customs of both races would merge on this holiday in a round of banquets and merrymaking.

Comforted by the festive atmosphere, Alana had been totally unprepared for what she saw. Her mind spun dizzily back to that first night she and Gilberto had arrived, almost a year ago to the day. All the Spaniards had taken local women, and a tall, handsome widow with burning eyes had chosen Brian. The breasts that thrust out so arrogantly then were now softened and expanded with milk . . . and in the crook of her arm where it could nurse easily rested a blue-eyed, red-haired child.

The widow had glanced curiously at the white woman as they passed each other. Blood drained from her face, and she closed her eyes as if in agony. Suddenly panic-stricken, the mother pulled her *huipil* over the child and hurried away. The foreigner might cast an evil spell. Nothing must happen to the seed of the huge male who resembled Quetzalcoatl. She would never bear again, but she had been blessed among women to bring this godlike child into existence.

When Alana saw Brian's child, born of the Indian's loins and not of her own, an ember of hate began to smolder. The acid of it ate into her. *Fray Mateo de Aldana. The Soul Seeker!* She spit and ground the saliva underfoot. *If it had not been for him, that child would have a brother. If it had not been for that psalm-singing bastard, she would not have fallen and lost her baby.* Alana devoutly wished she had let Finn tear him apart that night in the orchard. Her fingers slid over the dagger. If they ever met again. . . .

Picking up the embroidery, Alana forced herself to continue working. What made the situation even more bittersweet was the news she'd learned this morning from Bernal Díaz. She had teased him, saying he poked his nose into so many things he ought to write a book. He had grinned, saying he just might do that someday.

A few soldiers thought dead in the slaughter of the *Noche Triste* had returned after recuperating among wild tribes to the north of the Aztec capital. They were in sorry shape but when they reported to Cortés, they assured him that with a bit of rest and God's mercy they would help him rule New Spain. Or the world. He never doubted them a second.

Nomadic tribesmen had accompanied them to see if the grass was greener on the other side of what would be called the Sierra Madre. When queried, these Indians, whose tribe sent traders to Tenochtitlán with skins and game, said there *had* been an unusual captive on exhibit.

One with hair like autumn leaves? Yes, but they did not think he was a Spaniard. He was a giant with a chest like a shield and eyes like bluest stone. A fighter even the war-worshiping Aztecs admired for his strength and valor.

"Did you ask them what happened to this man?" she had begged Bernal.

But the savages did not have much to say. Only that the giant had been tied to a circular stone altar in the center of the city. And then he'd fought in the combat of five against one, the unequal survival contest Spaniards had appropriately named *el sacrificio gladiatorial*.

Besides, what did it matter? Who knew—or cared—if one more white man lived or died?

XXIV

"*Dios mío*, you can't travel with the army!" Pepe protested.

"Why not?" Alana challenged. "María de Estrada isn't the only Spanish woman in the country anymore. Beatriz Palacios and Isabel Rodríguez are here now, too. There's no reason why I can't serve as interpreter and help the barber-surgeon with the wounded."

He sputtered. "Why—why, you just can't, that's all. It's no picnic, eating dust and seeing—seeing what you'll see." He tried another tack. "Do you want to be taken for a camp follower?"

Alana's white skin reddened, but her mouth and chin were steady. "I am going. We're leaving at dawn." Her husky voice held a thread of steel.

Inmaculada finished pouring wine and sat down between the two, torn by conflicting emotions. On one hand, she was glad to have a beautiful rival out of the way. On the other, the Maya would always be grateful to the Irishwoman for saving her from the bishop's slavemasters and their dogs. Inmaculada certainly did not wish her harm.

Oddly enough, she trusted Pepe where physical fidelity was concerned. He had no cause to need other females, and she knew as surely as his eyes were gray that he loved her heart and soul. No, she worried that his foolish, unselfish attitude might lead to danger and loss. True, Alana MacKenna

238

was between the sword and the wall as Spaniards put it, with the Inquisition lying in wait and her protector gone for good. But there was no reason for Pepe to get involved.

"Not being a woman, I don't think you understand," Inmaculada pointed out.

"What is there to understand? Not only does she have the soldiers to think of, but the Aztecs as well. Do you think that ugly priest has forgotten her? Not by a long shot!"

Alana shuddered. Savage Serpent! She hadn't given him a thought for weeks. The last time they met he'd been wearing human skin and his voice had trembled with passion and anger. *Our paths will cross again! Depend on it!*

"I must go," she whispered. "I must. As long as there's the smallest chance Brian is alive, maybe hurt somewhere."

Pepe slammed the flat of his hand on the table. "Stubborn as a mule, that's what you are! Those Indians Bernal talked to said he was in combat *months* ago. Be reasonable, Alana. The Englishman is dead."

"You don't understand," his wife repeated.

"You bet I don't!"

Alana shot to her feet. "It's none of your business anyway!"

There was silence for a moment. She put a hand on his shoulder. "I'm sorry. I didn't mean that the way it sounded. But what do I have to lose?"

"Oh, not very much," he answered sarcastically. "Only your life, that's all."

"That's at forfeit either way I go." Alana patted his arm and kissed Inmaculada on the cheek. "Thank you for supper. And thank you again from the bottom of my heart for taking care of Blue Butterfly and Rose while I'm gone. I'll be sorry to miss the foal's birth."

Inmaculada helped her into the fur jacket. "What does the child think about your going away, Alana?"

"Oh, she's upset. She reminded me I'd promised not to go away, but I think she'll understand once she's a little older."

Alana fussed with the coronet into which her long hair was braided. "Look at this featherwork ornament she made. There really is genius in her fingers, just as her mother hoped."

Pepe grumbled. "You saved her. She's always felt she belonged to you. Do you want her to pine away for you?"

Alana laughed. "Stop playing on my sympathies. Blue Butterfly isn't nearly as fragile as her name suggests. She's as tough as a pine knot."

Before going out into the cold night, Alana paused in the doorway and smiled at the Spaniard and his wife. A handsome pair, this couple with a brand-new world before them. He like a silver-eyed falcon, small and swift; she like a glossy quail, curved and soft.

She blew them a kiss. "May God hold you in the palm of His hand, my friends, until we meet again."

By the bones of Saint Patrick, what a sight this convoy was! Alana began to have an inkling of the mighty adventure she'd accidentally become a part of.

The imagination, the gall of Cortés! He planned to convert every Indian to the True Faith and place a Christian kingdom at his monarch's feet. But to do this, he had to destroy the worm in the rose's heart; he had to humble the Mexica-Aztecs in Tenochtitlán and break their headlock on the other tribes.

And how was he going about it? What were these thousands of men around her bringing to place at *his* feet? A navy, for God's sake! A fleet of thirteen wooden brigantines of different sizes designed to carry brass cannon—a white-winged covey of death-spitting birds to attack the Aztec eagle. Shipbuilder Martín López had planned them, supervised their construction, tested them on a lake near Tlaxcala, and then had them taken apart. The convoy was now carrying hundreds of numbered pieces to the town of Texcoco, Cortés' campaign headquarters, where the ships would be reassembled and launched.

He planned either to win over or to destroy the towns along the shores of Lake Texcoco in which the Aztec island capital was located. Then, if necessary, he could crush the capital by force although he badly wanted to save it as the shining jewel in his crown of conquest. Cortés was more sensitive and cultured than was generally supposed. He considered Tenochtitlán one of the wonders of the world—it would be wrong to destroy it.

"*¡Señorita!*" Gonzalo de Sandoval had been sent to escort the dismembered fleet through hostile territory. It was a big responsibility, and he had a great deal on his mind.

"What are you doing here?" Clearly he was appalled to find the Irish-woman with the army.

"I've come to search for the Englishman." The green eyes brooked no argument.

Sandoval had listened to the warnings of his friends on the day she returned from the mountains. He had a great military future, one in which friendship with a woman wanted by the Inquisition had no place.

"You are a lovely fool."

"Yes. Well. . . ." She shrugged and smiled.

He touched two fingers to the steel cuirass. A pity. "Your servant, *señorita.*"

Alana lost sight of him quickly in the press. Eight thousand porters weighed down with logs, planks, anchors, cordage, sails, and ironwork formed the column's center. Around them marched ten thousand warriors and more than two hundred of Cortés' men. To the rear, where she rode, were the women, baggage, and livestock.

From her perch high on Conn's back, Alana saw loosely organized Aztec war parties harassing the fringes of the column, waiting to pick somebody off. When Sandoval and a Tlaxcalan chief with his unit dropped back to guard the rear, she felt more secure.

Someone had found her in that horde. Among the cursing, joking men on the road to gold and glory, one face leaped out at her, one feral countenance that turned blood to water and skin to ice. Their visual encounter would forever be bound up with smells of horse sweat and timber. In years ahead the memory of that terrifying moment in late January, 1521, would make her heart skip a beat. That endless moment when the eyes of Alana MacKenna and the crossbowman met.

When Cortés noticed Alana's arrival, his mouth hardened. By the end of the six hours it took for the convoy to enter Texcoco, however, she had long been forgotten. The next day she appealed to his mistress, Malinche.

"I can be useful while I search for the Englishman. I speak Nahuatl quite well and can act as an intermediary for Cortés. He has neither time nor men to deal with the little towns. And the more who turn their backs on the Aztecs, the better. I don't see that it matters how it's done, do you?"

Malinche felt a certain sympathy for this daring woman. Alana had found her resting in a luxurious apartment of the palace assigned to her lover by the royal family of Texcoco. The town's population had fled, leaving behind only those whose sympathies lay with the conquerors.

"What makes you think the Englishman is still alive?"

Alana sipped the chocolate she'd been offered. "I can't give you any logical reason. It's just a feeling I've had ever since the tribesmen from the country to the north said they'd seen him."

"But that was months ago," Malinche objected. "Even if he had managed to. . . ." She leaned forward, intent on making her point. "Do you know how the battle of gladiatorial sacrifice is fought?"

Alana bit her lower lip. "I believe so."

"Let me describe it so you won't entertain any false hopes. A prisoner is tied to the stone altar by a rope around his waist. Then he is given a wooden sword fringed with feathers. Five warriors in quilted cotton armor using standard weapons fight him one at a time. If he isn't too exhausted or isn't bleeding to death, occasionally a man wins and is set free—"

"There was a man from Tlaxcala who won once—"

"—but usually they don't win." Malinche fell back onto the bed piled with silky cotton coverlets in rainbow hues. Her blue-black hair fanned out over the pillows like splashes of ink.

"Nine times out of ten his heart is torn out right there on the stone to which he's fastened. No, my dear, I'm afraid he is long dead and his—"

"That's enough. Don't say it." Alana crossed herself, feeling a wave of nausea.

Brian's smile suddenly illuminated Alana's mind. She had relived their lovemaking so many times, dreaming of the ecstasy they had achieved, hugging his image to her heart. Oddly enough, it was something he said that she now remembered most tenderly. Those compassionate words he'd used to assuage her terror when he'd found her hiding in the blackness of Moctezuma's vast botanical gardens, her dagger stained with the blood of the man she'd killed.

Na, na, ma pet, Brian'll let naught harm thee.

She would find him. Then she would never let him go!

Malinche was tired from a busy week of rushing here and there, and the tension emanating from her guest began to put her on edge. It was obvious even physically. The Irishwoman looked wan, lean, and—dry? Was that the word she wanted? As if her body and soul were thirsty for the juices of love.

"I am sure I may speak for Cortés."

Alana rose with dignity and threw the black cape around her shoulders. *She means he wishes I'd go home and get out of the way.*

"You understand the situation. He plans to cut off support to Tenochtitlán. He will bring the cities and towns around the lake under his domination. Some will resist and be dealt with accordingly. Those saddled with garrisons to ensure obedience and tribute will yield immediately. Others will test the wind."

She stretched lazily. "Those are the ones you can contact. Try to sway them to our side. As a matter of fact, smaller places to the north and west will be better sources of information because gossip travels faster among provincials.

"If he's alive, your man may have hidden in the land of the Chichimecas which lies beyond the last civilized outpost. Don't, by the way, look forward to any reward. And don't depend on any help. You are entirely on your own."

She was surprised to see the white woman throw back her head and laugh. Rumors had been circulating that she was a witch. Perhaps she was mad as well.

Alana thanked the conquistador's mistress and left the harem quarters, her problems pressing in on her. Her first concern must be permanent housing, food for herself and the animals, servants, bedding, dishes. . . . Why was she setting up housekeeping on the edge of conflict, trying to nest in the shadow of death?

No, the household must be simple and protected. This meant she needed a trustworthy bodyguard, but Xicotencatl would help her with that.

Alana fingered the leather bag hanging around her neck. The pearls, diamonds, and emeralds. Everything had to be bought. How angry Gilberto would be if he knew his gifts were going to help her find Brian.

She headed toward the south entrance, where a large colonnade was being used as a stable. She had tethered Conn there while she ran her errand.

Finn had remained with him because Malinche had never been able to adjust to his presence. She found the idea of such an enormous dog unsettling.

To reach her destination, Alana had to run the gauntlet of hundreds of eyes. Cortés' army was housed here in the palace, and a steady hum of masculine activity surrounded her.

As many soldiers had recently come from Spain and the Indies, she saw no men she knew, nor did the Irishwoman speak to anyone. But Alana MacKenna could no more walk by unnoticed than lightning could strike and be ignored. The proud silver head with its striking eyes, the athletic, feminine stride, the enticing body completely covered and intensely desirable. . . .

Who cared if she was a witch? It did not seem to have hurt the men with whom she'd slept. On the contrary, Salvatierra had looked rejuvenated. That's what witches did, you know. And you should have seen the Englishman that particular morning!

Granted, she was fair game now, but watch out. This was no soft-petaled blossom that would fall into your arms wearing nothing but a smile. The woman had survived the *Noche Triste*, rode like a Spaniard, had stabbed an Aztec to death in personal combat, had recovered from a fractured skull and the loss of a child, and had spent a month in the mountains among the tough Otomis. A snow-white rose she might be, but her thorns drew blood.

Besides, the veterans said, her heart would not be in it. She had risked her life to come here and search for her Englishman. A lucky bastard, *if* he were still alive.

Alana walked through a doorway into a vestibule separating the palace proper from the horse colonnade. She heaved a sigh of relief mixed with amusement and uneasiness. Lord, she felt as if every shred of clothing had been ripped off. Head down, she caromed into a sweaty chest.

"Oh, I beg your—" The words strangled in her throat. She stood only inches from the crossbowman. Alana sniffed garlic, leather, and the oil used to clean his weapon. He wore no shirt, only a filthy suede jerkin spotted with food stains. He was as hairy as an animal.

Grinning at her alarm, he flexed the muscles in his upper arms. They writhed, big snakes underneath his skin. The man wielded the crossbow like a toy. He could handle her without effort.

"Looking for me?" His Spanish carried an accent Alana could not identify.

"No." Her knees began to tremble. His assault in the dungeon sprang vividly to mind.

"Get out of my way." She drew her dagger. As before, despite the needle-sharp point, it seemed pitifully inadequate. She had killed a man once. This fact revolted her, but at the same time it gave her courage. She tried to edge around him. Surely he would not try anything here.

Alana glanced up at the brutal features.

The crossbowman wiped away his slobber. He had often boasted with graphic prose and gestures, exactly what he planned to do to this woman. Now, being this close, smelling her, seeing the texture of her skin, he could hardly contain himself. Oh, he meant to have her, all right. But not in front of anybody and not for a single hurried time here in the corner either.

"All right." He reached out and ran a black-nailed finger ever so gently over the curve of her breast. She gasped and backed up, lashing out with the dagger but missing her target.

The man leered. "But some night. . . . " He did not have to say any more. She knew what he meant. He relished the fear his threat aroused.

Alana had continued to retreat and now whirled to run but found herself facing the men she'd just passed. Bolder ones stepped forward, their faces taut with lust. The big room fell silent.

She turned again, angered and frustrated.

The crossbowman's bulk blocked the way. He did not care if someone else took her. His time would come. In secret, when he could do with her what he willed.

Finally, Alana bolted, and the men moved swiftly, intent on capturing her. As she fled, she prayed.

Fray Olmedo had been reluctantly on his way to watch the branding of Indians taken prisoner during the fighting. This barbaric custom had prevailed for centuries in many countries, and God knows he had watched it often enough. Yet the stench of burning human flesh turned his stomach when he went to the brandings to baptize the poor wretches en masse.

The palace was so complex the priest had not as yet learned his way around; it was purely accidental that he'd come this way rather than past the archives which would have been a shorter route.

He saw the Irishwoman rushing toward him. Not quite running—too proud, he supposed—sheathing a knife, color surging back into her chalk-white face. A quick glance told him the old story. That Sicilian crossbowman, for example, a barbarian if he'd ever seen one. And those other men. He eyed their breeches reprovingly.

"Father!" Alana sank to one knee for his blessing and almost fell onto his feet. That had been a narrow escape. "I prayed," she said, breathing hard, "and you came."

He felt the trembling as he took one elbow to help her to her feet. "You shouldn't even be here alone. You should be on your way home to Ireland."

"I'm here to find—"

"I know. I know."

She huddled beside him like a young child who'd innocently caused a riot. "Please let me walk with you."

"You won't like where I'm going." Fray Olmedo's stomach had already begun to flutter. Pitiful cries and moans were becoming audible, although his companion, only now taking hold of herself, had not yet noticed them.

"Anywhere will do," Alana declared.

Without warning the voices soared to a crescendo of grief and then plunged into brokenhearted weeping. The priest's stern face became more bleak, and Alana began to lag behind him as they entered a large courtyard.

"Anywhere?"

She came to a standstill, transfixed by the drama of misery and degradation taking place before her eyes. Surely this was a scene from the depths of hell!

A cherry-red iron sank into the lip tissue of a middle-aged man as easily as a glowing coal melted through snow. The whites of his eyes showed as he rolled them in torment. Then he gagged violently on the stink of his own scorched flesh and fainted.

"Holy Mary, Father! The Indians at least drug their victims before they sacrifice them!"

The onlookers saw a line of women and one of men being kept in order by brawny soldiers. Pretty women were noticeably absent; they had been claimed as booty on the field of battle.

The huskiest men would soon be put to work with thousands of other laborers, digging a canal leading into Lake Texcoco. The brigantines were to be launched on it as soon as they could be assembled. The rest of the slaves would be parceled out to the army and its allies.

Anguish and horror hovered in the air like heat waves from the two braziers where the branding irons were constantly being reheated. Alana's tender heart ached for the Indians whose faces were masks of panic, dread, and helplessness. Most of them tried their best to be brave, but at the final moment some begged, some groveled, and some urinated or defecated in their terror.

"Maybe we can help," Alana murmured, her mouth compressed into a straight line. Whipping off her cape, she headed for the far wall, where a cloth awning had been stretched to protect the branded from the sun. Fray Olmedo followed her, rolling up his sleeves.

She passed the men doing the branding and those who gripped each captive by the hair so the hot iron could be applied in the right place. Her glare of scorn was so intense one of them accidentally burned his hand.

He swore. This was just his job, so much cattle to be marked for ownership. Why was she so angry? But for a reason he did not understand, he branded the rest of the women on the cheek rather than on the mouth.

Under the awning a native physician daubed paste on the terrible wound of the middle-aged man whose eyelids were fluttering. An assistant nearby held a cup to a woman's mouth, but she was sobbing so hard she was unable to drink.

"Let me." Alana took the weeping woman in her arms and held her head against her breast. Speaking to the physician, she asked, "What is this? Medicine to relieve pain?"

He glanced up. "Well, my lady, we meet again." She recognized the physician from Tlaxcala. "Yes, it is a narcotic to deaden sensation and let them sleep an hour or so."

With soothing sounds and friendly gestures, Alana encouraged the woman to drink. Then she propped her against the wall and turned to see what else she could do.

"What is in the paste?"

"Raw egg yolk, honey, and juice from the nopal cactus." The doctor applied it gently, gritting his teeth in an unconscious effort to avoid hurting his patient further.

"What are you doing here?" Alana cut up a dried root so the assistant could grind it more efficiently. "And I don't understand why you're treating these men and women. Aren't they your enemies?"

His shoulders slumped tiredly as he washed blood and spittle off his hands. "I'm here because Xicotencatl asked me to attend him and his unit. As far as these poor souls are concerned, yes, they are enemies of Tlaxcala. But the physicians have deserted Texcoco."

He paused to smooth back the hair of a homely young woman who'd fallen asleep with her hand on his foot. "All I can say is that my real foes are suffering and death."

Alana never forgot that afternoon. All around her she saw the obscene stigma of slavery irrevocably etched in living flesh. The brand—a capital letter *G* for *guerra*, or war—looked much like a capital *J*. The stem extended a short distance above the crossbar, and there was a dot on either side of the stem beneath it.

Alana noticed that it was close to dusk. Conn and Finn would wonder where their suppers were. The men who'd done the branding had disappeared and were replaced by the night watch. Fray Olmedo had gone. Several dead who had perished of shock had been removed. Food and water had been brought for the survivors.

When the royal notary stuck his head in to count the new crop, Alana asked permission to buy certain individuals. He named a price, and she paid him with a fine pearl. An honest man, he protested it was too much. She took the difference in supplies, forage, and a number of copper-headed pikes he thought the arsenal could spare. Alana told him she would send for everything as soon as she had secured lodging.

He brightened, anxious to be helpful. There was a handsome house not half a mile away on the other side of the canal. She would be separated from the palace by the canal, of course, but it might be wise to take possession quickly. It was partly furnished—if you could call these houses furnished! She would recognize it by the stone lions at the entrance.

He left then, wondering why he'd encouraged her to occupy the house. He'd had his own eye on it ever since the army arrived!

Yet the notary knew why. Romantic that he was beneath a severe exterior, he savored the idea of helping her even in the smallest way search for her long-lost sweetheart.

XXV

The Indian lord regarded his white visitor with respect. He remembered there had been talk in the marketplace about this woman, of her grasp of Nahuatl and of tribal traditions, of love for children and a warm heart. He would add bravery and a warlike spirit, qualities which appealed to him and had ensured her reception. An aristocrat did not usually deal with a female. But then these were extraordinary times.

"Be careful. He will crush your foot like a twig."

The man stepped backward hurriedly as the horse she rode moved impatiently. He would die before showing fear in front of the arrogant Tlaxcalans accompanying her, yet he would never grow accustomed to such large animals. The dog with the spiked collar, for instance. At least he *thought* it was a dog, poised there like a statue of obsidian. By the gods, if it stood on its hind legs, it would be larger than a man.

Alana measured the bronze-skinned chieftain from feathered headdress to jaguar-skin sandals. A dandy, this one! But a fighting man as well, to judge from multiple scars and his sinewy build. She admired his dress. A richly embroidered loincloth of fine white cotton, waist-length cape of pink and brown feathers, gold bracelets and earrings, a plug of turquoise in the nose septum, chains of opals, garnets, and amethysts, gold bands around his calves.

She liked the sweet balsam he wore as perfume and the pine oil on his long hair. Spaniards would do well to adopt a few of the Indians' grooming habits. Take daily baths, for instance, and clean their teeth; even apply herb juice mixed with ground bone and flowers to their armpits. They had that ridiculous idea of Gilberto's that bathing robbed a soldier of strength.

Alana had brought the chieftain and his townspeople Cortés' offer. If they swore allegiance to the Spanish sovereign, they would receive protection against the Aztecs who'd kept them subservient for many years.

"Please assure the great captain we are honored to become vassals of his king. As he requests, any Aztecs we capture will be sent to him immediately." He paused. "And should I hear about the red-haired man you are seeking, my courier's feet will sprout wings."

Alana flashed him a smile and turned Conn south toward Texcoco. She reached the road leading along the lake's eastern edge, and the stallion pulled at his bit, eager to gallop. But she did not want to get separated from her escort, nor did she dare.

Canoe-borne Aztecs hovered near the shore, whistling, catcalling, and yelling insults. The derogatory remarks were aimed not only at her, but also at the fifty Tlaxcalans who had volunteered as her escort. They considered it an honor to march beneath the circular standard featherworkers had completed for her at the palace. The design was a white cross on a black ground with bright green shamrocks in the quadrants.

Alana lectured them on the meaning of the shamrock. A great priest of her tribe had said it illustrated what was called the Holy Trinity. Each leaf had a name—the Father, the Son, and the Holy Ghost. They shrugged. What of it? They followed her, not the banner.

She did not return to the palace Cortés used as his headquarters until early March and then only to visit Bernal Díaz in the infirmary. Ten of her escorts came along to discourage suitors. Alana was too tired for any more of that nonsense.

When she entered and found the Spanish women clustered around Bernal, she felt a surge of pleasure. She'd missed the company of her sex. María de Estrada was there, the woman Brian had called a tomboy, who'd done valiant battle on the causeway. The experience had tempered her so that she became hard and deadly as the broadsword she now carried, and her smile was friendly but cool. Of the two worlds in which María had come to dwell, the one of men and of war remained the less complex.

Warm and comforting, Isabel Rodríguez had a reputation as a born nurse, who knew about such mysterious things as humors of the body—that yellow bile was prevalent in spring and black bile in fall and that bleeding and tonics were in order when humors became unbalanced. As a rule, she simply depended on common sense, cleansing wounds with water, and making the sign of the cross over them.

"So, Bernal," Alana called gaily, "you keep the ladies to yourself and let your comrades go unattended." She gestured at rows of the injured lying on pallets.

He answered in an odd voice. "None of them can compete with my charm." Everyone around him laughed, shaking their heads in fond reproof.

"What's the matter with your throat?"

Beatriz Palacios, a husky mulatto, chuckled. "He put it in the way of a spear point at Ixtapalapa and almost died." She jiggled his elbow. "But he was too tough, the old cock."

Pretending to be scandalized, the patient crossed himself. "Save me, Lord, from this hardhearted wife of Pedro de Escobar." He started to cough and turned beet-red.

The group drew in around him, patting him and making little noises with their tongues against the roofs of their mouths. Soldiers nearby complained smilingly about being discriminated against, and three women responded with good-natured scolding. Alana was slightly acquainted with Juana Martín and Beatriz Bermúdez, but she had not met the wife of Alonso Valiente.

Who would remember these six brave women, as well as all the others, Indian and Spanish, who accompanied their men to various parts of what Cortés called New Spain? Would anyone centuries from now even know they'd existed?

Oh, there would be plenty written about Hernán Cortés and his men and their horses, about Moctezuma and the Aztecs, about the collision of two great civilizations. Men who did important things were always mentioned somewhere by somebody. But no one ever called attention to the women who saw to it that those men got where they were going.

This seemed a serious matter to Alana. One that had never before crossed her mind. For instance, who would record the courageous answer the Spanish women gave Cortés when he urged them to remain safely in Tlaxcala during the battle for the Aztec capital? It was not right, they'd stoutly maintained, that women of Castile should leave their husbands when they went to war—where they were to die, their wives, too, should die with them!

Alana foresaw they might do just that in the months to come. Tenochtitlán would never surrender.

She drifted over to chat with María and make arrangements for yet another lesson in swordplay. She was determined to develop more dexterity. Not that she could ever use a blade as this woman did—like a flash of light!—but there was nothing one learned that one did not eventually put to use.

"Don't go yet, Alana," Bernal warned. "I have some information that may be useful."

Her tired eyes lit up, and those of the Spanish women warmed in sympathy. They took love very seriously. That this *señorita* risked her life almost daily to search for her man held deep significance. That she rode on a fool's errand lent additional luster to her quest.

They were aware of the charges of witchcraft leveled against Alana MacKenna—that the young monk had branded her the devil's handmaiden. At home they would have been the first to call for her execution. They had inviolable responsibilities toward their families, and protecting them from sorcery was among the most important.

But here in this bizarre world, where men ate men and children were walled up in caves to bring rain, whatever sins she'd committed had been overlooked. The women had decided to withhold judgment. There would be ample time later to study the ledger. Right now it sufficed to know she'd rescued a little girl from those vile sodomite priests, had lost a child in the early months, and enjoyed a good deal of respect from the army in general.

They made way for her at the pallet.

"Here," Isabel Rodríguez said. "Keep this slick-tongued rascal company. We have to see to food for the men."

"Can you use my help?"

"No, there are plenty of slaves to do the work, *gracias*.

Alana sat down, shaking her head. "What a reputation you have, Bernal."

He ignored the gibe and pointed at her warriors, who squatted by the doorway, relaxed but alert. "Brought your mountain lions, I see."

"Don't hurt your voice. What information do you have?"

Her pale face appeared strained as though in a subtle way her femininity were being threatened. He wished he were an artist. What a beautiful, sensual painting she would make.

"Have you heard of the Chichimeca tribes in the north?"

She nodded and motioned to one of her men, who came to crouch beside them. "Yes, Malinche thought Brian might be there."

The warrior spit before answering her questions.

"He says they are dirty, uncivilized dogs, Bernal. That they go naked and eat raw meat, are famous for their tortures and—take scalps." Her face suddenly crumpled. "Oh, the saints preserve us, I'll never find him in this awful country!"

"Here, here! You can't give up now. Remember what we say: When one door closes, another opens." The soldier took her hand.

Alana withdrew it immediately and blew her nose. No point in giving those avid spectators any more fodder for gossip. If Bernal had an unexpectedly swift recovery after this visit, it could be attributed to witchcraft. And then *he* would be in trouble.

She smiled tremulously as unshed tears sparkled in her eyes. "I'm all right. What about these tribes?"

"Hand me that wine there." He swallowed carefully. "Ah, that's better. Had to wet my gullet."

"Ask this fellow if he knows of a bunch called the Guachichil. He does? Good! Now I've heard—only heard, mind you—that they follow a chieftain called Eyes-from-the-Sky. Furthermore, these savages paint themselves red, including their hair. They seem to worship the color."

Bernal coughed. "Don't you think Phelps' red hair might make them think he was a god sent to live among them?"

"It's logical. But why stay there? Why not come back?"

"He could have been badly hurt in that gladiatorial combat. And I would guess his information gathering is poor. Primitives like that might lie and tell him we were all dead so he'd stay with them. And it's a long way from where he is to where we are without a horse!"

Isabel arrived with the evening meal and began to direct the slaves in serving it. Alana regretted having to leave the domestic bustle. Her house was lonely.

"*Muchas gracias, amigo.* I hope you get back on your feet soon. The army isn't the same without you, I'm sure."

Alana rose and wrapped the fur-lined black cape around her. Its severity enhanced her silver-blond hair and alabaster skin. But only the man she spoke to noticed her soft mouth tremble.

"Go with God, Bernal. If I find him, you'll be among the first to know."

She stopped at the doorway. "I nearly forgot! When you write that book, don't just list the men and horses that were here. Include the names of these *señoras*, too!" Alana was sure Bernal knew every mare and stallion that had trotted through New Spain—their colors, qualities, speeds, virtues, and shortcomings—and like his companions, the soldier had loved each horse like a brother.

He waved, more intent on his dinner than on the future. After all, one made his mouth water this instant, and the other might never even materialize.

Alana had bought six slaves at the branding, a married couple and two men and two women. None of them was young, but they sprang from strong peasant stock and had worked hard to stay in her good graces. On the evening of her visit to the infirmary they lined up in the inner courtyard of her house. She'd been treating the wounds on their mouths and arms every day with salve furnished by the physician.

"That looks good. This is entirely healed. I think we'd better treat yours again tomorrow. And these don't need any more attention." Alana studied the solemn faces. *My little family,* she thought glumly.

Taking the chin of the last slave in her fingers, she turned his head toward the torchlight. "I'm afraid those teeth will always show. If only you had not moved . . . ."

The man gazed at her mournfully. "I could not keep from moving."

"I know," she said. "I know." Then she smiled. "You have all done well. The house begins to come back to its original beauty." She began to hand out lengths of excellent cotton, which the servants took with murmurs of excitement.

"I understand twenty pieces of cloth are equivalent to a year's income. And I realize your homes and towns have been destroyed and that you have nothing but what I give you.

"Someday I hope to go back to my own home, and I will go with a lighter heart knowing you are not destitute."

They came forward clutching their gifts and bowing low as if to one of their priestesses. Alana shooed them away but was pleased to see they were laughing and relieved by their good fortune. The household settled down quickly for the night, as their everyday routine began before dawn. Finn came to stretch out beside Alana's pallet with a sigh and soon rolled onto his back and fell asleep. He snored so loudly she threw a boot at him.

"For heaven's sake, Finn," Alana complained, "I have enough trouble getting to sleep without you."

The dog had heard that tone before. He ambled to a corner of the bedroom where he collapsed in a heap, only to rise reluctantly a few moments later when she did.

"Oh, lie down! You don't have to tag along everywhere I go. Now stay here." She climbed the stairs that jutted out from the courtyard wall and led up to the flat roof. Like that of most Indian houses, it held a number of flowers and herbs in earthenware containers.

What a lovely idea this was. Of course, you could only do it with a level surface. But imagine the thatched roofs at home planted with roses and blooming in the spring! Looking down from a *teocalli* recently, Alana had compared the hundreds of colorful rooftop gardens to a featherwork mosaic.

It was close to midnight, and the moon was almost full. Across Lake Texcoco she could see pinpoints of fire on Tenochtitlán's pyramids. Far away a conch-shell horn was blown as Aztec astronomers marked the passage of the stars. It crossed her mind that two years ago this month she and Gilberto had made love for the first time. In April, 1519, so very long ago.

"Where are you, my dark darling?" Alana asked aloud as if her words could reach him across the ocean. His familiar image filled her mind, the black hair and tawny eyes, the wicked smile and lithe body.

"And where are you, my English love?" She faced the dark mountains to the north, yearning for him. "Oh, Brian, where are you? I swear on my mother's grave you're the only man in the world for me."

Seen through her tears, the moon shook and lost its form, an imperfect pearl in a blue-black shell. Alana dried her eyes and swore dejectedly. Her menses were due, and they had made her moody and despondent. She had no problems with their coming, praise be, but since the miscarriage her breasts swelled like melons and caused her much discomfort. Her thighs became heavy and engorged, too, and it was like being trapped inside another woman's body.

In her fit of pique Alana kicked a nearby pot. The clay broke with a satisfying clatter, and the scent of bruised sage filled the air. It made her feel better.

The hour was getting very late. She should be in bed. Reinforcements from Tlaxcala were due to arrive tomorrow. Her men were eager to head north along the lake and the fringes of Chichimeca country. The booty promised to be marvelous. But they expected some resistance from tribes closely related or allied to the Mexica-Aztecs of Tenochtitlán.

Before going downstairs, Alana knelt to pack dirt around the roots of the unpotted sage, thinking how good the earth felt between her fingers.

"I'm sorry I did that," she murmured. "I'll put you in another container in the morning." She'd believed since childhood that plants responded to kindness much the same as animals and people.

Suddenly the potpourri of fragrances triggered a picture of her mother tending daisies and foxglove, of her sweet face beaming down at a child from above a bouquet. A storm of longing swept over Alana in a bittersweet tide. Just once again to nestle in those arms which had held her from birth. Just once again to kiss her mother's hair and skin and bosom. Oh, to be a little girl again, precious beyond reason, with no fear of the future and all dreams unassailable within the fortress of love.

Alana's tearstained face lifted to an impersonal sky in an agony of the soul and a plea for understanding and with the knowledge that she could never go back—or be that young or innocent again.

And that was how he found her, crying her heart out.

He took her to a vacant house several streets away, one he had chosen with care. Although Texcoco was a large town, most of its citizens had fled to the countryside to get away from the army. This entire block stood silent and empty. No one saw the man carry the woman down the ladder from the roof garden, and no one saw him slipping steathily through early-morning darkness. Nor did his burden, gagged and bound, give him any cause for alarm.

He entered the house noisily and walked to a back room. A messy pallet sprawled beneath a pine torch spluttering in a wall bracket, and he deposited the woman there. His crossbow stood propped in a corner with helmet and cuirass, and there was a flagon of wine and half-eaten food not far away.

The green eyes which had raked him with loathing in the past were fastened on him. He admired their steadiness. She was a cool one, all right, but he would warm her up.

He shook a finger when she struggled against the ropes. "You don't like my company? When you get to know me better . . . " He winked lewdly, taking off his shirt and jerkin to reveal those immense chest and arm muscles. He posed and made them rigid for Alana's benefit like a yokel showing off for his sweetheart. Leather boots came off next and were followed by hose and breeches. She closed her eyes in horror and despair when his maleness bobbed into sight. He was huge. He would tear her apart.

The crossbowman placed a sword on the floor next to the pallet. She would not be able to grab it because he did not intend to untie her. She was too good with a blade. But if any barracks wolves had followed him intending to share this dish, he'd split them like capons. She belonged to him and him alone.

Alana made a muffled sound as he straddled her. She made another when he ripped the silken sleeping garment leisurely down the front, exposing her entire body bit by bit. A sigh escaped him.

"You are beautiful!" He slobbered over the white breasts, so full and luxurious. Touching her agitated him, and his face grew dark red. Fumbling in his eagerness, the man untied his victim's ankles. She kicked and tried to knee him, grunting behind the gag in fear and frustration.

He threw his head back and laughed. Torchlight flickered on his thick throat and herculean body. On his naked, throbbing phallus. He crouched over her, the personification of every woman's secret terror: the intruder, the female devourer, the pain giver. Then he pulled her legs apart, eyes glued to the target where he'd been aiming his bolt for so many months.

"Now you will have a real man!" His voice shook. Spittle dripped on her skin, and when he entered, she rolled her head back and forth in silent agony.

Alana tried to resist, but he was much too powerful. The panting, sweating body worked up and down on her, squeezing out her breath, hurting private places. He pulled her arms over his head so the tied hands rested at the back of his neck in mock embrace. Vaguely she was grateful he did not plan to remove the gag. At least she was spared that terrible mouth. She opened her eyes when he rolled off and saw him resting beside the pallet. He grinned and made an obscene motion.

"We had fun, eh?" He belched, scratched his chest, and fell asleep within seconds.

The house was as quiet as death. Only the spitting sounds of resin catching fire in the torch broke the silence. Alana gauged her chances for escape. They seemed good. He had not hurt her badly yet, and she knew approximately where they were. She would be running through the streets naked, but that was a chance she would have to take. If she could just get out of this house—

The crossbowman had turned on his side with his back to her. Alana stared at him with growing hatred and disgust. Actually he had not been as brutal as many men would have been. But then he had just begun. Alana sat up cautiously and then got to her knees. If he would only stay asleep a few more minutes. . . .

An arm like steel encircled her waist. "Don't go away. Your lover is awake now." A chuckle vibrated through the frame glued to the back of hers, and she felt him hardening against her buttocks. He'd been teasing her and had not been asleep. Savage that he was, he also knew the more subtle forms of torture.

The man ran an experienced hand down the length of her body, lingering here and there. How neatly she was put together. Elegantly, in fact, like a fine crossbow. Curved, taut, slim, and—he had no doubt—lethal. He would have to watch his back from now on. But it was going to be worth it.

He pulled her off the pallet onto the cool floor next to him and idly studied her disheveled beauty. The hair a coppery silver in the light, eyes almost black with emotion, a pulse pounding in the white throat, and that delectable mole on her left breast. She shrank away in repugnance when he leaned over it.

Her reaction angered him, and he cuffed her. Tears sprang to her eyes and spiked the eyelashes with tiny dewdrops. His cruel heart was unaccountably touched. She had been crying like a child when he'd captured her. Even though lust now sent him down upon her, proclaiming his mastery, he took care not to injure her. As his orgy continued, Alana discovered why. One did not damage a toy intended for constant pleasure.

Finally, the ordeal was over. The crossbowman was through with her. She glimpsed the dagger in his hand, but life meant nothing any longer. He might as well murder her. What did she care? No man would ever love her again. Sullied, used, broken, unworthy . . . the words tumbled through her tormented brain as she lost consciousness.

Alana did not open her eyes until the next morning when one of her slaves found her back on the roof, lying in a pool of blood.

XXVI

The horses had been so expertly stuffed and restored they almost seemed alive. As though the bay, the black, and the light gray were dozing until their masters came for them. Their feet were missing, sent to other tribes after the *Noche Triste* to prove the mortality of the iron-hoofed animals once thought to bring the lightning and fury of Quetzalcoatl's ambassadors. That had been at the beginning of the Spanish invasion when soldier and horse looked like a single monster.

Sunshine crept into the gory interior of the sanctuary atop the abandoned *teocalli* situated in a deserted inland village a few miles from the Valley of Mexico. It shone softly on slightly glossy hides and fell apologetically on eyelids sewn shut.

After death, priests had removed the animals' hearts and offered them to the gods, a strange new sacrifice for a strange new time in Aztec affairs. The remains had been left on display in standing position, front and hindquarters supported on wooden posts set into the floor. Considering the superstitious awe still surrounding these beasts, the taxidermy had been excellent. The legs reached and bent naturally as if the animals were running.

Alana caressed the stiffened faces. Her own hardened as it did so frequently now. "Take them outside in the fresh air and burn them. Then destroy the temple. It's no longer in use anyhow."

The Tlaxcalan commander motioned to his subordinates.

"Careful!" she reprimanded them harshly. "They were brave soldiers, too."

While fire consumed the three carcasses, the contingent that fought under Alana's banner of cross and shamrock watched from below. They stood in awe of the black-clad figure, her cape blowing in the wind, her head bowed in the sun, as from childhood they'd been familiar with the *ixtaccihuatl*, the "white woman" who had charge of sweeping holy places and lighting sacred fires.

Alana descended the steps, thinking what a barbarically handsome group the Indians made, with feathers and jewelry and copper-headed spears sparkling in the sun. A few had even duplicated her standard on their shields and shook them overhead.

One man who'd been fascinated with Conn from the first second he saw him brought the stallion for Alana to mount. When the horse snorted and pawed the ground, most of the warriors flinched and stepped back. They were not too comfortable with her man-sized dog either.

Alana placed the flat of her hand against the horse's shoulder and thanked God he had not been the black whose hide was burning. She mounted wearily.

"Rose should be throwing Bayard's colt pretty soon." Alana mused, gazing into the distance. "What a pretty poppet it will be!"

The commander touched the stirrup and spoke briefly. She glanced at the top of the pyramid where a pile of rubble and a column of smoke were all that remained of the horses' pyre. It was time to travel on. She had to keep moving.

Alana bent over Conn's neck, murmuring to him. The stallion tensed, anticipating her command. When she did not give it, he danced in place, curveted, and shook his head so the bridle bells jingled in his ears. He knew the game.

"Now, boyo! Now!"

The hundreds of warriors were taken aback. Was she leaving them? Surely not! They had come a long way from the lake into possibly hostile territory. Their eyes did not deceive them. She was gradually disappearing down the empty roadway with the dog in swift pursuit. Joyous barks roared out of the mighty chest and echoed in the empty streets.

Then the men began to smile and nod. Here she came like a flower on a thunderbolt, no weight at all for the horse to carry. She reined Conn in with a flourish only inches from the commander, who smiled thinly but did not budge.

Alana laughed. The jade-colored eyes studied the men. "I want to go on to Teotihuacán—the Place of the Gods." She paused and made a snap decision. "And then to Tlaxcala."

The buzz of excited comment rippled through the group. They'd been on the go for days; a respite with wives and courtesans would be very welcome. Spring crops and house repairs awaited them as well.

Foodstuffs had been in short supply at the towns they visited. Much of them had been confiscated by, or sold to, Cuauhtémoc, who now ruled Tenochtitlán and was taking precautions in the event of a siege. The young Aztec king had tried three times without success to destroy the brigantines on their stocks. He did not need an oracle from his holy men to tell him they spelled disaster once they were loose on the lagoon which embraced his island-city.

Alana had forbidden looting or fighting in communities willing to join Cortés and swear fealty to Spain. Most of these were inland, just as the largest number loyal to Aztec rule hugged the lakeshore. The Tlaxcalan warriors had accumulated a satisfying collection of luxuries, nonetheless, and each packed gold ornaments or gold dust in goose quills, cloth, featherwork, cacao beans, and gems.

Such prizes could not fill men's bellies, however. They were glad to forage in the vicinity of Teotihuacán where gods had once lived and where the sun and moon were born so long ago. That meant deer to eat and rabbit and grouse. Hunters and fishermen left the group while others went in search of wild honey and berries. Even the small force of hardworking slaves brightened. Maybe there would be enough for everybody to eat, for a change.

The village near Teotihuacán was small and peaceful, but to reduce the chance of ambush, Alana's commander chose to camp among the stone monuments. Here they could scatter and hide easily, coming together later at an appointed rendezvous.

"The men are uneasy," Alana commented, chewing on a meat-filled tortilla. Gawking at the huge monoliths that soared hundreds of feet into the air, she added in a hushed tone, "I can understand why. 'Tis a cemetery of phantoms." Although she'd visited here last year, she was as impressed now as she'd been the first time.

The commander cleaned his teeth with a twig. "The gods were gone from here more years ago than man can count, but their spirits linger."

Birds conversed mournfully in the twilight hush. Finn's ears pricked up at the howl of a wolf. Lavender-gray shadows lengthened as a stillness fell over the land.

Alana was bone-tired. It was the only way she could exist now. To be so exhausted nothing mattered. Her monthly flux had begun before she was discovered on the roof, but the shock of the night's atrocities had profoundly altered her personality.

She rolled up in the warm cape, placed a bolt of cloth under her head for a pillow, and tried to sleep. But the dead city insinuated itself into her imagination, and a wild fantasy took shape. Perhaps on certain moonless nights the shades of Teotihuacán escaped the underworlds? Did they stroll the earth-shrouded tombs between these looming colossi? Did the villagers shiver on their pallets when they thought they heard the faint sound of drums, flutes, and rattles of long-ago dancers?

Alana sat up, anxious and alert. But there was nothing. Only men twisting and turning in sleep and Finn stirring restlessly, haunted by the challenge of ancient foes. She snuggled against him so they lay back to back, and comforted by his warmth and bulk, she eventually slept.

She awoke just before dawn, stiff, chilled, and miserable. The hound had deserted her during the night. Was he pursuing a wolf? The good Lord grant he'd not enraged a pack of them.

Sleep had not refreshed Alana. Her body felt old and stiff, her mouth tasted foul, and her clothes and hair were dirty. How wonderful to reach Tlaxcala, take a steam bath, and get clean! Then there was some serious thinking to do. She had to face it. Brian was dead. There had been no news of him.

The men began to stir. Alana hurriedly got to her feet and walked past a sentry into a grove of trees. After relieving herself, she went several paces farther on into the woods, where she stood combing her hair with her fingers.

Riding through the greenery yesterday, she'd found a measure of peace. Birds had twittered and chattered overhead, and she had even whistled back. Now she turned to admire a deep-red warbler that sat singing in an oak tree growing along a game trail. As Alana watched and listened, dawn filled the glade with a breathtaking pink-gold radiance. Through an accident of light and the position of trees and shrubs at that exact instant, a cross took form on the trail. It glittered with pearl and topaz motes and flickered with the hues of pale seawater and spring leaves.

Alana fell heavily to the ground, one hand outstretched toward the image. "Oh, Lord, have You forgiven me after all? Is this the sign?"

The night of rape had become confused with sin, the sin of Alana Mac-Kenna whose lineage sprang from Ireland's High Kings and who had become a harlot. Living with the Spaniard, making love with the Englishman, losing the child—her defilement had been the punishment and it was right that she be chastised! But now forgiveness blazed in the crucifix of light. A weight lifted from her heart.

Concerned over her prolonged absence, the commander and a dozen men came for her. He helped Alana stand and, like the others, was struck by the radiant expression in her eyes.

"It's all right," she assured the warriors. "It's all right now."

But they were not so sure. They had seen such faces of rapture before. Like their male counterparts, priestesses inhaled, chewed, or drank narcotics to induce hallucinations for religious purposes.

They had to push on this morning, the commander said gravely. She must come eat. She did not eat enough to keep an insect alive. Then they would go. With luck they might reach the northern boundary of Tlaxcala's territory by nightfall and be in the city tomorrow afternoon.

"Come," he urged Alana, guiding her back to camp. A slave brought cold venison, tortillas, and water, but she only nibbled at her food. Finn bounded to her side, wet with dew and eyes shining, and she gave him the leftovers.

"I can't seem to get warm," she complained to no one in particular. "I'm cold inside and out."

"Reaction from the drug perhaps. Here. We have a few containers of *octli* from the last town. That should help." The commander unplugged a gourd and handed it to her.

Alana swallowed the fluid without a thought. Her eyes widened, and her face grew crimson. Then she started to cough and sputter.

"What in the name of Holy Saint Patrick is that?" she gasped in English.

He laughed. She did not have to translate. The intoxicant made from agave sap had a kick you remembered. Law forbade his people from drinking it except at certain festivals. *Octli* was reserved for the aged, the privileged, and those reaching their fifty-second birthday.

"Faith," Alana said contentedly, "it makes a fairly good substitute for Irish whiskey. I can feel it in my toes."

The warriors began readying their gear, kicking and cuffing the slaves. In between drinks, Alana saddled Conn and automatically inspected his hooves. She also examined Finn's feet for splinters or cuts. She had mounted and was regarding the landscape through a rosy glow when the murmur started. Men were pointing at the summit of a lesser pyramid which they'd passed while entering the valley last night.

Alana thought the edifice awesome and bizarre. Stone row upon stone row of huge plumed serpents' heads thrust out aggressively as if attacking onlookers with their fangs. Grotesque faces with snouts and great teeth lunged out, and sculptured snakes coiled everywhere. One felt the horror of the past. The sheer terror and the urge to run and hide.

"¡*Quetzalcoatl* ¡*Quetzalcoatl!*" The legend had never died. It had been bruised and battered by the arrival of Cortés, but since he had not been that god after all, it stood to reason he was still to come.

Alana spurred the stallion to a reckless gallop down the grass-slick avenue leading straight to the pyramid. Her warriors followed at a run. Everyone had now seen the figure standing in the sun on the summit of Quetzalcoatl's temple. The man-god. The warrior-priest. The Plumed Serpent!

It might be anyone. A farmer, curious to see the white woman and her army. A priest up before daybreak to chart the planets. Or an Aztec spy who had followed them. Yet hope flared. *Let it be Quetzalcoatl—let it be he!*

When they reached the foot of the structure, the Indians pooled around Alana, ignoring the horse's hooves. Silence fell. Breezes blew feather headdresses back and forth and flicked loincloths mischievously. Perspiration dried on expectant faces lifted to the dream.

The figure crouched with legs spread wide apart, a titan astride the temple, one that had emerged from the mists of time clad in furs and armed with a brain basher of a club. If it was a god, it was a deity such as they had never visualized! Then the mysterious being raised its club with a blood-curdling yell and leaped down the deteriorating stone staircase, sliding and shouting. The men gathered protectively around Alana and her standard-bearer.

Finn, unable to see the impending threat but feeling the apprehension in the air, pushed through the army to join its vanguard. Hackles up, fangs bared, the hundred-and-seventy pound wolfhound made their hair stand on end.

The figure neared the bottom of the pyramid, sending a cascade of stone, mortar, and earth before him. Finn snarled ferociously, hesitated, then launched himself at the stranger.

From the aerie where he had rested for two days, doing little but eat, sleep, and mend footwear, Brian Phelps could see for miles in every direction. He'd noticed the Indian forces enter the Place of the Gods at dusk the previous evening, but he did not reveal his presence. Better to do that in daylight after he'd found out which way they were headed. He hoped it was toward Tlaxcala.

Brian gnawed on dried fruit and meat without enthusiasm. He had to admit a stern beauty and remarkable engineering skill showed in the necropolis brooding around him. In fact, he had an idea it had once been a handsome city.

But, God Almighty, he was homesick! Homesick for smoky, raucous London and its crowded narrow streets, for haunches of rare beef dripping blood, for foaming ale and white-skinned women. But he could not go back. Not yet. He had a score to settle and a desperate need to replace the money lost in his baggage on the causeway. Otherwise, he could not buy passage home.

How time had flown. The retreat from the capital had taken place last summer. At home right now the hawthorn would be budding, grass growing green as fresh paint, and the luscious springtime beauty unfolding. The man chuckled, thinking of youthful antics and tumbles in the hay.

His thoughts brought Alana MacKenna to mind. Aye, *their* tumbles had been something to write home about! Had she survived that holocaust? For all her femininity Alana was a true Celt when it came to fighting, and she and the man from León had been at the third and last breach when Bayard had been speared.

Suppose she had escaped. How many times he had gone over that possibility! She might be back in Dublin right now, raising her precious horses.

On the other hand, if Salvatierra had survived as well, she might be with him. Brian hawked and spit.

You don't suppose she's still here, do you? You don't think for a minute she's stayed in case you showed up? During the months he was isolated from the army, he'd fallen into the habit of talking to himself. *Because we shared the same ecstasy for a while and I was head over heels doesn't mean she loved me the same way. Or remained faithful. Why should she?*

Gloomily he wondered whether there might have been a child. Alana would have been more than two months gone when the garrison tried to sneak out under the Aztecs' noses. Brian grinned reminiscently. She had never mentioned being pregnant, but she had conceived with their first joining in the gardens, he was sure of it. What a wild night that had been!

It grieved him not to know what had happened to his bonny poppet. If she had been captured and died in Tenochtitlán, he hoped her death had been quick and easy. If she were alive somewhere far away, he wished her the best. A woman alone had a hard row to hoe in the world . . . and perhaps someday he could forget her.

The Englishman rubbed several leg scars with his left hand, trying to ignore the absence of his little finger. Its loss bothered him beyond reason. The young Aztec who chopped it off had been the last of five to fight Brian and a sadist to boot, determined to hamstring the captive.

While recuperating in the territory of the Chichimecas, Brian had planned with grim zest how he would find and kill this Aztec, who belonged to the Eagle clan. He needed a good horse, decent clothes, and weapons in order to join Cortés. He knew the army was at Texcoco, but it would have been suicide to go there directly without arms or a mount.

Brian stared unseeingly at the monuments of Teotihuacán. He saw, instead, the face of his opponent, handsome as any Italian gallant with those melting black eyes women swooned over. That he considered himself the courtesans' prize stud had been obvious from his performance for those in the front row.

"But I fixed the bastard!" Brian exulted fiercely to himself.

Taunting him relentlessly, the warrior had gone far beyond the others. An eerie personal enmity developed, cutting across the ceremony's significance. Though he was on the verge of collapse after vanquishing the other four combatants, Brian had felt pure hate pour new energy through his body.

How long did we fight? I wish I knew. If I'd only been fresh, Brian thought, *I would have broken his back over my knee.* His eyes narrowed. His performance had been amazing considering his condition.

While they were locked in hand-to-hand combat, Brian had slashed his opponent's face with a knife. The scar would run from the hairline at the right temple, across the bridge of the nose and down below the left ear. Indians might value physical mementos of conflict, but this one would never forget that day. *And he won't ever kiss a woman who doesn't shrink from him either.*

The Englishman shook off his painful memories. He'd noticed activity in the Indian camp. If they traveled to Tlaxcala, he could follow at a safe distance. He hoped there were some Spaniards there. He was tired of wrestling with unfamiliar dialects.

Suddenly he leaped to his feet. Was that a black horse? And that smaller black animal a dog? Brian could see a rider swinging into the saddle, a dark-clad rider with what might be a light-colored headpiece. His whole being grew taut. Could it be Alana? Nonsense! It was merely one of the Spaniards on patrol or an Indian who'd learned to ride. Yet his heart thudded with excitement and hope.

Then the shout went up. "¡Quetzalcoatl! Quetzalcoatl!"

"Aye," Brian shouted back, "come see your god with the red hair and red beard. Come worship Eyes-from-the-Sky and bow down before the child of your sacred sun." Being mistaken for this god was nothing new. He'd soon learned it meant the best food and accommodations and the prettiest and most avid women.

The horseman approached at a gallop, leaping obstacles with a daring Brian had seldom seen equaled. He shot across the ancient city as swiftly as an arrow. Men ran behind in a column like the arrow's shaft and those remaining fanned out on both sides like its feathers. When they arrived at the foot of the structure where Brian stood, they ringed their leader. A standard with cross and shamrock fluttered in the wind.

Alana. Praise God from whom all blessings flow—it was she! Brian's chest tightened. He could hardly breathe. He tried vainly to speak. His eyes were filled with her, so small and valiant on the mighty horse and so cherished by that barbaric escort. She was staring up at him with her mouth open.

Irrepressible joy surged from deep within him. It tore through his vocal cords and turned into an unintelligible bellow. Shaking his war club at the sky, he shouted and guffawed in a delirious burst of relief and happiness. Then he tried to hurry down the crumbling stone staircase, but the risers were high and the treads shallow. He had to slow down. A broken neck would be an ironic climax to their reunion!

Stumbling down the final grade and digging in his heels to keep from falling headlong, he hit the ground off-balance. The wolfhound's onslaught almost sent him to his knees.

"Finn! Finn! You old rascal, you! For God's sake, Finn, you've grown into a big fellow!"

Fighting off the dog's affectionate greeting, Brian gradually progressed through the group of men. Smiling now and talking, they parted to let him through and then closed behind him. They shrugged good-naturedly. Not Quetzalcoatl, after all, but a warrior to be honored. They'd heard how he'd fought and won against the best Aztec champions in Tenochtitlán.

Brian finally arrived at Alana's stirrup and gripped a booted ankle in one hand.

"Hello, Irish."

She was stunned. For how long had this walnut-brown face with its cornflower-blue eyes obsessed her? Brian Phelps. Was this really the man she loved? This tough, fearless savage with muscles hard as oaken planks and a chest crisscrossed with scars?

He had changed. She could tell. Captivity, battles to the death, life among fierce scalp hunters. . . . This was no longer an English lion but a Viking *berserkr*. Her hands trembled.

She had wanted him and had risked her life to find him. Yet now that he held her ankle in his viselike hand, Alana felt frightened. Would he be the same as the others?

His eyes made her cringe; they were so shrewd, hard, and merciless. They were the eyes of a man who'd been to hell and back. Yet they grew more familiar as laughter began to melt their coldness.

"I'll be—why, you're drunk as a lord, Irish! Come here! Come to your Brian!" He reached up for her, and she fell into his arms. They kissed tentatively and then passionately. When they drew apart, Alana started to cry.

"I knew it! I'd have been disappointed if you hadn't done that." Brian held her tight. "At least I'm not wearing a doublet that will shrink."

He was being facetious, concealing worry. Alana's pale hair was as dirty as her fingernails. He smelled perspiration and unwashed clothing, and both Finn and the stallion were unkempt. Things were not as they should be. Obviously a firm hand was needed and at once.

Alana patted him like an old person touching a young one. She murmured under her breath and tried to smooth her hair away from her face. Brian suddenly became aware of how thin she was and that her forehead burned against his lips.

A middle-aged Tlaxcalan with an air of authority walked through the press surrounding the couple and saluted. He spoke to Brian hesitantly in Nahuatl. After almost ten months during which he had had no contact with his own kind, the Englishman had learned the tongue passably well.

"This woman is in no condition to be riding the countryside."

The man raised his eyebrows and glanced at Alana, who wept softly against Brian's chest. He looked up at the tall white man. "Who can tell her what to do and what not to do?"

Brian gave a bark of amusement, wrapping his arms more securely than ever about Alana. "I should know that."

Then he gestured with his head at the hundreds of warriors waiting for orders. "What battalion is this? And why is she with you?"

"We are Xicotencatl's men. We volunteered to escort her when she went to the towns in Cortés name. And to ask for information about you. She is a warrior's woman!"

The commander added, "We should be on the trail, my lord, not standing here. I have very little information on the enemy's strength in this region. I am most anxious to get into the mountains."

"What's your destination?"

"Tlaxcala."

"Good. Let's go. You can answer my other questions later."

Alana drooped like a wilted flower in Brian's arms. Poor little sweeting, she needed her man to take care of her. Brian wondered what she'd been drinking.

He slapped Conn's neck gently. "How about it, my black friend?" The stallion nudged the man inquisitively, smelling and lipping his bare arm.

"Make up your mind. We can do it the easy way or the hard way." Brian grasped the pommel.

Alana spoke for the first time. Her husky voice cracked. "As long as he's carrying both of us, I don't think he'll fight you."

"I thought you'd lost your power of speech, woman," Brian whispered, putting his cheek on top of her head and crushing her to him until she wiggled in protest.

"Oh, I can hardly wait until we're alone, Alana. I'll make up to you for every minute, every day and night . . . "

"What makes you think I missed you, Englishman?" She hiccuped and giggled. "I want you to have some of this *octli*. It's made of green lightning!" She peered around. "Where's that gourd I had?"

Brian mounted, reining the horse with an uncompromising hand. "Help me get her up here." How good it felt to have a fine animal between his legs! He had missed his loyal Bayard many times.

The commander placed Alana's foot in the stirrup and boosted her within the other man's reach. Brian grabbed her around the waist and pulled her into position in front of him. When he had circled her snugly in the crook of his arm, he said, "We're ready when you are."

Brian smiled down on his beloved burden. Thick lashes rested peacefully on the lightly tanned skin, and there was a faint snoring. Safe at last in his arms, Alana had passed out.

He threw back his head and laughed. He was ten feet high! A youngster with the world at his feet! He had found his woman. Now for gold—and his revenge.

XXVII

The Indian noble wandered through the gardens, gloomy and disconsolate. He paused in a grove of dahlia trees he'd developed through hybridization to twice his height. Last autumn the entire court had praised the amazing blooms whose width had been broader than two hands.

Xicotencatl slumped down next to a pool edged with alternating sections of bright-orange marigolds and crushed green rock. A statue of Xochipilli, god of flowers, presided over it; moss had begun to sketch velvet sandals on his feet.

The pride and enjoyment he had known in the mauve-pink, yellow-centered dahlias would not come again this fall. He knew instinctively he would not be alive to see them. An odd sense of impending doom saddened him, one that went deeper than a warrior's desire to perish in battle or on the sacrificial stone.

After all, he would go to paradise after such a death and there become a companion to the sun alongside other immortals. After four years he would be reincarnated as a hummingbird . . . and would perhaps come back to this very garden. Xicotencatl made patterns in the crushed rock with his fingertip. If the garden still existed then.

Life was about to change drastically for everyone. Because Cortés would reduce Tenochtitlán and grind the Aztecs into the rubble of their city like grains of corn under a stone roller.

Xicotencatl and his Tlaxcalan forces were Cortés' right arm. A certain dour condescension twisted his mouth. The man could not win without them. Yet he feared the Spaniards as a long-term proposition more than he had ever feared the Aztecs. The young chieftain had felt ambivalent about the situation; now his growing inclination was to go over to the Aztecs, his own race, even if they *were* the enemy, and resist the white men to the end. But he knew it was far too late for that.

A slave appeared to remind him of the banquet that would begin shortly. His wife knew he always lost track of time here. He rose to gaze for perhaps the last time on the trees and flowers, the herbal plots and botanical experiments. Part of his spirit would remain here forever.

Cortés had sent a message, asking for the fifty thousand soldiers Tlaxcala had promised, advising that the thirteen brigantines were to be launched with elaborate ceremony on April twenty-eighth. If those men could be in Texcoco by then, they would be a welcome part of the festivities with their white brothers in Christ. Otherwise, they should arrive as soon as possible. Praise God, The Virgin, and Saint James, the struggle was about to begin!

As he walked toward the banquet hall, Xicotencatl met Brian Phelps, now suitably clad in European garments. The men saluted and grinned.

"Have you been furnished with whatever comforts you need?" the Indian asked.

"More than enough, thank you. The only problem I had was getting clothing to fit. Most of the Spaniards are smaller than I am by far, but the women managed to alter a few pieces and put together a decent outfit."

Brian shook his head, now well groomed and barbered. "I was certainly glad to get rid of those untanned hides! It seemed as though all the lice in Chichimeca territory had taken up residence in them!"

The Indian and Anglo-Saxon made a handsome contrast as they went through the streets, though similar in their military bearing.

"Have you seen your son?"

Brian stopped, startled. "My son?" Teeth flashed in the chestnut beard. "She didn't tell me we had a son!"

His companion continued awkwardly, "I may have spoken out of turn. The woman who bore your child is the widow who stayed with you when you first came here the winter before last."

"Oh, the one with the—" Brian described the woman's physical attractions with his hands.

"Exactly."

They laughed, but Brian sobered quickly. "I've left a few offspring here and there like any young bucko. But I had hoped. . . . Damn, I had hoped."

Xicotencatl knew only too well the disappointment and frustration the words implied. When his beloved Yellow Plume wasted away and died, his sorrow over not having conceived a child with her had been deep.

"Look," he said, "it is not my place to tell you, but women can be so strange—"

Brian snorted. "Is that the only word you can think of?"

"I think I should tell you Alana was pregnant when she came here last July after the retreat."

"I wondered about that, but I suppose the night she suffered on the causeway could make any woman miscarry."

"No, it happened when she fell down the steps of a *teocalli*. A Spanish priest was with her at the time, but I have always suspected that he frightened her and caused her to fall. I hope he isn't typical of the holy men who are being sent to us from Spain.

"He took her prisoner right after the man she was with had left for Vera Cruz. The priest swore she was a witch and said she was wanted in Cuba for committing a crime. Of course, none of us believes *that*. Thanks to her guards' looking the other way, she escaped the first night, and I sent her into the mountains to hide."

"I didn't know any of this. There seems to be a great deal I don't know about. Tonight she's going to tell me what's been going on or I'll turn her over my knee."

The Indian was taken aback. "Is that a punishment you administer in your country?"

Brian roared. His companion's jet-black eyes glittered with amusement as the Englishman described what he meant.

"There they are." Brian waved at Alana, who stood waiting beside Corn Flower at the back of the hall.

He grinned wickedly. "If you don't see me for a few days, my friend, you'll know I am busy undoing the damage of that fall."

Xicotencatl smiled. "As soon as the troops get here from their farms, I am leading them to Texcoco to meet Cortés. Until then you won't see me either."

They shook hands, enjoying a special bond.

"If those aren't two little boys bent on mischief." Alana spoke more to herself than to Corn Flower. Nothing had ever been proved, but she was still convinced Corn Flower had murdered Moctezuma's beautiful courtesan. Because Alana was a guest at the family table tonight and in memory of past friendship, she felt obliged to be more courteous than she would have been under less formal circumstances.

The Tlaxcalan watched her husband approach, so handsome and virile it made her vitals ache. He had disciplined her for Yellow Plume's death. Oh, how he had disciplined her! He hadn't touched her once since the whore died four months ago.

He visited lesser wives often enough; they became more arrogant every day, preening and insinuating that she was no longer welcome in his bed. Now he was going off to war, and she had a sinking feeling that this time he would not return.

"Men are often like little boys," she agreed quietly. "Cruel, thoughtless children."

Xicotencatl halted in front of her with his back to the room so their faces were concealed from prying eyes. He studied her, watching the flush rise from throat to forehead. She was wearing pale rose this evening, the color he liked best. Fireflies glimmered like living jewels in the shining blueblack hair, coiffed in the latest style with two glossy loops above the forehead like small horns.

Corn Flower was not only the most gorgeous of his wives, but also the most aristocratic. She knew ways of love he felt eager to enjoy once again. Not only that, but this wife had produced excellent sons from those silken loins. The last seed he planted must be in the most excellent soil.

His heart softened. Her last child had been stillborn. The gods had punished her far more severely than he had. It was time to forgive. He despised what she had done, but he understood her behavior. Not every man was privileged to have a woman kill for him.

Xicotencatl said something Alana did not catch. Corn Flower paled and swayed toward him with a sigh of joy, her breasts touching him momentarily. She fastened radiant eyes on the stern face and replied shyly.

Alana did not hear the words. She had walked away. Such intensity threatened to crack the protective shell she'd developed during her lonely journey through recent months.

The banquet was still going strong at midnight. Poets recited, people danced to flutes and gongs, and guests consumed huge quantities of chocolate and tobacco.

No such cordiality prevailed in Alana's apartment, however, where she and Brian were alone for the first time since meeting at Teotihuacán. When they'd ridden into Tlaxcala, Inmaculada immediately took charge and gave him strict orders not to disturb Alana for a few days. Her regimen included sleep, rest, and regular meals but no men. And that was final. So Alana would know she was in his thoughts, Brian had sent enormous bouquets to her room and bathed and groomed her animals. Pleased to learn she was well enough to attend the banquet, he had fully intended to continue being solicitous. Yet when she came through the hall to meet him, he knew he could not wait much longer.

She was wearing an old dress he remembered, a pale-green silk trimmed in brown fur. The material slithered along her long legs, accentuating the inner thighs. Her ample breasts moved tantalizingly under a cape of silver fox tails. Brian sighed. He was falling in love all over again.

In the privacy of her quarters Alana changed to a high-necked tentlike garment of tangerine cotton. It lent a subtle color to her face, and its very shapelessness seemed to give her confidence. To Brian, however, the robe only made her more enticing.

He watched her pace back and forth, now and then revealing ankles and neatly shod feet. A vague uneasiness crept over him. This was a stranger who prowled the room, a dangerous silver kitten with green eyes that smoldered, yet were cold. No, not a kitten any longer but an adult feline with claws and teeth who had learned to defend herself and even to kill when necessary.

Brian had been deeply touched by her determined quest for him and impressed with her audacity. Riding the countryside, courting danger and discomfort when she really had no reason to hope he was alive. . . . Few men could boast a woman so loyal. Yet Alana was wild and rebellious by nature, a spitfire who loved adventure. Maybe she had only used him as an excuse to wander around, collecting treasure and accumulating slaves. He understood she now owned branded slaves and an expensive house in Texcoco.

He stepped in front of her to halt the restless pacing. Alana bumped into him, shying like a nervous mare.

"Hold still a minute." Brian buried his face in her hair. It smelled like honeysuckle. He ran a palm over one breast, closing his eyes as desire flooded through him.

"Alana, I love you."

She moved away quickly, heart hammering with his nearness, with the sensual, slightly cruel mouth and the curly beard glinting reddish gold. It was all she could do to stay away from that magnificent body.

But she panicked at the thought of intercourse. Painful sensations hurtled through her mind and made her pulse race. Calloused hands mauling her, spittle dripping on her skin, a penis invading her. Alana shuddered.

Aware of her fright, Brian reached out and pulled her close for comforting. It seemed natural to cup one buttock and press his groin to hers.

"Don't."

"Why not? Do you realize how long it's been since we made love?" Brian was piqued, but he released her. Maybe he had not been romantic enough. After all, they had not seen each other for almost a year. In a sense they were starting over. Then, too, it was late, and she was fatigued.

"All right, darling, all right. Get a good night's rest, and we'll talk tomorrow." He put out a brawny arm and gathered her to him again, ignoring her struggles. "But I get a kiss before I go."

She pecked his mouth primly.

He jeered. "Do you think I'm some milksop to settle for that?" The sapphire eyes glowed with ardor. "You're forgetting I know you right down to your little toenails."

She blushed but kept her face turned away.

"Remember what you said to me in the garden?" He shook her gently. " 'I am thy scabbard, Sword of Love!' You can kiss better than that!"

"Let me go, you big ox. Let me *go!*"

"Only if you kiss me good-night," he insisted genially.

"No."

"I won't be able to sleep if you don't."

"I don't doubt you'll find someone to comfort you."

Brian agreed. "Aye, I could."

"Faith, get on your way then! Go sleep with the widow. She would be glad to have you."

So that was how the wind blew. Carefully Brian said, "I am sorry about the babe, Alana. But I can only thank God you were not killed. We can always make another child."

"That's what Inmaculada said."

"How did she get into the conversation?"

"You've never liked her."

"Certainly I like her! Don't get Salvatierra's ideas confused with mine."

Alana pushed him away tiredly. She walked to the other side of the room near Finn and turned around. Brian was startled to see how remote and dispirited she seemed. "Please go. I have nothing more to say."

"Very well," he replied stiffly, sketching a bow. "Good night." As he stalked out of the room, he thought he heard an echo of his words.

Or had it been good-bye?

The colt was so young he had to spraddle his legs in order to remain upright. They traveled everywhere except where he wanted them to go. In fact, his mother often had to position herself in his way so he could nurse.

The dead Bayard's son peered shyly past his parent. Her bulk protected him from the creature making those interesting sounds, but his curiosity was as strong as his legs were wobbly. He took a few steps into the open, batting fawnlike eyes at the visitor.

"Tell the little sweetheart it's all right, Rose. Tell him I won't hurt him." Alana approached the colt confidently, caressing the mare and whispering soothing words. She had not slept well after the encounter with Brian, but being among the horses relaxed her, and wooing the adorable youngster had brought a smile to her face.

"That's the way I like to see you." Brian leaned on the stockyard fence. He wore a loose shirt open to his waist and a gold crucifix glittered against his ruddy chest hair.

"You mean wading in manure?" She lowered her eyes.

"No, with a smile on your face, you minx." He watched her touch the colt as gently as a butterfly alighting. She really had a way with animals.

"I can see Bayard's bone structure, can't you?" His tone was easy, gentle, one horse lover to another.

"Oh, yes. He'll be a hair more graceful, I think. Not a big fellow who carries armor but one light as wind singing over the moor."

"I want to talk to you." How incredibly charming she looked this morning with the silvery hair in long braids tied with orange ribbons. She wore a riding costume he'd always liked, a cream-colored linen shirt tucked into russet pants wide as a skirt and boots and jerkin to match them.

"We did our talking last night." Alana followed the colt's awkward journey toward the fence. "The only thing I didn't say was—if something should happen to me, I want you to have the animals."

"You're making mountains out of molehills. Why should the Inquisition be interested in you? It's that bishop who's causing the trouble. But if you'll feel better, of course, I'll take care of them."

After kissing the colt and his mother, Alana sighed. She supposed she had to leave the security of the stables and start thinking about how to get back to Ireland. Brian had not mentioned marriage; indeed, he never had. But even if they returned together, he would not keep a harlot like her for very long. She was sure he could have any woman in London he wanted.

She closed the gate behind her and strolled toward the orchards. "What did you want to talk about?" They passed Indians going about their daily chores, and Alana noticed Brian's smile. It lingered long after the person he had smiled at was gone.

"Well?" She paused beneath the apple trees, and blossoms drifted onto her hair and shoulders. In the dappled shade her skin gleamed ivory and gold, but he noticed a fine line between the emerald eyes that was new.

There was no simple way. He had to take the plunge and use all the winning ways he possessed. Brian took her hands idly and raised them to his lips.

"This morning I learned something else about you I didn't know."

Alana glanced around, not really listening. She wondered if this was the place where Fray Mateo had tried to seduce her. Blessed Lord, that was all men wanted.

Her attention finally settled on Brian. "Is that so?"

"I find out more about you from other people than I do from you." He held her hands tightly now, anticipating her pulling away from him.

"Inmaculada tells me you were . . . raped not long ago. Throughout an entire night."

"That was confidential." Alana's voice shook with agitation.

"She was right to tell me. You can't keep a bad experience like that locked up inside you. That's what friends are for."

"I'll never tell her anything again."

"Nonsense. Something like that is poison, and the only cure for poison is an antidote."

Alana stared at him. "No, I won't." Her face had gone dead white.

Brian put his arm around her shoulders and began guiding her out of the orchard toward the guesthouse where their separate apartments were located. She hung back, holding onto a tree.

"Don't," he insisted. "I've made up my mind. We need each other and want each other, and I know we love each other!"

"You've made up *your* mind!" She kicked him in the ankle hard enough to make him swear. "Let me go, you conceited bastard! Let me go or I'll scream!" Red started to stain her cheekbones.

"I wouldn't do that."

"Brian, it's broad daylight."

The Englishman smiled at her so sweetly her knees quivered. "It won't matter, will it?"

In her bedroom Alana panicked. He towered over her, huge and powerful, just like the other one. Her insides hurt. She could not go through with it! She tried to dart around him, but he blocked the way.

"Stop acting foolish, Alana. Act like the woman you are, not like a silly girl."

Brian undressed her so quickly she was naked within seconds. Then he pushed her down on the pallet and covered her with a blanket.

"You're not going to let that filth ruin your life, are you? I'll bet he's been blabbing about his conquest to anybody who'll listen, describing every detail of how he worked you over." Brian was taking his clothes off. "Don't let him get away with it."

When Brian slipped under the blanket with her, he was astonished. Alana was shaking like a leaf in a gale, and her flesh flinched from contact with his. "Na, na, darling, Brian won't hurt thee. Thou art my love!" What had that bully done to her?

She pushed his hands away, miserably aware of the clean, fresh smell of him and the warm, solid refuge of his arms. "Please. Please."

Brian stroked her back, taking care not to touch her lower body. He talked soothingly, took the ribbons out of her hair, and unplaited the braids. He kissed her face and throat, never forcing her to respond.

Damn that crossbowman to the depths of hell! This made another score to settle. He'd once threatened to amputate that organ the Silician thought so much of. *He'll wish he'd never looked at her when I get through with him.*

Alana froze in terror. A silken hardness against her thigh scorched the skin. A scream rose in her throat.

"I'm not made of iron," Brian admitted hoarsely.

A heavy weight slowly descended on top of her. A man's heart beat rapidly against her breast, and her own leaped violently. Who had taken her maidenhead? This man? And who had hurt her while she lay on the floor? There had been women, terrible women, fondling her and the nightmare of a hairy ape who'd mounted her again and again and again—

"No!"

Brian clapped his hand hard over Alana's mouth. "For Christ's sake, Irish, you sound like a banshee. Now relax. Relax. It's going to be fine. You've just forgotten how nice it can be."

He smiled at the eyes pleading with him over the edge of his hand. He did not want to hurt her, but he had not faced this dilemma before. Women were generally beating the door down to get into bed with him. Even the virgins he had deflowered had only offered token resistance.

The self-control he'd maintained since lying on top of the glorious body he knew so well began to dissolve. Holding her down, trying to keep from being bitten, he forced her legs apart. Brian almost laughed aloud. What a wildcat! She excited him so much he forgot everything but his own needs.

He had difficulty entering, yet once he rested in the passage, its tissues melted around him, a bud closing moistened petals on its pulsing center. Brian removed his hand, parted the still lips with his tongue and kissed Alana as he had dreamed of doing for so long.

Moaning, she tightened on him, and he took her in such an explosion of ecstasy he felt it in every muscle. Through a haze he heard Alana weeping and whispering love talk as she began taking part in the movements of her exorcism.

Brian thrilled with exultation and decided to stay right where he was.

XXVIII

Alana crossed herself as she and Brian rode past a corpse hanging by its neck and moving ever so slightly in the breeze. Downwind there was a stench of body wastes that had attracted the big black vultures. They hovered patiently overhead. These scavengers were accustomed to hunting for meals; here they had one ready-made.

"Who's that, the Lord save us?"

"Some fool who didn't know when he was well off. He was the ringleader of a group that's hand in glove with Narváez and the governor of Cuba. They'd planned to murder Cortés and his lieutenants and take over the army."

"The governor of Cuba is a conceited popinjay." Alana remembered his peeking into her bodice.

Brian glanced over his shoulder as the rope creaked. "What made him or anybody else think they could step into Cortés' boots, I can't imagine."

The couple had ridden into Texcoco earlier in the day. They were now following a path alongside a canal that ended at the shipyard. From there it was necessary to reverse direction on the opposite side of the waterway in order to reach the street where Alana's house was located.

They traveled slowly, examining the final touches being made on the canal. Eight thousand laborers had worked two months at top speed to enlarge a stream originating in the palace gardens and emptying into Lake Texcoco. Equipped with dams and locks and shored up with masonry and lumber, the mile-long canal now measured twelve feet wide and twelve feet deep. Tomorrow, April 28, 1521, Cortés would proudly launch the navy he called the "key of the war."

"Isn't that a sight!" Alana admired the brigantines. Fully rigged and ready to sail, they looked like predatory birds whose heads were tucked under their wings.

She saw Cortés strolling among them while he conferred with the shipwright, every inch the conquistador in black velvet, red cape, and shining armor. His new seven-man bodyguard surrounded him, ready to die for their leader.

When the Englishman and his mistress rode by, Cortés touched the rim of his morion courteously. He had watched them coming for quite a while. It was nice to see people in love.

Alana waved and smiled. "He has eyes in the back of his head."

"We're not exactly hard to miss," Brian remarked dryly.

He reached across the space between their horses and seized her by the elbow. "Where's that house of yours? I'm so hungry I may have you for supper. I think I'll start with your toes—"

"Oh, you oaf." Her pulse quickened at his touch. "There it is. See? The one with stone lions at the door. But let's go down the alley to the north to a stable I had constructed. Don't get your hopes up about food, though. The slaves may be gone by now."

"We can always go back to the soldiers' mess." He fingered the hilt of his sword. "There's a man there I want to find."

Alana said nothing. The crossbowman deserved what was coming to him, not only for what he'd done to her but for what he'd done in the past to other women—and might do again in the future.

When they rounded the corner, they were surprised to find a horse already munching corn in the makeshift stable as well as baggage stacked nearby.

"Isn't that Pepe's horse?" Brian asked as he dismounted.

"Yes," a voice answered, "and that's about the sum total of our possessions."

Inmaculada swept out of the house with a contrite Pepe in her wake. The

Maya's eyes burned with anger. "We never dreamed we would get here before you did. We're sorry to make ourselves at home without asking."

"Why, you're welcome. You know that," Alana replied. "We decided to get the horses shod and have Brian's armor enlarged before coming to the house. It won't be long before the army moves against the Aztecs, and he wants to be ready."

She glanced at her lover. To lose him so soon! He was champing at the bit, anxious to reimburse her for the diamonds that had outfitted him and to replace the money he'd lost on the causeway.

"That's exactly why we're here. So Pepe can risk his life to get the gold back he's gambled away. Just when I thought we were going to Spain!" Inmaculada burst into tears and hurried into the house.

Brian said, "What did you do? Try your luck with those cardsharps I warned you about?"

"Do you mean to tell me you've gambled away the gold bars Moctezuma gave you when you were married? And her jewelry, too?" Alana was aghast. She thought of the wealth that had wound up in the bishop's hands. Why, if she still had it, she would guard it with her life, not hazard it on dice or cards. She glared at Pepe Ortega and rushed past him to comfort his wife.

The culprit helped Brian unsaddle and groom the horses. Then he played with Finn for a few minutes. "At least you're my friend," he grumbled, pretending to box the dog's ears.

"Don't take it so hard," the Englishman advised. "There's so much gold in these towns every one of us will be a rich man when the war's over. Even after the fifth that goes to your king."

The Spaniard brightened. "You really think so?"

"Haven't you seen the loot from Xochimilco? It's magnificent! And we haven't even started yet. You'd better be careful about gambling though. Cortés has forbidden it."

"He has? *Por el amor de Dios,* the men have always—"

"Exactly. That's why they're always broke. And besides no gambling, there's to be no blaspheming, no treating the allies badly or leaving camp without permission. You're not allowed to remove your armor or sandals, even when you're asleep. And any booty you take must be reported on pain of death." Brian walked toward the house, unfastening the rewelded cuirass as he went. "I doubt I can be so obedient."

"I suppose he has to lay the law down with this collection of rough-necks. We aren't angels."

"You're so right." Alana had changed her clothes and stood in the open patio, instructing the slaves to prepare a guest room and start the evening meal.

Four female slaves had elected to stay, hoping she would return. Their villages were destroyed and their families scattered; here they had found kindness and stability. They gaped at the man with Alana and smiled behind their hands. He would give her sons!

Brian grinned at the twittering. He was used to it. What a shame to brand them. To wear the mark of the iron to your grave—how he would hate those who had done it!

He sat down in a crude chair Alana had had made. The whitewashed house, with its flowering vines and potted plants, was warm and cozy.

She had even had a regular table built on which she was arranging a cloth and dishes. Her house, though temporary, had the aura of good housewifery Brian identified with women in his family.

Alana turned to him, and his heart beat faster. He would have given a year of his life to be in a London salon with her on his arm, both of them elegantly dressed and faced with no more serious decision than whether to go gaming or to bed. He could be an important personage at court, too, if he could just get back to England and tell the king and Wolsey what was going on here.

"What *are* you thinking about? Your eyes turn such a deep blue when you're concentrating."

She perched on one knee and fussed with a loose thread on his doublet. When he did not answer, she kissed him. Since he'd destroyed her ground-less fears born of rape, she had been as hungry for him as a bride. Alana had not put it in so many words, but she was grateful to Brian for his compassion. He'd sensed that she was insecure and required constant assurance of her worth as a person and a lover.

"Don't do that, woman, unless you're willing to go without supper."

"That I'm *not* willing to do!" She jumped up, escaping his eager hands. "We have had a very long day, and I am famished."

"Don't forget we have to be up early," he teased. "The brigantines are to be launched tomorrow, and you said you wanted to attend Fray Ol-medo's early mass. Can't be a slugabed."

"In that case we must retire as soon as possible," Alana agreed solemnly, but her eyes shone.

After Pepe and Brian had gone, the women tried to occupy their days with household tasks and roof gardening, but their hearts and minds were across the lake with the army and their men.

The Maya girl agonized that she had sent her husband to war without a good-bye kiss. She should not have been so stubborn! But she had been so hurt and angered by the unexpected weakness he had displayed. Yet suppose he died and she had not kissed him good-bye! A stalk snapped in her fingers.

Alana brushed the hair out of her eyes with the back of her hand and carefully made depressions in the dirt for seeds. She was vexed by Brian's orders to remain in Texcoco like an obedient pet. Staying safely in the background while he fought for their future was not her idea of helping. There were services she could contribute. She could cook for him, mend clothing, tend his wounds, care for his horse, hide any gold he found. . . . Why, Brian had no idea how useful she could be. Faith, she wanted to be with him!

But he had insisted he did not want her anywhere near the action. The subjugation of Tenochtitlán promised to be bloody and vicious, and he had enough to worry about without being concerned about her welfare. Alana was to stay home and out of trouble!

She stood up to peer into the distance. Though the Aztecs were great fighters and brave men, the Christian attackers were equally fervent and steeped in fanaticism.

Since February, 1519, Cortés and most of his men had been conducting a holy crusade in the name of the Infant Jesus and His Holy Mother. The military campaign to win wealth and fame for each conquistador and an opulent Indian empire for the Spanish king ran such a close second to winning millions of souls for the Church that cross and sword were often indistinguishable.

Alana knew the valiant defenders of Tenochtitlán did not stand a chance. It was only a matter of time. Their besiegers boasted a navy, a strategy, cavalry, cannon and musketry, and a horde of vengeful allies. As auxiliary Aztec towns around the lake saw the noose tighten, hundreds of thousands more would join Cortés. The final conquest of the Mexica-Aztecs would be spearheaded by fewer than a thousand Europeans and their downfall assured by people of Indian blood.

"That's all I feel like doing, Alana. Stooping so long makes my muscles ache." Inmaculada straightened up with a palm splayed at the small of her back.

Alana rubbed her nose and sneezed. "This pepper plant! I give up, too. Let's wash and take a walk. Anything to get out of the house!"

"Where do you want to go?"

"Oh, we could wander through the library and the archives in the palace and watch the old codex makers. They're interesting to talk to. One of them told me that until a few months ago the Texcocans had a council of the arts. It passed judgment on teachers' qualifications, music, poetry, astronomy, oration, histories—that sort of thing. He also said those two rulers—you know, the father and son with those never-ending names—were avid patrons of the arts."

Inmaculada smiled. "Nezahualcoyotl and Nezahualpilli. The Hungry Fox and the Prince-for-Whom-One-Has-Fasted. The poet-lawmaker and the law enforcer."

"By Saint Bridget, these names are a mouthful! In any event, not, mind you, that I'd compare a heathen place like this with it, but the high regard for learning they had here was rather like Kells Abbey in my country. Our priests kept the Latin and Greek tongues alive long after Rome fell."

Inmaculada was descending the stairs. "Rome?"

"Oh, it's a city far, far away."

The women bathed and dressed and met later on the patio. Inmaculada was shaking wrinkles out of a *huipil*, which she handed to Alana.

"I've been so upset I forgot to give this to you. I found it at the hospital with Yellow Plume's other things."

Alana examined the garment. It was the purple one. "It's certainly lovely." She rubbed the fabric between thumb and forefinger. "Feels almost like silk."

"I believe it's fine cotton blended with rabbit hair."

"How do they get the vivid purple color?" She admired a geometric white embroidery done in bands at the neck and waist. The work on these was so thick and heavy they appeared to have been lightly padded in an effort to provide backing.

"The dye is from shellfish and is very rare and expensive."

Alana held the blouse to her heart. "Why did she want me to have this? What was so important about it? Poor darling, I suppose she was mixed up from being so sick."

Inmaculada hugged Alana impulsively. "I think she loved you."

"Love!" Alana exclaimed, clutching the dead courtesan's parting gift. "That's really what it's all about! And whether Brian Phelps likes it or not, I'm going to join him as fast as I can. I don't know if he's at the southern causeway with Cortés or the western one with Alvarado, but I'll find him."

"You might be killed."

"By all the saints, if Spanish women can take it, an Irishwoman can!"

Inmaculada protested that she could not go alone. It was at least a two-day trip to the north around the lake and then south to Tacuba. Sandoval had not yet been able to whip the region to the south into shape, and she could not go by water. Aztec canoes waited in ambush for anyone rash enough to attempt that route.

A wave of energy and excitement had galvanized Alana. "Now don't get upset. Two hundred Spaniards just rode in from Vera Cruz and are quartered at the palace. They can hardly wait to baptize their swords and fill their pockets. I'll ride with them and act as guide."

"But I can't go with you," the Maya said unhappily.

"Of course not! And endanger the child you're carrying? Pepe would be furious. And you mustn't stay here either. You had better go back to Tlaxcala, where you'll be perfectly safe."

Alana headed for the stable to check the saddle gear. "When you get there, will you keep an eye on that one-armed soldier Pepe hired to look after Rose and her youngster? If he's the one I think he is, he's part horse, but he also hits the wine bottle too much."

"Pepe said the man had spent several years at the royal breeding farms on Hispaniola. He thought he could be trusted."

"I hope so. The old sot will wish he'd never been born if anything happens to my horses." Alana frowned. "And tell Corn Flower I send my deepest sympathies. It was a blow to hear about her husband being executed. He was a good man. I was very fond of him."

Xicotencatl the Younger had been hanged in the square of Texcoco shortly before Cortés and his forces left the city in early May. His unexplained desertion had delayed the attack on Tenochtitlán, but such a serious breach of discipline could not go unpunished. Other discontented rebels, white or brown, had to be discouraged from such foolishness; every man was needed now.

Cortés, who had admired but distrusted the fiery patriot, had considered the execution a distasteful task. The Tlaxcalan had been the only one to turn his back on killing his own. A man had to respect that.

"It's the living who suffer, not the dead," Inmaculada reflected. "I understand his lands, slaves, and possessions are being confiscated by the Spanish crown. Corn Flower and her children will have to move in with relatives."

"Her life fell apart when Cortés came," Alana murmured sadly.

For the first time in months Inmaculada thought of Ah Tok, her young Maya husband. A wave of uncontrollable hatred swept through her for the woman who stood beside her and for those others who had crossed the seas and changed so many innocent lives, including her own.

"You turned pale. Are you ill?"

Inmaculada smiled shakily. "Oh, no. It was nothing. Just—just a pain in my heart."

XXIX

Standing in the center of the city on its highest *teocalli*, the Aztec generals studied the situation. Tenochtitlán was blockaded and under siege. The three principal causeways connecting the city to the mainland had been captured and invested by the enemy—Spaniards and Tlaxcalan dogs whose allegiance was to the foreign conquerors.

A fourth causeway paralleling a freshwater aqueduct into the capital from Chapultepec had been cut off in mid-May, almost a month ago. This loss had created an increasingly serious water shortage because of the lake's brackishness.

The captains discussed the precise information furnished by spies who'd slipped across the lagoon during the night. Sandoval was poised on the northern causeway at Tepeyac. His forces included twenty-four horsemen, four musketeers, thirteen crossbowmen, one hundred and fifty infantry, and perhaps thirty thousand allies.

On the western causeway at Tacuba blue-eyed Tonatiuh, Pedro de Alvarado, crouched like the huge, golden feline he was. He had thirty horsemen, eighteen musketeers and crossbowmen, three hundred infantry, and another twenty-five thousand allies. This had been the street of shame over which the Spaniards had fled stealthily last summer in the middle of a rainy night. Alvarado no doubt hoped to erase that memory forever with steel and shot.

Magnificent feather headdresses fluttered in the wind as the Aztecs transferred their attention to the great avenue bisecting the island and extending into the lake to become its southern causeway. More than two miles away, others fed into into it, coming from Coyoacán in the southwest and Ixtapalapa in the southeast. Stone watchtowers surrounded by twelve-foot-high walls had been built at the junction of the causeways to act as the capital's first line of defense.

Unfortunately the Spaniards had made this fort their command post, bringing cannon ashore from their ships and constructing additional shelters for their men. The officer named Olid had divided his forces, composed of thirty-three horsemen, eighteen crossbowmen, one hundred and sixty foot soldiers, and twenty thousand Tlaxcalans. Half remained at Coyoacán to guard the army's rear, and the other half came to the fort to join the valiant Spanish leader, the man the Aztecs wanted more than anyone.

Hernán Cortés, wily as the snake and courageous as the jaguar. Malinche. Each general would have flung himself to death on the pavement below if that would have guaranteed the conquistador's capture. No one wanted him killed. On the contrary! There were surprises in store for him: being painted black and blue, being crowned with a paper tiara and provided with a cardboard shield and sword, and—the juiciest joke of all—being placed under the influence of narcotics to make him play the fool so the city could see how far the mighty had fallen.

Only then could the high priest have the the honor and pleasure of cutting his heart out and offering it to the gods in the stone Eagle Dish. After that the man's skin would be flayed, and his arms and legs would go into the cooking pot with peppers and tomatoes; his torso, of course, was destined for the zoo.

Such a prospect buoyed their spirits. The military leaders grinned and nodded, and sunshine glinted on gem-studded lips, ears, and noses.

Perhaps they would also force him to witness the death of that horse he always rode, as well as the men closest to him—and then his mistress. They must think of something out of the ordinary for her. And they could not underestimate these whites who showed such disregard for discomfort, pain, or death. They cauterized wounds with hot oil on the battlefield. They marched and fought like demons for hours, even days on end, as at Otumba. They wept with emotion and bowed down before those strange idols of theirs and then rose up like wounded mountain lions at bay.

One had to be cunning to trap a crafty serpent. What an Aztec Cortés would have made!

Brian Phelps did not give a fig about converting superstitious natives. He never had. What they did was their business. His entire being was concentrated on just two things: killing the man whose face he had scarred in gladiatorial combat and laying his hands on as much gold and as many jewels as he could find and hide. There would never be another opportunity like this one.

The Spaniard from León, who had never quite recovered from the *Noche Triste*, stretched prostrate beside him. He was exhausted by the day's foray right into the sacred precinct and up to the top of the largest *teocalli*. Cortés must be part goat the way he ran and leaped, and he was in his thirties, too. It became a matter of pride to keep up with him. And with the Englishman who was equally tough. Made of iron, both of them.

Like his companions who sat, slept, or sprawled wearily around him, the man from León wore full armor. He had removed the dented helmet for the moment because of a bad headache. Brown hair curled damply against his scalp, and dried blood made an arc over one eye. He had got off easily this time.

"Is there anything to eat?" His belly was growling.

Brian grunted. "It's the usual. Tortillas, cactus fruit, and what passes for cherries around here. There was a bit of fish, but it's long gone."

Pepe Ortega, who was bandaging a lance cut on one arm, amiably suggested what the Englishman could do with the food. His answer was just as ribald, and laughter rippled through the barracks.

"How long do you think this will last?" someone asked idly.

"Who knows? These Aztecs are tough and strong-willed."

"I took part in the siege of an Italian castle once. Took two months to crack it. They were down to rats and their own piss by then."

"We divided half a ton of powder three ways, I hear. Will that be enough?"

"They're defending homes, families, and sacred ground. It's different from fighting them on the mainland. And let me tell you, taking a well-fortified island is a huge job.''

"But, *Madre de Díos*, don't forget the gold and silver waiting for us in there!''

Talk flowed back and forth in the drafty building as Brian yawned and closed his eyes. He slumped in a corner out of the wind. Their quarters were not yet completed, but any shelter was better than none.

The summer rains had started, making life miserable for men and horses alike.

What was Alana doing? Brushing that moonbeam torrent of hers? His hard mouth softened. How he loved that woman! He was glad she'd been amenable to staying home, where she was safe.

The night before he rode away with Olid's men, Alana and he had approached the ecstasy of that first time in the garden. In a way it had been better, thanks to new and more mature passions. Brian's body was much too tired to feel the tiniest tremor in the loins, but his mind's eye ranged over her image with sensual delight.

Those eyes dominated her personality. Sometimes they seemed to smoke with green fire, and other times they were like fresh spring foliage. And that skin, so milky white. Brian never ceased to marvel at it. Her mouth in its many moods, her graceful, competent hands, the lovely ankles and pretty toes. The long legs and her—

"Say, Pepe, are you asleep?"

"Not yet."

"Have you or your friends spotted the crossbowman yet?"

His friend whispered, "No. I think he's with Sandoval, as far away from you as he can get."

Brian chuckled coldly. "He's wise to be. Because his days on earth are numbered."

Pepe knew exactly what was going to happen to Alana's rapist if the Aztecs did not kill him first. He crossed himself. Filth like that deserved to be exterminated. The man reminded him of a rabid animal that foamed at the mouth; they both spread death of different kinds.

But that was not his problem. He shrugged and tried without success to get comfortable in his armor against the damp stone wall. What an ass he'd been to gamble away their tidy fortune. No wonder Inmaculada had been so furious. Pepe did not blame her, but he was upset that she'd refused to kiss him good-bye. He protested that he might be killed but she had kept on storming at him in a way completely alien to her normally solemn but sweet nature.

Pregnant women had their moods, he understood that, and Pepe Ortega knew well how much she loved him. A satisfied expression crossed the dark Moorish face as he drifted off to sleep. It was going to be a boy. A son to tell his sons how their grandfather fought at the side of the paladin of New Spain, the Great Conquistador, Hernán Cortés.

Alana rode into the fort at midday with most of her escort intact, although a number of men had splintered off to join Sandoval or Alvarado. She was surprised at the unceasing labor required to keep an army in the field. Porters trotted in and out with supplies. A band of them had accompanied her party, bringing in bales of tortillas from bakehouses that had been established at Tacuba to feed the ever-growing host of combatants.

Indians unloaded building blocks from brigantines for the barracks, and Spanish armorers and blacksmiths pounded and clanged on forges and anvils, repairing weapons and cuirasses. The cavalry would need plenty of horseshoeing tonight, too.

A few badly wounded men were in a corner with Isabel Rodríguez in attendance. Tying her horse to an unused anvil, Alana hurried to join her.

"What are you doing here?" Isabel gave her a little smile and then ripped the edge of a cloth between her teeth so she could tear it in half.

"The same thing you are." Alana stared with horror at the charred stump resting in the woman's lap. "God have mercy, Isabel!"

The nurse said grimly, "They *will* sear with hot oil or the hot iron. *I* think clean water, bandages, and the sign of the cross are better." The man screamed and quivered with agony when she touched the blackened flesh. The slaves had all they could do to restrain him.

"It will take months for that burned tissue to separate and come away, and the shock drives some of them mad. They wake up raving."

Off in the distance Alana heard a constant din. "Are they in the city? How far have they gone?"

Isabel finished applying the bandage and rinsed her hands. "Come outside."

The men who had ridden with the Irishwoman trooped along, tired but excited. When Tenochtitlán had come into sight earlier in the day, they could hardly believe their eyes. It was a barbaric Venice, a fairyland of luxurious temples and palaces with stucco gleaming like silver in the sun.

Standing beside Isabel, the spectators saw occasional flashes of musketry and columns of dust and smoke. "They forced their way into the suburbs a few days ago and went right into the area where they lived last year. You were there then, weren't you?"

Alana nodded, eyes wide and heart pounding painfully. She had been seized by a premonition of great danger. What was wrong? Was Brian fighting for his life while she stood here doing nothing?

"They had to do it over again this morning, I hear. They'd filled in the canals so the men and horses could walk across, but the Aztecs opened them up again during the night." Isabel paused to wave at men in a brigantine tacking near the fort. Indian corpses hung like grisly trophies from the yardarms.

A newcomer exclaimed, "Ships here in the mountains! Astounding! Have they been useful?"

"Cortés says he couldn't have done without them. Their crossfire on both sides of the causeways drives the dogs back into the city. They sail day and night, running down war canoes and cutting off supplies from friendly towns. Sandoval and Alvarado each have vessels, too."

She blushed as a sailor yelled a compliment that his companions echoed with cheers and laughter. "They bombard the shore when the infantry attacks, bring in provisions for us—Yes, *señor*, they are useful. "

Alana said, "I must find Brian."

"Don't be a fool. You can't go in there. It's hell on earth."

The green eyes blazed. "He needs me! I can feel it!" And before anyone could interfere, she ran back to the stallion, untied his reins, and vaulted into the saddle.

"*Adiós!*" she called to Isabel. "Go with God!"

The southern causeway was like the others, made of huge stones laid in cement, raised well above the water and wide enough for eight horsemen to ride abreast. Alana found herself alone on it except for Finn, who trotted confidently behind the horse. The brigantine crews were made up of soldiers, and many of them recognized the blonde who'd taken part in their adventures. And had had some of her own, by the mass!

"Want to trade me for that Englishman?"

"How about a ride, sweetheart?"

"You'll find it hot and heavy in there! Better go back."

"What do you think you are? A Spaniard?"

Alana threw back her head and laughed aloud, feeling an odd, reckless exhilaration. The long pale hair streamed out behind her as she cantered across the causeway, Conn's hooves thundering on the stones.

Several crewmen crossed themselves. *Perdición*, if she didn't look like a witch speeding into the flaming city. . . . Later some vowed the Irishwoman and her familiars actually flew from fort to island. *Dios*, the brigantines weren't even able to keep up with her!

When Alana entered the suburbs of Tenochtitlán, she found the reed and mud huts of the poor deserted. The better homes of red *tezontle* block lining the avenue had been leveled by Tlaxcalan work crews. These building materials were being dumped into the city's canals as fill in the absence of the drawbridges which the Aztecs had removed.

Alert and cautious, Alana felt no real fear until she neared the sacred precinct in the center of the capital. She suddenly remembered with dread how the Aztecs had hunted her in this area the night she ran away from Gilberto. The night she'd stabbed and killed a man and met Brian in the gardens.

Where could he be? What peril was he facing? He would very likely beat her within an inch of her life for disobeying him, but she could not help it. He needed her—she knew it in her bones—and she was here.

Conn reared excitedly when a disheveled woman with a small child under each arm darted out of the ruins. Her eyes started from her head and she screamed without sound. Alana started to speak, but the woman bolted down a side street.

The stallion pranced nervously, smelling the smoke of burning buildings and hearing the racket of battle. Alana had her hands full controlling him.

She knew exactly where she was now, proceeding along the eastern wall of Moctezuma's splendid palace and approaching that of his father, where the army had originally been quartered. It had already been fired. Spaniards ran here and there with torches, yelling like crazy men, destroying the place where they themselves had been blockaded and which held so many unhappy memories.

Cortés trotted into sight riding Morcillo, his favorite war-horse and one of the immortal sixteen that had come with the fleet. He pointed in her general direction, and soldiers with torches ran toward the aviary which stood nearby.

"No! Oh, no! Not the birds!" Alana made her way to the conquistador.

"What are you doing here?" The fine dark eyes were as cool as ice. "I can't spare any men to protect you."

"I'm looking for the Englishman." She motioned wildly, shouting to make herself heard above the growing noise. "*Must* you burn the aviary?"

"I haven't seen him." Cortés reined his mount away from her, giving orders to kill the large animals in the zoo but to release the smaller ones.

He glanced quickly over his shoulder. The first wave of men had seeped into the street from the sacred precinct. Musket fire rolled continuously, horses whinnied, and the shouting was deafening. The Aztecs were half out of their minds with hate and fury that he'd been able to penetrate to the heart of the city so quickly. He was almost at the end of his reserves for the day, however. All his men were wounded, and most of the horses as well. Better to retreat and fight again.

Alana held on to his sleeve. He jerked it out of her grip. "It grieves me to burn it. As God is my witness, it does! But I must!"

Of all people, she should know the significance of birds in Aztec worship. This would be a severe blow to the Indians. As for the birds—he pulled rein a second. The wood and bamboo enclosures had caught fire, and the cries of the feathered innocents seemed meant for his ears alone.

Cortés compressed his lips and put spurs to the stallion. Every fiber in him protested the destruction of Tenochtitlán. He had thought it a glorious and majestic creation from the first second he laid eyes on it. He now had no doubt the inhabitants were going to resist to the last man, but he planned to offer peace terms at every opportunity.

Alana looked around frantically. What a fool she'd been to think she could find Brian in this melee! She had forgotten how really big the city was. The army was funneling her way, however, back toward the southern causeway with cavalry acting as rear guard. She would wait until the last moment. He must show up! He must!

An anguished outburst from the dying birds wrung her heart. From atop Conn she was able to see only too well. Tears of pity and outrage stung her eyes. She couldn't just sit there. There was still a little time.

Alana jumped impulsively to the ground just as a stray arrow embedded itself in the horse's rump. Screaming in pain and terror, Conn jerked the reins from her hand and galloped back the way they had come. At least he was headed for the fort and away from the Aztecs. Holy Saint Bridget, that put her in a bad position!

She pulled her dagger and ran to the aviaries, many of which were practically in ashes. Others were beginning to smolder, and she rushed from one latticed gate to another and opened them. Small groups of birds darted out and vanished into leaden, smoke-filled skies. Most were unwilling to desert mates and nests, however. Confused by the stinking pall enveloping immaculate bowers, they huddled in abject beauty and were consumed by the flames.

Two figures stumbled out of the keeper's quarters, coughing and crying. A passing soldier menaced them with a sword, and Alana saw that death would have been welcome to the old man, whose entire existence had revolved around the aviary. The woman Alana had bought for him supported the keeper, her face tight with fear.

He clutched four of the rare quetzals to his wizened breast. Their yard-long tails fell forlornly almost to his ankles, scorched and smoking. The birds' eyes were closed in shock or death, and the ruby and emerald heads rested against his familiar flesh like inanimate ornaments.

"Aye," the voice quavered, "the plumes of the quetzal . . . the works of iridescent jade . . . they are all broken and gone . . . all broken and gone." The keeper's eyes passed over Alana blankly and the couple staggered out of her sight.

Alana had done all she could. The army was fighting its way back foot by foot, and she knew she must get to its rear or be caught in the maelstrom.

"Alana! Where did you come from?" Pepe Ortega appeared at her elbow, panting with fatigue and holding the hilt of a sword broken in half.

She stared at her friend. "Where is he? Oh, Pepe, where is Brian? I have to get him out of here!"

"What in God's name are you doing here? I thought I was seeing things." Pepe glanced around anxiously.

Alana took hold of him and shook him so hard his teeth rattled. "Tell me! Where's Brian?" she screamed hysterically.

"You missed him! He's already back at the fort. He took a spear in the thigh and couldn't walk, so he was sent back with the badly wounded. And that's where we're going! He'll break every bone in my body if anything happens to you!"

Pepe grabbed her arm and pulled her along, unresisting now and slack in his grasp. "Brian's safe. Do you hear me? He's safe. Come on, let's get out of here!"

Then, without warning, they were cut off from the main body of troops by a unit led by an Eagle Knight. A fierce bronzed face glared out of a helmet which imitated the beak of a fantastic bird.

"Oh, Jesus and Mary, don't desert me now," Pepe prayed, half supporting Alana with one hand and waggling the damaged sword with the other. They were in real trouble unless help came within the next few minutes.

Finn barked and snarled, dashing back and forth in front of them, putting his bulk between the enemy and his loved ones. He feinted, slashing and threatening, mammoth mouth open and dreadful. Warriors poured into the courtyard where Pepe had been driven. Someone threw a javelin that pierced the wolfhound's body, pinning him to the ground. His roar of agony as he writhed vainly trying to dislodge the spear brought Alana out of her trance.

"Hurt my darling dog, will you? I'll kill you for that!" She sprang at the Eagle Knight. Taken completely off guard he fell backward onto the ground with her on top of him. The dagger sank into the hollow of his throat, and he vomited blood.

Four warriors seized her, shaking their heads in amazement. She must be crazed by the fighting. Who would cry over a dog?

The serpent-skin drum on the great *teocalli* had begun to boom its funereal message. The time had come to sacrifice any prisoners taken today.

The Eagle Knight's unit gathered around their captives, fingering the female's hair. They were not certain, but this might be the foreigner wanted by the high priest.

As she and Pepe were led away, Alana tried to look over her shoulder at the wolfhound. *Oh, Finn, my faithful boy!* She wept as she kicked and bit and scratched. *Oh, Finn!*

Pepe and Alana had to be dragged up the steps to the summit of the truncated pyramid where Savage Serpent presided over his complex of altars and jewel-encrusted, blood-plastered sanctuaries. Neither of the prisoners could have walked at this point; horror and dread robbed them both of strength and will.

The Aztec high priest had fasted and prayed and mortified his penis with thorns in order that the gods might grant him the person of Cortés. He had even abstained from the handsome boy who was so enamored of him. Still, his city would survive, and there would be plenty of opportunity to apprehend the Spaniard.

But now . . . *now!* . . . he was going to deal with the woman who stood before him, gasping for breath and trembling in every limb. She was not so arrogant now that Moctezuma was not here to protect her. Savage Serpent would have danced with joy if his knees had not been so swollen and sore. At last he had her in his power! She would not escape death this time as she had in the past.

Here more than a hundred feet above the street, it was not necessary for him to raise his voice. Savage Serpent purred malevolently, "I told you our paths would cross again. . . . "

He gestured with triumph toward the concave stone altar, darkly stained with the life blood of thousands. "Now you will die."

Alana could hardly bear the sight of his filed teeth and ghastly hair. She gazed instead out over the Valley of Mexico and to the south, to the fort where her beloved Brian lay wounded. The man she had not been destined to have, after all.

Enormous gray and black clouds scudded toward the lake from the mountains, and thunder cracked loudly. Lightning rent the storm clouds as though the Aztecs' savage deities were slashing at them with knives. Gusts of wind tugged at Alana's hair and shrieked around the sanctuaries, blowing out sacred flames in the braziers. They sounded like banshees, she thought grimly, come like those supernatural beings to warn of impending death.

The die was cast. Any fool could see that, and she realized she was no longer so afraid. By all she held holy, she'd go out like other MacKennas before her—with a prayer on her lips and her head held high.

Alana looked at Pepe Ortega and smiled tremulously. He smiled back, bound and shaking in his boots but brave and cocky to the end.

"God bless us and keep our loved ones safe from harm, dear friend," she said, lifting her face to the first raindrops.

"Amen," he responded, trying without success to keep his eyes away from the altar.

"And this is for both of us, Pepe."

Summoning all her remaining strength, Alana stepped up to the high priest and kicked him in the knees.

BOOK FOUR

The Aztec's Slave

Thou art slave to fate, chance,
kings and desperate men.
—John Donne,
"Holy Sonnets," X, 1.9

XXX

June, 1521: beneath the great temple pyramid of Mexico-Tenochtitlán

Pepe Ortega heard the Irishwoman weeping quietly and wished he could hold her in his arms to comfort her. If they could only see one another, that might help, too. But the prison beneath the main *teocalli* was black as the pit and the wooden cages too far apart for them even to clasp hands.

He really should blame Alana for his predicament. Resentment and anger almost overwhelmed him when he thought of the son he would never see. Then the fatalism of the Andalusian won over, and Pepe shrugged. She had come to rescue Phelps out of love, and he, Pepe, had tried to save her out of love. Surely there was no better way to be remembered.

"*Amigo.*" The voice seemed tiny in the blackness.

"What?"

"Are you frightened?"

Pepe answered truthfully. "My bowels turn to water thinking about what's going to happen—"

Alana heard the tremor in his words. It was her fault, his being here. She would never forgive herself.

"They'll give us drugs to deaden the pain," she said lamely.

"That's decent of them."

She was quiet for a while. Then she began to talk about Brian, about Inmaculada and the unborn child, about her horses and gallant Finn, of Ireland and other things close to her heart.

Pepe reminded her of the night they had stolen her horses from the bishop's stables, and he smiled fondly reminiscing about his honeymoon at
Chapultepec in Moctezuma's palace.

"We have had good times."

"Aye, that wc have," Alana agreed.

The hours passed slowly. To their surprise, both slept a little, and then
they prayed together. It was impossible to know how long they had been
imprisoned; they were suspended in a time zone of sheer terror.

Then Alana murmured in consternation. A faint glow had appeared
which was brightening by the second. Someone was coming with a torch.

"It must be dawn!" As if to confirm her guess, conch-shell horns blew,
waking the city to another day of war.

"Oh, God, have mercy on this miserable sinner," Pepe whispered as he
crossed himself and kissed the crucifix hanging around his neck.

"Blessed Mary, remember Your servant in her time of need," Alana
pleaded haltingly. Her heart pounded. If only Savage Serpent had
sacrificed them yesterday right after she'd kicked him! It was just like that
devil to let them agonize through the night.

Their prayers faded as four burly guards armed with clubs entered the
cell. They were followed by two elderly priests, who carried with them the
stink of decayed flesh and dried blood. Each bore a golden cup.

"Do you speak our language, woman?"

"At least we're getting a royal farewell, Alana. Look at those cups!
Worth a king's ransom!"

"He wants to know if I speak Nahuatl."

"You know what you can tell them to do as far as I'm concerned."

The old man repeated his question impatiently.

"Yes, I understand the tongue of the Aztec dogs," Alana replied
haughtily.

They hissed softly at the insult but regarded her uneasily. The golden-
green eyes glittering like those of a trapped animal had hypnotic power.

Suppose this strange female was a witch of an unknown kind? One that could change into an awful beast right before their eyes? Aztec sorcerers were capable of such a metamorphosis—she might be equally cunning.

Pepe started to chuckle. "They're afraid of you, by the mass. *They're* afraid of *you!*" He went into a fit of mild hysteria and laughed so hard he brought tears to his eyes.

Alana shook the bars of the cage and tossed her head back and forth so her braids writhed like pale serpents.

"Don't you know I'm a black magician? Perhaps I shall turn into a war-horse and trample you to bits!" She menaced them, pretending to scratch at their coppery features.

She saw into men's souls! The gleaming cups were hastily shoved close to the cages. "Drink this. It will make you want to sleep." How anxious they were to nullify her spell!

"What's this?" Pepe asked.

"The narcotic I told you about. They want us to take it so we'll be drowsy."

Pepe grabbed his cup and threw its contents into the priests' faces. "You'll wait until pigs grow wool before I drink that, you boy-loving bastards."

A fifth guard arrived. "He wants the prisoners brought to him right away."

"Take them!" the priests snarled in unison.

The guards yanked Pepe and Alana from the cages and bound their wrists. Then the captives were hurried along a stone corridor, up roughly hewn steps and into the open near the staircase of the colossal temple pyramid dominating the island-city.

Pepe's gaze traveled fearfully over the blood-smeared facade of the edifice where he was about to die. How he regretted his folly! He wished now he'd swallowed every drop of that narcotic. His stomach churned, and he retched violently, but the Indians jerked him between them like a rag doll and started the ascent to the summit.

Above them Savage Serpent shifted from one foot to the other, trying without success to alleviate the excruciating pain in his knees. He was in a foul mood this mid-June morning, and lesser priests had made themselves as scarce as possible until needed for the sacrificial rites.

Never, in all his years at the altar, had a victim attacked him . . . until yesterday. His pulse hammered with hatred and fury. That woman had viciously and deliberately kicked him, hurling defiance at his authority, doubting, in fact denying, his awesomeness. That he had fallen, writhing on the stone floor—humiliating himself in front of everybody—had hurt nearly as much as the injured knees. He had originally planned to sacrifice the bitch immediately, but after the incident Savage Serpent had ordered her and her friend imprisoned for a while to think things over.

Looking up, Alana saw the high priest as a scarlet-clad predator in a robe decorated with black skulls and crossbones. When it blew against his body, wasted and abused by starvation and drugs, the hem fluttered to reveal skinny shanks. An enormous headdress of blue and red parrot plumes gave him the aura of a gruesome bird anticipating the delivery of hapless prey.

As she approached the top of the staircase, his half-mad eyes stared at her triumphantly. She straightened instinctively. Alana MacKenna would show these heathen how the Irish died!

Now that the participants in the daily drama of feeding the sun god had arrived, not a moment was wasted. The first rays of heavenly fire had already touched the ornate sanctuaries. Priests dressed in dark green and black ran back and forth to assist Savage Serpent.

Pepe struggled desperately, trying to hurl himself off the summit rather than suffer dismemberment after death. A holy man distinguished by earlobes hanging to his shoulders was aghast at such lack of decorum. He snapped his fingers, and a young novitiate blew fine powder off his palm into Pepe's face. His gray eyes glazed almost immediately, and his head fell forward.

The priests untied him, removed his doublet, and spread-eagled the unresisting Spaniard on the convex altar. Four of them seized ankles and wrists, pulling down in order to arch the chest and expand the ribs. Savage Serpent now chose an obsidian knife and ran a long-taloned thumb along its edge. He raised his arm, and Alana sank to her knees.

"Gentle Mary, brilliant diadem, pray for us! Pray for us that Your Son will forgive our sins. For the sake of the Fair Babe conceived in Thy womb, for the sake of His cross that will one day rise over these abominations. . . . "

She had closed her eyes but opened them when she heard an odd sound, a soft, hair-raising sound. The killer-priest had plunged the blade into

Pepe's breast right above the heart. With an expertness born of continual practice he had severed the chief veins and arteries with one stroke.

Savage Serpent dropped the knife, broke the ribs apart and plunged both hands into the chest cavity. As he wrenched out the still-beating heart of Pepe Ortega, hot blood spurted like a fountain, sprinkling corpse, executioners and altar. Onlookers nodded approvingly. The sun god should be pleased!

When her friend's blood splattered Alana, she shuddered with revulsion and pity; tears sprang to her eyes. His dead arm brushed her as they picked him up and threw the remains down the steps to the waiting butchers.

Alana's hands and feet were like ice, and her strength was draining away. Even prayer would not come to her lips. She had developed a horrified fascination for the diabolical scenes taking place around her.

Chanting paeans of praise, Savage Serpent held Pepe's heart up to the rising sun and then dropped it into the huge stone Eagle Dish on top of those taken the day before. Priests scattered fresh flowers here and there; a man dabbled fingertips in Pepe's blood, patting it into his gore-matted coiffure with the delicacy of a woman at her toilet applying perfume to her curls.

Whirling around and praying that they would kill her while her back was turned, Alana gazed down at the lake. Cortés' brigantines were sailing swiftly along the western and southern causeways which were dark with hordes of Indian invaders headed for the suburbs of their enemy's city. Punctuated by cannon fire from the ships, the hum of thousands of voices steadily increased in volume. Although she realized there was no possible chance of rescue, her spirits soared to see the army advancing. Alana turned, shaking a fist at her executioner.

"You Indian devil! It won't be long before you die yourself!"

He limped toward her slowly with a sinister smile. The words had been spoken in her tongue, but the tone was unmistakable. The priest felt a reluctant admiration for her courage.

They now stood face to face, the Aztec hunched against the wind, aching with disease and fatigued from severe fasting, the Irishwoman poised with arms akimbo, having been untied preparatory to sacrifice. Sweat beaded the white forehead, and she trembled visibly. Yet her lips moved in what he surmised was prayer, and she held herself proudly.

"Your time has come, warrior woman." He signaled.

Without warning a young priest grabbed her hair, and another one blew powder into her nostrils. Alana could not avoid breathing it in, and as she succumbed, she saw clouds of incense rising into the crystal air and feathered standards quivering in the breeze like butterflies at rest.

Gradually, her muscles relaxed, and her eyes closed. She felt her upper clothing being removed and tried to cover her breasts with her hands. Then there was a chill, hard surface underneath and a bright light in her face.

Laughing, Alana reached out to the sun god, her Sword of Love, whose eyes glowed more azure than the sky and whose embrace was stronger than death.

The young Aztec garbed in Eagle Knight regalia carried himself with the same pride and arrogance for which he was known in battle. He crossed the square swiftly, on his way to the *teocalli* where his uncle was officiating.

Tlacateotl tongued a broken tooth as he strode along. The white woman being sacrificed today had done that at the aviary. Because he would far rather face the fierce Otomis than a dentist, he had never had the tooth repaired. Now it had become a jagged symbol of revenge.

Revenge for being rejected and kicked like a dog or slave—but especially revenge for the scar her red-haired lover had dealt him when they'd fought in hand-to-hand combat last year. His primary purpose in watching the woman die was to see justice done. An eye for an eye and a tooth for a tooth. A pitiless expression that might have passed for a grin crossed his face.

Tlacateotl climbed the stairs and stepped onto the floor of the pyramid's summit, which was large enough to accommodate a thousand people. He recalled with bitterness how Cortés and his soldiers had fought their way up here shortly before Moctezuma died and again only a few days ago. The first time they destroyed the war god's bejeweled image, and the last they stole a golden mask from the new figure. He ground his jaws with frustration at such sacrilege.

A cluster of priests was gathered at the altar. Perhaps she was already dead. The warrior felt a twinge of regret. Too bad. She might have been interesting. But then, as he saw Savage Serpent's hand rise into the air,

Tlacateotl pushed in among those who were not holding the victim's limbs. He wanted a closer look at this ceremony.

The high priest glimpsed his nephew across the woman's alabaster-white flesh but thought nothing of it. After all, this sacrifice had a certain novelty; he could sense the well-disguised emotions of those around him. His arm tensed to strike.

"No." Tlacateotl's grip was unbreakable.

The priests drew in their breath with amazement at such audacity. Had he been crazed by battle? He was defying the gods! He would bring disaster down upon their heads!

"What do you mean—'no'?" Savage Serpent glowered at his valiant, but very foolish, relative. "Let me go," he commanded.

Tlacateotl released his uncle. How fragile those old bones were. He could crush them as effortlessly as the eggs of a lark. Yet he was aware of the rock-hard, implacable will inside that frail shell which had brought Savage Serpent to his pinnacle of power.

Alana moaned, and the Eagle Knight suddenly wondered why he had meddled. Certainly not for sexual reasons. She was a wretched sight with mouth open and eyes half slitted like an anesthetized animal. Half man from the waist down with legs encased in cloth and boots and half woman from the waist up . . . a very unattractive combination.

He touched the broken tooth absently with the tip of his tongue. Yes, that was why. Revenge. He had almost forgotten, he had been so astounded by his own actions.

"If you are quite finished, nephew. . . . " The sarcastic tone jabbed at him.

"No, I am not. I have urgent information about this prisoner you should know before proceeding."

"What *is* it?" Savage Serpent groaned inwardly. His knees were throbbing. Each rainy season they grew worse, and the physicians had exhausted their remedies. That kick had not helped matters either.

The warrior motioned respectfully, the plumes in his headgear dancing as he moved. "I must deliver that information in private."

"Oh, very well." The high priest cautioned his helpers to keep the victim sufficiently drugged until he returned and then hobbled after the younger man.

Tlacateotl walked across the great platform to its southern edge and studied the progress of Cortés' troops. They had been delayed once more by
having to refill canals with debris before crossing.

"They are as determined to get in here as ants into the honey pot."

His uncle nodded irritably. "Yes, yes, I know. But we have brave men
like you to see that doesn't happen. Now what's this information you're
prattling about?"

"That was only an excuse to talk to you alone. I want the white woman
for my slave."

"*What*? Are you out of your mind? I can't offend the gods that way!
You know that!"

Savage Serpent's nephew fingered a jade plug inserted in his lower lip.
"I had hoped you would be more cooperative."

The high priest almost lashed out at such insolence, but the young warri-
or's soulless black eyes sent a shiver down his spine.

"What do you mean?" he asked warily.

Tlacateotl leaned on his ten-foot spear with disarming nonchalance.
"Don't you think the Great Lord Cuauhtémoc would be upset, to say the
least, if he knew the head of the church was addicted to *octli*?"

His uncle started, and his tattoos sprang out in vivid blue against the sallow skin. How had the whelp discovered that? The entire Aztec priesthood
was dedicated to poverty, celibacy, and abstinence. Any deviation from
these vows meant swift terrible punishment. The very minimum he could
expect would be facial mutilation, removal from office, and banishment.
No, the Great Lord would probably order him strangled or disemboweled.
Thought of the disgrace after a lifetime of service to the state sickened him
more than anything else.

His drinking had begun innocently enough. He had asked his physician
for an analgesic for the increasingly painful arthritis. Then in a moment of
despair and anguish he'd swallowed *octli* which had been sent by mistake.
There had been no going back. He had never been drunk. Drunkenness was
forbidden. But *octli* helped him through those endless nights when his
knees refused to bend; it lessened the terror of the stiffening disease as it
crept through him inexorably, locking the rest of his aging joints.

Thanks to his supremacy in the religious hierarchy and to advancing
years, the high priest no longer rose so frequently at night to supplicate the

gods or to do penance. Taking a drink, therefore, was more easily managed. He had been careful to clean his mouth with wood ashes and honey and use a mouthwash, too, but someone had reported his lapse to his nephew. Which meant that a spy had been instructed—and no doubt paid—to keep an eye on him with blackmail in mind.

"You can't prove it. Even if it were true."

Tlacateotl smiled. If it could be called a smile. The scar that began at the right temple crossed the damaged nose bridge and finally terminated below the left ear. The plastic surgeons had been unable to avoid pulling down the right eye's lower lid, revealing its red-veined, unprotected inner lining.

The Eagle Knight no longer possessed the sensuous handsomeness that had once charmed his many willing conquests. Although women did not spurn him, neither did they put themselves in his way. The scar knifed far deeper than his physical appearance. He made love only in darkness now, so his strong, virile body might drive thoughts of the ghastly face from his partner's mind.

Tlacateotl's eyes flared with hate and misery, and his uncle took an involuntary step backward.

"Oh, I can prove it. What would you say if I told you there's a gourd of *octli* hidden in the base of the brazier in your room? And another cleverly fitted into the underside of your private altar?"

Savage Serpent flushed with rage. One little mistake, and now he would never hear the last of it.

"What reason am I going to give for not sacrificing her?"

"You'll think of something. Say she's a prostitute. That she's not worthy of acting as a messenger to the gods."

His uncle pondered a few seconds. "I suppose that would cover the situation. What are you going to do with her?"

Tlacateotl turned toward the immobile prisoner. Her hip-length hair fell in a silvery curtain, moving sensuously in the air currents.

"What am I *not* going to do with her? Her lover is with Cortés. My men saw him only a few days ago. Later, after we capture all the foreigners, you can kill them both. In the meantime. . . ." He paused significantly.

The young warrior scowled at his uncle. Having the whip hand over one of Tenochtitlán's most important men was very heady stuff, but the time for polite threats and conversation was over. He had to get his unit into action.

"See that she is delivered to the women immediately."

Savage Serpent inclined his head, hiding the animosity and dislike in his eyes. He would not forget this.

"It shall be done."

XXXI

Concubines who slept with unmarried warriors ordinarily enjoyed their own elegant quarters in the House of the Joy of Women. Because of fighting that had raged in the vicinity of that building, the women had been moved to another location. Unexpectedly uprooted and transferred to unfamiliar surroundings, they were disorganized and suffered from a sense of impermanence.

Although furnishings were scarce in any Indian residence, each concubine had been accustomed to her own room with arrangements reflecting her tastes and those of her lovers. Now the siege had forced them into a smallish structure, where they had to wait in line for daily baths and each one had to share a room with another woman. Tempers were on edge by the time Alana MacKenna was delivered to "those who gave their bodies for nothing."

When the temple guards dropped her onto the patio floor, she tried to stand up. Groggy from the narcotic, Alana struggled onto her hands and knees. Fingers grabbed her hair and yanked her head back.

"Why are you dumping this rubbish here?" a voice demanded.

"The high priest told us to. He was going to sacrifice her, but then he stopped the ceremony," a man's voice answered.

"Why?" The fingers released her, and Alana sank back on her haunches, her scalp tingling unpleasantly. Where in the name of Saint Bridget was she?

"How should we know? When Savage Serpent tells us to do something, we do it!"

Alana's eyesight began to clear, and she scrutinized the women gathered in the garden patio. She had thought for a minute this was the royal harem. Now she saw what it really was—the house of prostitution where warriors kept their mistresses.

Most of the courtesans were pretty, and a few approached real beauty. Some were rouged and dyed their teeth red, while others affected no cosmetics. Many wore their hair loose, though the more fashionable arranged it in two hornlike loops over the forehead.

Rich, delicate clothing glowed with embroidery, fringe, and feathers; jewels gleamed on ears, breasts, and arms.

Indian courtesans, unlike European whores, enjoyed a certain social status and were officially designated the warriors' companions at public festivals and religious observances. Pampered and proud to be desired by the mightiest men in the army, they were not about to put up with any competition.

"What are we supposed to do with her?"

"I know what I'd do with her."

"She could use a bath. Have you ever noticed how white people stink?"

"Should we lock her up?"

"Here comes Tlacateotl. He'll know what to do." A flurry of perfumed skirts parted to reveal the Eagle Knight.

He stared down at Alana broodingly. He was familiar to her, and yet he was not. His mutilated face suggested cruelty and strength, savagery and implacability. One long-lashed eye glistened, a liquid, melting black, while the other was a horrid caricature of veins and scar tissue. His mouth, shaped for passion, was stretched tight with bitterness.

His voice was deep and silky. "This is the woman Moctezuma called White Willow. She is to be a slave in the House of Joy."

A concubine with sharp features and long nails ran a hand down the length of his arm. "May I strip the willow of its leaves, lord?"

Tlacateotl grinned. He nodded, and the women fell on the interloper enthusiastically.

Alana tried to defend herself but was too weak and disoriented to put up much resistance. They stripped, pinched, and slapped her, and then a concubine came at her with an obsidian knife. Alana balled her fists, taut with fear.

"I'm not going to kill you," the woman assured her. "I'm only going to cut your hair!"

"Oh, my God, no! No! Don't!" Alana struggled, but her tormentors held her down, giggling and chattering. "Please! No!" She cried out again and again as the long strands fell.

Breathless and flushed, she was finally released by the concubines, who sneered at the dirty, shorn foreigner. Then their smiles faded. To them she also symbolized the foe who had unleashed smallpox and brought hardship and war. Now they stepped toward her with grim purpose.

Thunder had been rumbling overhead, and lightning flashed. Rain started without warning, flooding the patio and driving everyone to cover. Alana remained huddled on the floor, almost glad for the drenching. It was washing away incense smoke, blood, and perspiration. If she were going to die, at least she would be clean.

"Come in out of the rain." An older woman with hazel eyes, whom Alana had not seen before, gave the order with quiet authority and then dismissed the concubines. They dispersed reluctantly, piqued at losing their entertainment.

"I said—come in out of the rain."

Alana managed to get into her torn and soaking shirt before standing up. It clung to her body, making her uncomfortably aware of the warrior's intense appraisal.

The woman appeared neither hostile nor friendly and examined her with disinterest. "Follow me. I will see that you have clothing and a place to sleep."

"What am I doing here?" Alana was relieved to find that her voice was steady.

The shadow of a smile traveled to the pretty eyes. "You have been sent here to be one of our slaves. For the time being you will be my personal attendant."

"Oh, no," Tlacateotl objected harshly. "She is to be a *slave*, the lowest of the low." He loomed over them dangerously, resplendent in jaguar skin, golden ornaments, and fine cottons. He had removed the ferocious headdress, and a thick blue-black mane brushed across muscled shoulders.

"Get in there." He pointed to a nearby room.

The concubine said with disapproval, "Surely you won't soil yourself, Lord." She realized her comment verged on impertinence, but she had taught him many things and agonized with him when his face had been disfigured.

She also knew this exotic creature was the sweetheart of the great fighter who'd inflicted the scar. Taking revenge was completely understandable; still, the woman was not a spoil of war but an unsuitable sacrifice, which was a bird of a different feather.

"Not soil myself—relieve myself." He hustled Alana away.

The room was windowless but warm and fragrant with burning pinewood. Alana's mind raced. She would kill herself before she would let another animal do what the crossbowman had done. Slashing her wrists with this man's dagger should be easy, and she could only pray God would forgive her.

Yet the Aztec did not seem disposed to maltreat her. He acted thoughtful as he removed his gear. "You don't remember me," he commented.

"No, but I feel as if I've met you somewhere. At Moctezuma's court perhaps?" She shivered involuntarily with nervous tension and pulled at the short and unfamiliar hair at the nape of her neck.

He held out a towel. "Dry yourself off before you catch a sickness in the lungs."

When she glanced around, hoping for privacy, Tlacateotl muttered, "Don't be modest. You are a slave among those who undress for a living. You will do what you are told—or die."

Alana trembled. He meant it. "Is there a gown I may put on?"

"Later."

He peeled the shirt off, admiring the small, statuesque body. Since their encounters in the aviary he had been much too busy to think about her. Now the novelty of conquest renewed itself. Would she be as good as he had imagined?

He shoved her onto the pallet in the corner of the room and lay down beside her. He saw her stiffen. "Are you afraid?"

"Yes," she replied frankly.

His arm went under her, pressing her chilled flesh to his. Tlacateotl felt ridiculously pleased that his ruined face did not appear to be repulsive to the jade-eyed captive.

"I told you long ago," he whispered, "that I would not hurt you. That I but what about my hair? None of you cover yours. It will give us

e with me. The others have already run for their lives. Quickly!''
ubine ran with Alana at her heels, both looking around apprehen-
Vhen they reached her quarters, she daubed black mud onto Al-
d and combed it through the short curls.
should do. Keep your eyes downcast if you can. There's no way
e them.''
was surprised to find herself on the street that bisected the island,
ng at each end in causeways connecting with the mainland. The
eld hands tightly as they pushed through the stream of traffic head-
away from the Spaniards.
screamed at them for going in the wrong direction, kicking and
force them back. Alana saw fright in her companion's face, but
ed encouragement. They inched along, bruised and pummeled by

lana saw the cause of the panic. A wall of mailed men on ar-
ses swept up the avenue like alien creatures from another planet.
ttered in the sun, and swords flashed like light. The animals tram-
llen underfoot, their hooves stained with blood.
ncubine cupped a hand to Alana's ear. "We must go around,"
''or we'll be caught between them!'' She pointed in terror to an
horde of howling Aztecs, weapons upraised against the enemy.
men darted down one side street and up another, coming back
ain thoroughfare behind the Spanish infantry. Alana saw Bernal
ng by, lean face streaming sweat beneath his morion.
! Bernal!'' Alana ran after him and grabbed his arm.
nd wheeled, blade at the ready. "Who the— By the Body of
most ran you through! I didn't recognize you. What happened to

you later. Where's the Englishman?''
t the canal, making a new crossing for us.'' Bernal trotted away
with his comrades. ''Be careful! The—'' his warning was
the noise.
ubine leaned against a wall. "I don't know . . . how much
go,'' she panted.
ust! My God, you must! Look! There's just the one canal, an
n the center of the city.''

---

would give you enormous pleasure instead. But you kicked me in the jaw—''

Alana started with surprise, forcing her mind to concentrate on his words. Her senses had been directed toward resisting his advances. Of course! The sensual young Indian with slumbrous eyes who had been so determined to make love to her at the *totocalli*. How he had aged and changed!

''—and then your red-haired lover scarred me for life.''

She gasped. Blessed Jesus, of all the men in Tenochtitlán, she'd fallen into the hands of one with personal reasons for putting her to death. What better revenge to take on Brian?

''Are you going to kill me?''

''I may. When I am through with you.'' Tlacateotl reached down and removed his loincloth. ''You have nothing to say about it. I am the conqueror, and you the conquered.''

''I will never be conquered.'' She looked him straight in the eye.

His firm manhood probed gently. ''We will see.''

There was no sound but rain outside in the patio. Night had fallen, the day's battles were over, and warriors who were off duty had not yet arrived for meals, music, and feminine companionship. Alana resigned herself to the man's caresses; for some mysterious reason she felt reasonably confident he would not injure her. Afterward there might be a chance to escape.

Her resignation did not last long. Tlacateotl was an extremely skilled and experienced lover who had had access to concubines since boyhood. There was very little he did not know about arousing women, especially those hungry for love but who rebuffed him out of principle.

He kissed her, speaking against her lips. ''Have you ever heard what we say about the maguey cactus—that if it is opened when too small to take honey from the heart, it lacks substance and yields no honey? But if they allow it to grow and come to perfection, then the honey may be collected at a suitable moment. . . . Like this.'' He smiled as she responded convulsively. Good. The woman could not resist him now. He *had* conquered her. The warrior held back no longer, his climax made sharper and sweeter by the woman's degradation.

Tlacateotl rested briefly, rose, dressed, and left the room, paying no more attention to Alana. He returned with the hazel-eyed concubine who brought garments of the coarsest cloth. Alana slipped them on immediately, ashamed of her body gleaming pearl-like in the shadows.

"I have relieved myself in this poor vessel," he said, preening a bit. "Now put her to work until I need her again."

Alana refused to meet the eyes of the other woman. This was the nadir. She had relaxed her guard, thinking only of not being physically abused again. Then her instincts had betrayed her resolution and allowed her seduction by this. . . .

" 'Indian dog,' you called me once." He flicked his fingers painfully under her chin. "And you kicked me, just about there. See?" He opened his mouth and pointed. "You broke a tooth."

"Men from your unit have arrived." The concubine spoke respectfully. "Wouldn't you like to join them while I instruct the slave on her duties?"

Tlacateotl settled back into his clothes, a rising anger cooled by the opportunity to crow to his comrades of the subtle victory he had won. He turned and walked out.

"Listen to me." The concubine glanced out the door. "Were you not Yellow Plume's friend?"

Alana brightened. "Yes! She was very dear to me."

"As she was to me. Therefore, I will try to make your lot as easy as possible. But do as you are told, do you understand? The girls will be waiting for a chance to get rid of you."

Alana touched the woman's arm anxiously. "To murder me?"

"They are jealous."

"Of this?" Alana gestured contemptuously at her short hair, poor clothing, and bare feet.

"I doubt that you will attract the other men, and I will try to keep you out of their sight. But the girls hate you for what you represent."

"Can you help me escape?"

The hazel eyes widened and then narrowed shrewdly. "Will you take me with you? I do not want to starve under siege. I am still young enough to—" She cocked her head, listening, and then motioned frantically. "Straighten the sleeping area," the Aztec ordered in a loud voice.

Alana fell to her knees and was busily shaking out and repositioning the pallet's covers when a trio of concubines entered. They made unflattering comments, and one put her foot on Alana's backside, sending her sprawling.

"Now she must do the work over again," the older woman chided them. "I have other chores for her to do as well, so run along, please." She shooed them out.

That evening Alana labored at scaling hot peppers, grinding corn, and chopping task the cooks thought of was foisted off o takes or slowness were punished with thor to come.

Warriors and their mistresses ate, sang but Alana was not made to serve them. Pe and marked by battle, she gave thanks for

During the following week Alana had was watched every minute by other slaves heavyset women. Everyone treated her to the dirtiest jobs. Alana could bear feared.

He came each day to have his wound He would hurl her down and take her, n wiles. When his glaring eye transfixed he fought and scratched but eventually fou enjoy her again.

One afternoon Alana heard musket horses neighing, and the clash of arms. clamor louder than yesterday? She lea face.

Alana had no knowledge of military was having to take Tenochtitlán street b building. The Aztecs would die to a ma capital. She knew the canal network w the many thousands of besieged had b plies. When famine inevitably struck, growing in virulence as corpses went city's sanitation system collapsed.

Alana realized only too well that a position would become untenable. Th to die fighting than be murdered! Sh eyed concubine rushed in, cheeks ros

"The Spaniards have broken throu ing up the avenue toward the great they're trying to join forces from the them, can you guarantee my safety?"

"Yes, away!"

"Com
The con sively. ana's hea

"That to disgui

Alana terminati women h ed north,

People shoving t she shout the crowd

Then mored ho

Armor gli pled the f

The co she yelled oncoming

The wo onto the m Díaz passi

"Berna Her frie Christ, I a your hair?

"I'll tell

"Back a to keep u drowned i

The co farther I ca

"You m then we're

The woman sank to her knees, covering her head with her arms. "By the great *teocalli!* Oh, I am afraid!"

"But we'll be on the southern causeway in no time and safe with Cortés' army." Alana could hardly restrain herself.

"It's so far, and I am so frightened!"

"You think I'm not? Would you rather die right here? I thought Aztec women were brave," Alana scoffed.

"No, I don't want to die!"

"Hurry, then!"

They ran in the direction of the sacred precinct. Tiny figures of priests atop the pyramids stood out plainly in the clear atmosphere, and Alana shuddered. Pepe's death would always haunt her, and she hoped she would live to have a mass said for his soul.

"The canal! We're nearly there!" Alana craned her neck to see if Brian was truly there as Bernal had said. With battles raging throughout the island he might have been called elsewhere.

On the southern bank of the waterway Tlaxcalan demolition units were busily tearing down houses and heaving their timbers and stone into the canal. Twenty-five-feet wide and more than ten deep, the gap required large amounts of debris; the workers did not notice two women calling and waving for help.

But there were others who did.

XXXII

The Englishman stepped out of a nobleman's house just before the roof caved in. The wrecking crew enjoyed destroying their ancient enemy's city. It made up for a lot. A shame to destroy these lovely residences, but if the Aztecs were set on dying in the ruins, so be it.

Brian had lost much of his zest for finding treasure or settling scores; the reduction of Tenochtitlán had turned into a war of attrition, with the Aztecs slugging it out toe to toe, giving as good as they got.

Unlike Spaniards, who seemed capable of existing on gunpowder, steel, and prayer, Brian was constantly hungry. Rain kept him cold and damp and had rusted his armor; he was tired of fighting for Spain's benefit. Too bad the English had not arrived first.

He felt the packet of pearls against his body where he had hidden them. That was risking death under Cortés' regulations, as was the cache of emeralds and gold bars in safekeeping at Tlaxcala. But Brian knew he wasn't the only one, and what the conquistador didn't know wouldn't hurt anybody.

He had a hunch the loot from the capital would be disappointing this time; the Aztecs frequently taunted the army, saying they had hidden their gold and gems where they would never be found. And what did turn up would have to be reduced by the king's fifth and by Cortés' fifth before the balance could be divided among the soldiers. Chances were each man's share would be small.

Yet what did riches mean next to the loss of Alana MacKenna? Oh, why hadn't she stayed in her house in Texcoco and waited for him instead of being so reckless? Unshed tears dimmed his sight, and he rubbed his eyes impatiently.

It had almost killed him when he learned she had been sacrificed with Pepe. The thought of that body dismembered and the flame of that gallant spirit quenched had about driven Brian out of his mind.

The whole situation depressed and frustrated him. About all he'd got out of the past two years were a dead sweetheart, a dead horse, and a missing finger. By facing these Indian fanatics any longer, he risked being sacrificed himself.

Gloomily he walked along the canal's edge, keeping watch for arrows and stones from slingshots. War canoes with skilled marksmen had harassed his command ever since it began construction of the crossing. The same bastards had no doubt been responsible for its destruction earlier; cavalry and infantry would be trapped if Brian's men did not fill up the breach quickly enough.

A number of Tlaxcalans who had ridden under Alana's cross-and-shamrock banner had attached themselves to him. They were great fighters and good men, although they did nauseate him on occasion by eating Aztec flesh. He urged them on to greater effort as they staggered past, carrying heavy building blocks.

A shrill scream stabbed through the din. Two women on the north side of the canal were being dragged into a war canoe, the one with short hair putting up a fierce struggle. When her skirt tore, Brian was astonished to glimpse white skin.

The Tlaxcalan who had commanded Alana's men yelled, "They say it is she, Lord!"

The Englishman demurred. "Some of the highborn Aztecs have very light complexions."

"But this one has green eyes. Green as *chalchihuites*! She cannot be an Aztec!"

"Whoever they are, they need help. Obviously, they're trying to escape the city. See if you can get to them."

An Aztec toppled out of his craft with the captive in his arms. Tlaxcalans jeered loudly as a group of them jumped into the water. No wonder Tenochititlán was doomed with such weaklings to defend it!

As the couple splashed and fought, dye rinsed off the woman's hair, leaving a dark-streaked cap of pale hair. The Englishman stiffened with surprise.

"Brian! Brian!" Now he, too, saw those unforgettable eyes for just a moment before she went under.

He bellowed with rage and made a flying leap into the canal, forgetting he could not swim. His men surrounded him, pulling him back to stand on debris, waist-deep in the water. The spear wound in his thigh ached with the cold.

"Get her!" he shouted. "For God's sake, get her!"

But the canoe darted in, buoyant and swift as a dragonfly; its rowers seized Alana and lifted her in with the other woman, who sat petrified with fear. The Aztecs paddled toward the sacred precinct with the prisoners, leaving their companion to his fate.

Regardless of personal problems, Brian had to think of the armored cavalry and foot soldiers who might be coming back at any time. The horses, which were irreplaceable, were burdened by an average weight of more than two hundred pounds; they demanded firm footing on which to wade across.

Brian clambered out of the water, heartsick at not recognizing Alana sooner or acting faster. He pitched stones into the breach like a man possessed while he tried to think of ways to save her.

Then he told the commander, "Go find an Aztec for a messenger. And hurry, for the love of Jesus!"

Visions of that beloved figure bent back over a bloodstained altar flitted through his brain. Had those eyes been full of reproach or terror? Brian groaned. The twenty minutes it took to produce a defiant but frightened novice priest crawled by.

"Do you know who I am?"

The Indian's eyes were wide. Who did not remember the great fire-hair? Few men endured the five-to-one combat and lived. He who did survive was favored by the gods.

"You are to tell Savage Serpent that my woman has been captured by men in a war canoe, and I want her back." When Brian's eyes glittered, the other man shivered.

"Tell him I'll fight any warrior he chooses—with any weapon. If I win, she's to be set free."

"And if you lose?" the priest asked, feeling slight and insubstantial next to the white man's powerful bulk.

Brian shrugged. "Then he can add my heart to hers in that infernal dish of his."

By the time the priest returned with a reply Spanish forces were crossing the canal, bloody and angry. They had met more resistance than anticipated and failed to link up with Sandoval's men as planned. They were more than ready to take out their rancor on any islander that got in the way.

A horseman rode at Brian's messenger full tilt, lance aimed for the vitals, but a soldier kicked the Indian aside, and he scuttled toward the Englishman, his face clay-colored with alarm.

"Is she still alive? What did he say?"

"Yes, the woman's alive but—"

"But *what,* you stinking excuse for a human being?" Brian lifted the priest off the ground by the front of his bloodstained robe.

"He says—he says—come and get her!"

The Englishman's face grew dark with fury, and cords in his big neck stood out. The priest began to babble, and Brian tossed him into the canal like a discarded rag.

"Come and get her, he says! By the rood, boys, who's with me?"

A roar went up. The soldiers' chivalrous blood sang with maniacal, unthinking joy, catching fire from the light in those furious blue eyes.

"To the temples!" Brian thundered and swung up on Conn, who reared and pawed the air, bells jangling on his steel breastplate. The man was conscious only of physical sensations: the armor's weight and warmth; his sword hilt in one hand; the silken movement of the horse beneath him. His entire being focused on becoming a killing machine, capable of saving the girl he loved. He spurred Conn hard and within minutes was riding through the northern gate of the Serpent Wall. Fifty Spaniards and several thousand Indian allies followed him, falling on Tenochtitlán's center like ravenous wolves.

The Tlaxcalan commander, running at Brian's stirrup, shouted, "There she is, Lord! Up there!" He pointed at the main *teocalli.*

Aye, there she was, his Irish love, standing on the summit between a red-robed priest and a fierce Eagle Knight in elaborate headdress. Something about the warrior's stance was familiar, and Brian bared his teeth in a savage grimace. By the bones of Judas, it looked like the man he'd fought in the five-to-one combat on the stone!

Fighting erupted as Aztecs poured out of the arsenals to defend the holy city, and Brian was forced to hack his way to the staircase, leaning from side to side in the saddle.

He dismounted and then jumped aside as a warrior-priest vaulted off the steps at him, fell, and rolled under the horse's hooves. An Aztec foot soldier with broken arms attacked the Tlaxcalan holding Conn's reins, chewing and biting at him with the only weapons at his command. A crossbowman next to Brian launched his bolt as an Aztec archer loosed an arrow. They both fell, pierced through the heart.

Yet the carnage did not register with Brian Phelps. He plowed up the pyramid's face, brushing priests aside like insects when they tried to bar his way. Spaniards with red-edged swords were close on his heels, protecting him from the rear.

Brian's first thought when he sprang onto the platform was for Alana. Where was she? What had they done to her? He would carve this living carrion into bits and feed them to the mastiffs if she were hurt!

Then he saw her struggling with Savage Serpent and four lesser priests. The corpse of another woman with its heart torn out lay nearby, its hazel eyes staring sightless at the melee.

"I'm coming, Irish!" Brian bawled at the top of his lungs. "I'm coming!"

"No, you're not!" Tlacateotl came from nowhere, lithe and deadly. He brandished a *maquahuitl*, the lethal obsidian-toothed sword-club, in one hand and a short lance in the other.

"Yes . . . I . . . am," Brian replied, swinging his broadsword back and forth. He narrowly missed the Aztec's ribs but opened a gash in his arm.

"First blood, you son of a bitch," the Englishman growled.

The staring eye within the barbaric headdress leered mockingly. "The peck of a bird." The warrior made a lewd gesture. "Your woman may not even want you now that I've laid her. She's been my whore for days."

Tlacateotl laughed as his opponent's face grew dark red with rage. "Didn't you know she's been my slave? She might even bear my child!"

Out of the corner of his eye Brian saw the Tlaxcalan commander race toward Alana with at least thirty men. Relieved for the moment of his concern about her, he set about disposing of this hated adversary.

Those who saw the duel spoke of it long after. Of how well the men were matched: the Indian smaller but quicker and the Englishman slower but stronger, the former fueled by hate, the latter by love—and both driven by revenge.

They circled each other, slashing and lunging, feinting and cutting, oblivious to the chaos surrounding them. Froth dried on their lips, and they were no longer men but creatures caught up in primal conflict.

The end came when Brian penetrated the Aztec's defense with cold steel. His sword sank into the brown belly and ripped it open. Serpentine intestines spilled out of the terrible wound. Tlacateotl looked down in horror and disbelief and dropped the sword-club. As he collapsed to his knees, he made a vain effort to stuff the shining pink mass back into his body cavity.

With superhuman effort he jabbed upward with the lance, aiming for his enemy's genitals. Trying to avoid the spear point, Brian slipped in the man's blood, fell foward, and deflected the blow on his cuirass. Tlacateotl's last weapon dropped from a nerveless hand.

"I . . . will be a . . . long time . . . dying." A long time getting to paradise, where he would be perfect and handsome once more.

The once-lustrous eyes fixed on Brian's face, asking nothing, expressing much. True to his heritage, the Aztec made not one murmur of pain, and the Englishman respected his fallen foe for that. Putting him out of his misery was the least he could do. He ran Tlacateotl through the heart.

Blood dripping from his sword, he turned to find Alana's rescue at an impasse. The lesser priests had been disposed of, but dealing with their superior was another story; Savage Serpent had managed to retreat to the doorway of the war god's sanctuary.

Alana MacKenna stood in front of the devil-like figure, her face haggard with dread. Her captor had one hand entwined in her hair and the other clenched around the handle of a Spanish dagger. It pressed hard against her ribs, aimed for the heart.

Soldiers milled near Brian, concerned about their increasingly vulnerable position. From this high point Aztecs could be seen filtering through the streets, coming from northern Tenochtitlán to help drive out the white men and their despised allies. Bloodcurdling screams of vengeance carried on the rising wind.

"*Alala! Alala! Alala!*" We're coming, Spaniards—say your prayers! Jaguar Knights exhorted their battalions. "*Now is when! Now is when! Now is when!*" Now or never! Drive the spoilers off the island!

Savage Serpent grinned with satisfaction, displaying his filed teeth. He could wait. His people were on their way. Stabbing the woman would be easy, but every instinct leaned toward sacrifice. And when he died, that was the way he wanted to go—with a knife in hand, doing the job he had done for so many years.

Brian swore. Time was running out. Yet all it took was an inch of steel and she was gone. The priest held Alana so her body shielded his own, which ruled out a crossbow shot, and there was no way to get behind him.

The thunder and lightning that had preceded the afternoon rains had intensified during the fighting. Ash-colored clouds billowed toward the city. Lightning flickered ominously, and everyone jumped at a violent clap of thunder that made the stone tremble underfoot. Alana heard the high priest suck in his breath, and pain from the dagger's point lessened for an instant.

She seized on the diversion, acutely conscious of the danger Brian and the other men were in. Pretending to faint, she pulled the high priest off-balance. The arthritic knees could not respond quickly enough, and Savage Serpent released her hair and allowed Alana to slump at his feet.

Like the crack of doom a lightning bolt lanced through the crown of the high priest's head, and a weird bluish glow pulsated from his body. He vibrated uncontrollably, impaled on the white-hot spit of death, and a second before Savage Serpent's brain exploded, he realized all his bones had fractured into splinters.

Brian did not lose a second. He ran forward and dragged Alana away from the dying man. Lightning sometimes did strike twice! The air reeked with singed feathers, hair, and flesh, and his gorge rose with nausea.

The summit was strewn with the dead and dying when the ragged group of Spanish warriors and their Indian allies poured down the staircase with Brian and Alana in the lead. Once safely on the ground, the pair mounted Conn and headed for the causeway and safety.

Alana lay exhausted against the mighty chest, her face aglow with joy and thanksgiving. He had never looked so handsome as he did to her this moment in dirty clothing and battered, rusty armor. She would have gone barefoot across the coals of hell for the English lion who had risked his life for her.

* * *

The wolfhound was dozing in the kitchen, as he did so often now, sinking deeper and deeper into the shadows each day, grieving, caring for nothing. Unable to understand the absence of the creature he loved more than life itself, his heart had broken when she did not come. Had he done something wrong he could not remember?

Suddenly a voice in the distance called his name and burned through the mists in which he now existed. There! Finn heard the voice again. Panting and straining, he struggled to a sitting position. Was she coming? Was she?

Alana rushed across the room and knelt beside him.

"Oh, Finn, my dear, my *darling* Finn! Thanks be to God, you're alive!" She took him in her arms and kissed him, smoothing the massive head, laughing and crying on his fur. The dog sighed, his gaze luminous with pure bliss.

"Why, you're weak as a kitten! We'll have to put meat back on those big bones! We will, Finn, you'll see," Alana promised, her words trembling with emotion.

He whimpered, and the expression in the dog's eyes struck to the heart. "You thought I'd deserted you when you were hurt, didn't you? How could you understand?" She made him lie down again and examined the javelin wound.

"Don't worry, Pepe will know just what to—" Alana bit her lip. She still had not adjusted to her friend's death. Surely he would stroll in any second with his warm smile and a healing salve. *Requiescat in pace.* Brave Spaniard. *You are not forgotten.*

She looked up as the man from León came toward them. Finn's tail wagged feebly when the one-armed soldier spoke.

"By the mass, you'll get well now!" He squatted opposite Alana and petted the dog with affection.

"I am so sorry about your arm, *amigo!*"

He shrugged. "Fortunes of war, *señorita.*" A grin spread across his face. "But what do you think of this beast? Look at him! He's better already with you here."

"That's the way with love," she murmured. Then, more briskly: "Brian says you rescued Finn and have been nursing him."

"When I saw him with a spear through the guts, I ran to see if you or

Phelps were there, too. Then the dog moved, and knowing what the Aztecs would do to him—''

Alana stroked the wolfhound whose eyes were riveted on her. ''I can't tell you how grateful I am.''

''It took three of us to carry him. *Por Dios,* he weighed more than a man.''

His blue eyes examined Alana with interest. She had been through a war of her own: hair cut short, black dye on her cheeks, bruises and scratches, and torn clothing. Yet those long-lashed green eyes and the enchanting mouth, and *sangre de Jesús,* her glorious bosom! He had always envied the Englishman this woman.

Brian entered the kitchen with a flagon of wine in each hand. He had removed his armor and combed hair and beard. Here at Coyoacán, where the allied Indian forces had made their headquarters for the war's duration, a man could relax. He had helped himself to a house not far from those Cortés and his lieutenants had appropriated. Two other soldiers whom Brian liked, who were at present in Alvarado's camp, shared the house with him and the man from León.

Alana sipped the wine while the men discussed Finn's condition. She was content to rest a bit before getting cleaned up. The image of Savage Serpent frying on the lightning bolt crossed her mind, and she took Brian's muscled arm and leaned her head against him.

''Finish the wine, my friend,'' Brian said, setting his flagon down. ''I want to get her to bed.''

''Brian!'' Her cheeks flamed.

His laughter boomed through the kitchen, and Finn's eyes brightened at the happy sound. ''I meant, of course, that you must be exhausted after such a day. And I imagine you'd like a bath, wouldn't you, Irish?''

''Amen to that.'' She caressed the dog's head and commanded lovingly, ''Stay, Finn. Good boy. Stay. I'll be close by.''

Alana was trailing Brian through the quiet house when she asked teasingly, ''Are you saying you don't want me unless I've had a bath?''

He stopped so abruptly she ran into him. When he whirled and wrapped his arms around her, it was like being hugged by a bear.

''Woman, I'll take you any way I can get you.'' He crushed her to him, kissing her hungrily, and his maleness sprang up against her groin. She stood on tiptoe, pressing into it.

''God, to think I almost lost you again,'' Brian groaned. He was running his hands everywhere, nibbling at her throat and ears. "I ought to beat you within an inch of your life for disobeying me."

Eyes closed, savoring his touch, Alana crooned, "Don't ever lose me. Don't ever. . . . Beat me if you like. But don't lose me."

She was dimly aware of his carrying her somewhere. He pulled the coarse garment off, handling her like a piece of priceless porcelain; he went for a damp cloth and wiped the dye from her face, silently cursing whoever had cut her hair . . . and blotting out the gibes of the warrior who had said she was his whore.

It was close to dusk now and still raining. The house drowsed, dark and intimate, a cocoon for lovers tucked away where nothing mattered but being together again.

Their mouths met, and each sensed a mystery and loneliness and aching beauty about the other they could never completely possess but which was precious beyond their comprehension.

"I must have you this minute," he whispered urgently, covering her breasts with kisses.

"I am yours," she answered, and he blazed with passion in the emerald flames that devoured him.

Their bodies joined, the sword sheathed in its scabbard. The woman closed around her lover in all her volcanic heat, ready for him and excited beyond measure. Her near escapes from death had charged her senses to the hilt with a sweet, contagious madness.

They rocked in age-old rhythms, lost in desperate, delightful seeking. Ecstasy flooded them. She cried out once, wildly, then went limp and still. Alarmed, Brian shook her gently. She appeared to have fainted, but he saw color in her cheeks and a slight smile on her lips. He bent and kissed them.

The Englishman stretched mightily, filled with a boyish pride. Now *that* was the way to make love. He decided he was not about to share Alana MacKenna with anyone again. It was time to get married.

His wife. Aye, the loveliest, sauciest wench of a wife a man ever had. God blast it, this filly needed a tight rein. And he was just the bucko to pull back on the bit!

Brian settled a blanket over them and nestled closely in back of her. He put an arm around her and cupped a breast firmly in one hand. Snuggling against Alana's silky body, Brian fell into a deep sleep.

Alana placed her hand over his where it held her and sighed with pleasure and satisfaction. Now *that* was the way to make love.

BOOK FIVE

The Bishop's Captive

When the ashes had ceased to burn,
Quetzalcoatl's heart rose up. . . .
They say it was raised to heaven
*   and entered there.*
The old men say it became the morning
*   star which appears at dawn. . . .*
—Annals of Cuauhtitlán: Legend of the Suns
(translated from the Nahuatl by Irene Nicholson)

XXXIII

July, 1521: in the city of Tlaxcala

"Is she here in Tlaxcala now?" the midwife asked Inmaculada. As she spoke, she palpated the pregnant woman's belly to ascertain the baby's position. Ah, it seemed normal and the child active. That was good, because the mother-to-be felt as tense as yarn stretched on a loom.

Inmaculada glanced up into shrewd eyes that had witnessed much pain, sorrow, and joy. Closeted in the steam bath, they perspired freely; the midwife a wrinkled, old apple losing sap, her patient a firm, ripe, satin-skinned fruit.

"Who do you mean?" The Maya resented the question, interrupting as it did her absorption with the sensual pleasure of massage. It had temporarily freed her mind from the dilemma that had been tearing her apart.

The midwife patted her in gentle reproof. "The woman you hate." When no reply was forthcoming, she went on, "It is not good, this burden of bitterness and rage. Like an infant dead in the mother's womb, it creates poison. You should nourish good thoughts for the benefit of the child."

What a strange young woman! Even her physical appearance emphasized the distance she kept. The regal nose soaring without break from tip

337

*to hairline; the slightly slanted eyes, unusually dark and liquid; a bluish
mark near the base of the spine right above the buttocks where the gods
had marked her people for their own mysterious reasons.*

"I would like to get dressed now," Inmaculada said. "I promised to
decorate the chapel for services."

"Very well." The midwife sighed. "But remember what I told you.
Don't look at anything red, or the child will be born askew. And if you go
out at night, put a pinch of wood ash in your blouse so ghosts can't frighten
you. And under no circumstances chew *chicle* because the baby's palate
and gums will swell and prevent it from feeding. And—"

Inmaculada shook her head to halt the flow of admonitions. The old
woman meant well, but if she said another word!

"Thank you, grandmother. I promise to take care of myself and the
jewel I carry, truly I do." She bowed her head for the elder's blessing.

As Inmaculada strolled toward the chapel where she had delivered flowers and candles earlier in the day, she saw Alana on the other side of the
street. The Irishwoman stopped and held up a conciliatory hand, but the
Maya stonily ignored it.

They had had a falling out a few days ago when Alana returned from
Coyoacán at the end of the first week in July, and both had been in tears by
the time their hot words had been exchanged. Inmaculada had spewed forth
grief-stricken accusations rooted in jealousy, anger, and the inability to
come to terms with her conflicting feelings for the Irishwoman. Appalled
by such venom but concerned for the mother-to-be's condition, Alana had
tried to keep her own tongue under control.

"You know perfectly well Pepe and I were never more than the best of
friends."

"More like a knight and the mistress of the castle who was beyond his
reach, you mean. Oh, I know how he felt. Pepe used to tell me stories of
chivalry. How men rode into battle flying the colors of ladies they wor-
shipped from afar. I could have fought you if he had desired your body.
But it was your soul he adored—and it was a love in which there was no
place for me!"

So much pain vibrated in her voice that Alana had gone to her knees beside Inmaculada's chair and taken the trembling hands in hers.

"May God strike me dead if Pepe loved me more than you—in any way!

You were the light of his life, the beat of his heart—and that's the truth. I swear it on the holy cross.''

But nothing Alana said could allay Inmaculada's resentment and fury over the fact that her husband had sacrificed himself for another woman.

It only fueled the flame to learn Brian was coming to Tlaxcala. Pepe would never kiss her again or bury his manhood in her with tender, ardent murmurs or be there in the night when she was afraid—never, never. Alana would taste those joys while she wept alone in the dark.

"Get away from me."

Alana let her go, hurt by such treatment. "Don't be angry. Think of the child."

"I am thinking of the child, and I want you to get away from me. I've heard for a long time that you were a witch. You might harm my baby!"

"Oh, Inmaculada, you know better than that."

The Maya looked much older than her years. "Do I? Now that I think about it, your witchcraft must have lured Pepe away. He would never have deserted me of his own free will."

Alana smiled wanly. "That's what I'm trying to tell you. He *loved* you, and he *didn't* leave you for me. Like any good soldier, Pepe only tried to save a friend."

"He should have saved himself!" The young widow moaned and pressed her palms to her swollen abdomen. *Pepe, Pepe, my silver-eyed precious quetzal feather, are you here within me?* She was swept by a longing so intense she swayed. Alana exclaimed in alarm and took her arm.

"She brushed me off as if I were a loathsome insect," Alana mourned to Brian, who had ridden in shortly after the quarrel.

They had finished eating: rabbit and quail, baked squash, beans wrapped in flat, round corn cakes spiced with green *chilli,* tomatoes from the lower altitudes, chocolate sweetened with wild honey, and a dessert of nuts and berries. The meal had been tasty and satisfying.

The Englishman, replete with good food and visions of lovemaking to come, listened with half an ear to Alana's complaint. He, too, was at a loss, seldom having been at ease around females heavy with young.

Alana had arranged for dinner in her quarters, where they would not be

. disturbed. She wanted to spend every moment with her lover, to feast her eyes on him, to hold him close.

Sun, wind, and the experiences of the past two years had incised lines into Brian's handsome face, adding maturity's authority to youth's vigor. Heavy gold crescents gleamed dully in his ears, complementing a large golden crucifix inlaid with opals that hung around his neck.

Unlike so many of his comrades, the Englishman's teeth were sound. There was one damaged molar—he had been on the wrong end of a war club—but Alana thought it endearing, like that of a little boy who had been in a fight. In fact, she found everything about Brian of surpassing beauty and manliness.

"Bless the mark, Irish, are you going to gobble me up with your eyes?" Relaxed, indolent, and only half-dressed, he contemplated her lazily.

Shivers ran down her spine. One would think a person would tire of another's mouth and body, that familiarity would breed resignation. Yet his glance, touch, or word seldom failed to ignite her passion.

"You're blushing, darling," he observed teasingly and slid an arm around her. "Now stop looking at me like that, or morning will be here before we know it." He cupped Alana's chin and kissed her forehead. "We'd be man and wife by now if I'd been able to persuade Fray Olmedo to ride back with me."

Alana caught her breath with joy, and her great eyes sparkled. "You never proposed to me, you big ox." His wife! She wanted nothing more.

"Was it necessary?"

"Of course. A girl likes to be *asked*!"

Brian smiled, and her heart turned over. "Consider yourself asked then. I had to do something to keep you from becoming a sinner." He wrapped both arms around her, and they hugged each other, feeling giddy with emotion.

"As soon as the city falls," Brian continued, "which shouldn't be too long now, we'll get the father to marry us. Then we'll go back to England." He sighed. "I'd go now if my purse weren't so empty."

"I have a surprise for you! You can. I mean we can."

"How?" He watched her scramble to her feet and go to the other side of the room for a reed box she used as a sewing basket.

"Why wouldn't Fray Olmedo come? Did he feel he was needed there?"

She sat down next to Brian again, taking a small bundle out of the box and unwrapping it.

"Listen, those Spaniards celebrate mass morning and night, in rain or sun, among friends and foes. They always have. And no hypocrisy about it either. When those men bend the knee, the power and the glory of the Savior pours into every rascal's heart and sword arm. . . ." His voice faded.

Alana posed like an idol of ivory and silver, a bare shoulder gleaming in the torchlight, hair an aureole of glory, her face rapt. Her hands overflowed with emeralds.

"Lamb of God!" The Englishman touched the jewels reverently. "Where?"

She moved, and the emeralds shifted, revealing remarkable stones carved into roses, leaves, acorns, fish, and other imaginative shapes. Most of them were skillfully decorated with gold and pearls.

"Some are finer than the ones Cortés took from Moctezuma," Alana murmured, entranced by the treasure and what it meant to her and her beloved. "We're rich, Brian. *Rich!* Rich as Croesus! What do you think of that, my darling man?"

"What do I think? That you're wonderful! They're wonderful! Life is wonderful!" Brian drew a fingertip along her cheek. "I can see you now, my sweet, smothered in satins, laces, and furs!"

He chose an emerald made like a rose and held it delicately between thumb and forefinger. "Magnificent! Imagine, a hard substance like this carved with a bronze tool. The Indians don't know about iron, did you realize that? Oh, I can name some Genoese merchants who will give their eye teeth for these," Brian exulted. "But you haven't told me where you got them."

Alana poured the gems into her lap. "You remember Yellow Plume, don't you? Moctezuma's courtesan?"

"Oh, yes. The one who screamed for hours on the causeway."

"The Lord rest her soul. When she lay dying last December, she was insistent that I have her purple *huipil*." Alana began rewrapping the emeralds.

"I thought she was simply out of her head with fever. Then, the other day, because purple isn't one of my favorite colors, I decided to rip off the embroidery bands from the neck and waist and sew them onto another garment. And there they were; sewn into the stuffing beneath the bands, bless her heart. Our stepping-stone to wealth for the rest of our lives and for the lives of our children.''

Alana rested her head in the hollow of Brian's throat. ''No more fighting for you, my love. We're going home—so I can have my baby in England.''

''Baby?'' he asked stupidly.

''Yes, baby,'' she echoed.

His grin warmed the room. Then Brian grabbed her shoulders and exclaimed loudly, ''I did it! I did it!''

''It's not a thing to be marveled at. Holy Saint Bridget, you've had plenty of opportunity.''

The man kissed her breasts, arms, wrists, neck, and ears. ''When do you think it happened?''

''Does it matter?''

''Indeed it does! We're going to make a baby on that date every year!''

''I'm not a brood mare, Brian, and I'll thank you to keep that in mind.''

''Tell me, Alana. When?'' He had carried her to the bed and was undressing her.

She quivered as he fondled her. ''In May,'' she whispered raggedly. ''In Texcoco—before you went with Olid's forces.''

''Aye,'' he whispered, taking off his clothes. ''Aye, that was a night. Just as tonight is going to be.''

Flames from the torches reflected in Alana's extraordinary eyes. He stared into them, spinning, falling.

''Take me as if we were never going to meet again,'' she demanded. ''As if this were the last time.''

''How grand that it's not,'' Brian said hoarsely, entering without delay, drawing in his breath with excitement at the perfect fit of their bodies and climaxing almost immediately.

''Brian!''

''You know better than to worry about a little thing like that.'' He kissed her lightly, teasingly. She moaned with frustration, and Brian laughed. Give me a few minutes, and I'll make you glad you're alive. When did you know we had a son?''

''Maybe we have a daughter.''

''No, it's a boy. But why didn't you tell me before?''

"I wanted to be sure. I'd been hoping in early June, and then when I was in Tenochtitlán—"

"You reckless spitfire, going in there alone."

"—I still wasn't certain because I might have missed my menses out of fear and tension. That happens, you know."

Brian entered his woman firmly but gently, prolonging the act to give her maximum pleasure. "Aye, I'm expert in a lot of things, wouldn't you say?"

"You're—"

He lowered his mouth to hers. "You talk too much, Irish. Shut up and kiss me."

The Toltec girl had matured during the past year and grown away from her childhood companions. It was not only Blue Butterfly's coloring—hair yellow as poppies, skin the shade of dark honey, and eyes shining turquoise one moment and morning-glory-blue the next. The aura of the man-god Quetzalcoatl, her ancestor, embraced her and set her apart.

Blue Butterfly had never felt superior to her friends. She was simply different. And the girl had found the essence of not being like everyone else to be loneliness.

She frowned. Learning to be alone—inside—was frightening and painful. But what else was there to do? At first she had stayed with Pepe Ortega and his wife. When they went to Texcoco to be with Alana and Brian, she had moved in with Corn Flower. Then Xicotencatl had been executed, and Corn Flower had been forced to live in another town.

When the bereaved Inmaculada refused to take her, the council had placed Blue Butterfly with a respectable couple for her protection until arrangements could be made for a proper marriage. She had thanked the gods when Alana returned. The mere idea of living with a strange man frightened and repelled her. Men were so troublesome!

Her real parents had perished of smallpox not long ago, and the gentle giant, Finn, had almost died. Blue Butterfly knew well the danger inherent in loving too deeply.

"Don't do that," she scolded the *xoloitzcuintli,* swooping down on him as he made a final lunge at the colt's heels. Blue Butterfly gripped the dog between her hands and rubbed his nose with hers.

"Yaotl, you are naughty, do you know that? How many times must I tell you not to chase the little horse? He might fall and hurt himself." But she laughed when the animal licked her face with the energy tiny dogs apply to their activities. During Alana's absences from Tlaxcala, the girl had been drawn to the mare and her charming youngster, identifying them with the white woman she loved, who was often as elusive as a morning breeze.

Like the colt to whom she had become passionately attached, Blue Butterfly's body was developing swiftly: legs long and gangling, yet with promise of grace, eyes alert, innocent and eager, a deceptive appearance of delicacy and fragility.

This morning would be one to remember. She was going to have a riding lesson! Blue Butterfly put the little dog down with a final scolding and started to brush the mare. At least she supposed Alana was planning to keep her word.

The big Englishman had ridden back to Tenochtitlán yesterday, much against Alana's wishes, and she had been in a bad temper ever since. Blue Butterfly had taken her latest featherwork creation to Alana's rooms shortly before Brian rode off, hoping for a hug and words of approval. The fan was her best work to date, and she had used colors that reminded her of the Irishwoman: green from jungle parakeets' wings, white from canyon wrens' breasts, and coral from flamingos' throats.

But the gift had gone unpresented, because a full-blown argument had been under way. Alana had been so angry she had shifted from one language to another, weeping, shouting, pleading with Brian not to return to the Aztec capital.

All Blue Butterfly could make out of it were references to a soldier, possibly an archer, who had done something for which he had to be punished. And Brian was not going with Alana—where?—until he had found this man.

The cold spot in the girl's stomach grew in intensity, and she wielded the brush so hard the mare turned her head reproachfully. Where was Alana going? Was she, Blue Butterfly, to be left to face the future alone?

While she had no way of estimating the cataclysmic forces loosed on her land, Blue Butterfly's instincts told her life would be full of confusing changes the tribal wise men had never dreamed of. She found herself caught between two worlds, bound to each and unable to comprehend either.

She leaned her forehead against the horse's side, drinking in its pleasant odor, it's comforting heat, absorbing into her being its divine patience and its gentleness of soul.

"Here, here, Rose doesn't want you lying down on the job." Alana stood at her elbow, patting Blue Butterfly fondly.

Then her voice grew husky, and she said in rich, harmonious Nahuatl, "Why, my pretty dove, my golden feather, you're crying!"

The Indian girl turned and with as much dignity as she could muster asked, "When are you leaving Tlaxcala again?"

Alana said, "Leaving? When Brian gets back, I suppose." She gazed blindly around the enclosure. "If he does get back, the stubborn fool."

She had insisted she no longer gave a fig about the crossbowman. Not that she would ever forget the experience, but what did it matter now? She and Brian had their health; he had his four limbs; the child grew lustily within her; they had enough wealth to keep them in lifelong luxury. Why risk injury, capture, or death when the wretch might already be dead?

But, oh, no, you'd think the insult had been dealt to the Englishman personally. What peculiar views that stiff-necked race held about property, which law and custom decreed her body to be. No such written word or tradition could ever bind her spirit, that she vowed by all that was holy!

And speaking of property, what about her lovely stallion Brian was riding everywhere over the countryside? She had only lent the horse to him until he bought a good mount. She certainly had not anticipated Conn's being exposed to battlefield conditions yet again.

Alana's concern shifted once more to her protégée. "Why are you crying? Has someone hurt you? Are you afraid? Tell me!" If one of the Spanish veterans living here had touched the girl, she would kill him!

"It's . . . I don't want to be left alone. I . . . don't know where I belong."

Aye, that is pain enough, Alana thought ruefully, *especially at this age.* "As a matter of fact, I have decided to take you with me when we go back to England."

Hope flared in the turquoise eyes, although the finely chiseled features remained grave. Alana reached out and took Blue Butterfly in her arms. She had been mulling over the question for some time. Was it morally right to remove the girl from her native soil? Despite startlingly European coloring, she was an Indian, a Toltec, born of talented and cultured people.

Would she pine for the sun in cold climates? Would she miss familiar customs or the language and spotless cities of her own kind? Would she languish and sicken in the great English houses without open spaces, without snow-topped mountains and clean, crisp air?

There would be no problem of acceptance in social circles or of finding a suitable spouse when the time came for Blue Butterfly to marry. But was it wrong to deny her the opportunity to choose a husband from among Indian men, many of whom were equal, if not superior, to European men in looks, breeding, sophistication, and assets?

The girl could easily mix with Venetian nobility, Scandinavian royalty, Spanish aristocracy, or Germanic patricians. Within a few years men would give a fortune to possess her exotic beauty. Until then she needed to be guarded and loved.

"Come now," Alana exclaimed, holding Blue Butterfly at arm's length.

" 'Tis too pretty a morning to be gloomy! Let me bridle Rose and lead her around with you on her back. That's a good way to learn the feel of a horse. If you get along well after several days, we'll graduate to the saddle. But you have to remember that when you're saddling a horse, he has one thing in mind, and you have another."

They laughed, and while Alana prepared the mare for the girl's first riding lesson, Blue Butterfly fussed over the wolfhound, who had been leisurely patrolling the stockyard.

Finn had put on weight but tired easily; he still suffered sharp pains in the midsection where the javelin had pierced him through. He was on the road to recovery, however, and seldom strayed far from his mistress. The dog did not wish to be left alone either.

XXXIV

Summer nights were cold and frequently rainy in the highlands of the country that would eventually be called Mexico. The name would immortalize the Mexica tribe that also called itself Aztec and had once possessed most of the land. In Santiago de Cuba, on the other hand, nights were hot and humid, making it hard to sleep.

Gilberto de Salvatierra, Count of Altamira, having performed husbandly duty and sown his seed, as well as put his business affairs in order in Madrid, enjoyed the heat. He had suffered a chill, miserable winter there, aching in every bone. The tropics were in his blood, and not until he had returned to the Indies had he felt truly warm.

Now here—ah, *Dios,* one's bones might give a twinge now and again, but the sun warmed a man to the guts. He ran an appreciative hand over the bare breasts of the young half-breed sitting on his lap. There were other things here to heat the guts as well—

He kissed the woman, and she wound her arms around his neck, moving her naked body against his. "Go to bed, *querida.* I have something to take care of, and then I'll join you."

Gilberto started to get out of the chair, but the woman held him down

347

and excited him to take her. He blew out his breath with exhaustion . . . no, he was no longer the quick, vigorous cock he used to be.

"You are a jewel," Gilberto complimented the sloe-eyed prostitute. "Almost as good as she used to be." Scowling and tired of being compared to some harlot he knew in his salad days, she stalked away.

Too bad you don't have her brains and verve, he mused, watching her disappear down the corridor.

Gilberto put on slippers and a lightweight robe of dark-red silk and went into the library, where he lit a single candle. He did not want to be any more conspicuous than necessary. For all he knew, the woman waiting in his bed was a spy of the Inquisition, and he had to get a warning to Alana.

The message was to be picked up before dawn—he would hide it under a certain bush in the garden—and delivered with a cargo of pork at Vera Cruz. There a man with whom he had made arrangements a few weeks ago waited to rush the letter inland to Tlaxcala.

The Spaniard felt confident of his accomplices this time; they were both comrades-at-arms who'd fought with him at Ravenna in 1512; they were down on their luck but men of honor, more than willing to help an old friend and make a tidy sum to boot.

Perhaps it had been ungentlemanly of him not to mention that the Inquisition was getting ready to arrest the letter's recipient for witchcraft. On the other hand, they might not have cooperated if he had, and chances were excellent they would keep a closer mouth if they believed it *una carta de amor.*

Gilberto de Salvatierra was not the most sensitive of human beings, but he had felt guilty about the men and women seized by the Soul Seeker last winter. This had been after the ascetic had intercepted his letter to Alana in which Gilberto instructed her on whom to contact in Cuba for help in escaping to Ireland.

As soon as Gilberto returned to Cuba, he had prevailed on the Bishop Bartolomé de Zamora, the inquisitor general, to release those unfortunates. In his compassion and pity for poor sinners, His Worship surely realized they had seen the situation only as a lark—playing Cupid in a romantic affair in which a lost sweetheart flew in secret to Gilberto's arms.

As for himself, at the time of the arrests he had still been besotted by the cat-eyed witch. Now, *gracias a Dios,* the spell was broken. Application of his energies to conjugal duties in Spain had cleared his mind and saved his soul.

Gilberto was careful to see that the churchman received kegs of the best wines, sweetmeats from Madrid's most famous confectioner, laces delicate as spider webs for his undergarments, and—the *pièce de résistance*—one of his own relatives, a beautiful virgin whose reputation had been ruined by a foolish flirtation. He personally guaranteed her gratitude at finding herself in such luxurious surroundings instead of a nunnery.

What was Alana doing this minute? Drinking that chocolate she liked so well? Sleeping with one foot out of the covers as usual? Gaming with that infectious giggle she had when she made a mistake? Gabbling with the Indians as if she were one of them?

How many glorious times they had made love between April, 1519 and November, 1520! He laughed aloud.

Perdición, those were the nights—and days!

Yet the memories he treasured had no carnal character. He saw her kneeling beside her dog, brushing her long hair, giving her servants extra money, gasping at the diamond and emerald jewelry, climbing the ratlines of the ship en route to Vera Cruz.

Oh, he could see her in so many ways! How she often sang with joy as her stallion cantered along. How lovable she had looked with her pink cheeks and little red nose that night in the mountain pass. How inexpressibly lovely she had been the day they visited Xochimilco, and the Indians had wreathed her with flowers. How. . . .

What did it matter, *hombre*? Alana MacKenna was no longer his. Yet in a way she would always be his, forever young and fair in his mind's eye, ready to be conjured up in a second from a past that could neither change nor fade. *Oh, you are mine, preciosa, forever.*

And as he wrote the letter in the light of the guttering candle, tears trickled down the ravaged face, and Gilberto de Salvatierra tasted the gall of encroaching age and of lost and golden hours.

As luck would have it, the letter traveled on the same caravel that brought the two churchmen to La Villa Rica de la Vera Cruz. From there the inquisitor general and his companion, Fray Mateo de Aldana, the Soul

Seeker, planned to ride inland and apprehend a dangerous criminal.

With them were two dozen well-armed ruffians to do the dirty work. These "familiars," officers of the Inquisition employed to arrest the accused or suspected, were bullies and sadists in the mold of their masters. Born killers, they answered to no discipline but that of the dreaded Holy Office.

The ship captain and then the port authorities were relieved to be rid of such uncomfortable company, the latter in particular being hard pressed to explain why the town's population had suddenly melted away to almost nothing.

"Is this the magnificent New Spain I've been led to expect?" the bishop grumbled. Pigs rooted in muddy streets, vultures fed on carrion, and scrawny fowl clucked over offal. He slapped irritably at mosquitoes feeding on his dark jowls.

Mopping his brow, Fray Mateo replied, "By no means, Your Eminence. The large cities you heard about are at least a hundred miles inland. If I am not mistaken, you will be very interested in what you see."

That he unconsciously dismissed Vera Cruz, a creation of his own countrymen, for the squalid, dismal hamlet it was said much for the fact that Fray Mateo had been impressed by Indian culture in spite of himself. He had not reached Tenochtitlán, having arrived after the *Noche Triste*, but he had toured Cempoala, Jalapa, Xocotlán, Tlaxcala, Heujotzingo, and Cholula, admiring the immense structures raised without the use of draft animals, wheels, or iron tools; the dazzling featherwork, the pottery, embroidery, and jewelry; the masterful urban planning; the architecture tastefully adorned with fountains, gardens, and birds; the sophisticated herbal remedies and medical skills.

"My sole interest is in getting out of this steaming pesthole, Mateo. First, I suppose, we will have to dine with the local priests."

"The fathers would be disappointed indeed if the Sword of God did not accept their meager hospitality," his companion agreed.

They were walking toward the church beneath a canopy carried by leading citizens of Vera Cruz when a horseman pulled rein beside them. Doffing his battered morion, he asked the prelate's blessing as he entered the land of infidels.

Raising his hand in benediction, the bishop said unctuously, "Go with

God, my son. Bow down before Him who is the Father of us all and who
will protect you in whatever trials you may have to endure.''

Chanting of a Te Deum drowned the petitioner's response, but he made
the sign of the cross, clapped on his helmet, and trotted off on the road to
Tlaxcala.

The bishop picked his way carefully over a crude boardwalk specifically
constructed to protect his satin shoes. He felt petulant and put upon. ''At
least that man is on the way to comfortable lodgings.''

His pallid skin, like melted wax in the afternoon's torrid heat, was
splotched with bites, and the bishop had to resist a mighty urge to scratch
crotch and anus, both of which stung and itched with perspiration.

He glanced at his companion, who sloshed through mud and manure
without protest. By the bones of Saint James, what a clod! If Fray Mateo
had not been such an incomparable man-hunter, he would have sent him
back to Spain long ago.

''Will our horses be rested by morning?''

''Without doubt, Your Eminence. The ship made a quick run this time,
and they aren't as stiff as they might be.''

''Then see to it we are riding at dawn. I am anxious to get on our way
and sleep between cool sheets. What with the voyage and these, ah, festivities, I have never suffered so.''

The monk snickered. Tomorrow night the pompous windbag had a real
surprise coming. Wait until he discovered that there were no beds and that
he had to sleep on a pallet on the floor!

Reading, writing, and doing sums were not among Alana's strong
points, although she had learned a bit of each in the convent as a girl.
When Gilberto's courier arrived, she had dropped her sewing on the floor
in excitement.

A letter! A rare event in one's life, to be sure— She saw to it the bearer
had refreshments and then directed him to the company of Spaniards now
living permanently in Tlaxcala.

The man from León, who had left Coyoácán because of a chest complaint, was one of them. He had attended the university of Salamanca as
Cortés had done and, like a remarkable number of conquistadors, read and

wrote with facility. This particular day he happened to be playing with the colt, who was kicking up his heels and pestering his mother in an excess of youthful energy.

"Look!" Alana called, beaming with pride and anticipation. "I got a letter!"

The man smiled. "Are you going to open it or just wave it around in the air?"

"Of course, I'm going to open it." She and the one-armed soldier had developed a camaraderie based on mutual respect and affection for the Englishman. In his way, he had come to fill the void left by Pepe's death.

"From an old lover?" he asked slyly as she broke the seal.

Alana winked and began to read. Then she put a hand to her heart and staggered back against the fence.

"What is it?" The man from León cursed and spilled the basket of corn he was holding. He was not yet adjusted to the loss of his arm.

When she did not answer, he took the letter out of her unresisting hand and read it. He whistled. "Woman, you *are* in trouble."

"My God, what should I do?" Alana was panic-stricken. She had deliberately buried any thought of this happening. Her voice shook. *"What should I do?"*

The man from León was as superstitious as the next person. He knew *el diablo* would appear in a flash if summoned. That forgetfulness vanished if a lapwing's eye hung about the neck, and that a piece of apple inscribed with a Latin invocation cured hydrophobia. Like any enlightened Christian, he also knew a great deal about witches—and he felt certain this woman was not a witch.

He did not intend to put himself in conflict with the Inquisition, however, an act tantamount to suicide. Yet there must be something he could do to help her. In gratitude for rescuing and nursing the wolfhound, Alana had given him a whole bag of gold coins, more than enough to buy a cozy wineshop back home and support himself with *dignidad*. Like most of the army, he had lost his portion of Moctezuma's treasure on the *Noche Triste*. Then the arm had been lopped off. If it had not been for her, he would have been a crippled veteran with no future.

Alana's confidence and quick wit had deserted her. In the absence of the Englishman's counsel, the soldier took charge. He reread the letter. Written more than a month ago, it warned her that the inquisitor general and the

Soul Seeker were ready to embark for Vera Cruz to hunt down and arrest her!

It went on to say she should flee without delay and, if able to reach Cuba, contact the writer in the roundabout manner described. There was more that had nothing to do with Alana's peril. The soldier shufflled his feet, embarrassed at peeking into another man's soul, and handed the letter back.

"You should burn that, you know." Realizing he defied his own church frightened him; he kissed his crucifix and silently asked forgiveness for the sin of helping a friend.

"I will." Alana's mind began to clear. She must make plans that in no way involved this dear man watching her with such concern.

"Let's approach this like a military campaign," he suggested, sitting down among the baskets of corn. "You mustn't go off in every direction, dissipating what strengths you have."

"You might get into trouble. There may be those here—"

He pressed her hand to his lips. "Those charges listed in the letter were completely new to me. After all, I'm a simple soldier in the service of our Lord Jesus Christ and His Sacred Majesty, Charles the First of Spain. If we handle this right, no one will pay any attention to me."

Tears of thanksgiving brimmed in her eyes. *"Gracias, amigo."*

Because time was short, Alana had to find a hiding place immediately. She decided to slip out of the city after dark and go first to the Otomis patrolling Tlaxcala's borders; after all, they had hidden her from the Soul Seeker once before. They held fierce loyalties, and Alana was sure of her reception. After resting a few days, she would go on to the Place of the Gods at Teotihuacán. A person could hide among these ruins for months.

"Will you find Brian and tell him what's happened and where to find me?" She hesitated. "And that the baby and I are well."

"Right away."

"What about the animals?"

The soldier scratched his head. "What about them?"

Alana shuddered. "The monk called Finn a hound from hell. He said he'd—he'd *burn* Finn at the stake with me. *After* hanging him from the ceiling with twenty-pound stones attached to his feet."

She remembered the Soul Seeker's threats vividly. How he would put her to the question, shave off her hair, use red-hot pincers on her flesh.

How he would rupture her joints on the rack, bind her with chains to the stake, and no doubt thrust the torch into the fagots heaped about her feet with his own hand. The smell of her burning flesh would be like incense to him.

The colt came running to her outstretched hand, mouse-soft muzzle nibbling hopefully at the palm. "The horses must not be anywhere in evidence. Anything and anybody connected with me will be suspect, and for Rose and Bayard's son to be destroyed would be a terrible waste."

The friends then decided the man from León would accompany her into the mountains, taking the colt over his saddle. From there he'd ride to Tenochtitlán via the Place of the Gods, around the northern perimeter of the lake and south to the Spanish camps. As for Finn, too weak to travel far. . . .

"I guess we'll have to ride slowly and rest often. We have no way of carrying him."

Distressed about the effect of her disappearance on Blue Butterfly, yet determined not to involve her, Alana wept while packing her jewels, warm clothing, and a minimum of personal possessions. Why did this have to happen when the future had seemed so bright?

They met in the orchard as agreed upon. Rose was saddled and ready for Alana; the soldier had tortillas, cooked beans, and fruit. Finn wore a heavy, quilted cotton coat made to shield him from the cold.

The colt's legs were tied, much to his consternation, and then he was positioned as comfortably as possible on a blanket in front of the man's saddle. Nudging her mistress, the mare whickered anxiously.

"Don't worry, *mavourneen,* you'll be right beside him," Alana whispered.

A sliver of a new moon cast hardly any glow on the sleeping city as the fugitives headed for safety in the mountains. It was purely by chance that a restless sleeper noticed their departure and filed the information away for future use.

By the time the inquisitor general and his retinue arrived at Tlaxcala he was thoroughly out of sorts. He had most assuredly come to a land of savages! No beds, no chairs, no sugar, beef or pork, no cheeses, wines or bread, no olives or citrus. . . . By the blood of the blessed saints, it offered nothing to a civilized man.

The absence of the city-state's most important chieftains increased his irritation. He found it demeaning to deal with lesser dignitaries and old men. He was an enormously influential and powerful individual! Didn't they understand that? Not until a one-legged, one-eared Spaniard fluent in Nahuatl was ordered to act as interpreter did the bishop learn that the great lords were away fighting with Cortés.

He was well aware the armies of Tlaxcala had been instrumental in the conquistador's victories; that as a tribe they had been generous and loyal to the Spaniards; that many of them, including chieftains, were already Christians.

But the churchman had no way of knowing his hosts were not overly impressed by his credentials. Naturally, they had no knowledge or conception of the Inquisition's grim and merciless purpose, nor was torture ever used in Indian courts to elicit confession as it was in the dungeons of the *Casa Santa.*

They knew what their eyes saw, however. While their monastery schools produced tough, disciplined priests respected for sanctity and austerity, this person who waddled and complained like an overfed duck apparently denied his stomach nothing, lacked good breeding, and had too quick an eye for women.

Cortés had promised to ask his emperor to send holy men of unblemished purity to preach the Faith; he definitely did not want bishops and pampered prelates who squandered the church's substance in riotous living. The revered Fray Olmedo personified the type hoped for, but this man posturing before them—let him not be an omen of the future!

The interpreter, nevertheless, was visibly affected by the presence of his countrymen. His voice shook as he pulled nervously at his remaining ear.

"Stand still, man," the inquisitor chided. "Are you unwell?"

"Oh, no, Your Reverence! No, no. Just a . . . ."

"I'm not interested in a recital of your infirmities. Do your job and ask these men where the witch is."

The man gaped. "What witch?"

He jumped, almost losing his crutch. Fray Mateo stuck out his neck like a striking snake and hissed, "The woman with green eyes and blond hair. The one with the big dog."

Like a number of Cortés' veterans, the interpreter had benefited from Alana MacKenna's nursing. What's more, he liked her—she was a good campaigner. But a witch! To have abjured Jesus Christ and dealt with the devil! He made the sign of the cross.

"I myself have not seen her recently." He conversed with the Indian officials. "They say she is a guest and not kept under surveillance. She is well liked for her good works in the city."

The Soul Seeker rubbed his useless arm without thinking. The gray eyes smoldered with hate. "You see, Your Excellency, I told you she put them under a spell. *Good works!* They are the works of the devil!"

The Spaniards looked around, fully expecting His Satanic Highness to appear. Fortunately the inquisitor's presence, as well as that of a monk renowned for driving out demons, proved an excellent defense.

The inquisitor had been unable to transport his coach aboard the tiny caravel, and he was exhausted from riding horseback. The familiars had tried carrying him in a litter, but he had been uncomfortable that way, too. Right now he had to have a bath, a bed, and a good meal. The woman could wait until tomorrow.

Sober Indian eyes appraised him, and he felt grimy and overdressed beside the natives' immaculate white garb, brilliant headdresses, and glossy hair. Frustrated, he began to complain. Then he noticed all eyes had shifted to the entrance of the room. He turned.

It was the betrayer.

Alana covered the wolfhound with a blanket. The return trip from the hiding place in the mountains, so soon after getting there, had almost killed him. The familiars who came for her had kept a steady pace, pulling Finn by a rope tied to one of their horses.

By the time the party reached Tlaxcala, the barely healed javelin wound had broken open and was bleeding badly. One of them had carried the colt, thank God. Not out of pity—these cutthroats did not know such emotions!—but because the colt was to die with the witch. The inquisitor would have been irate if it had perished from fright and fatigue.

She sat down beside her faithful companion and leaned against the wall. He licked her hand, and Alana leaned over to kiss the top of his head. Wouldn't it be kinder to kill him herself? Better that he die by the sword of love than suffer a grisly death at the stake. When, oh, when was Brian going to ride in and rescue them?

Tlaxcala and Spain had a treaty, but none of its terms seemed to apply to her situation. Although a member of the Christian faith, she was not a Spaniard. Was she then, the Indian judges asked, subject to Spanish law when said law did not exist under their jurisdiction?

And as for being a witch, what was so objectionable about that? According to their astrologers, benevolent sorcerors were born under the rain sign and were destined to practice witchcraft; they held a certain status in society. Because men—and gods, for that matter—were good and evil, black magicians were also known. Such individuals were put to death if found guilty of harmful witchcraft.

But this woman had been in the public eye for an entire year, and the judges were in possession of no evidence that proved her guilty of any crime. With due respect for the honored inquisitor and Tlaxcala's position as Spain's ally, they could only approve of her being put under house arrest pending future developments.

"God blast it!" Alana jumped to her feet and paced back and forth. "Who told them where I was?"

Could it have been the jealous widow who had borne Brian's son? A soldier denied her favors who harbored a grudge? Was it a slave from her house in Texcoco, hoping for a reward? Or a spy of the late Savage Serpent's . . . even Corn Flower, afraid Alana might accuse her of murder? Who? Who hated her this much?

"If only Brian hadn't been so obstinate, we'd be on the way home," she murmured aloud. "Instead, the emeralds have gone into the pocket of that fat swine and the Lord only knows where Brian is. I'm—"

The biggest and roughest of the familiars pulled aside the door hanging and stamped into the room. Finn growled, and Alana spoke to him soothingly.

"Are you ready for a visit from the inquisitor, *bruja*?" He was not aware his voice grated like the ratchets he spun so often when torturing victims on the rack.

"I am not a witch." Alana fastened her robe closer to her chin. He had manhandled her when taking her prisoner and confiscating the emeralds. Had it not been for the Otomis, she had no doubt she would have met the fate of other women taken for questioning.

He sidled closer, leering suggestively. "I'll make it easier for you if you . . . cooperate."

"You whore's bastard, I wouldn't spit on the best part of you."

The coarse features reddened, and the nostrils flared. "Wait—" he choked. "Just wait—"

His superiors swept in, garments rustling. The familiar made a servile bow and then hurried away while Alana stood petrified with fear and loathing. How she hated these terrible men!

The Soul Seeker. This canting hypocrite had caused the loss of her first child. Now he endangered a second babe who slept and flourished in her womb.

The young monk was taken aback by the fury in her eyes. Muttering a prayer, he stepped away from her. In doing so his sandaled foot nudged the wolfhound, concealed under the blanket. Finn raised his huge head and snarled at the scent of an old enemy.

"Oh, my God!" The monk grabbed his bad arm and involuntarily passed water in his terror. The spatter of urine on the smoothly stuccoed floor sounded plainly.

The inquisitor glanced at him in disgust. "Go to your quarters and remain there until I send for you."

Faint with humiliation, the monk rushed out as Finn rose painfully and lifted his leg over the stain. Alana laughed shortly.

"Your beast has an unsettling effect on poor Mateo. But then you yourself have always made men lose their composure."

The Irishwoman was as lovely as—no, lovelier than—the bishop remembered. Maturity became her. Right now at least, he had no desire to possess her. Burning the first witch in New Spain offered sufficient fame and stimulation at his age, yet he had had a pang of nostalgia for the young goddess who had ridden out of the sea.

"In fact," he purred, "you seem to unsettle a lot of people." He paused, relishing the drama of the scene and his role in it. "Wouldn't you like to meet your Judas?"

Alana drew a deep breath. "Faith, and indeed I would!"

The door hanging moved, and she gasped as if struck. "You!"

The woman kept her eyes downcast. "Yes," Inmaculada whispered, "it is I."

XXXV

The man from León regaled the familiar who guarded Alana's room with tales of Aztec treasure and honey-skinned women. His audience was fascinated; his experiences so far had amounted to trailing after the inquisitor and lounging here by the witch's door. What good that did, he couldn't tell. Everyone knew witches vanished and reappeared at will.

Had he ever heard of the red-haired Englishman who fought five Aztecs in what Spaniards called *el sacrificio gladiatorial*? He hadn't? Oh, it was a good story! The soldier laid it on thick.

"And after all that, he went and got into bad trouble a couple of weeks ago."

Alana's heart skipped a beat. She had been hunched by the doorway, listening for the message her friend had hidden in the narrative. Bad trouble? Sweet Jesus, what did that mean? She ran a hand across her abdomen and tried to wet her lips.

"He killed a crossbowman . . . a personal matter, I understand. Broke his back and then drowned him in a canal. Now he's on the run up north where the primitive tribes are. If he's not already dead from a musket shot in his back, Cortés will hang him. But the siege is at such a point right now Cortés has more urgent matters to take care of. It's been dragging on almost sixty days, you know, and whoever holds out one minute longer than the other wins."

Did he hear a muted sob? He was sincerely sorry to bring her this news and sorrier still he dared do no more. Yet he did think of one item—

"I can't help admiring those Aztecs. How brave they are! Their women are every bit as fierce as the warriors. They throw stones, fire slingshots, string bows for the men, sharpen spear points. . . ."

His voice lowered. "I tell you, enemy or not, I salute them. Crammed into one corner of their city, walking on their dead and dying, watching their children and babies starving. . . . *Dios.*"

Faces of Aztec women she had known drifted across Alana's mind—the bird keeper's slave, courtesans, featherworkers, weavers, palace serving girls, healing women, embroiderers, tortilla makers, cooks, gentlewomen and peasants, maids, matrons, and priestesses.

Were they gone now? Ground into the foundation of Tenochtitlán by pain, famine, and sorrow or sword, shot, and iron hoof?

She felt sick and empty. They would be dead soon, she and the Indian women who had fought so faithfully and loved so deeply. Alana sank to her knees. Oh, Merciful Father, what shall I do? Guide me, I pray You, strengthen, me, give me courage.

The wolfhound pressed his body to her knee, knowing she was worried. She put an arm around him.

"Oh, Finn, we're so alone, you and I. What will we do?" Brian was gone, probably food for the vultures by now. Alana groaned in almost physical agony. She rocked back and forth, keening to herself.

How Brian's warm, sweet glance danced with love and laughter in her memory. But those same eyes which evolved in the tiny babe she carried would never smile up at her. Because he, too, would be charred to ashes! She fainted.

When Alana returned to consciousness, Finn was washing her face and whining with anxiety. The room was quiet, and the guard outside yawned audibly. Evidently he had heard nothing. She crawled to the bed and covered herself, glad not be seen prostrate with grief.

Someone scratched politely at the doorway, and an Indian girl delivered a flagon of mulled wine Alana had requested earlier. Its steaming spiciness was cheerful and comforting, and it occurred to Alana that she had not eaten since yesterday morning. Why, she was ravenous! The servant, gathering soiled clothing, promised to bring a tray of hot food as soon as possible.

In the meantime, Finn no doubt needed to attend to his natural functions. Because the dog tolerated no one but his mistress to lead him on a leash, the inquisitor had given reluctant permission for such emergencies. *Naturalmente,* familiars would accompany her. She called to the guard.

Ah, it was good to be outside! Alana shook her curls in the breeze. She smelled roses, freshly ground *chilli,* horse manure, wood smoke, and the perfume of sun-kissed pine blowing down from forested slopes.

Passersby smiled, exchanging greetings and ignoring the men with her. How somber and unattractive they appeared to the Indian eye, garbed so severely in rusty black with the green cross of the Inquisition worked on their tunics.

In the distance a Spaniard tossed his head much the way Gilberto used to do. He, too, had hair like a raven's wing in the sun, touched with white at the temples.

Her dark darling who loved her so much. Whatever his faults, they faded into nothingness beside the gallant gesture of the letter. It so easily might have fallen into unfriendly hands. *Gilberto, my dear, I send you my love. Love from another time, another world.*

The Soul Seeker walked out of a nearby street and stopped in front of the escort. Alana gazed with grim satisfaction at his emaciated figure.

"Take the woman to that building there." He pointed with his good hand, the useless arm hanging from a voluminous sleeve. Alana pulled Finn closer. Fray Mateo would hurt the dog if he could do so without the knowledge of his superior.

It was with the greatest sadness that Alana sat on a low stool at the front of the Council chamber. When she had first seen this room, she had felt at home, as if she were in the hall of an Irish mountain king. Garlands of pink tuberoses and pine branches had been draped along the walls; fires had burned in big tripods; laughter and conversation had rippled through the crowd; dusky skins, limpid Indian eyes, jewels, and metals had gleamed in the torchlight.

Xicotencatl the Younger had been alive then, and Corn Flower had glowed with love and desire. Brian had flirted with the haughty widow and conceived a child with her. Pepe Ortega had been gay and vibrant, eager to marry his Maya sweetheart. Moctezuma, Yellow Plume, the men lost on the *Noche Triste*—Lord, how many people had died. Her stomach contracted with fear. Was it her turn next?

Local carpenters had hurriedly made four chairs and a long table for the witch's hearing. The furniture was arranged on a platform. How typical of her persecutors to force her to look up at them, as if beseeching indulgence and compassion.

Alana heard onlookers settling behind her with interested murmurs of Nahuatl and Spanish. From the little she knew about inquisitorial practices, it was a stroke of luck the hearing was not taking place in Cuba. As the accused—guilty until proved innocent—she would have confronted the inquisitor and his torture master there in total secrecy, weighted with chains, half-starved, filthy, and abused.

Here she had a measure of security beneath the stern but impartial eye of Tlaxcalan judges. Like those in a majority of the advanced tribes, they administered a complex, efficient, and honest judicial system. In the absence of lawyers, judges were final arbiters; their responsibility was heavy since any decision not rendered impartially was punishable by death.

The wolfhound growled softly. The inquisitor, Fray Mateo, and the chief familiar, who presumably acted as *fiscal*, or public prosecutor, were taking their seats. They were out of place in the simple chamber decorated with bear, puma, and deer skins.

Tlaxcala's feathered standard behind the dais was picturesque and dramatic: a golden eagle with wings outstretched and sparked with emeralds and silver on a pure white ground. Shrouded with veils of black crepe, the Holy Office's banner hovered over the eagle like a harbinger of doom. Against a sable ground an oval medallion displayed the green cross of the Holy Office; on one side an olive branch assured God's mercy; on the other a sword pledged death to the unbeliever.

The inquisitor was nettled by the number of elderly Tlaxcalan judges who had expressed concern for this woman sheltered by their laws of hospitality. Did they think he didn't know what he was doing? It was bad enough having all these other people privy to the proceedings.

He bumped his gout-swollen toe and almost lost his poise. A man liked to work his own way in his own establishment. He glanced at the woman sitting in front of him, pale but serene. Better make this a simple hearing instead of a trial in order to put her Indian friends off guard.

Matters would be better served by taking her to the capital, in secret if necessary. There he would have the support of Hernán Cortés, whom these natives respected so highly. Bind her to the stake! Fire the fagots around her feet! That would make the desired impression on Aztec and Spanish rogue alike. What did it matter if the Irishwoman was truly guilty or not? Only he and Mateo would ever know.

Alana sensed something evil going through the man's mind, and the way he glowered at her made her flesh creep. She smoothed the folds of her flowing robe, ordinarily worn in private. Public exhibition in undress was merely one stratagem the Inquisition used to catch the accused unawares, as was arrest after midnight and before dawn when physical powers were at the lowest ebb.

The inquisitor leaned forward to position a tall, silver crucifix and two very slender burning candles more to his satisfaction. Then he spoke to a notary, the tribunal's fourth member, and pointed to a large volume of the Gospel.

Dry and impersonal as his records, the notary quickly arranged quills, ink, and paper, lit a small candle to provide wax for seals, and then picked up the Gospel. Alana failed to suppress a jerk of apprehension. Here it came, dear God, here it came. She clasped her hands to conceal their tremor.

Fray Mateo commanded, "Administer the oath."

Alana stood without being told when the notary halted in front of her. "Repeat after me.

"I swear by the Living God and by the Holy Virgin, Mother of Christ, that I will truthfully answer questions pertaining to the matters about which I am to be questioned and that I will not withhold information pertinent to them or refuse to divulge names of associates involved in them."

Alana repeated the oath, kissed the pages of the Gospel, and crossed herself reverently.

"The defendant will stand during questioning," the familiar said. Whore's bastard, was he? Wouldn't spit on the best part of him, wasn't that what she said? He crouched in his chair, a ruthless tomcat waiting to pounce.

The notary lifted the pen. "Your name?"

"Alana MacKenna, descendant of the High Kings of Ireland."

"Your birthplace?"

"Dublin, Ireland, near the river called Liffey." Oh, God, would she ever see it again?

"Are you a Catholic?"

"Yes."

"Where did you learn to speak Spanish?"

"My father was a horse breeder who sold much of his stock to Spaniards, especially in the southern part of Spain. When I was old enough to travel, he often took me with him. And you'll remember, the Spanish and the Irish have traded with each other for a long time."

"Where is your father?"

"My parents died of the sweating sickness several years ago."

The inquisitor asked in a silky tone, "Have you ever been married?"

"No, but—"

He struck. "Of course, you haven't! Because you are a witch!" The spectators gasped, and the judges frowned when his statement was translated.

"How else could you work your obscene magic on men who are unprepared for the onslaught of such malevolent powers?" The inquisitor felt pleased. He already had the defendant on the hook.

"When did you last confess?" Fray Mateo's voice flayed the nerves, but she met his glare without flinching.

"In Coyoacán in early July." Alana knew he would pounce on the answer, and the monk did not disappoint her.

"Early in July! This is the first of August!" He threw his hand into the air theatrically. "What better proof that this female, vile sorceress that she is, has renounced God!" His words boomed in the hushed chamber.

Alana's indignation brought spots of color to her cheekbones. "I'll have you know I've always been a devout Christian. But there's no priest in Tlaxcala. They're off with the army."

"*We* are here and have been for some time. One of us would gladly have heard the confession of such a sinner."

The Soul Seeker smiled frostily as she covered her throat with one hand. It was a gesture often made by proud prisoners trying to hide the rapidly fluttering pulse that betrayed a pounding heart.

To cover her confusion, Alana studied Finn, who rested at her feet. The wound in his side still suppurated, and he grunted when he changed position. Unaccountably she began to feel better. If she lost this battle, it would not be for lack of courage. Why, thanks to His hand, she had faced many dangers and survived.

Alana thought back to the sea voyage from Spain, the shipwreck, the

Noche Triste, her fall and miscarriage, the forays while searching for Brian, rape by the crossbowman, the two brushes with Savage Serpent. . . . Faith, she planned to go down fighting! Life had taught her how to fight!

The men on the dais watched the change incredulously. There she was, this small woman, friendless and alone and about to be charged with the most heinous crimes. A prisoner in the grasp of the most awesome of authorities, the Holy Office. And what was she doing?

Smiling. Lifting her head and straightening her shoulders. Folding her arms as if chatting with a neighbor. Could she be calling on demons to come to her aid? Don't forget there were seven million four hundred and five thousand nine hundred and twenty-six of them! And take care with the glint in her eye!

"Well, now, Father," she said politely, "there are very excellent reasons why I didn't come to the pair of you to take confession."

"Read the charges!" The inquisitor's face had turned bright red and the monk's paper-white.

"Alana Mackenna, single female," the notary hastened to say, "is here charged with the practice of witchcraft and sorcery and with using the *Book of Ballymote*, an Irish textbook on magic."

The notary sat down, anxious to listen to what had the elements of the most dramatic hearing he had ever attended. Thinking of his big, fat wife who had the courage of a mouse, he mentally applauded this valiant defendant. Perhaps she wasn't a witch. But then she had not been tested by the iron boot or thumbscrews, nor had had her fingernails been torn out. Women almost always confessed after those tortures.

"The others! The others!" the inquisitor gritted. "Where are your wits, man?"

"Oh, forgive me, Your Holiness!" The notary shot to his feet with a paper in his hands. He had better keep his mind on what he was doing.

"Adultery. Murder. Theft. Wearing men's clothing. Blasphemy." He paused impressively after each word. "Worshiping the devil. Talking the language of animals. . . ."

The soldier-interpreter hesitated to interrupt, but he was between the sword and the wall. No sane Spaniard would dream of irritating an inquisitor, yet he had married a Tlaxcalan widow and planned to remain in the City of the Eagle. He gulped.

"The honorable judges wish to know why the woman has not been given the opportunity to continue with her reasons for not confessing. They are also concerned that no advocate has been appointed to assist her in these legal matters."

"This is only a hearing, not a trial," the familiar grumbled.

"Even so, she is a woman without learning and entitled to representation," the Indians persisted.

"Women are sinks of iniquity!" the Soul Seeker suddenly yelled, half rising from his chair. "That is why they are witches!" He pointed at Alana, his finger shaking visibly. "She is Melusine, Satan's own whore!"

Finn scrambled to a standing position, disliking the voice of violence aimed in his direction. He lifted his upper lip, fangs bared in warning.

"See? See how that hound from hell is threatening me?" The monk almost frothed at the mouth. How he wished he might put that cursed dog to the torture! He would never forget losing control of his water in front of his superior because of this animal. Never!

"Sit down, Fray Mateo," the inquisitor ordered. "Now, Alana Mac-Kenna, how do you plead?"

Removing the chain from around her neck, Alana kissed her crucifix and raised it into the air. "I swear by the holy cross, by the Only-Begotten and His Blessed Mother, that I am innocent of witchcraft and sorcery and that I have never even seen the *Book of Ballymote.*"

She turned toward the native magistrates and repeated her words in Nahuatl. These men were her only hope. When an Indian invoked the gods in his defense, touched a finger to the ground, and then to his lips, his innocence was usually taken for granted. The gods punished liars more severely than any human court.

Murmurs rippled through the audience when the oldest Tlaxcalan queried, "What of the other charges, daughter?"

Alana was beginning to feel faint from lack of food, nervousness, and standing too long. She passed a hand over her forehead. "The other charges, revered sir?"

The inquisitor rapped the table sharply. "Speak Spanish! Speak Spanish!" He admonished the soldier-interpreter sternly. "Look alive there if you know what's good for you."

"I—I will freely admit to two of the charges."

"Freely admit?" her accusers chorused in triumph.

"It is no secret that I lived with two men. Men I loved," she said softly. "Adultery is a sin—" Alana grasped her crucifix tightly to her heart. "But I loved them. That is my only defense."

The notary noticed the majority of onlookers appeared uneasy with that answer. Idly, he wondered how many had felt love when they committed the crime. Oh, the climate in New Spain was indeed ripe for the word of God!

"I swear I am not guilty of murder or theft. As for wearing men's clothing, I have done so only because it has been necessary to spend much of my time here on horseback. As for blasphemy, which is profane speech about God, I am His humble servant, not His reviler."

Alana sat down suddenly. "I'm hungry," she explained. "I haven't eaten since yesterday morning, and I don't think I can go on."

"One final point," the old Tlaxcalan said, "then the hearing will be bound over until midmorning tomorrow." He ignored the spluttering from the Spanish quartet.

She stood again, reeling a trifle. "Yes?"

"I object!" the inquisitor thundered. "We have not dealt with her worshiping the devil or talking to beasts. Nor have we heard the letters from witnesses who swear they saw the witch and her evil spirits fly. And that when they did, there was a stink of brimstone, a flapping of leathery wings, and voices in strange tongues!"

Alana shivered. He had overlooked nothing in his eagerness to convict her and take his petty revenge.

The Indian judge went on as if uninterrupted. "Although we confess only once in a lifetime, we know those who worship the Woman and Child do so often to cleanse their souls." The dark, wrinkled features revealed a slight disdain for a race so undisciplined it required constant absolution of sin.

"I believe an important question has gone unanswered," he continued. "What were your reasons for not confessing to these representatives of your faith?"

Alana knew she was signing her death warrant, and her earlier confidence fled. Was it intuition that sent such a chill down the spine—or the Soul Seeker's deadly stare? Then she remembered the baby she'd lost.

"I did not confess to either man," she declared in a clear, high tone, "because I had no respect for them as men of God. They have both tried to seduce me, Fray Mateo de Aldana as recently as last winter, right here in Tlaxcala.''

In the stunned silence Alana added, ''My wolfhound attacked him to save me. That's how the priest lost the use of his arm.''

''I deny it! I deny it!''

The inquisitor was shouting over the hubbub. ''Clear the court! Clear the court! Take the defendant to her quarters!''

A squad of familiars marched to the front of the chamber, surrounded Alana and Finn, and hustled them toward the door. As they pushed through the crowd, she saw the man from León drop his cap and bend to retrieve it. She was past him before she realized he had hidden his face so she would not accidentally betray him.

As the familiars and their prisoner filed through the door, a unit of Tlaxcalan warriors fell into step. Among them were several men from her little army that helped her hunt for Brian and act as intermediary for Cortés. She smiled fondly.

''You won't smile for long, *bruja*,'' the chief familiar snapped. ''I can promise you that.''

XXXVI

How cold it was all of a sudden! Tired out, Alana had gone to bed after eating a light meal, sleeping naked as usual between fur robes. But they had been yanked off, and her skin shrank from the chill air.

Who held that candle over her? She felt distant pain when hot wax dropped on her thigh. Terror raced through her brain at the sight of two well-known faces, but her body refused to budge. She could hear and see but not move or speak.

"I do believe she's with child," the inquisitor said, eyes glued to his captive's globular breasts. "See the swelling of the bosom? Not much as yet, but the evil fruit grows each second."

"Yes," his companion agreed, almost overcome with his old weakness, yet incapable of turning away. *Oh, Lord, why have You sent me this burden again? Have I not proved that I could conquer temptation?* Surreptitiously, Fray Mateo pressed the hair shirt painfully to his private parts. *Forgive me, I pray Thee, forgive me. But she is so beautiful!*

The inquisitor wished the younger man would leave the room. He vibrated with desire. Such a glorious body, seductive even in its helplessness! However, now that each man was accused of the same transgression, he was not letting the other out of his sight. Furthermore, Fray Mateo had politically powerful relatives at court who might cause difficulties.

369

"Abandoned bitch! She has lain with the devil many times and conceived by him."

"Is she not Melusine? You may be sure the babe will have hooves and be furred!"

Alana listened, motionless and dumb. God save her, what drug had been in the food? Out of the corner of her eye, she saw an immobile Finn lying on the floor, breathing quietly. At least he was alive. Then her eyes widened in panic. The chief familiar, who reminded her so much of the crossbowman, had entered the room.

By the tits of a virgin, what a sight! The man's mouth watered as he grinned expectantly. Most women did not resist abuse. They hoped against hope that surrender and cooperation would lessen future punishment or make imprisonment easier for themselves or their loved ones. It never did, of course, but he savored having the whip hand in the dungeons.

Then his grin faded. Evidently this strong-willed wench was not going to be his to play with. Both his superiors wore proprietary expressions. *Bueno,* they could keep her then, even though it would have been enjoyable to teach her a lesson.

"Begging your pardon, Your Worship. The mules have been loaded, and the men are saddled and waiting. But the witch's horses have vanished."

"What?" The inquisitor popped a sweetmeat into his mouth.

"Both mare and colt are gone, and the guard swears he saw a figure with horns before he fell and hit his head."

Alana closed her eyes. Bless the man from León.

"We did find this near the corral gate. A blue butterfly made out of feathers."

The inquisitor tossed it aside. "A native must have dropped it. They make a lot of useless things. Once Holy Church gets here, they'll begin to do real *work.*"

He pondered a moment. "She's spirited the horses away, but we have no time to wait for the drug to wear off so she can cast a spell and get them back. We have her and the dog. That will have to do.

"Chain the animal on the biggest mule and make sure its muzzle is bound and its legs securely tied. Then dress the woman warmly—I don't want her to die of exposure—and bring her outside. I want to be on the road by midnight."

He bustled away to attend to last-minute details, but Fray Mateo remained behind with the chief familiar, whose assistants, after one lip-smacking look, hoisted the wolfhound off the floor and staggered out with him.

"Here," the monk said, "put these on her. I could not bear to touch the flesh of a succubus." He handed the man Alana's clothing—an underskirt, russet boots, a heavy greenish blue cotton *huipil* and skirt, and her white rabbit fur jacket.

I'll bet you wouldn't touch her! No more than any of us. The familiar took care not to let his hands wander. This monk was touched in the head.

"That was like dressing a doll." He chuckled, pulling on a boot.

"Get her out of my sight." The monk sank to his calloused knees.

When Alana had been taken away, the Soul Seeker stared blindly into space. Then with a groan be buried his face in the bed furs, faintly warm and fragrant from her nakedness. As he rubbed his face back and forth like a dog in a favorite scent, he feverishly ripped the fur out in clumps with his one good hand.

Burn the witch, he moaned. *Burn the witch!* Only that way could he rid himself of this canker eating at his soul, weakening his body and will, softening his heart, weening him away from the Lord's work. *Burn. Burn.* Burn the woman for whom he lusted.

He fell back on his haunches as the inquisitor hurried in to see what was keeping him. Yes, it was his holy duty to burn the lovely witch without delay. The exalted expression on the gaunt face left the older man puzzled and unsettled.

Headed west, the company had covered almost twenty miles by the next evening, staying overnight in a town allied with Tlaxcala. Alana's paralysis, as well as Finn's, had disappeared during the day.

The following morning she was able to ride, and they made better time. With the wolfhound chained to grain bags atop a husky mule, the riders followed a road across the northern flank of the volcano called Ixtaccihuatl. Because this route was at a much lower altitude than the alternate path between the two great volcanoes taken by Cortés, no one suffered from the cold.

Alana's apathy and feeling of hopelessness grew. Another day and a half at this pace, and they would reach the lakes and the Spanish fort that controlled Tenochtitlán's southern causeway. There had been no chance for escape. Wrist manacles were chained to a wide iron band around her waist that padlocked at the back. As yet no chains had been fastened on her ankles, but she realized that was only because the inquisitor was anxious to reach the capital.

And poor Finn! Her heart ached for him, bouncing up and down, cruelly bound in one position the entire day. His whimpers of pain and entreaty finally reduced her to tears.

"I said you wouldn't smile for long, *bruja*. I was right, wasn't I?" the chief familiar jeered.

Watching her, he exclaimed, "Aha! You'd like to scratch my face to ribbons, wouldn't you?" Their mounts trotted side by side.

Alana wiped her eyes. "Hog. Turd. Misbegotten son of a murderer and his faithless trollop."

Because the epithet happened to be true, it provoked him. The man struck her cheek with a mailed fist, not hard enough to stun but enough to make her cry out and cause hemorrhaging beneath the skin.

"Keep your lousy mouth shut, or I'll shut it for you," he threatened.

Alana's temper flared. She shook her chains with anger and began to curse the familiar in loud, ringing tones.

"May the grass grow at your door and the fox build his nest on your hearthstone. May the light fade from your eyes, so you never see what you love. May your own blood rise against you—"

The Soul Seeker rode up to see what the disturbance was. "Be quiet. Be quiet, do you hear me?" The chant made hair brush up along the skin.

"—and the sweetest drink you take be the bitterest cup of sorrow. Aye, may you die without benefit of clergy. May there be none to shed a tear at your grave, and may the hearthstone of hell be your best bed forever!"

The wolfhound howled forlornly as if calling down his own malediction, and the riders crossed themselves with a shudder. The chief familiar dropped back, away from those untamed eyes. He felt badly shaken at being the target of such a virulent curse. A witch, after all, was no one to fool with! Especially an alien such as this Irishwoman. At least he knew what to expect from those of his own nationality.

After the outburst, which had drained her energy, Alana rode silently through what had been a fruitful, orderly region, along the southern banks of the lakes called Chalco and Xochimilco. As the armored Spaniards and their prisoners passed, bands of Indians watched sullenly from a distance. They looked wretched and starved.

"How far are we from Coyoacán?" The inquisitor's petulent question whined above the hoofbeats.

A familiar who had ridden ahead to make arrangements answered, "We should be there by the end of the day, Your Excellency. There will be comfortable lodgings and hot food waiting."

"Thank God for that!" His behind had never been so sore. The prelate turned in the saddle and motioned to Fray Mateo to join him.

"I've lost track of time. Is this the thirteenth or the fourteenth?"

"Wednesday, the thirteenth. Blessed Saint Hippolytus' Day, the thirteenth of August, 1521."

They were now passing Xochimilco—or what remained of that rich and elegant city with its two-hundred-and-fifty-year-old gardens—and Alana bit her lip. Cortés and his Spanish-Indian army had sacked and burned it in the spring, leaving behind a desolation softened only by the artificial islands on which vegetables and flowers grew in neglected disarray.

Were the flowers rotting in the heavy afternoon rains? A nauseating odor wafted over them with the wind. As they drew nearer their destination, the stench intensified.

The inquisitor covered his mouth with a lace-trimmed handkerchief. "What *is* that?"

The same guard who'd been to Coyoacán blew his nose. "It's from the Aztec corpses. I hear they're stacked so thick you have to walk on them. When you can see it, the ground is soaked with blood. The infidels are still resisting and have been driven into the northwestern section of the island, a district called Tlatelolco." He stumbled over the pronunciation.

"What barbarous names! Give me a good, honest Christian name like San Salvador or Santo Domingo any time!"

"Amen," the familiar muttered, bored with the subject.

Jubilation roared through Cortés' headquarters by the time the tired, hungry party rode in at dusk. Cuauhtémoc, Great Lord of the once-mighty Aztecs, had been captured that very day! And with his surrender all hostilities had ceased on the bloody, war-torn island.

By the sacred bones of Jesus Christ, our Savior, the siege was over! After seventy-five days of hell on earth, the siege was over! New Spain now gleamed in the crown of Old Spain, courtesy of Hernán Cortés from Estremadura, himself a great lord of men and conquistador *extraordinaire*.

If the gem dripped with blood for the moment, that was simply the way of the world in 1521. Someday the city he planned to build would take its place among the capitals of the most polished nations.

As it happened, everything went wrong for the inquisitorial group the minute it came to the end of its journey. The riders had entered a courtyard not far from houses kept by Cortés' lieutenants when Alana fainted from hunger and fatigue. As she toppled out of the saddle, an Indian in full battle regalia rushed out of the gloom to catch her.

The two dozen familiars, nervous as only cowardly men are, drew their swords. Not to save the woman, God save the mark, no, but to save the priests and themselves.

At least fifty more Indians leaped into sight, hideous in paint and feathers and ready to protect their comrade, who knelt on the ground with an arm around the captive's shoulders. It was the Tlaxcalan chief who had led her army under the cross and shamrock. He frowned at the manacles and iron belt. How fortunate that he and his men had been quietly looting nearby while the Spaniards drank and sang. What had she done?

A brief fight quickly ensued in which three familiars were killed. The melee excited the inquisitor's horse, which subsequently threw and trampled him; the pack mule kicked out in agitation and broke a man's leg; the Soul Seeker, trying to reach his superior, tripped over combatants rolling on the ground and fell, knocking himself out.

Horses neighing, men cursing and shouting, the wolfhound barking, mules braying. . . . A squad of Spaniards finally came on the run to investigate the noise. They were much the worse for wear, having battled in heavy armor for weeks in the rain on a starvation diet, witnessed companions sacrificed, and waded in gore. They were anxious to get back to the women and the wine that was flowing freely in celebration of victory.

"Bring those lanterns! Over here!"

"That's enough, that's enough! Get up, you whoresons!"

"Holy Mother of God, here's the inquisitor general, out like a snuffed candle. Certainly I know him. Seen him in Cuba many times."

"Who's this?"

"*Dios mío,* handle him carefully, too. That's the monk known as the Soul Seeker."

"And here's the Englishman's woman in chains. Her dog, too."

A soldier glanced around the courtyard and yawned. "What a mess. Where's the blasted Indian that started it? I swear they can vanish like a puff of smoke."

"Don't turn up your nose. You'll wish you had the same talent some night when a husband's banging on the door, *amigo.*"

Laughter lightened everyone's mood, and order gradually prevailed. The two priests were quickly transported to a house that had been allocated to them. A messenger was sent to Cortés, and Fray Olmedo and a soldier with a gift for mending broken bones were sent for. Animals were unloaded, unsaddled, and stabled, and the familiars guided to lodgings and refreshments.

A hard rain had begun to fall by the time Alana and Finn were taken care of. The Chief familiar, nursing a broken hand and a ragged temper, blamed their troubles on her. On the witch who had been brought to Tenochtitlán to be burned at the stake.

They planted the stake at Tacuba, where the western causeway met the mainland. Although the inquisitor general remained in bed with multiple injuries, he gave specific instructions for his captive's exhibition. The pagan dogs leaving their dens must see the wrath of the Christian God who had brought them to their knees! And when the time came to light the fires for New Spain's first *auto de fé*, he would be there, never fear.

Oh, where were the princes and the grandeur over which they had reigned? The latticework of canals shimmering in the sun, the temples and houses of shining stucco and ruby-red stone, the gardens and statuary, the zoo and aviary, flower-edged pools, the people, arrogant and brilliantly dressed like tropical birds? Gone, gone forever. Bernal Díaz had been right; no place like it would ever be discovered again.

What Alana had heard Cortés describe as "the most beautiful thing in the world" no longer existed. Nothing remained but a piteously barren plain of rubble and a *teocalli* here and there slated for future demolition.

The Aztecs' last stand had been made at Tlatelolco, at one time the empire's commercial center and its prime marketplace. Its cannon-scarred walls smoldered stubbornly despite a tremendous storm that had shaken the earth during the night. The stench of thousands of corpses sickened even the most hardened soldiers.

Dully, Alana watched refugees evacuating the island stagger across the causeway toward her, some falling into the lake and drowning from sheer weakness. When they reached land a short distance from the platform on which she stood, waiting Spaniards searched them for hidden gold. They also took the strongest warriors as slaves and branded them on mouth and cheek.

Contrary to the inquisitor's expectation, however, few surviving Aztecs paid any attention to his prisoner and the huge animal tied at her feet. Homeless, grief-stricken, feeble and diseased, wounded or maimed, wasted from eating lizards, rats, worms, weeds, bark, corn cobs, they had their own calamities to face. Those of the white race were less important to them than the death of a larva. And they knew everything there was to know about death.

Had they noticed, they would have seen the manner in which Alana MacKenna, descendant of kings who once sang in Tara's wondrous halls, had been fettered.

She was bound to the stake with ropes at the ankles, below the knees, at the groin, around waist and neck, and beneath the arms. Chains were often used, but in this case the inquisitor had decided against them in view of the prisoner's frailty. She must not die in advance of punishment.

Her feet rested on fagots; more fagots and straw were stacked at neat intervals about the platform. When the time for execution came, a mixture of these would be piled to her chin and fired. But only after she had confessed her sins and been given absolution, for these acts permitted death by garrote before fire consumed the victim. If she refused to confess, she would be burned alive.

Alana's guard the first night turned out to be a grizzled old grouch with an empty eye socket and a bad stomach that no longer tolerated wine. Rather than sit on the sidelines of the drunken festivities, he had volunteered for the night watch. And a melancholy duty it was! He had forgotten how pretty the city used to be with altar fires blazing on the temple summits and processions of partygoers wending along canals with flutes playing and torches mirrored in the water. It was black and as silent as a crypt over there now.

The prisoner moaned. Following orders to keep her from dying, the soldier mounted the platform. Her wolfhound growled weakly.

"Still her champion, eh?"

He had campaigned with Cortés from the very start and had lifted a few with this woman and her lovers before his stomach gave out. Now that he thought about it, after the *Noche Triste*, she had kept his socket cleansed and free of infection while he recovered from other wounds.

He hesitated. This *was* a witch. Yet she asked for water so sweetly he could not refuse. Nor could he deny the dog that had always defended her.

"They could not win," she muttered. "They couldn't, you see. Not in court. They had to cheat."

"*Sí, sí.*" He held water to her lips again.

"*Gracias, hombre. Muchas gracias.* Do you have a cloak? To cover the dog?"

The iron heart melted a trifle. Poor baggage. He untied the ropes except for the one at her waist, helped her work it down the stake so she was able to sit and tossed her a blanket. Alana immediately threw part of it over Finn and put his head in her lap. Within minutes she had fallen asleep, utterly spent. When dawn reddened the sky, the soldier gave them more water and tied her in place again.

The green eyes seemed opalescent with the new day's pearly glow. "You are a good man." She looked away and did not speak again.

As the hours wore on, Alana's will to live began to ebb. Where the night had been cold, the day was hot, intensifying her thirst. The ropes chafed cruelly and brought blood. Her own excreta insulted her nostrils, and muscles denied a change in position ached intolerably. It became harder and harder to breathe normally, and delirium started that afternoon.

When people came to stare and speculate on how she would meet death, Alana ignored them. Cortés, grown haggard and morose; Malinche, impassively regal as ever; dear Bernal and Sandoval; the sad and dejected Aztec ruler; Spanish women marked by battle; others her tired brain refused to recognize.

It was those she loved who came to console her and stayed as ghostly confidants, and she hailed them in the many languages her facile tongue spoke so well.

Brian was there, smiling and marvelously handsome like the son he cradled with such tenderness. Her parents and the Irish sweetheart of her youth beckoned to her. Gilberto offered a string of pearls and kissed her hand. And Pepe Ortega had brought Conn, who whinnied in greeting and shook the gleaming floss of his mane in the wind.

For an instant Alana regained consciousness, aroused by the racket of thousands of Cortés' Indian allies crossing the causeway to act as burial parties. Then she heard the crackle of a thousand fires as the conquerors set about the business of purifying the charnel house they had created. She lapsed back into a more peaceful world of her own.

Here Blue Butterfly led the mare and her colt, so small and eager for life, and Yellow Plume gathered roses for a banquet. Ah, how blessed she had been to have had so many to love! Yet there was someone, someone dear to her who had cast aside that love, though that person remained indistinct and refused to take form.

"Finn, Finn, my good dog." Tears streamed down her face when she felt the warmth of his body against her foot.

"Soon we will join the others, and you will hear them shout, *'Cead mile failte sa bhaile romhat'*—a hundred thousand welcomes home to you! And you will course with Conrac, the proud hound of the princely Fionn, who led the Fianna . . . that's what you shall do. . . ." Her words trailed off.

The wolfhound knew the voice. Oh, how he *loved* that voice! But he, too, had slipped into oblivion where pain could not follow. He did not want to fight anymore.

But a smell brought him back to his senses, one he detested, one that reeked of danger and hate. Finn tried to move, but the ropes held him fast. He growled with all his might.

Alana opened her eyes slowly, uncomprehending. There was nothing to be seen. Night had fallen. Yet instinct quickened at the dog's warning. Where was the guard? Why wasn't he here? Who was that behind her, busily piling up fagots and straw? She felt a jolt of shock over the heart as pure fright poured adrenaline into her system.

"Who's that? What are you doing?" Alana struggled in vain against the ropes, gasping for breath. My God, were they going to burn her now?

A torch flared, bringing the visage of Fray Mateo de Aldana into focus. The pale, metallic eyes, utterly devoid of pity, studied her with unholy glee. The prematurely gray hair had been plastered to his skull, so the monk resembled a death's-head in the flickering light.

"I have come to burn you, witch! Burn you to ashes and cast you out of my soul!" He kicked Finn again and again. "And get rid of this hellhound, too."

Shouts of merriment and music sounded clearly in the distance. No one had any interest in a condemned sorceress this evening, nor had the date of execution been advanced. Her enemy had simply come to take his vengeance in private.

He poked her in the abdomen with a heavy silver cross. "Is the child in there? Or have you lost it?"

"Damn you for the devil you are! *Damn* you! You are not fit to wear that habit."

"You will meet the devil soon enough, whore."

The priest jammed the handle of the torch between stones so as to free his good hand and illuminate the platform. He began to heap fuel around the helpless figures. He swore wildly at the useless arm and took every opportunity to bury a foot in the dog's ribs, exclaiming delightedly when they cracked.

To Alana's terrified eyes the Soul Seeker was a fiend from hell. His stooped figure scuttled back and forth, bent with the weight he bore. Fagots soon reached her thighs, then her waist, then her breasts.

"Don't! I beg of you! In the name of the Immaculate Virgin, *don't!*"

But he heard nothing, his mind cracking at last beneath pressures of love and hate too overwhelming to withstand. Finally, the man stood back to admire his handiwork. His victim was enveloped in wood and straw. She now resembled a grotesque tree trunk topped by a small, pale human head.

"*Incantatrix! Incantatrix!* The Gospel commands that 'Thou shalt not suffer a witch to live!' " He grabbed up the torch, and Alana screamed.

"I swore to you that night in the orchard that you and your familiar would burn at the stake!" Peal after peal of hysterical laughter marred the gay Spanish tunes rollicking in the distance.

"I said fire would lick up from your pretty feet—did you know I wanted to kiss them once? But I whipped myself until I hated them. And now that milky flesh will char and fall off the bones, and you will never tempt me again, woman. Because you are going to die. Now *burn—burn!*"

The Soul Seeker leaned forward—and jabbed the flaming torch into the straw and fagots.

Alana heard the straw catch fire. She shrieked in terror, and Finn whined pathetically. Tendrils of smoke drifted upward and made her cough, and she inhaled additional smoke as she breathed more and more rapidly in abject fear.

A few pieces of wood caught fire and crackled ominously. Much of it was damp from an afternoon shower, but she knew there were only minutes left before the combustible structure would begin to burn in earnest.

Suffocating from the smoke, Alana managed to say, "I commend my soul to thee, oh, God, and those I love."

The monk looked on in silent fascination. Tired from his exertions, he let the torch drop to the platform. There was no longer any need for its light.

Her voice drifted faintly from the stake. *"I hope you rot in hell!"*

He giggled, so engrossed in the prisoner's agonies he never noticed the flames licking at the hem of his robe, and by the time the scorching pain in legs and feet penetrated his consciousness, his habit was on fire. His howls filled the air as he beat at himself with his one good hand. The Soul Seeker jumped to the ground and rolled about frantically, trying to smother the blaze.

"Witch! Wi. . . . *Ahhhh!"* The man turned into a pillar of fire, a burnt offering to gods he had worshiped over and above the One to whom he had been so devoted.

Plunged into the solitude of impending death, Alana was unaware her torturer had perished. Her spirit had leaped wild and free into the night wind—she was going home at last! Home! Across the wide, wide sea. . . .

The Englishman rode through the dark at a steady trot, a horde of naked Chichimecas running behind the horse like silent panthers. He had headed south along the banks of Lake Texcoco and was now nearing the Tacuba causeway, where Alvarado's camp had been located during the siege.

His mouth was grim and sullen as he wrestled with the fact that he was now an exile, a renegade, and cut off from England. Why hadn't he listened to Alana? Brian struck the pommel of the saddle with a hard fist. If he had, they could have been in London this minute.

Instead, he had signed his own death warrant by deliberately searching out and killing the crossbowman. At a crucial point in the siege when Cortés had needed every soldier, the conquistador had suffered the loss of one of his best marksmen. There'd be no forgiving, that was certain, and the hangman's noose would always be waiting.

Suppose he went to Vera Cruz? Could he commandeer a caravel and cross the Atlantic to England? Hardly. No self-respecting Spanish crew would put up with that, and he had no one to help him.

Granted, he had attracted a collection of followers in the brief period he'd been on the run but no individual equal to such a complex and dangerous undertaking. A few malcontents from the army had joined him, and seasoned, fanatical warriors from tribes throughout New Spain had been pouring into his camp in hopes of revenge against the white invaders.

The majority, however, were primitives who ate raw meat and scalped their fallen foes. Warlike, brave, and aggressive, they were capable of being welded into a tough fighting force. One was going to be needed to resist the Spaniards who would soon be probing into the country's northern regions in search of silver mines.

Brian snorted. Once he had dreamed of being a famous personage in the glittering court of Henry VIII, of being respected and admired for his explorations and adventures. Now he himself was to be king—king of barren mesas and hostile mountains, of refugees, outcasts and scalp takers who painted themselves red.

He cursed, bringing his thoughts back to the matter at hand. Hopes of finding Alana and his unborn son were slim; yet the Otomis living on Tlaxcala's borders claimed she had been taken to Coyoacán. Their messenger said a pregnant woman had brought them the information and later died in childbirth after coming all the way on horseback to beg his people to contact the Englishman. Poor, miserable Inmaculada. He made a mental note to have Pepe's child brought to him as soon as possible.

God, but the silence was deafening! As they approached the causeway, they passed campfires ringed by Aztecs sleeping like the dead. Those who were awake watched impassively as the big white man and his barbarians passed by.

"By the rood," Brian murmured, "Tenochtitlán must have been totally destroyed." Nothing but a tiny light showed here and there on the island where a scavenger or survivor roamed the ruins.

"Look!" One of his men pulled at his leg.

Brian grunted, already observing the flames ahead, as well as some suffering wretch who had caught on fire and was screaming like a skinned cat.

He slowed to a walk, wary of spectators who might be viewing the show from a distance. His mission was to save Alana, if she were still alive, not to be captured and executed. As soon as the scouts reported, he would decide his next move.

"Lord! Lord! The woman!"

Brian leaned down to stare into the face of his best scout, who had appeared like a wraith at the stirrup. "What woman?" His heart lurched painfully.

"It is a woman burning. One with hair like silver, like the one you have come for."

"*Sweet Blessed Jesus!*" Brian spurred Conn to a gallop, heedless now of being recognized.

The stallion skidded to a halt next to the platform, and Brian vaulted out of the saddle.

"Alana! Alana!"

He kicked and tore at the smouldering pyre. Sparks caught fire in his hair and doublet, and his men extinguished them with their hands. They glanced at him with awe. He was bigger than life! This was indeed a leader to idolize! Laboring at his side, ignoring their own injuries, they pointed with amazement when Finn's body was uncovered.

"Get him out of there! Hurry! He belongs to her. Hurry!"

Emaciated as the wolfhound was, it took two men to raise him onto the shoulders of another; he carried the dog over the back of his neck like a dead game animal with Finn's legs hanging down in front.

Brian had by now whipped out a dagger and was slicing through Alana's ropes with the power of a lunatic. What if they had been chains! Brian pulled her away from the stake and pressed the singed and smoke-grimed form tenderly to his breast.

"My darling . . . darling." His voice broke.

"You've . . . come." Tears fell on her face, and she coughed when she whispered, "Home, Brian. Me and the baby. Take us home."

"Aye, poppet, I'll take thee. And we'll never be apart again." He turned to step into the saddle with her in his arms when a musket ball whizzed past his ear.

Attracted by the monk's cries, a group of drunken soldiers had converged on Brian, waving torches and firing their weapons. Blade in hand, one more sober than the others climbed onto the platform. When he saw who it was, he stopped to reconsider. *Dios,* the crazy Englishman! But he waited too long.

Easing Alana down, her lover attacked so ferociously that the smaller man went to his knees. Wrestling the sword away from him, Brian brought the gleaming death over his head with the hilt in both hands and split the soldier's skull in half like a ripe melon.

Picking up his beloved, Brian shouted an order—and the rest of the Spaniards never knew what hit them. Arrows poured out of the night, and any soldier lucky enough to withstand them fell beneath the scalping knives.

When the massacre was over and battle lust satisfied, the natives found that their leader had left them. His face stern and white, he waited for them at the edge of darkness astride the great horse.

Heartless brutes that they were, somehow they sensed he was brooding over a pain beyond their comprehension. To cheer him and demonstrate their prowess, the men held up the bloody scalps for his approval just as the woman he carried put an arm around his neck.

Huge, strong lord of them all, Brian motioned imperiously and reined his black stallion toward the north.

There he and Alana MacKenna would find their destiny.